OTHERWISE ENGAGED

AVERY KEELAN

PLAYLIST

Stonecold – machineheart
Cold-Blooded – Zayde Wolf
Gimme – Banks
Small Doses – Bebe Rexha
Slower – Tate McRae
Belong to You (feat. 6LACK) – Sabrina Claudio, 6LACK
100% – Goldilox
Say – Ruel
Torches – X Ambassadors
Move On – AJ Mitchell

OTHERWISE ENGAGED

CHAPTER ONE

Thayer

MY SPANX WERE KILLING ME. SO WAS BEING STUCK IN THIS ballroom decorated with Swarovski chandeliers and pretty lies. But all I had to do was put in a brief appearance. Shake a few hands, smile at a few faces, and then I could duck out.

Elegant notes from the string quartet floated in the background as I leaned against the bar, clutching a glass of 2007 Gaja Barbaresco in one hand while scanning the crowd. Movers and shakers, the big-deal kingmakers—and the strivers clawing their way to the top. At a glance, I'd spotted a handful of CEOs, the mayor, countless socialites, three senators, and my twin sister, Quinn, with her fiancé, Adam. None of the options were appealing.

Attending these events was squarely at the bottom of my list, right next to having laser hair removal on my bikini line and getting a root canal. Well, I'd never had a root canal, but I assumed it was about as pleasant as these ostentatious parties.

Unfortunately, my mother cared more about keeping up appearances than about my feelings. Or at least, that was the only explanation I could think of as to why she continually guilt-tripped me into attending.

Her new husband, Charles Horvath, had thrown this charity fundraiser tonight to support endangered sea turtles. He was a big oil magnate, and I assumed this event was intended to create the illusion that he cared about the environment—even though I was fairly certain that wasn't the case. When I remarked that I could support the cause equally well by giving a donation from the comfort of my own home, my mother had looked at me like I'd suggested we go slaughter the turtles en masse.

If I wanted to remain in her good graces, my presence wasn't optional. But I couldn't explain why, as a fully grown adult, I cared so much about what she thought. I didn't want her life. I knew first-hand it wasn't nearly as nice as it looked from the outside.

"Thayer!" a voice called out from behind me. My grip on the crystal goblet tightened and every muscle in my body tensed. I'd been spotted, and not by someone I wanted to see. I took a gulp of wine that my mother's finishing school would have frowned upon while Matilda 'Millie' Pruitt barreled toward me like a heatseeking missile locked onto a target.

She gave me an air kiss on each cheek, wrapping me in an embrace with her spindle-thin arms, while I made a half-hearted attempt to do the same. Releasing me, she held me out at arm's length, giving me a once-over with laser-like precision. I'd had less invasive X-rays.

"Have you lost weight?" Millie asked. "You have, haven't you? You look amazing. So much better."

"Thanks," I said, though I wasn't sure I should. Still, it was easier to go along with the pretend niceties than get dragged down into the weeds of what she truly meant.

"Love the dress. It's almost like we're twins." She gestured to the both of us in semi-formal black lace dresses. My Badgley Mischka hit at mid-thigh, with long sleeves and a plunging back. Millie's Valentino was a sleeveless boatneck that ended just above the knee. The styles differed, but the material was still too similar for my comfort. I'd have chosen differently had I known. Millie wasn't exactly someone I tried to emulate.

"Right." In reality, the only thing we had in common was thinly veiled contempt for one another. If Millie could have straight-up assumed my life, thereby eliminating my existence, I'm sure she would have at least seriously considered it.

Quinn trailed up from behind Millie, a vision in a pale yellow chiffon cocktail dress that I couldn't have pulled off in a million years. My sense of dread multiplied tenfold, churning in my belly. One-on-one, my sister was perfectly pleasant. With Millie, the two formed the ultimate passive-aggressive duo.

"There's my beautiful sister." Quinn repeated the same fake air-kiss routine, enveloping me in a vanilla-sugar-scented hug.

It was an interesting compliment, given that we were identical twins. And especially given that she was arguably the prettier one of us two. Other people seemed to agree, though they'd never openly admit it. Her features had always seemed softer to me, more feminine, with fuller lips and bigger eyes. Not to mention, she hadn't broken her nose playing softball senior year like I had, creating a small bump on the bridge that our mother had not-so-subtly encouraged me to have surgically repaired.

The slight discrepancy between our appearances mirrored the differences in our personalities; she was known for being warm and effusive while I was, well, not. There was probably something to be said about the underlying theme of her dressed like an angel tonight while I was wearing black.

"You look great," I told her.

Quinn scoffed, waving a perfectly manicured hand. "Hardly. I look ragged." My sister couldn't accept a compliment to save her life. It went way beyond humility and well into false modesty territory.

"Where's Adam?" Millie asked, craning her neck.

"He had to duck out to take an important call with an investor. Not optional, unfortunately." Quinn tacked on the last sentence a little too quickly; I wasn't sure whether she was trying to convince us or herself. "What are you doing hanging out at the bar all by yourself, Thay?"

"I was just getting a refill before coming to find you." False, but now I could get credit for pretending. It's not that Quinn and I had a bad relationship, at least not one-on-one, but it was strained when we were within the suffocating confines of this gilded cage.

"I haven't seen your sister in ages," Millie said to Quinn like I wasn't standing right in front of them. She turned back to me and touched me on the arm, sizing me up once more. Looking for, I knew, signs of injectables, fillers, or nips and tucks. Bonus points for spotting roots or grey hair. But too bad for her, I had my balayage touched up and toned yesterday.

"What have you been up to, Thayer?" she asked.

Code for, why did you drop off the face of the planet? But nobody knew the answer to that, and nobody needed to.

"Oh, you know." I waved airily. "I've been super busy with work." Running the two boutique lingerie stores, Lace & Grace, that I co-owned with Quinn consumed most of my time.

It started off as a one- or two-year project after college, a breather between undergraduate and graduate school for me. Quinn managed our merchandising and marketing, while I oversaw the finances and business side. The plan was for Quinn to eventually take over all the responsibilities when I headed back to school to obtain my MBA, but somehow, I'd gotten sucked into staying much longer than I'd intended.

At this point, I could reconcile our books in my sleep. Part of me yearned to move on to a new challenge, but that was easier said than done when dealing with my steamroller of a sister.

"That's all she does," Quinn chimed in with a sing-song voice. "All work and no play, this one." As my business partner, you'd think she would have seen this as a positive thing.

Millie made a faux sad face. "That doesn't sound like fun. You should come out with us one night."

To be clear, I had plenty of friends to go out with. I just chose not to subject them to this particular form of torture. In fact, I was meeting my best friend Lola for brunch tomorrow, if I ever escaped this lions' den in one piece. And my friends didn't sharpen their knives while my back was turned.

"Maybe when things calm down at work," I said. "Things have been hectic lately with preparing our quarterly financial statements, not to mention tracking the budget for our new build-out." Someone had to do it; the only thing Quinn was keeping track of these days was her list of wedding RSVPs.

"Aren't you excited about your sister's big news?" Millie beamed, revealing her slightly-too-big, whitest-white veneers. Her face was long and thin, which made the overall effect equine.

"So excited," I said, trying to sound like it.

"I mean, look at that rock!" She grabbed Quinn's left hand, proudly showing off the cushion-cut three-carat yellow diamond like it was her own. My sister at least had the decency to feign embarrassment at the attention.

I forced a smile. "I'm familiar."

"And don't fret about not having a date for the wedding." Quinn withdrew her hand, tilting her head sympathetically. "I know the dating scene is rough these days. Not many good fish left in the sea."

It wasn't clear how Quinn would know about the dating scene when she'd barely ever dipped her toe into it. She was a serial monogamist who'd been on three first dates that resulted in three long-term boyfriends, the last of which was her fiancé, Adam. Unlike me, she'd never combed the dregs of Tinder, trying in vain to find a decent date. It was more than rough; it was a nuclear wasteland.

"Fortunately, there will be lots of eligible bachelors at the party," Millie said. "Ocean Heights' most desirable."

Unlike Millie, who was perpetually trying to sink her talons into a well-to-do white collar business bro, I wasn't interested in my own Adam 2.0. I had vibrators in my nightstand that were better company than that. Better conversation, too.

"Oh my gosh, yes," Quinn cooed. She liked nothing more than playing matchmaker. "We have to set you up."

"We totally do," Millie agreed.

"That's so sweet of you," I said. "But I already have a date for the party."

I'm not sure why I said it. Maybe it was their tone, laden with saccharine and superiority. Maybe it was because I hadn't eaten dinner and hanger had assumed control of my brain. Or maybe it was that my own sister—my twin sister—was marrying my college boyfriend.

Adam and I dated for most of senior year in college. I was the one who ended things shortly before graduation for a myriad of reasons, including, but not limited to, the fact that he was kind of a jerk. While that was more than four years ago, the two of them "running into each other" at a Starbucks and ending up on a weekend-long first date was still weird. Getting engaged after two months? Weirder still.

Yet, the only one in my life who gave the situation the side-eye was Lola. Everyone else seemed to think it was perfectly fine.

Quinn's ice-blue eyes widened. "A date?" The string quartet's song ended just as she spoke, causing the two words to echo throughout the ballroom.

"You do?" Millie looked like she'd sniffed a carton of spoiled milk.

"Yes. I've been seeing someone," I told them, lowering my voice. "It's getting serious, actually." Apparently, my lifelong drive to overachieve extended to self-sabotage.

"That's great, Thay." Quinn ducked her head, leaning in closer. Her eyes danced as she studied my face. "Who is it?"

Who knew? Certainly not me.

"I don't want to say yet. It's still new. Might jinx it." I bit my bottom lip. With any luck, my evasiveness would create intrigue rather than suspicion. I knew I was backing myself into a corner, but I couldn't stomach another pitying look, consoling comment, or pushy matchmaker attempt in response to my perma-single status.

"It's new, but it's serious." Millie frowned, gesturing with her half-full martini. "And it's a secret."

My stomach flip-flopped. As the biggest gossip in town, she took pride in always being in the loop. Hell, she wanted to be the loop. Millie's mouth set in a thin line, clearly irked she hadn't heard about this before. Now she would be going straight into hardcore recon mode, digging for dirt. Millie could be relentless about things like this. I needed to manage her somehow, but people-ing wasn't my strong suit.

"It's not a secret. We just haven't done the whole meet the friends and family thing." Could they see my heart pounding beneath my dress? Hopefully not, but Millie did have freakishly good vision.

Quinn nudged me with her elbow. "Come on, tell me. I need to know who finally made the cut."

"Soon." Soon? Why did I say that? As if the hole wasn't deep enough, I kept on digging. Maybe I could hide in it later when this came back to haunt me.

"Give me a hint, at least. Do I know him?" Quinn furrowed her brow as if she was mulling over the possibilities.

"You might…" I said, trying to keep the details vague. If I said no, she'd ask why I couldn't at least tell her his name. If I said yes, well, that was even more problematic.

Adam swaggered up and threw an arm around Quinn's shoulder, planting a kiss on her cheek. She giggled, batting her eyelashes and leaning into him.

"Hi, sweet cheeks. Millie, nice to see you." He glanced over at me, giving me a finger pistol. "Hey, sis."

I fought the urge to roll my eyes. At six feet tall with sandy-blonde hair and a cleft in his chin, Adam looked every bit like Quinn's dream man. His bespoke grey suit and swanky property-development career were the icing on the cake. The only problem was, he was obnoxious. For instance, our relationship was anything but sibling-like given our history, but he enjoyed annoying me with weird, passive-aggressive comments.

"Thayer has a date to your wedding," Millie announced.

"Oh, really?" Adam raised his eyebrows, taking a sip of his red wine. "Who's the lucky guy?"

Heat flared up my cheeks. "You'll find out soon enough."

"Hello, darlings." My mother appeared out of nowhere, as she tended to do, in a cloud of judgment and Chanel No.5. Her hair was pulled back in a sleek, blonde chignon, complimented by an understated, royal blue dress that showed off her lithe, former-ballerina frame. She placed an icy hand on my shoulder, gigantic emerald engagement ring from husband number four sparkling in the dim light. "I see you four are off in the corner all alone. What could possibly be more pressing than socializing with our lovely guests?"

Quinn turned to her. "Thayer was telling us she has a date to our wedding."

My mother looked as shocked as Quinn had. If her forehead hadn't been recently Botoxed, she might have even raised her eyebrows.

"Really. Well, that's good to hear." She offered me a forced smile, as if she didn't quite believe it herself. "Who is it?"

The million-dollar question.

I swallowed. "I was just—"

Quinn cut me off. "She's playing coy with us." She stuck out her bottom lip, forming a glossy peach pout. "Won't cough up a name."

"It's still new," I said. "You'll meet him when I'm ready." They all knew I was notoriously private. Or "emotionally unavailable," as they liked to say. More like an expert in self-preservation, which was necessary when you traveled in these circles. Either way, hopefully this would put an end to their prying.

"Ah." My mother nodded regally. "Well, the wedding is still three months away, dear. Are you sure you'll still be seeing him by then?" I suppressed a flinch at the verbal dagger. My past relationships may have been short-lived, but I was always the one who cut them loose.

"Positive." Coffin, meet final nail.

"It's new but moving fast, Alexandra," Millie added, butting in. "Maybe there will be more wedding bells soon." Her tone was aspartame—sweet on top, bitter aftertaste beneath.

I nodded. "Maybe so."

In reality, I didn't see wedding bells in my future ever, and certainly not any time soon. Marriage was an antiquated tradition that, in heterosexual relationships, benefitted the man more than the woman. Studies even said as much. On average, wives still did something like 1.9 times as much housework as their husbands, even if they both worked full time. That was a total rip-off; any man who freeloaded like that deserved to be downgraded from husband to was-band, stat.

Plus, my mother's marital track record only reinforced what I already knew: promises of till death do us part meant nothing in the bitter end—and the end was always bitter.

"Excellent." My mother's expression was pleased, if uncertain. "I can't wait to meet him. I do hope I can have the chance prior to the engagement dinner. You know, to ensure that he's a suitable choice."

"Of course. I'm sure we can make that happen." I took a sip of my wine, wishing it were cyanide instead.

CHAPTER TWO

Bennett

LIGHTNING FLASHED OUTSIDE THE FLOOR-TO-CEILING windows of my corner office, reflecting off the polished marble floor. In the distance, the low grumble of thunder followed like an ominous warning. Sheets of rain began to pelt against the glass, turning the street below into a blur of colored lights and movement. It was unusual for a storm of this magnitude to hit the city in the middle of the day. But then, it was also unusual for a potential investor to show up twenty-five minutes late for a meeting, especially without even bothering to call.

Sure, we were technically still trying to woo Callaghan to invest in Flux Development's latest project, a mixed-use building with commercial tenants occupying the bottom two floors and residential condominium units above. The deal wasn't signed, sealed, and delivered—yet. But last we'd spoken, Callaghan had been on the hook. Sold on the investment, happy with the return we were offering, and ready to cough up the five million that we desperately needed to secure the city-owned parcel of land. All that we had to do was reel him in and get him to sign the papers. Now he was missing in action after rescheduling on us twice, and things were starting to look increasingly grim.

Ian ducked his head in my doorway and rapped on the glass. "Got a minute?"

"I've just wasted twenty-five," I said dryly. "What's one more?"

He strode in, settling into the cream leather chair across from my glass desk. Crossing an ankle over his knee, he adjusted his grey silk tie with a frown. His dirty blond hair was mussed, like he'd been raking his hands through it as he tended to do when he was stressed or struggling to perfect his Gantt charts for project scheduling.

"We have a problem."

"You mean the big fish that's managed to wriggle off the hook?"

"Yes and no." His expression was neutral, poker face in full effect.

Ian was the quiet, analytical one. Coolheaded with an aptitude for organization and scheduling, he was all about analysis over emotion. It made for a great COO, and it was a useful counterbalance for my own personality, which was not always calm and collected. But sometimes he bordered on being downright cryptic.

I waved him on impatiently. "Details, please."

Ian opened his mouth to speak and then closed it again. He hesitated, like he was weighing what to say.

"What?" I pressed.

I was having a bad day. Some might have called it a bad week. A bad month would also have been an accurate descriptor, and it was rapidly threatening to turn into a bad year. I didn't have time for Ian's dancing-around-the-point act. Something was standing in the way of getting our deal past the finish line. I just didn't know what it was.

"I think I know why Callaghan seems to have cold feet."

My desk phone rang, interrupting Ian. I held up a finger, gesturing for him to be quiet, as I hit the intercom button. "Yes?"

"Mr. Bradford?" My assistant Shane's voice echoed through the speaker. "There's a Mr. Jared Callaghan here to see you."

"Send him in, please. Thanks." Releasing the intercom button,

I glanced over at Ian. "Well, so much for cold feet. Maybe he got stuck in traffic."

"No, that's what I was—" Ian started to say but stopped short as the glass double doors swung open and Shane escorted Jared Callaghan into the room. He was a portly man in his fifties, with a thick head of white hair and a tanned, lined face. His navy suit was well-tailored, designer loafers shined to perfection, and he looked every bit the part of a big fish. Ian stood up to greet him while I walked around from behind my desk.

"Hello, Mr. Callaghan." Ian extended his hand.

"Ian," Callaghan said warmly, embracing Ian's hand in his own briefly before breaking apart. "Please, call me Jared."

Then he turned to face me, and his tone cooled a hundred degrees, gaze hardening. "Bennett."

"Nice to see you again, Jared." I stepped closer, offering my hand. His gaze dropped to it, and he eyed it with disdain, failing to extend his own in return. Rude, but okay. I was willing to look past it. We needed him—badly. The economy was sagging, almost no one was liquid, and anyone that had money was hoarding it like Gollum and his ring.

I withdrew my hand, walking back over to my desk and sitting down. Jared settled into a chair beside Ian across from my desk while I tried to get my game face on, telling myself whatever just transpired wasn't personal when it so clearly was.

After some brief banter about the record-breaking rain as of late, Ian and I cut to the chase: the closing. "As we discussed," I started, "the projected return is significantly higher than industry average. The fundamentals are solid and with a payback period of—"

Callaghan waved me off, holding up a pudgy hand. "Enough numbers. I know what the prospectus says. But numbers only tell one side of the story. I want to know more about you and your company. Get to know you as people."

I stopped short. What did that even mean? Our biographical blurbs were in the investment package. Ian and I had attended top tier business schools for our undergraduate studies before starting Flux from the ground up together, and since then, we'd completed numerous successful projects. We both possessed various other credentials, including membership with our respective professional organizations, and volunteered for causes like the local chamber of commerce. Granted, Ian forced me into the last one, but it still counted.

What more did Callaghan want to know? My shoe size? Favorite movie?

He draped his arm over the back of the chair, shifting to face Ian. "Are you married, son?"

I tried to hide my confusion. Married? What did that have to do with anything?

"Two years in June," Ian replied, holding up his left hand, complete with platinum wedding band.

I wondered if married couples ever regretted giving up their freedom or if it was something they made peace with, like people supposedly do after other tragic life events.

"Ah, in the honeymoon stage!" Callaghan chuckled, belly jiggling. "Those were the days."

His smile faded as he turned back, setting his sights on me. "And you, Bennett. Are you married?"

"Er—no," I said. His glare intensified. "Not yet." Nor ever, actually, but I got the sense that he wouldn't be keen on that answer.

His eyes went cold. "Still living the bachelor life, then." He spat out the 'b' in 'bachelor' like it was a dirty word.

"No, not—"

"I think the way a person lives says a lot about them, don't you?" He reclined, folding his hands over his round belly, and his shirt buttons strained. "We show our true selves in our private lives. Our morals and ethics, those things that matter. And I have to say, I have some serious reservations about yours, Bennett."

After another twenty minutes of my character and personal life being raked over the coals, Ian and I managed to steer the conversation back to the topic at hand: the five million dollar investment we were seeking. Unfortunately, neither of us could close Callaghan. We did, however, narrowly convince him to meet with us one more time before completely shutting the door on the deal.

Cloaked in a cloud of defeat, we escorted him to the elevators and exchanged a terse goodbye. Once the elevator doors were safely shut, I turned and looked at Ian in disbelief. "What the hell just happened?"

Ian's lips pressed into a line. "That's what I was trying to tell you." He inclined his head in the direction of his office. "Come on. This is a closed-door conversation."

We strode down the brightly lit hallway adorned with framed black-and-white architectural photos, rounding the corner into his modest workspace. Ian's office was smaller than mine by choice, tucked away in the northeast side of the floor. He said he didn't like the visibility of the glass-walled corner office and wanted the ability to close a solid door in the middle of the day and disappear, losing himself in his work. In retrospect, it did have its advantages, like better privacy for the occasional afternoon delight. The pull-down shades I had were questionable at best.

Ian walked past the shelves lined with signed baseball memorabilia and photos of him with his wife, Laura. He pulled out his chair and sat down with a leaden sigh, resting his elbows on the solid walnut desk. I followed him in, locking the door behind us and easing into the buttery leather seat across from him. We stared at each other blankly, still processing the bloodshed that just transpired.

I shifted my weight, looking at him expectantly. "Again, I ask, what the fuck was that?"

"I did some digging earlier," Ian said. "Word is, Callaghan doesn't trust you."

"No shit." That much had been crystal clear during our interrogation. "Why?"

He gave me a withering look. "Maybe it has to do with your

penchant for dating models, fucking in nightclub bathrooms, and snorting coke off strippers' tits."

"I can neither confirm nor deny those allegations."

In my defense, I wasn't actually doing cocaine in the situation he was referring to; I would never be foolish enough to ingest narcotics in public. I was taking a body shot of tequila and the angle of the freeze-frame video happened to be highly misleading. Second of all, Staci wasn't a stripper, she was someone my friends and I met at a Vegas nightclub and brought to the strip club with us. But Ian wouldn't know that because he wasn't there. He wouldn't be caught dead at a strip club. More accurately, if he did go to a strip club, his wife Laura would see to it that he was dead immediately after.

"You do know that article comes up when people Google you, right? Pictures and all? Have you looked into having that removed?"

"I asked our lawyers," I grumbled.

Ian raised his eyebrows. "And?"

"Apparently, as a private business, that club has the right to do whatever they want with their security footage as long as they have a sign warning patrons they're being recorded. And turns out, they do. A teeny tiny fucking sign beside the bathroom that no one would ever notice, let alone read." I blew out a breath. "Which means I have no recourse with them or the news outlets that ran with it."

As for who bought and leaked those photos to the press, I had a pretty fucking good idea. My slimy cousin, Adam.

My cell phone vibrated in my suit pocket, and I pulled it out to find Millie's name flashing on the caller ID. I watched the screen, tempted to decline the call, but thought better of it. Then she'd know I was at my phone, and she'd keep calling. If it rang through, I could pretend I'd missed her by accident. I didn't have patience for her nonsense at the best of times, let alone when everything was on fire.

"Anyway," I said, silencing the ringer and sliding my phone back into my jacket. "Back to Callaghan. How did you find out?"

"He told his assistant, and his assistant leaked it to someone I know." Ian was one of those friendly, easygoing types that people naturally trusted. He was great at making connections, digging up dirt, and the occasional low-key corporate espionage, which was useful because people were less inclined to air their dirty laundry with me.

"And you think it's because of my 'reputation?'" I said, making air quotes.

"He's old school. The guy has been married for something like fifty years. He has three daughters, six granddaughters, and everyone says he's wrapped around their little fingers."

"I get it. He likes rainbows and butterflies and tea parties and shit. What does any of that have to do with business?" I asked through gritted teeth. "I'm trying to do a deal with him, not get one of his daughters' hands in marriage."

Ian shrugged but said nothing.

"This is ridiculous." I slapped the wooden arm of my chair. "My private life has nothing to do with this deal."

"Look, I don't disagree. But I've done some digging and everyone says the same thing: your lifestyle is an issue. It's killed deals for Callaghan in the past. He prefers working with wholesome, reliable people. He's all about family values."

The unspoken part was clear: Ian was an asset, and I was a liability.

"You mean boring married people like him."

"I guess you could put it that way."

"Well fuck, man. I didn't know we were back in 1960." I pinched the bridge of my nose. What was this, an episode of Mad Men? "If that's the case, we should be drinking whiskey and smoking cigars before I go bang my secretary."

"I'm still trying to work on Callaghan," Ian said pointedly, ignoring my snarky comment. "I've been trying to convince him to meet us for dinner next week so that we can discuss things. And so that you can show him what a well-behaved, mature adult you actually are."

"Good plan," I said. "I can do that."

"Can you, though?" He raised his eyebrows.

"You wound me, Ian. Have a little faith."

I could rein it in if I had to. At least, temporarily.

"Faith is the only thing keeping me going." Ian scrubbed a hand down his face. "I'll keep you posted."

"Just let me know where and when."

We exchanged a grim glance and I stood up, pushing the chair back and heading for the door. Strolling down the hall, I mulled over possible strategies and angles of attack.

In the past four years, Ian and I had triumphed over nightmare scenario after nightmare scenario. Paper-thin margins, unreliable general contractors, impossible city permitting departments. Bank loans that fell through at the last minute, a handful of potential lawsuits, and more late-night emergencies than I could count.

I had learned how to not only function, but thrive, on nothing but coffee, spite, and three hours of sleep.

I didn't come this far to only come this far. I could do anything. Would do anything. Except lay down and die.

Unable to focus or accomplish anything of value, I fired off a few emails before bailing at five o'clock to pick up my dry-cleaning before hitting the gym to work out some frustration. I sprinted to the bank of elevators, fueled by defiance, denial, and too many espressos. As the elevator car zoomed down to the ground floor, I gave myself a pep talk. There was still hope. There had to be.

The stainless doors slid open on parking level three and my text notification vibrated again, a reminder that I still hadn't read Millie's message. Millie and I weren't friends, exactly, more like peripheral acquaintances who kept in touch to serve our own purposes. Mine was to stay ahead of the curve, and Millie was the authority on all things gossip-related within our social sphere. Usually this involved trivial matters I didn't care about, but once in a while, there was a diamond in the rough, like the time she gave me the scoop about a rezoning proposal before the news went public. Flux scooped up a nearby property and made a killing off the development.

And in Millie's case, well, she wanted to get into my Hugo Boss boxer briefs—she'd made that abundantly clear on more than one occasion. That was never going to happen. For starters, I suspected she would be the lights-out, missionary-only type in the bedroom. But the bigger issue lay in the fact that I'd pegged Millie as the type who'd stalk you relentlessly after a one-night stand while practicing her signature as 'Millie Bradford' and photoshopping pictures to create likenesses of your future children. Having dealt with that before, I could spot it at a hundred yards away and knew when to keep my belt buckled, pants on.

I pushed open the metal swinging door, greeted by the asphalt and gasoline scent of the underground parking garage. A car alarm beeped in the distance as someone locked or unlocked it from afar. Pulling out my phone, I navigated to my texts as I headed for the row of parking stalls on the north side, reserved for Flux.

Millie: Did you hear Thayer had a new boyfriend?

Unlike the vast majority of Millie's breaking news, which was banal at best and catty at worst, this piqued my interest. Thayer had spurned every desirable bachelor in the greater metro area, leaving a trail of broken hearts—or bruised egos, at the very least—in her wake. At this point, she was verging on legendary; a mythical man-eater.

On her first and only date with legendary womanizer, Pierce Cunningham, Thayer criticized the condition of his Mercedes Maybach S-Class and recommended a better detailing shop. Although Pierce doesn't exactly float my yacht, he's heir to a massive fast-food dynasty, richer than God, and isn't exactly wanting for dates. I mean, there were women who would fight each other just to blow him in that car. But after finding himself on the receiving end of Thayer's criticism, Pierce was so embarrassed that he sold his beloved Mercedes.

Allegedly, Thayer also made Will Abbott, highly sought-after hedge fund manager, cry when she publicly dumped him on his birthday. And she walked out on Crosby Richards, uber-wealthy founder of a well-known dating app, in the middle of dinner at Culina. I'd been told by other women that Crosby turns into a handsy octopus after a few glasses of scotch, so to her credit, that one was probably warranted.

I wondered who the lucky guy about to be ripped to shreds was this time.

Bennett: No, hadn't heard.

Millie: You don't know who it is, then? She was kind of cagey about it.

I continued walking to my car, mind whirling. Thayer was a cagey person, so this wasn't a huge surprise. When I didn't reply, Millie followed up, planting a seed—one I knew she hoped would take root and travel all the way back to Thayer. There was nothing Millie loved more than starting a vicious little rumor, especially about her arch-nemesis.

Millie: I think he might be married.

Bennett: Thayer, playing second fiddle? Doubtful.

Millie: She wouldn't tell us ANY details. Not even his first name.

Bennett: What do you expect? I mean, this is Thayer we're talking about.

Millie: True. But she's hiding something, and I'm going to find out what it is. I'm still going with the mistress theory myself.

Standing in front of my driver's side door, I stared at the screen, trying to piece it together. I got into my car and continued mulling it over, intuition niggling at me. And by the time I pulled out of the parking garage, I realized Millie was right: something was going on. But I had a feeling it wasn't what she thought.

As I turned into the parking lot across the street from the dry cleaners, Ian called me.

"I made some progress," he said.

"Okay. Where are we at?" I asked, popping in my Bluetooth earpiece as I walked onto the street. Flat grey skies loomed overhead, accompanied by pissing rain. Not a steady downpour, at least, but enough of a drizzle to be annoying as hell.

"I had to twist his arm," Ian said. "But he committed to dinner next Friday. At a swanky steakhouse on our dime, of course."

I did a silent fist-pump as I kept walking. Fuck yes. My excitement was short-lived; I had another commitment the same night that would have to be rescheduled. There were few things I hated more than being flaky, especially when it came to my mother. I didn't make many promises—or any at all if I could get away with it—but I kept the ones I made.

"Sometimes you do pull your weight after all," I said, narrowly dodging a slow-moving pedestrian. The burly, red-headed woman turned and glared at me, which was unfair considering that she was the one blocking the sidewalk. Just like how freeways have fast lanes, there should be a fast side of the sidewalk and a slow side of the sidewalk. It only makes sense.

He snorted. "Yeah, now it's your turn. We still have to close him."

"Let me handle that."

Until recently, closing had been my forte. Hell, there were times I'd talked circles around investors until they begged me to get in on the deal and fought each other for a bigger share. This situation might require a little more finesse, but I'd get it across the finish line.

"Oh, and there's one more thing you should know." Ian's voice was careful, like he was trying to sound casual and failing.

"What is it?" I quickly looked both ways before darting across the street. A car veered around the corner, slamming on its brakes with a screech to avoid hitting me.

"Watch it, pal!" The beefy, red-faced driver leaned on the horn, flipping me off through the glass.

I grinned and gave him a friendly wave, which angered him

even more. He leaned out the window, cursing at me and shaking his fist emphatically, his skin turning an even deeper shade of scarlet.

I loved the city. So full of energy.

"He thinks you're bringing a date."

"A date," I echoed, my attention snapping back to Ian. "Is this a business dinner or the fucking prom?"

"He's bringing his wife and I'm bringing Laura. If you show up alone, you'll be the awkward fifth wheel. It'll only reinforce Callaghan's perception of you as an overgrown frat boy."

I grunted but said nothing. I was never a fraternity bro, not even in college, and I certainly didn't resemble one now. Nor did I think having a date on your arm magically made you mature or trustworthy. But I wasn't in a position to argue.

"A *respectable* date," he added.

"Got it. Thanks, Dad." Who exactly did he think I was going to bring?

"If we don't get that money..." Ian trailed off. But he didn't need to finish his sentence. It was even more dire than he realized. If we didn't get Callaghan on our side, we were done. Closing up shop. Kaput. Uncle Sam would be the lucky new owner of some prime pieces of waterfront property waiting to be redeveloped.

"I am aware of the severity of our situation," I ground out. "I just don't see what a date has to do with that."

Ian sighed. "Look, no one is asking you to get married. Or to even settle down. Just, you know, pretend to be a mature adult for a few hours. Eyes on the prize."

"Fine," I snapped. "I'll find a date."

"I'll make a reservation for six people at eight PM."

"Super," I said sarcastically, ending the call.

To Ian's credit, he took my foul moods in stride—just like I put up with his cryptic ways and circuitous path to the point. We had the whole yin/yang thing going on. Whenever I was ranting and raving, unable to see things objectively, Ian was the level-headed one who stopped me from going scorched earth. Or tried to stop me, at least. And when the situation required, I played bad cop, so he didn't have to. Our dynamic worked, which was how we had gotten a start-up off the ground without strangling each other.

Clenching my jaw, I ducked into the storefront of the dry cleaners and handed the woman at the front my numbered tag. As much as I had a 'reputation', as Ian had put it, I never led women on. I was perfectly upfront about my intentions, which were always short-term, non-exclusive, and X-rated. Take it or leave it, and they usually took it.

But the minute meeting my friends, attending fancy parties, or other remotely relationship-like activities entered the picture, it was like blood in the water—cue the Jaws theme song. Everything I'd said went straight out the window and they would think I had either changed my mind or was open to having my mind changed. Which goes to show how little they knew me to begin with. Ian couldn't even persuade me to go for Chinese food instead of Thai yesterday; being hard-headed was practically my hobby. There was zero chance my position on serious relationships would budge any time soon.

With an armload of clean dry cleaning, I pushed open the door. Thunder sounded overhead and rain began to pour down, soaking through my clothes just before I reached my car again. A fitting end to the day. I started the ignition, still stewing over Ian's orders. The last thing I needed was to bring a woman to this dinner and have her get the wrong idea. It always resulted in hurt feelings, tears, and pain-in-the-ass drama. If I wanted drama, I'd watch shitty reality TV.

But regardless of whether I wanted a date, I needed one for this goddamn dinner. Someone appropriate who would help me make a good impression. Someone willing to accompany me, but who wouldn't want it to lead to anything more.

Someone who needed something from me, too.

CHAPTER THREE

Thayer

AFTER TWENTY-FIVE YEARS ON THIS PLANET, I HAD punctuality down to an art. A customized black-and-gold Erin Condren planner outlined my days, weeks, months, and years. Everything went in that spiral-bound book—morning workouts, weekly blow-outs, monthly book club. I'd even blocked out my free time each day. And, as an additional scheduling security measure, I replicated every single appointment in my phone's calendar.

I was never late. Unless it was on purpose.

When I pulled onto 5th Street, the clock in my Lexus SUV dashboard read 1:10 PM. I was supposed to meet Bennett ten minutes ago. My belated arrival was intentional, meant to throw him off-guard. Meant to make him worry I was standing him up. Sweet irony, given his track record with women; it was usually the other way around.

At any rate, I hoped he was sweating in his Gucci dress socks. Especially after he summoned me so cryptically.

We need to talk. Starbucks on 5th, one PM tomorrow.

When I asked why, he'd refused to elaborate. It was bizarre, not to mention irritating. Bennett and I didn't do coffee dates. We weren't even friends. We barely tolerated existing within the same social solar system.

I could only think of two possible explanations: Bennett was dying of some rare, incurable disease and wanted to make things right between us, or he wanted something. My money was on the latter.

It was quarter past one by the time I pulled into an empty stall, shifting the ignition into park and hitting the engine on/off button. Before sliding out of the car, I gave myself a once-over in the rear-view mirror, fixing a stray mascara smudge and reapplying a coat of Charlotte Tilbury Love Bite. What I really needed was a suit of armor, but bright red lipstick was the next best thing.

The aroma of freshly brewed coffee greeted me as I pushed open the glass door to the cafe, immediately spotting Bennett at a small wooden table off to the corner. He was hard to miss. His broad frame filled the black leather armchair, the body of an athlete from playing competitive rugby throughout high school and college. Rumor had it, you could bounce a diamond off his abs, which was a pity when you considered who they belonged to.

Streaks of sun-kissed copper graced his chestnut hair, which was immaculately styled. It matched his neatly trimmed stubble, creating the effect of effortless and groomed all at once. Bennett basically rolled out of bed looking perfect every day, which made me hate him that much more.

He'd already purchased two drinks and he was scrolling his phone, seemingly at ease—and decidedly not sweating over my late arrival.

The bastard knew I would come.

My heeled Rag & Bone booties clicked on the ceramic tile flooring as I approached, drawing his attention. Our eyes met, and he locked his phone, flipping it face down. A pretty blonde girl a few tables down watched the two of us with ill-concealed envy on her face.

I knew Bennett looked appealing from the outside, but she wouldn't be jealous if she knew what he was really like.

"Thayer." He stood up to greet me and his handsome face lit up with a movie-star grin, courtesy of good genetics and modern dentistry.

It was difficult to tell whether he was genuinely happy to see me or merely wanted me to think he was. Bennett was difficult to read at best and impossibly opaque at worst—one reason I shouldn't have even been here. Yet here I was, against my better judgment.

"Bennett." I sank down into the armchair across from him, unwinding my Burberry Classic cashmere scarf. He eased back into his seat, unfazed by my frosty tone. I crossed my legs and tried to gather my thoughts, bracing myself for whatever battle of the wits was sure to follow.

"I assumed you encountered some traffic." Bennett gave me a look that said he knew that wasn't the case. "So I ordered for you." He slid the cup toward me. Grande dark roast, no room, black as the midnight sky. My usual to a T. On the surface it seemed like a nice, harmless gesture, but I knew better.

"Trying to butter me up?"

"Just trying to be a gentleman," he said. Bennett was anything but. He flashed me a disarming smile that had the opposite effect, and I scrambled to fortify my emotional walls.

"How do you know I still drink the same thing?"

Until the eleventh grade or so, you could have called us friends. We even bonded while studying for AP Chemistry, which was where my penchant for strong black coffee began, necessitated due to the all-nighters I pulled before exams. But something changed between us not long after that, and in the decade that followed, Bennett made it abundantly clear that he could not stand me. It was a two-way street.

"Call it a hunch."

Irritation simmered within me. The worst part was, he was right. I was still perpetually early, I still drank my coffee the same way, and I was still a creature of habit. He had my number. And that's what bothered me most.

"Thanks," I said grudgingly. I accepted the cup, taking a sip because coffee was coffee, even if Satan was buying. "Now, why am I here?"

He dodged my question by completely ignoring it. "How have you been? I feel like it's been ages since we had the chance to catch up."

"Fine." I didn't ask him the same in return, because I didn't care.

"How's work?"

I clutched my cup like a shield. "Also fine."

Then I remembered what Millie told me last week about his mother's cancer relapse and my hostility waned. I'd known his family for two decades and beneath it all, I wasn't a total monster. An unwelcome pang of sympathy stabbed at my gut.

"How's Lydia?" I asked softly.

Bennett's face fell, composure faltering. "She's doing okay. You know, taking it day by day." He cleared his throat. "She's a fighter."

I nodded. "She definitely is."

"Circling back to you." He leaned back in his chair and crossed an ankle over his opposite knee, revealing dark purple dress socks. "How are things with you and your new boyfriend? I've heard you two are getting serious."

I shouldn't have been surprised that Millie told him. Sometimes, my life was like being trapped in a never-ending reality show—whatever came before the Real Housewives phase of life. Though, I hoped that wasn't my future because it was seriously depressing.

"They're great," I said. "We're great. So why did you—"

Bennett cut me off. "What was his name again?"

My mouth went dry. Bennett's steel-blue eyes pinned me, watchful and waiting. I took a sip of still-scalding coffee, buying time. I hadn't committed to giving my 'boyfriend' a name. I thought fewer details would make it easier to keep my story straight, but now I didn't have a name to pull out of my back pocket.

"John?" It came out more like a question than a statement.

Bennett smiled pleasantly, like a well-meaning friend that we both knew he wasn't. "And does John have a last name?"

Of course, John didn't have a last name, because he wasn't real. I fumbled, landing on the first thing that popped into my head.

"Uh, Hamilton." I'd been listening to the Hamilton soundtrack in the car on the way over and John Laurens happened to be one of the main characters. Hopefully, Bennett wouldn't make the connection.

"Hmm, can't say I've heard of him." He pressed his lips together, stroking the groomed stubble on his chin. "And I know everyone who's anyone around these parts."

Dammit. He did, too.

"Different social circles, I suppose." I shrugged, trying to conceal the panic rising in my chest. I liked to think I was an okay liar; passable, at least. But you can't lie to a liar, and I was dealing with a pro.

"That's one explanation for it." He took a sip of his coffee, watching me over the rim.

My heart stopped cold. "Excuse me?"

Bennett set down his cup, leveling me with a look. "Thayer." His voice was low and velvety, full of promises and threats. "Let's be honest. There is no boyfriend, is there?"

My pulse kickstarted, resuming at a frantic pace. Fighting the rush of heat to my cheeks was impossible. I was sure the glowing red emergency exit sign behind him matched my face.

"Sure there is." As if on cue, the coffee grinder roared to life in the background like some sort of lie detector.

"Okay, let me see his Instagram page." Bennett held out his large hand, beckoning.

This wasn't a meeting; it was an ambush.

"He doesn't do social media."

"I see." He withdrew his hand, leaning on his elbow, and his gaze turned razor-sharp. "Then show me a picture of you together. In this digital age, a happy young couple should have lots of those, right?"

My stomach did a nosedive. Was it possible to perform an internet search at light speed to find a stock photo of a smiling couple with a female model that closely resembled me? In less than a minute, to avoid arousing Bennett's suspicion? Unlikely. I debated making a dash for the exit, but I knew I'd never outrun him in these heels.

"I don't have to prove anything to you."

"That's true." Bennett shrugged, draining the last of his coffee. There was menace in the way he set down the empty cup. "You don't. But I can't be the only one who's curious about your mystery man. Bet your family can't wait to meet him."

I fought the urge to squirm. "All in due time."

In the background, the milk steamer screeched. He raised his eyebrows innocently, a smirk playing on his full lips. I glared at him, wishing I'd stood him up.

My palms began to break out in a sweat as the afternoon sun pouring in through the window went from pleasantly warm to stiflingly hot, and the thin cashmere sweater I was wearing suddenly felt more like a parka. I drew in a breath, trying to steady myself and failing. Why did Bennett care so much about my fib? It's not like it affected him.

Seconds crawled by while the low din of coffee shop chatter filled the silence between us. Bennett tilted his head and gave me a questioning look, waiting me out.

"Fine," I hissed. Embarrassment simmered in my gut, syrupy and sickening. Leaning in closer, I lowered my voice. "I may have embellished the truth a little. You caught me, Sherlock. Are you happy now?"

There was the gleam of triumph in his eyes—mingled with a hint of something that, on anyone else, I would have called desire. But this was Bennett so it could only have been the desire to win. It was the only thing he cared about, other than himself.

"True happiness comes from within, Thayer."

Great. Now he was speaking in riddles. He wanted something.

I rolled my eyes. "I know you're enjoying this little cat and mouse game, but I'm growing bored." I twirled my freshly manicured index finger, urging him on. He'd already found my weak spot, but I couldn't let him know just how weak it was. In our world, the only thing worth more than your reputation was your last name. "Get to the point, please. What do you want?"

His lips curved. "I want to help you."

"Why?" I asked flatly.

Bennett didn't do anything unless there was something in it for him. He didn't volunteer for charity unless there was a photo op involved; didn't make donations unless his name would be on a big, shiny banner, front and center on a stage. Besides, I wasn't sure how much help he could be, unless he knew a reputable rent-a-date company.

"Like you," he said, "I have a small problem of my own."

Word had been going around for a while now that Bennett's real estate company was in a bind financially. Well, more than a bind. According to rumors, it was practically insolvent. I hadn't known how much credence to give it; sometimes, stories like that were fabricated to further someone else's interests.

But Bennett actually admitting there was a problem? Smoke, fire, inferno.

"Oh, I hear it's far from small."

"That's what they tell me." He smirked.

I glared at him, fighting the urge to kick him in the shin with my bootie. "First of all, gross. Second of all, I don't see how your problems have anything to do with me."

"They don't," he said. "Yet."

He placed both elbows on the table and leaned forward, encroaching on my personal space. I knew he was trying to establish the upper hand, and I refused to let him have it. I didn't budge. I didn't even blink.

Notes of leather and rosewood mingled with vanilla wafted over to me. I stilled my expression, keeping it impassive, but inwardly I was fighting the insane urge to lean closer and bury my face in his neck for another hit of his cologne. It wasn't fair that someone so horrible smelled so good.

We remained in a silent standoff, slightly too close together for either of us to be comfortable. Each of us daring the other to move.

To back down.

To lose.

His cold blue eyes captured mine, pinning me to the spot. "Your story's flimsy, Thayer. It didn't take long for me to figure out the truth."

"Not everyone is as nosy as you, stalker."

"It's only a matter of time before someone else figures it out too."

"So you're blackmailing me." Not even Bennett could pretend this was a level playing field.

He shifted in his seat and his knee grazed mine under the table, sending an electric current down my spine. It was just the physical embodiment of my distaste for him. Repulsion, that was it. Had to be.

"No, I'm offering you a deal."

CHAPTER FOUR

Bennett

THAYER GLOWERED AT ME, HER CHEEKS FLUSHED ROSY PINK. Likely out of embarrassment that I detected her mistruth, but this was actually her best-case scenario; better me than Millie or her mother. At least I had some sense of discretion.

"A deal," she repeated.

"Exactly."

"What's in it for you? Explain, Bradford." She leaned back in the black leather chair, crossing her arms tightly against her body. The neckline of her grey cashmere sweater shifted, revealing the slightest hint of cleavage. I made a concerted effort to keep my eyes above shoulder level.

"I need a date," I said. "Or a girlfriend, rather."

Between due diligence and the other items that would need to be negotiated, finalizing the deal with Callaghan would take at least a couple of weeks. After further reflection, it was clear that a date for the dinner would be insufficient—a girlfriend was the only logical solution. I couldn't risk Callaghan getting cold feet and pulling out partway through the closing process over his doubts about me.

Being in a committed relationship was the perfect way to cultivate a stable, reliable image and put Callaghan's mind at ease for good.

But a real girlfriend was obviously out of the question; I was desperate, not insane. Which brought us full circle to this table at the coffee shop, where Thayer and I both needed the same thing.

"I fail to see how that has anything to do with..." Her eyes widened, realization dawning on her face, and her expression hardened. "No. Hell no."

"In name only, for appearances' sake," I said smoothly, like this was the most normal proposition in the world. "Pretend to be my girlfriend and I'll pretend to be your mystery man everyone's been talking about."

Thayer's fall-themed paper cup crumpled halfway in her hand, causing the lid to pop off. Her upper lip curled into a subtle sneer. "If you think there's a chance that I would ever—"

She stopped short as a tired-looking woman in a messy bun pushing a black jogging stroller approached, trying to reach the restrooms behind us. The stroller's oversized rubber tire jostled our table, sending my empty cup rolling onto the floor.

The woman's hand flew up to her mouth. "Oh, I'm so sorry."

"Don't worry about it," I said. "Here, let me move the table over for you."

Thayer scooted her chair aside, and I grabbed hold of the laminate tabletop, dragging the base over a couple of inches. Leaning down to retrieve my cup, I caught a glimpse of Thayer's long legs beneath the table, clad in black skinny jeans. Unbidden, the mental image of her legs over my shoulders invaded my brain. As much as I resented Thayer for selling me out back in high school, there was no denying how attractive she was.

Thayer flashed the woman a warm smile, waving at the chubby, dark-haired baby in the stroller. "Hi," she cooed. "Your baby is adorable."

With everyone else, she was the epitome of class and manners.

Then her eyes fell to me, and her stare turned so menacing that I wished I'd worn a bulletproof vest underneath my charcoal suit.

"Thank you." The woman gave us a frazzled, apologetic smile and darted off.

"You were saying?" I maintained a neutral expression, pretending not to notice that Thayer was trying to bend the laws of physics and murder me from afar.

She took a hearty gulp of coffee from her rumpled red cup, apparently no longer concerned with decorum now that we were alone. Leaning closer, she lowered her voice to barely above a whisper. "You think I'm some cheap date for hire now?"

Of course, I didn't. Even if Thayer were for hire, we both knew she'd never be cheap.

"I didn't offer to pay you, I offered to help you. We both know I don't need to pay women to go out with me."

"Then ask one of *them*," she said through clenched teeth.

"Ah, but dating brings about its own set of complications I'd rather not deal with. This is simply an innovative solution to our respective problems."

That's right, I was practically goddamn Elon Musk. She should be thanking me for being so forward-thinking.

Her delicate nostrils flared. "You have problems, all right."

"It would be a mutually beneficial arrangement. Quid pro quo." I gave a one shoulder shrug. There were at least dozen women in my contacts list who would volunteer for this job. Problem is, they'd want a permanent position with a promotion to wife in the future, and I wasn't hiring.

"But why?" She studied my face, her pale blue eyes wary. "Why do you need a fake girlfriend?"

Progress. If she was asking, she was interested. Or at least curious.

"It seems I have, shall we say, a slight image problem." No thanks to Adam, that backstabbing shit. I was sure he was the one who leaked those photos. Someday, I'd prove it and exact revenge accordingly.

"You could say that again." Thayer pressed her lips into a thin line, and she nodded, gesturing impatiently for me to continue.

"For our next round of financing, I'm wooing a high-net-worth investor, Jared Callaghan. He's all about old-fashioned family values. You know, those silly antiquated things. And due to some of the things he's heard—not all of them true, of course—he's not much of a fan of yours truly."

She drained the last of her coffee, slamming the empty cup down on the table. "Smart man."

"Long story short, my reputation is a problem. In order to gain Callaghan's trust, I need to sell myself as a changed man—which includes a respectable, serious girlfriend. I need someone who can help me win him over, and you're the perfect person for the job."

In elementary school, Thayer finished her work early and read quietly until everyone else was done, sternly shushing other students who were talking or goofing off (and by other students, I mean me). And in junior high, when most of our peers were experimenting with smoking pot and making out at parties, she hung out with the choir nerds and volunteered on weekends.

Even in high school, she'd refused to participate in the senior prank. I thought filling the teachers' lounge with helium penis-shaped balloons was harmless, but she had disagreed. I even offered to add breast-shaped balloons for parity, but gender equality must not have been her objection.

Really, the worst anyone could say about Thayer was that she was the definition of Type-A, known for holding everyone else to her impossibly high standards. And, in my opinion, not a whole lot of fun. But on the flip side, she was morally upstanding, trustworthy like a vault, and her reputation was squeaky, soapy clean. She would pass anyone's background check anywhere, at any time. Once I decided I needed a fake girlfriend, she was the only one who fit that bill.

"You want to con your investor into trusting you," Thayer said slowly. "Solid plan, Bennett."

"I prefer to think of it as repairing my image." Which I still contended shouldn't need to be done in this day and age, but I needed that money more than I needed the self-satisfaction of sticking to my guns on that point.

"But being linked to you would tarnish *my* image."

"Not as much as getting caught inventing a boyfriend."

She narrowed her eyes. "If this is your idea of persuasion, I have news for you."

"I don't think you need persuading," I said. "Your circumstances are dire enough."

"Why would I agree to this?" Thayer shifted her weight, crossing her legs under the table. Her foot grazed mine, and she yanked it away like she'd been burnt.

"Have you got better offers beating down your door?" I rested my chin in my hand in mock interest, leaning closer with an expectant smile.

"Well, no." She blinked, long lashes fluttering. "But—"

"Then pray tell, what is the alternate solution to this problem you've created for yourself? This whole fake boyfriend thing?"

We both knew she didn't have one. Her lie was a grenade, and she'd already pulled the pin.

There was a telltale pause before she replied. "I'll tell everyone I broke it off." She jutted her chin defiantly, but fortunately for me, and unfortunately for her, she had a terrible poker face. Good thing she was too prissy to gamble; she'd get taken to the cleaners.

"You sure that will put the issue to rest?" I leaned back in my chair, watching her squirm. Then, I went in for the kill. "You know, Millie is floating the idea that your new beau is married. She's painting you as the other woman."

Thayer's right eye twitched. "So?"

"Our friends are starting to wonder if she's right."

"Please." Her expression was tight. "You know I would never do that."

I did, and I'd said as much to Millie. But unfortunately for Thayer, the rumor mill didn't care much for logic or reason.

"It's not about what I think," I said. "It's everyone else you need to worry about."

Sunlight poured in through the window, casting her in a golden glow as she sat quietly for a moment, mulling over what I'd just said.

Thayer heaved a resigned sigh. "What's the catch, Bennett?"

"There is no catch."

"Of course, there is." She snorted. "What is it? Do I sign over my soul, too? The deed to my condo parking stall?"

All solid ideas, but what I really needed was her.

"I wouldn't call it a catch, but we might need to commit to the charade for an extended length of time. You know, for believability's sake."

"Have you lost your mind? I told people I had a date," she hissed, bracing her fingers on the table and glancing around the coffee shop. "Not this warped scenario you're trying to drag me into." The flush returned to her cheeks, and she raked a hand through her hair, mussing the perfectly styled blonde waves.

Thayer was the picture of composure most of the time, almost never flustered. It was a good look on her; softer and less walled-off. Made me wonder what else might be beneath her frosty veneer. Like pink satin, maybe, or black lace. Or better yet, nothing but silky skin. I doubted Thayer was the type to go commando, though, especially given her line of work.

"You told people you had a boyfriend and that it was serious," I corrected her.

"Either way, this will never work." She looked down at the black laminate tabletop, drumming her pale pink fingernails in thought. Then she shook her head and lifted her chin, eyes glacial and tone to match. "No one would ever believe I'd date you."

"Ouch," I said dryly.

She shrugged. "Truth hurts."

"Lots of women would jump at the chance to become Mrs. Bennett Bradford."

Thayer curled her cherry-red lip in disdain. "There are also people who eat laundry detergent pods. I bet the Venn diagram for those is a perfect circle."

Despite myself, I laughed. Thayer was one of the few people who could successfully burn me. It didn't happen often, of course, and she had to work for it, but once in a while she landed a jab.

"What's your real objection?" I set down my cup. "Scared you won't be able to keep your hands off me?"

"More like scared I'll end up strangling you." She held out a hand, examining her flawless manicure. "I'd rather avoid jail time. I hear the food is dreadful."

"That's a risk I'm willing to take."

She heaved a sigh, pressing her lips into a thin line. "Look, I might consider it, but I don't think anyone will buy it."

"You're running out of other options, as am I." I stood up, pushing my chair back. "Just say yes. We both know you're going to."

Her gaze drifted from my face to my chest, continuing past my waist. Then her eyes snapped up to meet mine and she blinked rapidly, like she'd caught herself and was reverting back into Thayerbot mode.

Thayer pursed her crimson lips and exhaled, the hardened mask slipping back on. "Or what? You're going to tell everyone?"

It was strange how little she seemed to think of me, when I'd never actually do that. I knew firsthand what it was like to be burnt at the societal stake. Then again, Thayer thinking that was a risk wasn't the worst thing right now, either.

"They'll figure it out on their own pretty quick."

She snatched her leather purse off the back of her chair, pushing to stand. "Maybe, maybe not. I'm willing to take my chances."

"I doubt that very much," I said. "Offer's good until Friday. Then you're on your own."

CHAPTER FIVE

Thayer
September 4th
Grade 11

THIS WAS A BAD IDEA. A BAD IDEA THAT, AS PER USUAL, I'D *gotten talked into going along with by my sister and her friends, because I didn't want to be known as the 'boring twin'—though realistically speaking, I already was.*

Of course, it was marginally less bad before Bennett sauntered up, beer in hand, and joined the game. Now he was sitting directly across from me at the oversized wooden table in Millie's dining room. If I chose truth, I knew exactly what my sister was going to ask. And if I didn't, that was a different risk on its own.

My nails dug into the cream suede chair beneath me. "Dare."

Next to a pile of discarded red Solo cups, Quinn shifted on Porter's lap, giving me a knowing smile. "Okay…" She tapped her mouth with a finger and pretended to think, but I could tell she already knew exactly what she was going to say. "I dare you to spend seven minutes in heaven with Bennett."

Bass throbbed in the background, rap lyrics shooting rapid-fire out of the speakers, but the table fell silent, and all eyes turned to stare at us. Bennett shot Quinn a look of mild irritation, while I tried to keep my face as blank as a sheet of paper. I didn't know whether to thank her or strangle her when we got home. Frankly, it depended on what happened next, which with my luck, was going to be absolutely nothing.

Reluctantly, we both stood and began to make our way to the powder room just down the hall. Porter glowered at us—no, at Bennett. One of the other guys at the table made a wisecrack I didn't quite catch, and Bennett flipped him off on his way by.

"That was some shade Porter was throwing your way," I said under my breath. He was a senior at our school who played on the rugby team with Bennett, and my sister had lost her virginity to him the week before. Quinn was head over heels with the idea of dating an older guy, but I thought he was a jerk.

Bennett chuckled. "He's pissed because he choked at tryouts last week and I took his spot in the starting line-up."

One problem with going to an exclusive prep school? Parents sent their children to give them a leg up in life; an edge; an advantage. Which meant that our classmates weren't just our peers—they were our competition. It was like growing up inside an image-conscious, label-loving pressure cooker designed to turn us into carbon-copies of our parents.

With the exception of Lola and Bennett, dealing with everyone was exhausting. Actually, dealing with Bennett was exhausting in its own way too. Our friendship used to feel natural, but lately things between us were strained. Something had changed over the summer, and I wasn't sure if it was good or bad.

Bennett followed me into the silver wallpapered powder room and closed the door with a soft click. My heart pole-vaulted into my throat. He'd been locked in dark rooms with a lot more people of the opposite sex than I had. Not that I should have cared, because we were just friends.

He leaned against the white vanity, stuffing his hands into his pockets. I hopped up onto the granite counter next to him in an attempt to compensate for our height difference, which, thanks to his growth spurt last year, now verged on comical.

"Don't worry, Thay. We don't have to do anything."

Translation: he didn't want to do anything? I knew he'd kissed other girls. Like an idiot, I was waiting around for my turn.

I groaned. "I don't know why I agreed to play this stupid game."

"That's a good question." Bennett grinned. He reached over and gently tugged on the end my hair, sending a little thrill through my body. "Maybe the two coolers you drank had something to do with it."

"Why'd you agree to play?"

There were so many other things I wanted to ask instead of this. Things I would have asked without thinking twice, not long ago, but that now seemed awkward and potentially intrusive. Like did he really have sex with Caroline Phillips over the summer while I was staying with my father in Geneva? That's what the rumors said, but I could never trust those.

"Because you agreed first, and I figured something like this might happen. Better you get stuck with me than someone like Will or oc-to-hands Henderson."

"Nah, I think you were hoping to get some time with Millie."

He snorted. "She'd probably slip me some chloroform and hold me captive in the basement."

"Sounds about right." My eyes drifted down to his hands, still hidden in the pockets of his jeans. "How's your hand?"

Bennett glanced down and pulled out his right hand, straightening his fingers and making a fist, evoking a barely concealed wince. "It's fine."

"Looks like it hurts."

"Not as much as Reid's face."

I stifled a laugh. "You didn't have to do that."

"After he grabbed you?" In his profile, his jaw tensed. "I don't think I could have stopped myself. What a dick."

Somehow, word about Millie's party had made its way to

Hillside, one town over, and half of their senior class had shown up. When I had tried to squeeze by to get another drink from the fridge, Reid Hampton, captain of the Hillside's rugby team, not-so-subtly grabbed my boob.

He'd either been really drunk, really stupid, or both, because I wasn't even alone—Bennett was standing right behind me and had immediately punched Reid in the face, thereby almost instigating a brawl in the middle of Millie's marble kitchen. Fortunately, Millie's older brother and his friends had been home to play bouncer and kick out the party crashers.

"But now Hillside's going to be out to draw blood when you play them next week."

Bennett smirked. "They can try, but I doubt they'll have much luck."

It was true that he was one of the stronger players on the team, but I still didn't like the idea of them gunning for him. I fought a yawn, trying to hide it. Maybe he was right; maybe two drinks had gone to my head, because suddenly, I was exhausted. Or maybe that was the six AM wakeup for jazz choir practice before school.

With a sigh, I leaned against Bennett's shoulder, realizing only too late the bodily contact between us lately was charged with an electricity that didn't exist before. A few tense breaths passed, but neither of us spoke.

"Thay?"

"Yeah?" I turned to look at him in the dim lighting of the tiny chandelier. On the other side of the door, someone murmured something indecipherable, and a burst of laughter rang out.

Suddenly, he looked uncharacteristically nervous. He reached up and rubbed the back of his neck, giving me a sheepish smile. "Want to go to homecoming with me?"

It took at least five full seconds for me to process what he'd said. "I thought you didn't want to go."

"But you want to," Bennett said, nudging me with his elbow. "So let's go together."

Was this a pity ask, or a real date? I wasn't sure. But I hoped it was the second.

"Only if you really want to."

"With you? I really do." His gaze dropped to my lips, tension between us multiplying exponentially with a single look.

Someone banged on the door, and we both jumped, the fragile moment between us bursting like a bubble.

"Time's up, lovebirds!" Millie's voice carried through the door.

"Was she standing outside with a fucking stopwatch or what?" Bennett grumbled.

Heart racing, I slid off the counter. "Probably."

CHAPTER SIX

Thayer

A LONE CAR SPED PAST ME AS I SPEED-WALKED DOWN THE
block, shivering in the chill of the early morning. Streetlamps
illuminated the thin layer of frost glimmering on the windows
of vehicles left parked overnight. The neon green sign of Spinfinity
Cycle Studio at the end of the block glowed, beckoning to me like
a sanctuary.

All I wanted was to throw myself into a strenuous workout and
forget the whole week had ever happened.

Better yet, erase it altogether. If only I could.

I pulled open the glass double doors and exchanged hellos with
the receptionist, Pamela, before heading for the women's locker
room. The comforting, familiar eucalyptus aromatherapy greeted
me as I changed out of my joggers and tee, yanking on my black
sports bra, black racerback tank, and black leggings.

Then I plopped down on the bench and slipped into my cy-
cling shoes, fighting my ten-ton eyelids. My fingers slipped, accidentally tying a knot in my laces instead of a bow. I cursed under
my breath, pulling the knot out with my fingernails. I'd already been

awake when my alarm went off at five AM this morning. In fact, I'd been awake most of the night, because as soon as I turned off my bedside lamp, my mind had latched on to one inescapable fact: I was screwed.

After my slip of the tongue at the fundraiser, I'd planned to lay low while things blew over. In time, I figured I could simply pretend that my nonexistent boyfriend and I had broken up. A week or two of hiding at home, dodging calls and invitations, and I'd claim we'd gone our separate ways. Irreconcilable differences, incompatible lifestyles, infidelity on his part, something like that. Preferably something that painted me in a sympathetic, but favorable, light.

But things weren't blowing over. Not even close.

What I hadn't accounted for was the serious lack of interesting gossip circulating within our social stratosphere. No one else was newly dating, mating, or doing much else of interest. For lack of other things to focus on, my friends and family were far more interested in my pretend paramour than I had expected.

It was like a breaking scandal on a slow news day. Ever since the gala, my phone had blown up with texts: *Who's your new boyfriend? When can I meet him? How did you two meet?* The attention was overwhelming, not to mention a little insulting. Just because I hadn't had a boyfriend in a few years didn't mean I couldn't get one.

But that didn't change the predicament I was in now, solidly without a boyfriend or an escape plan. At this point, joining the witness protection program seemed like the only option. Maybe there was a for-profit division where you could pay to disappear after making humiliating, life-altering mistakes. Surely, there had to be a market for that kind of thing. Then I could start over on a white sandy beach somewhere, selling coconuts filled with colorful tropical cocktails. It would be money well spent.

"Sorry I'm late!" Lola breezed into the locker room, tossing her lavender Lululemon duffle onto the teak bench beside me. She rummaged through her gym bag, yanking out her clothes. "Pearl threw up on the floor because she found a hair elastic and ate it again. Cats, am I right? Then there was construction on the freeway, and I couldn't find the valet to come park my car..." she trailed off.

After more than fifteen years of friendship, I'd accepted Lola for who she was, tardiness and all. I wasn't sure why she still bothered making excuses or apologizing, but I guess it was the thought that counted.

Glancing at the stainless-steel clock on the wall, I checked the time. "We're good. Still have four minutes to spare." I stood up, closing my locker and securing it with the digital code.

"Phew." She yanked off her baggy white t-shirt and stepped out of her hot pink flannel pajama pants, cramming them into her bag and standing before me in nothing but her purple underwear.

Unlike me, Lola had zero qualms about her body or anyone else seeing it. She also literally rolled straight out of bed and came to spin class, sleepwear and all. Personally, I needed an extra fifteen minutes to caffeinate beforehand.

"I'm thinking we should hit Riverside Bistro this weekend," I said. "Carbs and mimosas?" If there was ever a time for emergency pancakes, this self-inflicted crisis was it.

"Sure," Lola said, yanking on a pair of black leggings. "Hey, how was the fundraiser the other night?" She shimmied into a neon orange sports bra, followed by a lime green crop top, both of which glowed against her tawny skin. Gathering her dark, gold-streaked ringlets, she secured her hair into a high bun with a spiral elastic. "I know you said you got cornered by some of your mother's friends, but you never filled me in."

Cornered was putting it mildly. Shortly after my mother learned about my newly invigorated love life, the entire hospital fundraising board waylaid me near the women's bathroom, drilling for details about my new 'suitor.' I'd complained about it to Lola in my quick recap text before bed, without thinking about the fact that she'd want to know why I'd been cornered.

"It was fine."

"Fine?" She wrinkled her nose, tossing her belongings in the locker and locking the digital keypad. "Those parties are never 'fine.' Mixing alcohol with that crowd is like lighting a stick of dynamite; something always explodes. That's why I let you take one for the team and tell me about it later."

Lola's father was heir to the Van Sant fortune and worked in Swiss banking. Her mother was a reclusive semi-famous artist, but neither cared for the pomp and circumstance of the society pages. This provided Lola the freedom to enjoy her generous trust fund while also embracing her inner hippie. The perfect unicorn scenario.

Her parents did force her to attend our stuffy prep school for K-12, but the moment we graduated, Lola headed straight for a tree-hugging, pot-smoking small liberal arts college in New Hampshire. She'd threatened to stay there after graduation, too, but that only lasted a couple of months. After a disastrous one-week marriage to a lumberjack named Phil while she worked as a barista, she got an annulment and moved back to the city.

Now she was an art curator at a ritzy boutique gallery downtown and had a rotation of hookups on speed dial. In other words, she was my polar opposite, and that's what made our friendship work.

"It was pretty uneventful, that's all. Boring as usual." I shrugged, following Lola down the hall to the fitness area. Pulsing pop music tumbled out of the dimly lit spin studio as she pulled open the door. We grabbed our familiar two bikes off to the left, setting our water bottles in the holders and spreading out our gym towels across the handlebars.

Lola clipped her feet in and began pedaling. "Did something happen that you don't want to tell me? You always come back with at least one good story about a handsy senator or a drunken television personality."

Trepidation swirled within my gut, low and uneasy. I hadn't yet decided whether to tell Lola the truth. Objectively, it seemed like the logical thing to do—best friends should tell each other everything, right? And unlike most people in my life, Lola never judged me. But pride was a powerful thing, and it was difficult to own up to my humiliating lie even to her.

"Slow night, I guess."

She shot me a sidelong glance. "You're acting off."

The problem with having the same best friend for nearly two decades? She could read me like a book. Better than my own sister could, even.

"What?" I took a sip from my white S'well water bottle, avoiding her eyes. "No, I'm not."

"You totally are."

"Not." I pedaled faster, wishing I could outrun my lies.

"Are too," she insisted.

Our instructor, Celeste, walked in and hopped onto her bike at the front, facing the rest of the class. At six feet tall and ripped, she could have passed for a professional volleyball player or a fitness model. With a Disney-princess voice and a sadistic streak a mile wide when it came to hill climbs, she was a confusing combination of drill sergeant and perky cheerleader. The result was both motivating and terrifying, which made for brutal workouts.

"Good morning, everyone! Time to get going. Let's begin on a flat road, aiming for 90-100 RPM to start." The loud pop music got louder, bass reverberating through my body.

"Something is up," Lola whispered loudly, "and you're going to tell me."

A blonde girl in the next row glanced over her shoulder, shooting us a dirty look for talking. Lola shot her a sickly-sweet smile in return.

We pedaled along without speaking for the rest of the five-minute warm-up. Lola reached down, grabbing her water bottle and taking a drink. Courage seized hold. Now was the time; if I told her what I'd done, we could laugh it off and by the end of class, it would be old news. Then, she could help me concoct a way out of this mess. Lola was no stranger to unusual predicaments.

"Well, I kind of—" I started to come clean, to tell her the truth, but my self-preservation instincts kicked in and my throat clamped shut.

"You're seeing someone, aren't you?" Lola turned to face me, watching my reaction.

"Um…yes." As much as I hated lying, it did seem easier to play along. Plus, this way I wouldn't have to worry about the truth getting out by accident.

Her eyebrows shot up. "I knew it! Millie's dirt is never wrong." She snapped her water bottle shut, placing it back in the holder. "That's awesome, Thay. I'm happy for you."

"Ladies!" Celeste shouted over the mic. "If you can chit-chat, you're not working hard enough!"

"You knew, but you were waiting to make me tell you?" I hissed, facing forward so Celeste wouldn't call us out again.

"Obviously." Lola wiped a trail of sweat off her brow with her white gym towel, shooting me a mock-offended look, but beneath it lay genuine hurt. "I can't believe you didn't tell me. I'm your best friend."

"Let's turn it up now! I know you came to work," Celeste boomed, which felt a lot like a dig at us.

"It's been moving fast, and I needed some time to wrap my head around it." I increased my resistance and stood up out of the saddle for our first hill climb. That wasn't untrue; one minute I was single, the next I had a fictional boyfriend. Wham.

Lola nodded, breathing heavily from the exertion. "I didn't mean to give you a hard time. Who is it?"

Before I could formulate a reply, Celeste's voice carried over the mic again. "What did you come here for today?" The throbbing bass got louder, nearly rattling my teeth. "Results! Hit that dial and turn up your resistance some more. Come on, everyone! Halfway through our two-minute standing hill climb."

Looking down, I adjusted the dial on my bike to avoid Lola's prying eyes. "We can talk about it later," I huffed, thighs starting to burn as we climbed the hill. It was unfortunate that the spin bike was fixed in place, because riding away seemed like the only solution.

After class, we headed for the studio's steam showers and got dressed for work, primping at the makeup station by the sinks. Lola leaned over the white quartz counter, gazing into the mirror as she carefully filled in her eyebrows with a pencil. She worked quickly, using short, feathery strokes until her arches were sculpted perfection.

"Are you going to make me guess who it is?" She caught my eyes in the mirror, pursing her raspberry pink lips in thought. "Is it that Devon guy you went out with last month?"

"No..." I rifled through my makeup bag to find my liquid eyeliner, trying very hard not to think of Devon, who'd hinted at a threesome with my sister at the end of our first date. Like I said, the dating pool was a swamp.

"Sebastian from your stepfather's company?"

"Definitely not." Steadying my elbow on the counter, I carefully traced a thin, inky line along one eyelid, followed by the other.

"Really? He was super hot. Definitely had that boss daddy energy."

"He took that energy a little too far," I said. "He basically told me how lucky I was to be out on a date with him. And he ogled the woman seated at the table next to us the entire time." Admittedly, she'd been gorgeous, but if that was Sebastian's idea of wining and dining me, it was a hard pass.

"Ugh." Lola made a face. "It must be that guy from the dating app, then. Vince."

"No. He was vegan." I tilted my head back, carefully wiggling the black mascara wand up from the roots of my lashes. Lola shot me an exasperated look in the mirror, and I held up a finger, silencing her. "Judgy vegan. I already knew where my bacon came from, I don't need to be reminded over dinner."

My phone buzzed in my purse on the counter. It was still early, so it was probably Quinn with some sort of 'emergency' at one of the stores. Her definition of emergency was pretty liberal. Last time, she'd spotted a spider on the roof that she couldn't reach with a broom. I was pretty sure she didn't even try.

When I checked the screen, it was even worse.

Bennett: Four days. Tick tock….

Insufferable jerk. I quickly locked the screen, cramming my phone back in my bag. I'd handle Bennett—or try to handle him, at least—later.

Lola huffed a sigh. "Fine, I give up. I guess I'll find out when you send me a wedding invite."

"Look, I'm not trying to be difficult," I told her. "I just need a few more days to fully vet him."

Or decide whether to go along with Bennett's scheme, thereby making a deal with the devil. One or the other.

I tossed my mascara back into my gold makeup bag, zipping it shut and examining my reflection in the mirror. Even with a full face of makeup, the lack of sleep showed. Full-coverage concealer and clever contouring could only do so much. I'd disguised the purple circles and highlighted to hide my pallor, but sadly couldn't magically remove the undereye bags I was sporting.

Maybe it was time for some injectables. Then again, I was going to die alone, so why bother?

"I'd say I need to vet him for you too, but anyone who passes your test will pass mine with flying colors." Lola laughed, but we both knew there was truth to it—she had a defective bullshit meter.

Combined with her heart of 24-karat gold that she wore on her sleeve like a Hermès bracelet, it was a recipe for heartbreak. Repeated heartbreaks leading to emergency girls' nights with pints of her favorite chocolate almond-milk ice cream, organic Sauvignon blanc by the bottle, and Netflix marathons. I didn't mind being there for her, but I found the whole cyclical aspect perplexing. Having your heart stomped on seemed like an experience you'd want to avoid repeating.

Yet, despite that, Lola was never deterred from her search for 'the one.' As endearing as I found her oversized heart to be, I knew the one didn't really exist. It was a fictitious concept fabricated to sell books and movies. Just look at my mother—first she thought my father was the one, then her second husband, then her third husband, and now her fourth husband, Charles. Each and every time, she was convinced.

It completely violated the entire premise. You're only supposed to get one.

Which brought us to the second problem with this concept: Planet Earth, population 7.8 billion. Are we really supposed to believe that out of all the people around the globe, there's one person solely meant for us? That out of billions of human beings on the planet, a single one could fit you like no other? It's statistically impossible. Not to mention, if that was the case, the odds were not in your favor of ever finding them.

CHAPTER SEVEN

Bennett

Afternoon arriving at Flux a little after eight, I'd barely had the chance to boot up my computer before Ian barreled into my office and threw down a sheaf of papers on my desk.

"Well," I said. "Good morning to you, too."

"Someone else put in a bid on our parcel of land yesterday," he snapped. "This third party is trying to edge us out. They've triggered a competing bids process with the city, which means the clock is ticking. We no longer have the luxury of waiting to nail down our financing."

"Who?" I could only think of one person stupid enough to consider that, but even he wasn't dumb enough to actually do it.

"Who do you think?" Ian said. "AM Developments."

My jaw clenched so hard I nearly broke a cap. What in the ever-loving fuck did my cousin Adam think he was doing? Some people get to where they are in life because they've earned it. People like Adam Matthews, on the other hand, get to where they are because they're opportunistic assholes that ride everyone else's coattails to the top. No leadership skills, business acumen, or even grit to back any of it up. Just good old-fashioned freeloading.

And now he was marrying into the Montgomery family. Connections like theirs, combined with the weight of their old-money name, would go a long way in compensating for Adam's meager business sense and milquetoast personality. I'm not saying it was a marriage of convenience, but it was certainly convenient for him.

I balled and unballed my fists, wishing my hands were around Adam's throat.

"He'll never get it," I said, for my own benefit as much as Ian's. "They already accepted our conditional offer."

Ian looked less than convinced. "Exactly. Conditional. We have less than two months to come up with the funds, satisfy those conditions, and convince council to approve our rezoning and variance requests. Even then, if they decide his project is a better fit, we could still lose."

"It'll be fine."

"Will it?" He sighed, leaning back in his chair.

"Your connection at the planning department said it's as good as ours, right?"

"Right." But Ian sounded unconvinced.

The worst part was, Adam and I went way back. My mother was his father, Richard's, younger sister, and growing up, Adam was like another brother to me. We'd attended prep schools in neighboring cities, enjoying the friendly rivalry between our schools and playing each other in varsity sports. Even throughout college, we'd remained close.

After graduating, we struck out on our own and founded a real estate development company with Ian. The three of us invested blood, sweat, tears, and every penny to our names. It just so happened that I was the only one with any appreciable amount of capital to sink in, but we called their portions sweat equity and considered it equal—as an act of good faith.

First and last time I ever did anything in good faith.

Right before Christmas last year, the disloyal bastard decided to divest himself of his ownership interest. The three of us collectively held a total of fifty-one percent, with the remaining forty-nine percent distributed among twenty-odd smaller investors. Allowing Adam to sell his shares on the open market would have meant Ian and I lost controlling interest—and Adam knew it. We were forced to buy him out ourselves on short notice, nearly bankrupting us both in the process. Happy Holidays indeed. The icing on the double-crossing cake? Adam used his proceeds to start a rival company, leveraging his internal knowledge to compete.

Until now, Adam had been little more than a mosquito in my ear. A nuisance, perhaps, but not a real threat. Now that he was fucking with my project, however, he was more like a venomous spider in need of extermination.

"What do we do now?" I began to entertain a variety of revenge scenarios in my head that were wholly illegal, and sadly, never going to happen. Unless, possibly, I hired someone...

"You tell me," Ian said.

Time to initiate Plan B. "Let me go talk to Richard."

He braced his hands on the arms of his chair, gaping at me. It mirrored the way I felt. Approaching my Uncle Richard was an absolute last resort. In our family, gifts didn't come with strings—they came with nooses. And so did favors.

"Richard?" Ian repeated.

"What choice do we have?"

I knew asking Richard for a business loan was risky. Not only was he family, but he'd also been my father's boss ever since I was in high school, when my father ran into trouble with the Securities and Exchange Commission. After a lengthy, stressful investigation, my father admitted to lesser charges and was permitted to continue working in the financial field under specific, limited circumstances subject to the supervision of someone else. That's where Richard came in. I'd like to say Richard hired him out of the kindness of his heart, but Richard didn't have a heart. Richard was the reason he had to cop a plea in the first place.

It didn't help that Richard's only son, my cousin Adam, was shady as fuck too—I gave Adam the benefit of the doubt that he was different from his father and learned only too late that the apple didn't fall far from the two-faced tree.

For those reasons, among many others, I promised myself I'd never ask Richard for help. Unfortunately, I was breaking a lot of promises lately. This was my last resort. After the frosty reception I'd received from Thayer at Starbucks yesterday, I couldn't count on her agreeing. And asking my father wasn't even an option, because he didn't have that kind of money anymore.

Besides, it was temporary—or at least, it was supposed to be. That's why I was proposing an extortionate interest rate. That's why I was willing to sign my life away. That's why I'd offered a personal goddamn guarantee, another thing I swore I'd never do. I just needed to stop the bleeding so we could keep moving forward with construction. Then, we'd be able to close the next round of financing, get a large cash injection, and everything would work itself out.

Or everything would go up in flames. But at least there'd be a resolution.

"Okay, son. Let's skip the pretense, shall we?" My uncle Richard gestured to the black plastic folder in front of him, which contained the report I'd spent the better part of the past twenty-four hours compiling. Painstaking attention to detail, line-by-line proofreading, double- and triple-checking the figures. Lost sleep, lost hair, lost sanity.

All for nothing, as the folio was still closed, and Richard apparently had no plan to read it. I'd sent him an electronic copy too, of course, but Richard was old school and preferred paper.

"The pretense?" I echoed.

"Talk to me about what's going on. Cut to the chase." Richard adjusted the sleeves of his light blue French-cuff shirt and placed his elbows on the oversized mahogany desk, fingers clasped. His bespoke grey suit hugged his mid-sized frame, and combined with his commanding presence, the two created the effect of him being much larger than he was.

I squared my shoulders and strapped on my mental battle armor, preparing for psychological warfare. The plush, black leather seat I found myself in felt more like an electric chair.

"In the interest of full disclosure," I said, "the funds I am seeking are to finance the purchase of a property Adam is also bidding on with his new company. If that is a conflict of interest for you, I understand."

When Ian, Adam, and I founded Flux four years ago, Richard had declined to invest, claiming start-ups were "too risky" for his portfolio. But when Adam decided to strike out solo last year, suddenly Richard was more than happy to write him a seven-figure check. In other words, I was asking Richard to fund a company that was in direct competition with one he'd already invested a significant amount of money into.

"That won't influence my discussion." He waved me off.

"Are you sure?"

Though, it wasn't a huge surprise. The list of things Richard cared about was short, and money was at the top. If I could convince him this was a lucrative arrangement, it would be a done deal. It didn't matter if he was family or that he'd seen me running around in diapers at one point. We were both professionals, discussing a potential contractual agreement. Business was business.

And really, helping me was the least he could do after the other things he'd done.

A wry smile played on his lips. "The business world isn't going to go easy on him, so why should you? Let's circle back to the details of the offering."

"Okay," I said. "I need bridge financing. Five million."

He sighed, combing a hand through his slicked-back, artificially darkened hair. "Tell me the truth: is your company in trouble financially?"

"No," I insisted. Technically, we weren't—if we got this money. "I just need short term funding until we close this next round of financing. We're ninety percent of the way there."

Richard reached for the folio and flipped it open with a disinterested expression. He slipped on his wire-rimmed reading glasses, peering down at the document. "You're asking for a term of six months," he observed, running a finger down the front page of figures. "My bridge financing arrangements are for a period of ninety days or less. I'm concerned that you won't be able to get the capital to repay before our usual ninety days. Frankly, it's a red flag."

I shifted in my seat, resisting the urge to flinch. He looked at me like I was still seven years old. Like he was reprimanding me during t-ball, back when he used to coach the team I played on with Adam. I use the word coach lightly, because it was more like yelling at us for missing the ball or not running fast enough.

Or like the time when I was fifteen years old, and Adam and I took his beloved silver Porsche out for a joyride. Adam scrubbed the curb and blew a tire, and Richard had blown a gasket in response.

"I'm trying to allow for some cushion. Of course, it's my intention to pay you back as soon as possible." I just didn't know when that would be.

Richard tsked, nodding. The dim lighting that he favored for his office cast shadows on his jawline, which was sharp enough to cut stone. He was hawkish—and he looked it.

"You understand my position."

"I do," I said. "That's why I'm here. I want to work something out that is favorable for all parties."

He fell silent, studying the proposed terms sheet on the front page. "I would need to take some security," he said, closing the plastic folder without bothering to read the rest. "Half of your interest in the company."

"Pardon?" I was certain I'd misheard. No one would ask for that. It wasn't reasonable.

"You have what, 25.5% now? Let's round that up to 13%."

How did he know that off the top of his head? This is why he didn't bother to read the report. He'd already done a deep dive on our financials. I should have known.

"To be returned upon repayment of the loan," he added. "If you repay it."

My jaw ticked. Of course, I'd repay it. What did he think I was, a thief? An idiot? The company was doing great on paper. We were just having some issues getting through a growth spurt. No thanks to his golden son, Adam.

Of course, he provided Adam with a steady stream of cash whenever he needed it, no strings attached. While I couldn't expect my uncle to treat me like his son, was it too much to ask for him not to destroy me like a ruthless corporate raider?

I bit back a retort and swallowed a mouthful of sand. "I'm open to it." The words were bitter, hard to get out.

"And I would need a seat on the board—permanently."

I blinked at him, dumbfounded. While many people would kill to have access to his expertise and business acumen, I preferred to dodge his tendency to steamroll everyone else in the room. Having him on the board in any capacity would basically be akin to making him Chairperson. And I was Chair.

I cleared my throat and made an effort to keep my voice even. "I'm not—"

"We also need to talk about crafting some conditions into your employment contracts as well as the contracts for the board," he said.

"Conditions?" Speaking of steamrolling, I was flat as a goddamn pancake. Worse, I didn't even know how to stop this death spiral. But I wasn't in a place to push back, let alone make demands. If we didn't get some funding, Flux would go down in flames and cremate me along with it.

Richard nodded. "Stipulations regarding acceptable and

expected behavior. You know, to avoid issues in the future. I can't be associated with a corporation of ill repute." He rifled through his desk drawer, emerging with an ivory business card, sliding it across the desk to me. "David McCarthy at Blake Miller McCarthy LLP. He specializes in employment law matters and he does stellar contract work."

Suddenly, my tie became a noose around my neck. Beads of sweat broke out around my hair line, and I resisted the urge to wipe them away. Fidgeting or looking nervous would only add fuel to this bonfire.

"What kind of stipulations did you have in mind? And to what end?" My mouth was desert dry. I picked up the glass of water sitting on the marble side table next to me, gulping back half in two swallows.

"Anything that would cause embarrassment or disreputability for either company."

Anything? I didn't like the sound of that, especially not after Strippergate last year. My uncle's lawyers would craft something they could drive a bus through, and then they'd throw me right under it. They'd probably turn around and flip my shares to Adam for good measure. I stared at the card, mind working overtime. The word 'disreputability' alone was a clear red flag. I was many things, but a pillar of society wasn't one of them. There had to be an alternate solution. Had to be.

"Bennett?" His voice brought me crashing back down to reality. "What do you think of the terms I've outlined?"

I thought they were exploitative and unreasonable, especially from my own uncle, but even I wasn't stupid enough to say that out loud. Not that I should have expected anything else from Richard William Matthews. His specialties included leveraging other people's vulnerabilities to strong-arm them, squeezing every last dime out of business deals, and playing puppeteer with others to further his interests.

I crossed an ankle over my knee, trying to pretend like I wasn't inwardly losing my shit. "To be clear, I wasn't looking to divest myself of any equity."

Richard looked at me skeptically. "I realize that. But you're over-leveraged. At this point, I have serious doubts you'll be able to pay the money back, and I have to protect myself in case things go sideways. Or when they go sideways."

In other words, he'd rather give me the money and consider it a write-off—with multiple, handcuffing conditions that benefited him—than extend a legitimate business loan to me. My uncle had already decided I was going under, and he was more than happy to strap cement boots on my feet to help speed up the process.

"Not everyone is cut out to run a company," he added.

Like father, like son, but he didn't need to say that part out loud.

"No." I drew in a breath, pushing away from the mahogany leather chair to stand. "I'm sorry, but I can't agree to those terms."

"I don't think you're in a position to refuse."

My jaw tensed. "I came to you for help, not to get screwed. I already have enough people willing to fuck me."

"Watch your mouth." He glared at me, straightening his forest green silk tie. "Let's not pretend this is a level playing field. If you want my help, you play by my rules."

"That's funny," I said. "Rules never meant anything to you before."

"Son," he warned, tone dripping with venom.

"I could tell my mother the truth, you know."

For nearly ten years, I had been sitting on the acrid knowledge that Richard screwed over my father. Richard masterminded their entire insider trading scheme, neatly designed to make the already rich even richer. It carried on for two years until the feds swooped in. Then Richard let my father fall on the knife for him, and we lost everything. The only reason I hadn't exposed Richard was my mother.

"Bennett." His demeanor turned eerily calm. He tilted his head, pity across his face and malice in his eyes. "You'd never do that to her."

He was right. It would be the equivalent of blowing up her world for a second time. I couldn't bring myself to be the one to do that, even if he did deserve it.

"Forget it." I stood up, turned on my heel, and stalked out of his office, slamming the solid wood door behind me. It echoed down the corridor, causing everyone in the vicinity to turn and watch my hasty departure.

Back to Plan A, regardless of what it took to get Thayer to agree.

CHAPTER EIGHT

Bennett
September 7th
Grade 11

EVERYTHING HURT, FROM MY BODY TO MY BRAIN. MAKING THE starting line in rugby meant Coach Hansen was riding my ass even more than usual. What little spare time remained was consumed with tutoring and SAT prep class. Thanks to constant parental reminders, I was hyper-conscious of college admissions looming in my future. Battling a bunch of other privileged kids with their own private tutors while being graded on a curve, like some sort of academic Hunger Games.

Not to mention, my mom was still sick. Ever since she'd been diagnosed with breast cancer, Holden has turned into a shell of his former self. My sociable, athletic younger brother had taken to lurking in his bedroom, glued to a screen, refusing to come out for anything other than school—and sometimes not even then. Therapy, meds, nothing seemed to help whatever the hell was going on with Holden. He'd only stayed on the swim team this year under the threat of losing his phone.

I poked my head into the living room, where my mom was lying on the couch, resting.

"Where's Dad?" Family meals were more like half the family, lately. Me and my mother, and she wasn't eating much these days because chemotherapy had killed her appetite. I offered to hook her up with some marijuana to help with the nausea, but when she connected those dots, I nearly got my ass grounded for life. According to my mother, Bradfords didn't do drugs.

"Working late."

"Again?" I snorted. "What's the excuse this time? Someone going to die if he doesn't answer an email within two minutes of arrival?" He'd been working all the time for the past couple of months; supposedly out of necessity, but my father ran his own firm so it's not like he had a boss. Coming home for dinner with your sick wife once in awhile was the least the guy could do. Granted, he made sure she had a housekeeper and part-time chef, but you couldn't outsource being a husband. Or a father.

My mother set down her paperback, hesitating. Her eyes traced my face and as they did, I realized they were bloodshot like she'd been crying.

"Where is he really?" I asked. Was he having an affair? It wouldn't have been a huge surprise. Among the families we knew, infidelity wasn't exactly uncommon. "I'm not a little kid, Mom. Just tell me the truth."

She dropped her gaze to her hands, shoulders rising with an inhale, and lifted her chin. There was a sadness I'd never seen across her face before, not even when she broke the news about her cancer diagnosis.

"Your father was arrested this afternoon. He's under investigation for insider trading."

My gray backpack slid out of my grip, landing on the hardwood floor with a thump that echoed through the hall. Her words ran through my brain again, my heart picking up pace as I processed what they meant. Or tried to, because they didn't make sense. "What? He'd never do that."

"I know." Her voice wavered. "But sometimes these things are gray from the outside looking in, honey. I'm sure they'll realize he's innocent once they complete the investigation."

Panic clawed at my throat. "Does this mean they're going to freeze all your assets? Are we going to lose the house?"

"Everything will be okay," she said, but it seemed like she was telling herself as much as me. "I already spoke to Richard, and he said he will make sure your father has the best legal defense money can buy. He'll cover tuition for you and Holden, too, so you don't need to worry about changing schools. It's only temporary until this gets sorted out, anyway."

"Right." I nodded, but school was the least of my worries. "Wait, does this have anything to do with the IPO that Dad and Uncle Richard were working on together?"

She shook her head. "I don't think—I don't think Richard was involved."

I bent down, retrieving my bag from off the floor. Did Adam know? He was like a second brother to me, but somehow, even him hearing about this seemed embarrassing. I didn't want everyone to know my father had been carted away in handcuffs like some kind of criminal. Especially when he was obviously innocent.

My mother stepped forward and placed a hand on my shoulder. "Do you want something to eat? Maria left a plate for you in the fridge."

"Thanks, "I said, "but I've lost my appetite."

"Are you sure?" Her face fell in a way that made me wish I could eat, but it truly wasn't an option.

"Maybe later, after I get some studying done." If I could focus on AP Chemistry while my father sat rotting in a jail cell somewhere.

Turning away, I threw my bag back on my shoulder and headed for the hall. This couldn't actually be happening. It had to be a mistake. Some kind of misunderstanding or legitimate trade gone wrong.

"Bennett," she called. "Please don't say anything to your brother. Let me talk to him when he gets back. I don't want him to find out while he's away on his first swim meet of the year."

CHAPTER NINE

Thayer

"**O**FFER'S GOOD UNTIL FRIDAY. THEN YOU'RE ON YOUR OWN," I mimicked under my breath, easing my SUV out of the Starbucks drive-through. "Asshole."

Doing a quick shoulder check, I pulled onto the main road that led to the flagship location of Lace & Grace, on the south side of town. With our third store due to open in four months, I needed to find a more efficient way to track orders and inventory. We also planned to float employees between the three stores, which required tweaks to our payroll system. Between the two tasks, I had a full day of work ahead of me.

Unfortunately, not even the fresh black coffee sitting in my cupholder could take the edge off my sour mood.

My mind was reeling, full of a thousand conflicting thoughts per minute. A fake relationship? Really, what was Bennett thinking? No one would believe a womanizer like him would settle down. The guy had more skeletons in his closet than a graveyard. I'd never known someone less suited for a second date, let alone a serious relationship. And I certainly wasn't the only one who shared that opinion.

Even more ludicrous would be trying to sell the idea that I would get involved with Bennett. I mean, please. I was picky—and everyone knew it. He would never even have a shot.

Sure, most people got hung up on his superficial appeal, like his broad shoulders, chiseled jawline, and earth-stopping-smile. The packaging *was* pretty. But there were flaws beneath his shiny exterior that ran right down to the foundation. Bennett was a master manipulator; he could make you feel like you were the only one in a crowded room, but if you crossed him, he could make you feel like you didn't even exist. Or in my case, sometimes he did that even if you didn't cross him and he just deemed you unworthy of his time.

Moreover, I wasn't stupid, which was what you'd have to be to believe someone like Bennett could be monogamous, even just for show.

But if everyone else believed it, it would solve my self-inflicted problem.

When I pulled into the parking lot in front of Lace & Grace ten minutes later, Quinn's silver BMW coupe was conspicuously absent. My grip on the tan leather-clad steering wheel tightened, a flicker of irritation sparking in my belly. She was supposed to be here, preparing to open in ten minutes. If I hadn't come in and a customer had shown up, we would have lost a sale. Hell, if a customer showed up now, we *still* might lose a sale. There was a reason my role was relegated to the back office: I couldn't close to save my life. If anything, I tended to inadvertently talk people out of purchases.

Why was it so difficult for everyone else to be on time? Exasperating. I should buy them all watches for Christmas.

My phone lit up from the charging station in the center console. Dread surged as I reached for it, praying it wasn't Bennett again. Then I regretted thinking that, because what I found was worse.

Mom: Will your boyfriend be joining us for Sunday dinner this weekend?

Thayer: Let me just make sure he's free.

Mom: Please let me know so Henrietta can plan accordingly. Or we can reschedule for a day when he's available.

Thayer: I'll let you know.

I shook my head, sliding the phone into my bag and climbing out of my car. Sadly, I couldn't even begin to think of a solution that didn't involve Bennett.

Speed walking up to the storefront, I jabbed my keys into the lock and shoved the glass door open with my hip, flipping on the LED track lights. My mood softened as I drank in the sight of the blond hardwood floors, clean white walls, and recently changed-up displays. Our fall inventory had arrived, and the racks were full of satin-trimmed robes, cozy waffle-knit sets, and lace negligees. The entire retail floor was bedecked in rich, inviting hues like burgundy, forest green, and a gorgeous shade of navy.

Though Quinn's work ethic left much to be desired, she had a brilliant eye. Specifically, she had a knack for predicting trends and a gift for arranging merchandise. Most of our new items would sell out within a week.

Leaving the front unattended wasn't an option, so I stashed my wool coat and handbag in the back office, praying we didn't have any customers until Quinn arrived. Then I perched at the front desk with my laptop and began to pore over my spreadsheet. I couldn't balance the tax deduction figures for this quarter to save my life and I wasn't sure if it was the program or my brain that was glitching.

Usually, I enjoyed math and took comfort in the black-and-white aspect of it. Either it was right or wrong, and if it was wrong, then you simply had to find out why and fix it. The solution was eluding me today—a perfect metaphor for my life.

At a quarter past ten, just as I'd started to make progress un-tangling the web of numbers, Quinn bustled through the door in a blur of balayage and pink. I glanced up, debating whether to call her out for being late. But adding a fight with her to my list of problems didn't seem like a wise decision. Quinn didn't accept criticism well, no matter how legitimate, and she held grudges like our mother. That was how I'd gotten sucked into still working here four years later, while my MBA applications gathered dust.

"Did the new shipment of corsets come in?" Quinn adjusted her dusty rose shift dress and smoothed her hair, which was flat-ironed bolt straight.

Unlike Lola, whose time management skills were genuinely lacking, Quinn was usually punctual. But while I didn't mind working mornings, she secretly—or not-so-secretly—resented it. This, combined with her immaculate hair and makeup, made the timing of her arrival seem intentional. Quinn's interest in our company took a sharp nosedive the moment she got engaged.

Unfortunately for my sister, she would be working the morning shift for a while because our lead sales associate recently quit, leaving us short-staffed, and I was an abysmal salesperson.

"I think so," I said. "There are a few boxes in the storage room, but I didn't open them yet."

"Great. I'll go check." Instead of heading to the back, Quinn lingered by the rack of white terrycloth spa robes. She tilted her head, studying me—trying to use her twin telepathy powers to probe into my brain. But after over twenty years of practice, I was Fort Knox.

I kept my gaze fixed on the screen. "What?"

"Nothing." Quinn shrugged, fighting a sly smile in my peripheral vision. "When Kaitlyn arrives after lunch, I'll get her started unpacking the boxes and doing an inventory check."

"Sounds good," I muttered, saving and closing the program. I rebooted the computer before I unplugged it, moving into the back office. If only I could reboot myself.

By the end of the day, the spreadsheet was more of a mess than when I began. I was fairly certain I'd have to scrap everything I'd done and restore from an old version, starting over. An entire day's worth of work down the drain. It didn't help that I was starving. All I wanted was to hit the shawarma shop a few minutes away, order a Greek salad with pita the size of my head, and lose myself in my new book. But there was one minor problem: I was trapped, a hostage in the office.

Laughter floated from the front end of the store where a bride-to-be and her friends lingered, chatting with Quinn and squealing over boring wedding-related things. Objectively, this was a good thing—we made some of our biggest sales with brides and bridal parties—but I didn't want to get roped into a conversation about wedding night 'attire' with my sister. Way TMI, considering it involved my ex-boyfriend.

Sighing, I re-opened the original file and started over, but I couldn't focus, and all the numbers turned to a blur. It was like being a contestant on some twisted TV game show: Wheel of Misfortune. All of my options were horrific.

Door Number 1: A pact with the player. Enough said.

Door Number 2: Pretend I broke up with my imaginary boyfriend and pray no one else finds out the truth.

Door Number 3: Come clean about my little white lie.

Scratch that. The third option wasn't even remotely an option. Even I knew that. That left the first two: fake it or break it.

People didn't actually fake relationships...did they?

It didn't fit with the picture of myself in my head—it wasn't something an upstanding, principled person would do. I'd always prided myself on having a strong moral compass and for doing the right thing even when it was difficult, which made the lie I told even more bothersome. If I went along with Bennett's charade, I had to face myself in the mirror every day knowing that.

But it might be better than getting caught and having to face everyone else.

When I finally heard the door chime, followed by a lingering silence that confirmed our customers had left, I grabbed my laptop and my purse and headed for the front. Quinn stood by the retail display near the window, frowning at the wall with one hand on her hip. She'd taken the satin camisole and short sets from the bottom rack and put them at the top, replacing them with the new jewel-toned fuzzy robes that arrived last week.

I thought it looked appealing enough, but she could spend all day rearranging the merchandise displays. And she probably would. Possibly—I often thought—to get out of doing other tasks, like paperwork. Somehow, all the boring responsibilities got delegated to me because I was 'better with details.' Convenient.

"Hey," I said, giving her a little wave. "I'm going to head out for the night."

Quinn turned to face me, her brow furrowed. "Wait. Do you think that bra display looks okay?" She pointed to the merchandise stand in the middle of the room, covered with lacy black and nude bras. Each was arranged in a neat row, with a circle of matching thongs and bikinis on the lower shelf.

Generally speaking, it was hit-or-miss as to whether I liked the things she brought in. While we may have looked alike, our tastes were polar opposites. Quinn favored bright colors, and I lived exclusively in monochromatic neutrals. The high-heeled pink pompom slippers from last month weren't my style, though to her credit, they'd flown off the shelves almost immediately. But these lace sets were delicate and understated; sexy but classy. The kind of thing you'd wear under your clothes like a secret for yourself.

"It looks great," I said. "I'll probably cave and grab a set later."

Being able to obtain pretty little things at cost had turned out to be dangerous for my shopping budget. Since starting our business four years ago, my lingerie collection had grown extensively, though I wasn't sure why I continued to acquire fancy items no one else would see.

Her eyes danced. "For your new boyfriend?"

Oh God. Let's not go there right now. Or ever.

"Exactly." I shifted my weight. "Anyway, I should get going.

This spreadsheet is a real mess. I mean, it's a disaster. There are ones where there should be zeroes, and—."

"Are you sure you don't want to grab some dinner together?" She stepped away from the rack, coming to stand beside me. "If we wait until Kaitlyn gets back from her break, I can go with you. I was hoping we could catch up a little."

That's what I was afraid of.

"Uh…" I tried to come with an excuse on the spot. Normally, I'd have said yes, but right now I couldn't risk slipping up with Quinn like I had with Bennett. "Yeah, I'd like to. But our accountant is going to have my head if I don't straighten these numbers out for our quarterly report." In fact, I was ahead of schedule on delivering this, but Quinn didn't need to know that.

Quinn narrowed her eyes. She hated anything to do with numbers or money, so as long as I handled them, she wasn't inclined to argue with me.

"Fine," she said. "Come over for wine night later."

I fished around in my purse for my keys, hitting the remote start button. My phone buzzed against my fingers, and I slid it out, revealing another text from my mother. Great. Exactly what I needed right now.

Locking my phone without reading the message, I glanced back up at Quinn. "Oh. Uh, maybe."

"Adam is working late again. We can watch The Bachelor," she added.

I suppressed a shudder. I never understood what she saw in those cheesy dating shows. Thirty women throwing themselves at some guy they wouldn't look at twice if they saw him in a Walmart? Hard pass.

And Adam sure seemed to work late a lot.

"We'll see," I said. "I'm supposed to talk to Dad later, but I'll text you if it's not too late after I'm done."

When Quinn and I were three, our father moved overseas to accept a high-level position with an international bank. I didn't see him much outside of major holidays, when I usually went to see him, but we had weekly video chats and always had a game of Scrabble going remotely. Somehow, the idea of lying to him bothered me more than my mother.

The store's entry bell chimed, interrupting us. A brown-clad delivery courier poked his head inside. "Good afternoon. I have a delivery for Thayer? Thayer Montgomery?"

Quinn shot me an inquisitive look, but I was as lost as she was. I hadn't ordered anything to the store and wasn't expecting any deliveries. If anything, I'd been trying to curb my shopping habit.

I walked over to meet him at the front. "That's me."

"Sign here, please." The courier handed me an electronic tablet and pen, heading back outside to retrieve the item from his white delivery truck. A moment later, he returned with a pale lilac cone-shaped parcel and handed it to me, retrieving the tablet. "Have a nice day, miss."

"Thanks. You too." I cradled the paper package in my arm, gently lifting up the piece of tape securing the top. Inside were a dozen flawless, long-stemmed, deep purple calla lilies.

Generally, I wasn't a big fan of flowers; they only lasted a couple of days, which seemed pointless, and most bouquets verged on tacky. This was anything but tacky, however. It was the most stunning bouquet I'd ever seen.

"Ooh." Quinn sashayed over, studying the parcel in my hands. "Is that from lover boy? Can I see?"

"Um, it's—" I faltered, cheeks heating. "It's kind of private."

"Too late!" She plucked the small envelope from its clear plastic holder and darted away behind the counter. My heart hit full throttle while I waited, wondering what the card might say. If it mentioned the words, 'fake' or 'deal', I was sunk like the Titanic.

Quinn slid out the card and read aloud, "Can't stop thinking about you. -xx." She held the card to her chest, pretending to swoon. "Thay! That is so sweet."

"It's something, all right."

I was going to kill Bennett. Then I was going to resurrect him and kill him again. He did this to trap me. So other people would see the flowers and think my boyfriend was still in the picture—not just still in the picture, that things were going well. To make it that much harder for me to break things off with 'him' and get myself out of this predicament.

Judging by the look on my sister's face, it was working, too.

"Mom is going to die when she sees these," she said.

"Mmm-hmm." I forced a smile. "I'm going to let him know I got them." I set the paper package down on the counter, retrieving my cell from my handbag.

Quinn leaned over, taking a photo of the flowers with her phone. Millie would know about this within the next fifteen minutes, Quinn would loop in our mother shortly after that, and the entire town would hear by the end of the day.

Scrolling furiously, I found my conversation with Bennett and composed a new message.

Thayer: Flowers? Really?

Three little grey dots appeared, because Satan was nothing if not speedy in his replies.

Bennett: You're welcome.

Thayer: I didn't thank you.

Bennett: You should.

My unread message notification popped up again and I backed out of Bennett's thread, navigating to my mother's.

Mom: Does Sunday work for the two of you, or should we pick a different day?

I stared at the screen, unblinking. What if Bennett was right? Even if people did give our fauxlationship the side-eye, the alternative was even worse. One that surpassed being linked to Bennett: my falsehood being revealed. I could already see how that would play out. I would be the laughingstock of all my friends, my mother would practically disown me, and I'd never get a real date again.

Glancing down, I composed a quick reply to Bennett and hit send before I could think twice.

Thayer: Fine. I'm in. But I have conditions.

CHAPTER TEN

Thayer

EITHER THE APOCALYPSE WAS NEIGH, OR MY SANITY HAD GONE out the window.

Bennett Bradford was on his way over to my place.

I wiped my clammy palms on my black jeans, surveying my apartment. The white quartz countertops were so shiny I could re-touch my lipstick in their reflection. All the throw pillows on my couch were perfectly arranged. And a Diptyque Tilleul candle glowed on the glass end table, bathing my apartment in the sweet honey-scent of linden trees and early summer. Not a seasonally ap-propriate scent for autumn, but it was my favorite—and given the situation, I needed something to soothe my frazzled nerves.

The intercom chimed and I jumped, gaze snapping over to the alarm panel. With knees like jelly, I walked over and buzzed Bennett up, fingers almost trembling too much to do so.

I must have had too much coffee earlier. Surely, that was the problem.

Moments later, there was a tap on the front door. I froze with my feet glued to the spot for a good couple of seconds. Another knock followed, snapping me back to reality. I quickly gathered up the stack of MBA school brochures I'd been poring over earlier and set them off to the side of the coffee table. Then I rushed over to the front door and unlocked the deadbolt, reluctantly swinging it open.

"Hey." Bennett's lips tugged into a devastating grin, sending my already speedy pulse into a full-on arrhythmia. I couldn't remember the last time I'd had a guy at my place, least of all one that looked like him.

The exterior was so appealing. Too bad the inside didn't match.

"Hi." I moved out of the way to let him pass, pointing to the mat in the entry. "Shoes off."

"Pardon?" He raised his eyebrows, lingering in the doorway.

I sighed. "It's just my thing, okay? Shoes track in all kinds of dirt and bacteria from outside."

Yes, I knew people considered it uptight. Some even said it was rude to ask of your guests. But I walked around on these floors barefoot. I could not get past the idea that someone might have stepped in dog excrement, rotten food, or heaven knows what before coming up to my apartment, tracking in E. coli or other toxins. Blame the New York Times for running the article that put those ideas in my head in the first place.

Bennett's gaze fell to the charcoal mat, lifted back up to me, then dropped back down to the mat. My breath stilled and I braced myself for an argument.

"Okay." He shrugged, slipping off his brown leather loafers. "When in Rome."

Maybe he was in an agreeable mood. That could be a good sign as far as negotiating went. Or it could be a trap. He was probably trying to get me to lower my defenses so he could go in for the kill.

I stiffened, locking the door behind him. This was a bad idea. Wasn't there some rule about not inviting vampires into your home?

Bennett strolled in, scanning my condo appraisingly. "Nice digs."

"Uh, thanks?" I had no idea what his apartment looked like, so it was difficult to know how much weight to give his opinion. Most men weren't exactly arbiters of interior design.

His place was probably bachelor central: oversized flatscreen TV, modern finishings, and lots of black leather. Probably lots of chrome, too, so he could admire his reflection at every opportunity.

"Let's set up over there." I pointed to the living area where my papers and laptop sat on the wooden coffee table. "Would you like something to drink?" Being polite felt weird but being impolite seemed equally odd.

"What do you have?"

"Herbal tea, La Croix, or water." I paused. "Or there's an open bottle of Sauvignon Blanc in the fridge, but I'm guessing you don't drink white."

Most men didn't. Then again, Bennett was a bit of a wildcard in general.

"No scotch?" Bennett trailed behind me.

"Do I look like I drink scotch?"

He shrugged. "It was worth a shot."

I hurried ahead of him and returned to my spot on the loveseat, where my makeshift office was set up. Bennett sauntered into the living room, weaving past the ottoman over to the two grey couches that formed an L facing the gas fireplace and television. The loveseat sank under his weight as he sat down on the other end, a mere foot away from me. Instead of, you know, sitting on the totally vacant couch beside it like a normal human would.

His presence swallowed up the room, like he was the only thing in it. And his long legs and broad torso took up so much space, mentally and physically, that it was almost impossible for me to focus.

If he tried to manspread, I was going to bash him with my MacBook.

I gestured to the stack of notes beside me, written neatly in blue ink on loose leaf paper. "I had a few thoughts, but I didn't have time to type them all out yet."

Because I was speed-cleaning my apartment before his arrival like some kind of idiot. I always tidied before anyone came over, just not quite to the same degree. I didn't know why it was so important Bennett thought I had the cleanest kitchen sink in the metro area. It's not like I cared what he thought.

"You wrote all that down?" He craned his neck and looked over at my notes, amusement tinting his tone. "And now you're typing it up?"

I glanced up from my laptop. "Of course. It serves us both to have the scope of our arrangement clearly delineated. That way everyone knows what to expect."

"Still a keener, just like back in high school." Bennett smirked, placing his arm along the back of the couch. His right hand rested in dangerously close proximity to my left shoulder. "Precious."

"I prefer to think of it as thorough."

"But you're creating a paper trail," he pointed out, expression sobering. "What if someone else finds it?"

"I'll destroy it later." I was meticulous about records management—notes would go in the cross-cut paper shredder and the electronic file would be wiped clean. "This is to keep us honest. To keep you honest, specifically."

"I haven't the faintest idea what you're implying."

"I'm not implying anything," I said, selecting 12pt Times New Roman and formatting the line and paragraph spacing. "I'm straight-up saying it."

Bennett made a face at me, and I made one back, like the two mature adults that we were. Then I rolled my eyes, returning my attention to the blank word processing screen. The cursor blinked against the stark white page like a silent alarm bell. A dull throb of low-level irritation replaced my nervousness from earlier. Was this how it would be for the next couple of months? The two of us bickering all the time? I was exhausted just thinking about it.

Maybe I would be better off feeding my reputation to the wolves.

Sifting through my notes, I found the list of questions and

outstanding items that I'd compiled over the past few days. "There are a few details we haven't settled on yet."

"Like what?" Bennett shrugged. "Not much to it. We'll tell everyone we're dating, accompany each other to social events, and act the part in public for a while."

"For starters, we need to decide how long we've supposedly been dating. We need to make sure we get our story straight." If someone else cornered me verbally like he did—which was inevitable—I couldn't afford to come up empty-handed.

He furrowed his brow, falling silent. "Let's say dating for a month and we recently got more serious."

Nodding, I made a note under the 'relationship background' header. I hoped a month was enough of a buffer between me and any other women, so that nothing would come back to haunt us, but part of me was afraid to ask.

I, on the other hand, had a buffer the size of the Atlantic Ocean. It had been well over a year since my last relationship and even that hadn't been exclusive.

"And how long do you intend to hold me captive?" I looked up from the laptop screen, expression rapt.

Bennett shot me a look. "We'll help each other for four months. That's long enough for me to close this deal and be well into the construction stage. Then we can tell everyone we parted ways mutually. My reputation will be repaired, yours will be preserved, win-win all around."

"Four *months*?" I recoiled. That was longer than a season. It was two entire haircut cycles. "Not a chance."

"Going to interfere with your packed dating calendar?"

I scowled at him, sorely tempted to use my pen as a dart. "Three months, until after Quinn's wedding, and I get to dump you. Preferably in a public and humiliating manner."

"Humiliating like, say, faking a boyfriend?" He raised his eyebrows and my level of irritation ratcheted up a notch. "Four months and we say it was amicable."

It wasn't lost on me that Bennett's idea of negotiating meant going straight back to his initial ask; he hadn't budged at all on the duration issue. Four months was too long, though. That would bleed into the following year. It was one thing to put up with Bennett until the wedding; it was another to ring in the new year still chained to his side.

I picked up my mug of lukewarm peppermint tea, fighting the urge to throw it at him. "Three months. I get to say I ended it, but you can tell people it was already circling the drain. Final offer."

Ninety days. I could last ninety days without strangling him with his silk tie. Right?

"Sold." He leaned back, reclining against the grey fabric and propping his sock-clad feet on the ottoman. His navy dress socks had tiny, colorful cartoon robots all over, and I couldn't decide if it was endearing or annoying. Grabbing the remote, he switched on the TV and began shuffling through the cable guide while I returned to the computer.

"You don't need to draw up a literal contract. You know I'm not going to renege on our deal," Bennett said, idly channel surfing. He seemed way too comfortable for a first-time guest. "I always keep my word."

"You have a tendency of twisting words to suit your agenda. This contract is black and white." I mistyped as I spoke, resulting in 'Badford' instead of 'Bradford.' While amusing in a Freudian slip sort of way, I was trying to replicate a real, legally binding agreement as much as possible. Frowning, I backspaced and re-typed it correctly.

While I continued to draw up a rough draft, Bennett turned the TV to a baseball game and leisurely scrolled his phone. I sincerely hoped he was checking his texts and not Tinder.

As I finalized the last item, my stomach growled insistently, so loud that I thought Bennett might have heard it. But if he did, he was polite enough not to comment.

The first thing I was going to do after he left was stress-eat a massive plate of nachos and scream into a pillow. And polish off that half-bottle of Sav Blanc. Straight from the bottle.

He leaned closer, trying to see the screen. His cologne drifted over to me, and I did my best to ignore the cartwheel in my stomach. Ironic that someone so evil could smell so heavenly. "Are you done yet?"

"Just about." I turned the laptop to face him. "What do you think?"

CHAPTER ELEVEN

Bennett

T HE MORE I READ, THE WORSE IT GOT. THAYER'S DRAFT contract wasn't just thorough—it was over the top. I didn't know I'd needed to bring a lawyer with me to her place tonight. We were faking a couple of dates, not drafting a fucking prenup.

If this was any indication of what things were going to be like with her, I was in for a bumpy ride.

Agreement for services between Bennett Bradford (hereby known as "Bradford") and Thayer Montgomery ("Montgomery")

Scope of Work: Both parties agree to engage in a short-term, exclusive partnership for a duration of three (3) months for the purposes of reputation enhancement and social networking. Duties will include escorting the other party to personal or professional functions as required and other behaviors consistent with creating the outward appearance of a serious, committed relationship.

Terms, Limitations and Exclusions

1. Both parties agree that the arrangement will not include sexual intercourse or other sexual relations. For added clarity, sexual contact is explicitly excluded from the arrangement and all related activities are forbidden.

2. Both parties agree to exercise the utmost discretion regarding the arrangement and will refrain from sharing the details of this agreement with any outside third parties. Such parties include but are not limited to Ian Fenmore, Lola Van Sant, Quinn Montgomery, Millie Pruitt, and Adam Matthews.

3. Both parties agree to work jointly toward a common goal for the enrichment of both parties, fostering the public perception of a healthy romantic relationship.

4. Both parties agree to inform the other party should any issues arise that interfere with their ability to perform their duties in good faith, such as illness, death, or other unforeseeable emergencies.

5. Both parties agree to maintain a professional, cordial working relationship at all times.

6. Bradford acknowledges that he has unfairly coerced Montgomery into this arrangement and that he owes Montgomery one (1) favor in return at some future date. The nature and timing of said favor is entirely at the discretion of Montgomery.

7. Bradford agrees to provide Montgomery with a copy of recent comprehensive STD testing results.

8. Both parties acknowledge that the arrangement is strictly for business purposes and no romantic entanglements or other future relationship will result.

I turned to look at her, trying to conceal the terror brewing within me. "Did you go to law school when I wasn't looking, or what?"

Thayer shrugged. "Thought about it at one point. I took the LSAT, but then I changed my mind."

"Let me guess," I muttered, returning my attention to the screen. "You nailed the LSAT."

"172."

"Figures."

Based on what I remembered from my younger brother's LSAT prep, that was somewhere around the ninety-nineth percentile. Sounded about right. Thayer had always been insanely smart—one reason I was about to have my hands full trying to manage her and this situation. I couldn't just verbally steer her around like I could most other people.

On the other hand, unlike some of the women I knew, Thayer wouldn't get wasted and dance on tables in front of Callaghan and she wouldn't develop feelings for me. And those things were what mattered most.

I skimmed the page for a second time, scanning for any hidden land mines contained within the clauses. Everything was fairly reasonable except—wait a minute. What the hell? I paused, re-reading number four, and my gaze snapped back up to her face.

"You want me to inform you if I *die*?"

She smirked. "Well, I might get lucky."

"Hilarious," I said. "And did you really need to slip in number six?" I wasn't sure what kind of favor Thayer had in mind, but the idea of being indebted to Her Majesty the Ice Queen was less than appealing.

Then again, if it was a sexual favor, count me in.

"Can you honestly say you didn't coerce me?" She quirked a slender brow, eyeing me over the rim of her mug.

"I'm saving you from Millie's wrath." I rubbed my chin thoughtfully. "One could say I'm your knight in shining armor."

Thayer snorted. "You're definitely the evil dragon in this scenario."

Well, I'd been called worse.

"This is a perfectly fair deal, and you know it." If I didn't rehabilitate my image, we'd lose our bid on the property—and everything else along with it. If Thayer's lie was exposed, she would be too humiliated to leave her apartment ever again. Pretty level playing field.

"You have leverage over me. Call it blackmail or not, though I maintain that it is. How could I possibly say no to your offer, knowing you could turn around and tell everyone my secret as payback?"

I opened my mouth to argue, but she held up a slender finger, holding me off.

"One might even say I'm entering this agreement under duress. The sixth clause is intended to ensure that I receive equal and adequate consideration, and it shows you're acting in good faith."

Good faith was no longer a part of my vocabulary, but whatever she needed to tell herself.

"Can I at least get a veto or two?"

She smiled, full of sugar and spite. "No."

Perfect. I'd finally done it. I'd found someone who was even more strong-willed than I was. And I'd decided to chain myself to her for several months.

"Fine." I sighed. A picture popped into my head of my freedom growing wings and taking flight, dragging my sanity along with it. This had better fucking work.

"What about the seventh item?" Thayer nodded at the laptop. "Did you read that one?"

Ah yes, the STD clause. Another nice little dig on her part.

"Why do we need that if we have number one?"

She scooted over to the far side of the couch, placing a tan throw pillow between the two of us. Then she shot me a look so chilly, I practically developed frostbite beneath my clothes. "Because I don't need someone from your past resurfacing saying my 'boyfriend' gave her chlamydia."

Look, I wasn't claiming to be a Boy Scout by any stretch of the imagination. But if there was one thing I made sure of, it was always, always using protection and getting tested regularly. I was far too fond of my manhood to put it at risk of disease or disfigurement. Not to mention, mini-Bradfords weren't part of my five year—or forever—plan.

"I don't have any STDs. But if you need me to prove that to you, I will. Would you like a copy of my vaccination record as well? Driving record, perhaps?"

"Those would be great." She smiled earnestly. "I'll give you my email address before you leave, and you can send them over at your earliest convenience."

Well, fuck. I was being sarcastic, but I couldn't tell if she was being serious. Maybe her poker face was better than I thought.

On the flatscreen TV playing in the background, the Yankees hit a ground ball with the bases loaded in the bottom of the ninth. I watched as the ball rolled and the left fielder sprinted for it. Thayer snatched the remote from my hands, turning off the television.

"Let's stay on task, shall we?" She scrolled back up, tapping the screen emphatically with a dark red fingernail. "Speaking of item number one, any issues there?"

It was the sex clause. Or no sex clause, rather.

"Why would there be?"

I mean, other than the fact that it was total bullshit.

"Because you're Bennett Bradford, womanizer extraordinaire."

"The tales of my conquests are greatly exaggerated."

Christen one nightclub bathroom, land in the gossip section of the papers a handful of times for questionable decisions, and all of a sudden, everyone thinks you're some kind of Lothario. It was totally unfounded character assassination. I mean, I was still in the double digits. Approximately.

Plus, compared to Thayer, anyone would seem promiscuous.

"You won't try any funny business with me," she said evenly.

"Hate to break it to you, doll, but you're not my type."

This was an epic lie. Thayer was exactly my type, at least on a superficial level. While technically identical to her sister, Thayer was definitely the more appealing twin. Quinn was wide-eyed and pretty in a bland way, but Thayer had an edge that made her hot. Her full lips were pouty and pillowy soft, calling to mind all sorts of sinful acts. Don't even get me started on her perfect round backside, the kind made to be spanked.

But personality-wise, I preferred women who were a little more pleasant and a whole lot less uptight.

I also preferred women who didn't hate my guts and threaten

to kill me with office supplies, which had happened twice since I'd gotten to her place.

At any rate, admitting that Thayer was a ten wouldn't help, so I had to bend the truth a little. For her sake—and mine. The truth was, it didn't matter whether I found her attractive. I needed Thayer just as much as she needed me, even if it meant agreeing to her ridiculous rules.

"Thank God for that." Thayer crossed her legs primly, drawing my eyes right to them. My gaze traced the curve of her thighs, lingering for a beat. I was exercising significant restraint not to check her out—and failing. It didn't help that her entire place smelled delicious, scented with some kind of sweet, feminine perfume.

"But you know you can't have sex with other people either, right?" she asked, snapping me back to reality. "Getting caught with another woman while you're supposed to be committed to me would defeat the whole purpose of rehabilitating your reputation."

"No shit." Did she think I was a total idiot? "Believe it or not, I'm capable of self-control."

Thayer studied my face for a moment, considering, then shook her head. "Yeah, I'm firmly in the 'or not' camp on that."

Her remark wasn't entirely unwarranted, but it's not like I was some kind of maniacal sex addict. While I liked to have a good time, I could keep it in my pants, especially with this much at stake. Besides, I could always make up for lost time later.

"You're not the only one with a lot on the line here."

"Two months in, when you're missing your bachelorhood freedom, you'll remember that you agreed to this?" Thayer's teeth sank into her crimson-painted bottom lip, and she studied my face. Her expression was somewhere between worry and hope.

"I will."

Of course, I'd remember, I just wouldn't care. Who gives a shit about some arbitrary rules we thought up on the fly? I would stay in line to save my own ass, not because of her little contract.

"No sex. At all. None," she emphasized, pointing at me with her blue pen. "Forgive me if I'm skeptical."

Hell, I was skeptical too. Three months without sex? Not even a blowjob? Signing on for that did sound like self-punishment, but I didn't have much of a choice, I'd make it work somehow.

"No sex," I echoed. "Not with anyone, not with you. Not even if you beg me for it."

Another lie. If Thayer decided to throw herself at me, it's not like I was going to say 'Sorry, can't because we're contractually forbidden from fucking.'

"Beg you for it?" She barked a laugh. "Hate to break it to you, *babe*, but you're not my type either."

"Because I actually exist?"

"Because you don't have a soul."

"Fortunately, I more than make up for that in other departments. You'll see."

Thayer huffed, looking down into her black ceramic mug. "Never going to happen. Ever."

Challenge accepted. One month in, I'd have her thinking it was her idea to break rule number one. Repeatedly.

The printer screeched from the other room as it spat out a copy of the contract. Thayer stood up and walked down the hall, returning with a sheaf of papers a moment later. She handed them to me along with a blue pen. And by handed them to me, I mean violently shoved them in my face, nearly slicing a paper cut across my cheek in process. I suspected it wasn't accidental.

"Sign here, here, and here." She pointed to the signature lines she'd inserted on the first and second page. "And initial here by number six. You're not getting out of that one, so no pretending you didn't know about it or didn't agree."

"Sign a hard copy?" I glanced back up at her, my hand hovering above the page. "I thought you were destroying this."

"Didn't say when," she said. "I'm keeping a copy in my safe until this is done. Now sign."

CHAPTER TWELVE

Thayer

SUNLIGHT FILTERED THROUGH THE TREES OUTSIDE CAFE Allegro's window as I took a sip of coffee and crossed my legs, examining the menu for the tenth time. While I liked to arrive early to avoid feeling rushed, rushed was Lola's default setting. Factoring in her usual fifteen-minute delay, I had roughly five more minutes to wait before she'd arrive for our standing ten AM Saturday brunch date. Or ten-fifteen, if you were going by her time zone.

I scanned the array of omelets, steel-cut oatmeal, and green juices, trying to focus on the food, but the menu items kept blurring together. My chest tightened, mouth turning sticky. I had to tell Lola about Bennett. She was my dry run—my practice for my family, other friends, and frenemies. If I could convince her, I could easily convince the rest.

Lola strolled up and pulled out the chair across from me, her gold-streaked ringlets bouncing as she flopped into the seat. "Sorry. I sat down to open my mail for a minute, and when I looked up, it was ten. My bad." She slid her mustard yellow purse off her shoulder, hanging it on the arm of the chair.

"No worries." I glanced up from the menu, giving what I hoped was a natural-looking smile. At the moment, her tardiness was the least of my problems. "I was debating between the banana French toast and the blueberry pancakes. Do you want to get both and share?"

Weekends were my one and only time to eat processed carbs. At least, until after Quinn's wedding and I didn't have to worry about fitting into my bridesmaid dress, which had mysteriously been ordered at least one size too small. I tended to think Millie, who'd been tasked with handling the dresses, was somehow responsible. She was still bitter that I was named Maid of Honor instead of her.

And lucky me, I had the pleasure of heading to a bridesmaid dress fitting with Millie and my sister after this.

"Sure." Lola reached over, pouring a generous splash of cream into her coffee, followed by two packets of sugar. The spoon clinked against the sides as she stirred it in and took a sip, making a face. Unsatisfied, she added more cream and sugar, repeating the process until the contents of her cup had nearly turned white. I'd tasted Lola's coffee before and it was so sweet it made my toes curl.

We ordered and fell into small talk about our jobs for a while. She'd acquired some new pieces by an up-and-coming artist for the gallery, then ended up going out on a date with said artist in Paris via his private jet. Only Lola.

I tried to keep the topics of conversation on her, so I didn't have to say as much, even though I knew that was only prolonging my agony.

Halfway through our meal, I gathered up the courage to break the news. I reasoned it would be like jumping out of an airplane— not that I ever had. Just hold your breath and leap. No turning back.

"I have to tell you something." I set down my fork, still loaded with a massive bite of blueberry pancake. I'd boomeranged from losing my appetite due to stress, into stress-eating all the carbs in sight.

Lola looked at me over the rim of her Bloody Mary, her

expression a cross between concern and confusion. "What is it? Is everything okay?"

Okay, so maybe my approach was a little abrupt.

I shook my head. "No, no. Everything is fine. It's, er, great. It's about who I'm dating."

"You mean you're finally ready to reveal your mysterious new beau?" She shimmied in her seat, raising the roof with her hands. "Yes! I've been dying for this moment. Who is he?"

"Well, he's—" I paused, suddenly feeling like I'd jumped out of said plane without a parachute. "It's going to come as a bit of a surprise."

"Ooh, is he famous?" Lola seized a forkful of waffle laden with syrup and butter. "Or is he in politics? A silver fox, maybe. Or…" Her amber-gold eyes flicked back up to mine, brow furrowed. She winced, lowering her voice. "He isn't married, is he?"

Goddamn Millie and that stupid rumor. It had grown legs and run all over town. Now everyone believed it, including my own best friend. Guess Bennett wasn't the only one who needed reputation rehab.

"Nothing like that." I swallowed, pasting on my best impression of a lovestruck smile; it was more of a best guess, as it wasn't an emotion that I had firsthand experience with. "It's Bennett."

Lola's jaw dropped and she froze, the fork full of waffle halfway to her lips. A thin trail of golden syrup dripped down onto her plate. "Bennett…who?"

"Bradford." I shoved the bite of pancake in my mouth.

"The same Bennett Bradford we went to prep school with?" She glanced around the cafe as if checking for hidden cameras, turning back to face me. "But you hate Bennett."

"Hate is a strong word." Though entirely accurate, in this case. I looked down at my plate, nudging my turkey sausage with my fork. "I've had strong opinions of him in the past. But you know what they say, where there are sparks, there's a flame."

"Isn't it, where there's smoke, there's fire?"

"Same idea," I said, even though it clearly wasn't. Unfortunately, I wasn't nearly as good as Bennett at dodging and weaving verbally.

I should have written myself a script and rehearsed it. Or drawn up a flowchart, perhaps, to account for the various possible outcomes for this conversation. Yes, definitely a flowchart.

Maybe I could download an app for that in the car later, before I faced the interrogation squad at the bridal boutique.

Lola blinked slowly. "I'm confused."

Chewing her bite of waffle, she studied my face, waiting for me to continue. To explain the inexplicable. I threw back a gulp of mimosa and drew in a breath, scrambling inwardly for words. She looked at me like she was trying to determine whether I needed a psych hold. I was questioning the same thing myself. The alone time did sound kind of nice.

Suddenly, the weight of the lie came crashing down around my shoulders. I couldn't do it. Not with Lola. She was the one person I didn't have to wear my mask around, the one person in my life who accepted me as I was.

"It's more of an arrangement," I admitted.

"Even more confused."

I sighed. "Millie was needling me about not having a date to the wedding. Then Quinn jumped in, and they started threatening to set me up with one of Adam's banker bros. Again. I got annoyed and said I had a date to get everyone off my back."

Guilt washed over me. I just broke one of the rules in the contract. It hadn't even been a whole day since we'd signed it. If I couldn't follow the rules, what hope was there for Bennett?

"But how does Bennett factor into this?" Lola prodded.

"Well, that part just sort of happened." It wasn't untrue. First came the impromptu lie, then before I knew it, a fake relationship landed right in my lap. Like dominoes in a series of terrible decisions, which left me worried about which poor choice I might make next.

I began to explain from the beginning, recapping our meeting at Starbucks, followed by his sneaky flower stunt and our negotiations at my place. Lola leaned forward and listened intently, interjecting with the odd comment or question along the way. I concluded my story and stared at her from across the table sheepishly, my heart racing.

"This is kind of awesome," she said.

"It is?"

"It sounds like something I would do."

Oh, God. It did. I loved Lola, but she wasn't exactly a bastion of good judgement.

Lola set down her fork, dabbing her coral-painted lips with the ivory cloth napkin. "To be clear, there are no 'benefits' associated with this arrangement?"

"Just the opposite. Like I said, it's strictly forbidden in our agreement."

"I mean…" she shrugged. "You could have a little fun."

"Not a chance."

Lola raised her eyebrows, watching me over the rim of her glass. "Are you sure? Anya Switzer slept with Bennett a while ago and she said it was, and I quote, 'fucking mind blowing.'" She took a sip and set her glass back down. "Anya said she still thinks about him when she—"

"Okay, okay." I held up a hand, squeezing my eyes shut. "That's quite enough of that."

I couldn't explain why, but the mental image her story created was strangely unsettling. It was unreasonable, considering Bennett wasn't even mine. Not for now, and definitely not to keep.

"Anyway, that wasn't my point. I just want to make sure he's good to you, whatever the 'arrangement' is. I don't want you to end up with a selfish fucker like Adam." Lola giggled and clamped a hand over her mouth, her shoulders shaking. "Oh my God, selfish fucker. Get it? It works both ways."

After a few too many martinis last month, Quinn had confessed that Adam was only interested in his own pleasure in the bedroom. That summed up my disappointing college experiences with Adam as well. Apparently, some things hadn't changed. I still had no idea why my beautiful, sweet sister was marrying the guy.

Despite myself, I snorted; then I made a mental note to veto Lola's third Bloody Mary. Otherwise, she was going to end up passed out by noon. She was a lightweight.

Lola hummed thoughtfully to herself. "Though, I always did think Bennett had a thing for you."

A laugh escaped the back of my throat because that was ridiculous, even crazier than Bennett being my boyfriend. "Yeah, right."

"Have you told your parents yet? Or Quinn?"

"Not yet. You were going to be my dry run, but I guess that crashed and burned." The server came by with our bill and I snatched it off the table before Lola could grab it, slipping my credit card inside the folio.

She grimaced. "Yeah, your delivery could use some work."

"I'm aware."

"Fortunately, you have me. Let's run through your story a few times. Rehearse a little, get you more comfortable. Then I'll send out texts to a few key people telling them about the hottest new couple in town."

I nodded and my shoulders relaxed as the tension I'd been holding all morning started to dissolve. Having someone in my corner was a massive relief. And Lola was right, I could do this. I just needed some practice. Or a lot of practice, likely.

"You'll make a smoking hot couple," she added. "I'm sure you guys will be able to sell this."

"If we don't kill each other first."

She grinned. "I'd tell you to tread carefully, but if anyone was going to serve Bennett his balls on a silver platter, it would be you."

An hour and a half later, I was standing in Belle Bridal boutique, glass of champagne in hand, wishing I was anywhere but here.

The seamstress, Ingrid, tsked and adjusted the straps of my pale pink dress to account for my utter and complete lack of boobs. She'd been fussing over me for twenty-five minutes and couldn't have seemed more disappointed in me for being flat-chested if she tried, like it was a choice I'd made to make her job more difficult.

Unfortunately, the style flattered the other bridesmaids' figures and Quinn was dead set on all the dresses being identical, so Ingrid and I were both out of luck.

Millie came to stand in front of me, tilting her head. A flute of champagne rested in her long, slender fingers. Immediately, I knew Lola's promise to help spread the word has succeeded.

"You and Bennett, Thay?" Her eyes scanned my face methodically, watching for my reaction. "That's wonderful. I'm so happy for you."

Translation: She wasn't.

A familiar uneasiness settled into the pit of my stomach. "Thank you."

"He must be the one who sent you that stunning arrangement at the store. Lucky girl."

"Yeah, he's really great." I gave her a bland smile, letting Ingrid rearrange me a quarter turn. The champagne had taken enough of the edge off to make this encounter tolerable.

"He's a catch," she said. "I just hope it won't be too awkward with Adam at family dinners."

I huffed a dry laugh. "Ancient history, Millie. We've all moved on. Or else we wouldn't be here, right?"

"Oh, I meant because of their business dealings." She smiled sweetly, but it was sour beneath the surface and completely disingenuous. "You know, because things between them turned hostile when they split."

Bennett hadn't told me that. I knew they parted ways when Adam struck out on his own, but not that it had been on bad terms. Quinn hadn't mentioned that, either. Was Bennett using me to get back at Adam?

"Mmm," I said. "It'll be fine. We're all adults."

The seamstress placed her last pin into the hem of the dress, guiding me off the platform while Millie continued her interrogation. "How long have you been together, exactly?"

Remember the script, remember the script.

"We've been serious for about a month."

"Really." Her thin eyebrows jumped. "How serious are we talking?"

"Well—" I began. Just then, Quinn swanned out of the dressing room, ensconced in satin and lace. The dress was beautiful, if a bit much, which meant it was perfect for her. We all ooh-ed and aah-ed over her for a few moments until her ego was sufficiently fed. Then she swung over to me and touched me on the arm gently.

"Can I talk to you for a sec?"

"Sure." I tipped back the last of my champagne, setting it down on the nearby marble counter.

Quinn led me over to the mirrors, away from everyone else. I gulped and dutifully prepared my lines. Recently dating, newly serious, I was head over heels...

"I have some great news," she said, adjusting the sweetheart neckline of her dress. "Style and Society had a last-minute cancellation, and they want to feature Lace & Grace in their next issue."

Thank God. It wasn't about Bennett. Style and Society was the biggest local magazine around, featuring luxury homes, local fashion, and the biggest trends. A feature would be great publicity for the store.

"That's amazing. They have a huge readership, don't they?"

She nodded, beaming. "Especially within our target demographic. They want to include us in the feature too." Her pale blue eyes sparkled with excitement.

"Both of us?"

"Of course." Quinn looked at me funny. "That's like, the entire point of the feature. It's a family-run business. You know, the whole twin thing. It's our hook."

Dread took root in my belly, blossoming up into my chest. "Define feature."

"A photoshoot and interview, that kind of thing."

In other words, my worst nightmare.

"I don't know, Quinn." I hated being the center of attention. This was hard for Quinn to empathize with, however, because she thrived on it; she would have thrown herself a daily parade if it were possible. I often thought she'd missed her calling as a social media influencer.

She waved dismissively, nude nails glinting. "It's just a photo shoot."

"Which isn't in my job description."

I was nervous enough about being the Maid of Honor in the wedding, having all those people watching me walk down the aisle. Or worse yet, tripping and falling flat on my face. I couldn't think of anything more awkward than posing for a photographer like Quinn was describing. Just the idea made me want to hide.

"Yes, it is," she insisted. "Part of owning a business means you have to promote it."

"And I do. On social media." Behind the scenes and behind the camera, not in front of it.

"But this is a huge opportunity for us." She blinked in disbelief. "We can't say no."

"We're not," I said. "I am. But I'll meet you in the middle and do the interview, just not the shoot."

"That's even worse. Then everyone will think you're a recluse."

Or maybe just not thirsty for attention, but I didn't want to start a fight in the middle of a bridal boutique, so I shrugged.

"Why are you always like this?" Quinn glared at me. "You're being so selfish."

The level of irony in her accusation was staggering. Our lives had revolved around her for as long as I could remember. She was the one who needed to be coddled, which meant I had to have everything under control. Or at least, had to appear like I did.

"I'm selfish? You're trying to force me to do something I don't want to do." After dealing with Bennett, I had no patience left for being coerced into doing anything.

She stamped her foot, and in her poofy bridal gown, the effect was not unlike a tantruming child playing princess. "Good lord! I'm not asking you to pose nude. I'm asking you to be in some pictures to promote the store. *Our* store."

"This is really more your thing, Quinn." That was the deal. I shouldered more of the work on the back end, but Quinn was the public face. The people person. The meet-and-greet sister. That way, we both played to our strengths.

Quinn deflated, evidently realizing that she wasn't going to be able to pressure me into agreeing. She switched gears and turned on her charm, flashing me a hopeful smile that worked ninety-nine percent of the time with other people.

"Can you at least think it over? Please?"

Normally, I'd have said no. But in light of the Bennett situation, maybe I should go along with it. My brain could only grapple with so much conflict at one time.

"Fine," I said. "I'll think about it."

Millie rushed over. "The seamstress needs you again, Quinnie."

My sister gave me a meaningful look. "They need to know by Monday. Let me know at dinner tomorrow night, okay?"

"Will do."

CHAPTER THIRTEEN

Bennett

OPERATION FAKE RELATIONSHIP: TAKE ONE.

"There sure are a lot of cars parked outside for a small dinner party." I let off the gas, easing my car into the circular driveway outside Charles and Alexandra's sprawling white stucco mansion. We weren't exactly late, but we weren't as punctual as I would have liked. That's what happens when you squabble over who should drive for twenty minutes instead of getting the fuck on the road.

"Sure are," Thayer murmured, looking out the window at the array of luxury vehicles. It was like a catalogue of high-end cars—a bright red Tesla, a handful of dark-colored Mercedes, a silver Bentley, Quinn's white Lexus SUV, and Adam's tinted-out black Range Rover. Briefly, I indulged in a fantasy of digging my keys into the immaculate black paint on my way past, but I knew I'd never get away with it here.

If I ever saw it parked in public, though, all bets were off.

Switching off the ignition, I climbed out and walked over to the passenger side, pulling open the car door for Thayer. With practiced elegance, she grabbed her clutch and slid off of the black leather seat, coming to stand beside me, perched on impossibly high stilettos.

She didn't thank me for getting her door, not that I really expected her to.

"You think you can handle this?" I slammed the car door, locking it with the remote.

Thayer's gaze cut over to me. "Of course."

We climbed the stairs to the front entry and hit the intercom button, waiting in front of the wooden double doors to be granted access. Even in her tall heels, I towered over her. Her sweet perfume drifted over to me, and something stirred in my body in response. Not entirely surprising with the way her little black dress hugged her figure. It was sexy but still understated, leaving a little bit to the imagination—unfortunately, all that did was make my imagination start to run wild.

I drew in a slow breath, trying to banish the sordid images swirling through my mind. All that mattered was Thayer had nailed the attractive, respectable girlfriend look. Now if we could get through the evening without her killing me, we'd be set.

That was a big if, though.

Charles and Alexandra's household manager let us in and took our coats before directing us to the dining room, even though I was sure Thayer had been here a hundred times before. Or maybe the need for directions was legitimate, because the place was enormous—more of a compound than a house.

No amount had been spared when it came to the finishings, either; there were ornate crystal light fixtures and solid wood-paneling as far as the eye could see. I'd been around money for my entire life, but I was used to hedge fund managers and generational money, with a dash of newly minted well-to-do professionals thrown in. Charles, her mother's husband, was more on the level of an oil sheikh in terms of wealth.

Our footsteps clicked on the marble tiles while we navigated the hallway. A murmur of voices spilled out from the room ahead, hinting at far more than a small family dinner. Suddenly, I realized this wasn't going to be the informal test run I'd been hoping for.

I bumped Thayer with my elbow, keeping my voice low. "You didn't tell me this was some huge dinner party."

"I didn't know," she hissed.

We drew closer and the chatter became more audible. "Jared," a female voice echoed. "So lovely to see you again."

"Jared, as in Jared Callaghan?" I grabbed her arm. "Callaghan is here?" The stakes just multiplied exponentially.

I guess it shouldn't have come as a huge surprise. Alexandra and Charles knew everyone with money, like they belonged to some kind of big-bank-account club. But I hadn't known they were friendly enough with Callaghan for dinner parties, either.

"Sounds that way," Thayer said under her breath. "Thanks for the heads up, Mother."

I placed a hand on her lower back, hyper-aware of the need to appear like a legitimate couple. "Come on."

The click-clack of her stilettos slowed, and she came to a halt, fingers digging into her leather clutch like a life preserver in a storm.

"Thayer?" I urged.

"Huh?" Thayer looked up at me, expression vacant. She blinked and gave her head a little shake, taking another step. "Yeah, let's get this over with."

I stepped in front of her, blocking her path. "Hold up."

"What?"

No way could I drag her into the dining room with the deer-in-headlights thing she had going on. I steered her backward a few steps to the small powder room we had just passed. Something that felt a lot like guilt bubbled up within me. Maybe I should have known to expect this, but with the impenetrable front she put on these days, I didn't think it would be an issue.

I ushered her into the room and closed the door behind us, flipping on the lights.

"What are you—" Thayer started.

"Talking to you privately for a moment, as boyfriends often do."

"Okay." Her scarlet lips formed a thin line, and she crossed her arms, focusing on the black-and-cream patterned wallpaper behind me. "Talk."

I ducked my head, trying to catch her eye. "Do you still have panic attacks?"

Thayer's attention snapped over to me. "Why?" She eyed me suspiciously, like showing weakness meant I would go in for the kill. And in most cases, she would be right, but not with her.

"Are you on the verge of having one right now?" I already knew the answer; her face was the same as it was the time that I had to talk her out of the girls' bathroom to convince her to come write our English Lit final in sophomore year. Her panic was for nothing, because she ended up with an A+.

Her mouth pulled into a sulky pout. "No."

Bullshit.

"I need the truth because it's going to dramatically influence my response here." I stepped closer and cupped her chin, tilting her face up to mine. The look I received back was nothing less than pure defiance. "Now, are you being difficult to fuck with me, or are you nervous?"

"Neither."

"So the latter, then." I let my hand fall away but I didn't move, the two of us still only inches apart. The tension in the room was palpable, either from attraction or animosity or both. The briefest inappropriate urge shot through me, and I immediately clamped down on it.

Our eyes stayed locked, and her expression shifted, uncertainty flashing in her eyes. "Maybe."

It was the strongest admission I was going to get. Hell, I didn't blame her. Most people would be nervous in this position. But I didn't have the luxury of being nervous, because that would merely harm my ability to pull this off, and failure was not an option.

Without thinking, I gently touched her upper arm. The instant my fingertips connected with her smooth, bare skin, it was like the contact completed an electrical circuit, lighting me up from the inside out.

Only problem was, I had no idea if she felt it too, or if I was randomly working myself up in a bathroom over nothing. While I liked to think there were signs it was mutual, I wasn't getting my hopes up of her defrosting anytime soon.

Her gaze dropped to my hand, then moved back up to my face, the hostility in her expression waning.

"Look, everything is going to be fine. Most of that"—I nodded to the door beside me— "is fake anyway. We're just doing the same thing everyone else does. Only difference is, we're smart enough to be honest with ourselves about it."

"True." She gave a tiny nod.

"If anything starts to go sideways on you, make an excuse to come grab me, and I'll smooth it over."

The emotional walls shot straight back up and she squared her shoulders, eyes hardening. "I can manage just fine."

I unlocked the bathroom door, pulling it open to let her exit first. "I know."

Despite the shaky start, the first half of the night flew by without incident. Alexandra was clearly happy to see Thayer with someone. Not just happy, in fact, she was visibly relieved. Though I suspected she had mixed feelings about it being me. I could practically hear her mentally cataloguing the pros and cons, but I was fairly confident it added up to a net positive in her eyes.

Dinner was served not long after we arrived, which was a solid opportunity to gradually ease into our charade. A few times, I caught Thayer stuffing a bite of food into her mouth to buy time before answering questions about our 'relationship,' but she'd done an impressive job pulling it off overall.

With the plates cleared, however, it was time for the most arduous part: making small talk and socializing. While pretending to be madly in love with Thayer and like I didn't want to punch Adam in the throat, no less.

"Bennett," Alexandra said, cornering me solo while I topped up my drink. "Adam tells me you and Jared are in talks about an investment."

And how the hell would he know that? Despite the havoc he wreaked on my company when he left abruptly, Adam wasn't some corporate espionage mastermind, he was merely a douche.

"Yes, we are." I cleared my throat, checking on Thayer from across the room. She was engrossed in a conversation with Charles, which seemed a hell of a lot better than my current situation. Remaining diplomatic when speaking about Adam was always a challenge. "Didn't realize you and Jared were friends. It was a surprise to see him here tonight."

"Yes, we know him from the club. When Adam mentioned they were also discussing a business opportunity, I thought it would be a great way for everyone to get to know each other. Jared is lovely, as you know."

"Indeed," I murmured. First Adam goes after my property, then he goes after my investor? Why didn't he just hit up the Bank of Richard as per usual? Did Richard cut him off? It would explain why he was going after Quinn. The good old Montgomery trust fund.

"Did I hear my name?" Callaghan chuckled, sidling up to join where we stood. "Alexandra, you flatter me."

Alexandra laughed. "Always."

"Bennett." He extended his hand, clamping mine in a firm handshake. "Good to see you again."

Being seated at opposite ends of the table, we hadn't had much opportunity to talk over dinner. Now it was time to make a good impression or die trying. Unfortunately, before I could get a word in edgewise, Adam sauntered up and inserted himself into the conversation.

"Jared." Adam clapped Callaghan on the back like they were old frat brothers. I maintained a neutral expression, but inwardly I wanted to punch him in the throat. "How was your daughter's wedding?"

"Fantastic. Napa is lovely in September. What about you, son? Are you getting excited for the big day?"

"Can't wait." Adam smiled, oozing with smugness only I seemed to detect. "Don't worry, Bennett. You'll join us at the adult table someday."

"I'm sure." I returned his fake smile, grip on my glass tightening.

In a twist of unfortunate timing, Millie strolled by and caught the tail end of what Adam said. She spun around to face the four of us, tucking a lock of mousy brown hair behind her ear. "Actually, I heard Bennett and Thayer aren't far off from walking down the aisle themselves. Is that true, Bennett?"

Her eyes scanned my face with such precision that I was scared to blink. I doubted that Millie had, in fact, heard such a thing. My money was on fishing or trying to stir up trouble, but there was nothing I could do about that now.

Alexandra, Callaghan, and Adam all looked at me expectantly, waiting for a response. It was go along, or look like our relationship wasn't serious. And if there was one thing I needed to appear, it was serious.

"We've talked about it," I lied. "Just waiting for the right time to pop the question."

One by one, like a domino effect, everyone reacted. Millie's eyes widened; Adam's expression clouded over before returning to his default self-satisfied setting; Callaghan appeared impressed; and Alexandra looked pleased, if somewhat surprised.

"That's excellent," Alexandra said.

Callaghan held up his glass of red wine as if in a toast. "Well, that is exciting news. Shows a lot of personal growth on your part."

"Shows something," Adam muttered. I wanted to dump Callaghan's wine on his white dress shirt, but I refrained. Barely.

"Maybe we'll see a ring next time I see you," Callaghan added.

I nodded. "Here's to hoping." Guess I was committing to this, then. Thayer was going to lose her mind.

Fucking Millie.

After some additional, superficial small talk, Callaghan and Alexandra excused themselves and Millie followed suit, evidently having lost interest once the juicy gossip dried up. Or more likely, she was about to go tell the whole damn town that I was next to walk down the aisle.

Their departures left me alone with public enemy number one: my backstabbing cousin. An awkward silence hung between us while I scanned the room, searching for Thayer without any success. We'd talked about me rescuing her, but never the reverse. Wish we had, because I could use it right now.

"I didn't know Callaghan was going to be here," I said, turning back to Adam. Might as well call him out on his machinations.

He met my gaze evenly, like he wasn't blatantly trying to fuck me over for a second time. "Up until yesterday, I didn't know you were going to be here."

"Clearly," I said, taking a sip of scotch. "I'm sure you didn't want me to know you were wooing him."

"No different than all the other people who are pursuing Jared for funding." He shrugged. "Just a little friendly competition, cuz."

"Of course." Except it was different. Entirely different. I was sure Adam went after Callaghan specifically because he'd heard we were courting him. "Why do you need Callaghan, anyway? Richard cut you off?"

"He wanted to diversify instead of investing more at this point in time."

"Ah." I didn't even try to hide my grin. Good to know I wasn't the only one Richard had zero faith in.

"You know," he said. "I've been hoping we could bury the hatchet. Especially now that you and I will be around each other more. After all, business is business."

"It sure is." Just like it would be 'business' when I stole his company out from beneath him.

Adam gave me a calculated smile. "Perfect, because I wanted to ask you to be a groomsman in the wedding."

The skin on the back of my neck prickled. It's almost like he knew my relationship with Thayer had an expiration date.

"Would love nothing more," I lied. Except for skydiving without a parachute, waxing my balls, and doing basically anything other than that. But obviously I couldn't say no right now. I'd figure out an exit strategy closer to the wedding date.

"No hard feelings, then?" Adam extended his hand and I accepted it, but our handshake was a little too firm to be friendly.

"None at all."

Forget the hatchet. I was going to bury him.

By the time Quinn swooped in and rescued me from Adam—or rescued Adam from me, as I was dangerously close to smashing a champagne flute over his head—Thayer had been cornered next to the bar by someone tall and lanky with dark hair.

I weaved past clusters of people scattered around the room, making my way over to them, and Louis Sullivan came into focus. He was a friend of Adam's and to say I wasn't a fan of his would be putting it mildly.

He leaned against the wooden rail, glass of amber liquid in one hand as he spoke to Thayer, body angled toward hers. They were standing a little too close together for my liking.

As I drew within earshot, Louis gave her a wolfish smile. "Adam and Quinn were going to set us up, you know. We're set to walk down the aisle together at the wedding."

A bolt of irritation shot through me. While we weren't actually together, Louis didn't know that. Disrespectful dick.

Thayer let out a strangled laugh. "Oh, well. As they say, timing is everything."

"It really is," I said, coming to stand beside her. My arm slipped around her waist, the movement feeling a little more natural than it should. I stared Louis down. "Guess you missed your chance, Sullivan. Not that you had one."

Surprise glanced across his face, like he genuinely didn't expect to be called out for hitting on someone else's girlfriend. "Relax, Bradford. I didn't mean it—"

"I'm sure you didn't." I smiled, but it was more like baring my teeth. "Either way, you're not her type. Timing or not."

A silence fell over the three of us. Thayer gaped at me like I'd lost my mind. Louis's jaw ticked as he glared at me, weighing whether to engage, but he apparently thought better of it.

"I should go find Adam." He turned and made an abrupt departure, disappearing into the room.

Thayer shot me a look so pointed it practically pierced my skin. "We need to talk. Now." She took my hand and yanked me through the room, barreling out the door. It wasn't lost on me that all eyes were on us as she did.

She led us down a different hallway than the one we'd entered through, making a series of left and right hand turns. I nearly had to jog to keep up. Given the height of her stiletto heels, her speed was impressive.

With a few more steps, Thayer pushed open a glass door leading into a massive indoor atrium filled with trees, plants, and flowers. Floral scents drifted in the air, humid and warm, creating a tropical atmosphere despite the chilly early winter outside.

"What the hell was that?" She set down her empty wine glass on a rock ledge, glowering up at me through her long eyelashes. "Not my type? You don't even know what my type is."

"Trust me," I said. "I was doing you a favor."

"A favor, huh? You sure seem to do a lot of those for me."

"Louis Sullivan is an asshole."

The things I had heard about him made my skin crawl. Like that fact that he allegedly had a poor understanding of the word 'no,' which I'd heard from more than one reliable source. I had no idea why Adam would try to set Thayer up with someone like that, but Adam wasn't great at thinking of other people. Or thinking, period.

And with Millie at his disposal, there was little doubt Adam was aware of those rumors. Quinn should have been, too, but maybe she was buying whatever bullshit Adam was peddling these days.

"Like you?" Thayer shot back.

"No, he's a creep. If you think we're comparable in any way, you're sorely mistaken." I stepped closer to her, lowering my voice. "And we could have company, you know. Just keep that in mind before you say anything more."

Her eyes darted around the atrium, then landed back on me. She drew in a long breath, holding it, then exhaled slowly. "Fine. But you're still an ass."

"Noted," I said. "While I've got you here, I should let you know that everyone thinks we're getting engaged. Like, imminently."

She was already pissed, so what better time than now to break the news?

Thayer's jaw dropped, crimson lips forming a tiny O of surprise. "What?! How? And why?"

"I got railroaded."

"Aren't you the one who told me you could, and I quote, 'handle anything'?"

Obviously, I was full of shit, but I wasn't going to admit that to her.

"I said handle, not control."

"But you can't—" She gestured and dropped her voice to a whisper. "Just change the terms like that."

"Didn't exactly have a choice, Thay. One minute, I mentioned we might be talking marriage, and the next, everyone was asking for a wedding date. It snowballed. You of all people should understand."

"Ugh!" She threw her head back, dark glossy hair tumbling down her shoulders as she looked up at the glass-paneled roof. "I don't even want to get married, Bennett. Everyone knows that."

"Newsflash: I don't either. But people change their minds about wanting to get married all the time. It's called growing up, or so I'm told. And if we don't follow through with an engagement now, it's going to make it look like our relationship is on the rocks."

"Fine," she snapped. "Put a ring on it."

Not the reaction most guys hope for when discussing an engagement, but good enough.

Voices echoed from afar, followed by footsteps. Thayer spun back to face me, her light blue eyes fraught with panic. "What are we going to do? They all know we're arguing."

"And? It's fine."

Her voice climbed a register. "It is not fine."

"Shh, keep it down, okay?" I made a calm down gesture with my hands, which only made her look angrier. Mental note not to do that again going forward. "It's called a lovers' quarrel for a reason."

"What?" she looked at me like I was insane. "Is this code for something?"

"People in relationships," I said quietly. "They fight. I may not be an expert, but I know that much. And what do people do after they fight?"

Thayer's immaculately groomed brows knit together. "They make up?" Realization dawned on her face. "You mean like…? You can't be serious."

"Do you want to sell this or not?"

"Of course, I do," she ground out.

"Then play along."

CHAPTER FOURTEEN

Thayer

"**P**LAY ALONG?" I REPEATED.

"Right." Bennett nodded. "I'm going to kiss you." He enunciated the words slowly, like he was exercising a great degree of patience. It was truly ironic, considering how much patience dealing with *him* required.

He dipped his head, lips nearly brushing my ear, and I fought the most ridiculous urge to lean in closer. "You need to at least pretend to kiss me back." His warm breath danced along my skin, sending a thrill through my body. I told myself was just a physical response to the sensation; nothing to do with him.

"But we said—"

"No sex," he finished.

I blinked slowly while my brain worked overtime to process what he'd said, but staring at him only further impaired my ability to think. Because while our contract said no sexual activities, I hadn't defined what that meant.

Naively, when I pictured a fake relationship, I'd envisioned G-rated activities like dinner dates, holding hands, and hugging.

Maybe a slow dance or two at Adam and Quinn's wedding. You know, a level of physical contact appropriate for a Hallmark movie.

What I hadn't accounted for was the honeymoon period. Most new couples still in the throes of lust were all over each other—and they definitely weren't keeping it G-rated. Especially not someone like Bennett. If we wanted to sell this, kissing was a more than reasonable expectation. It was a requirement.

His lips tugged into a smug grin. "If you're worried a kiss will lead to sex, allow me to clarify. Generally, sex involves removing at least a few key layers of clothing, not to mention this thing called foreplay, where you both—"

"I'm familiar with that process, thanks." The sudden mental image of Bennett getting undressed—or him undressing me—did little to set my nerves at ease. If I was being honest, it did something else entirely.

"If you're not comfortable, we can pull the plug on our deal." Bennett shrugged. "No hard feelings."

Although he was doing a respectable job of acting indifferent, I knew it was a bluff; Bennett needed me as much as I needed him. If this went up in flames, so did he. It would validate Callaghan's objections about his unstable personal life and kill the deal. Even worse, it would send Callaghan straight into Adam's arms.

Bennett raised his dark eyebrows, waiting for my response. From the distance, Quinn's laugh carried, and a low male voice muttered something indecipherable. Time was running out: it was either make nice or risk everyone thinking this sham of a relationship was already in peril.

"Fine," I hissed. "Kiss me." Heat shot through my body, panic mingling with the slightest hint of curiosity.

"You know, women usually sound a lot more enthusiastic when they say that to me."

I had the nearly overwhelming urge to drown him in the Koi pond next to us. But sadly, he was more useful to me alive than dead.

"Are you trying to ruin this whole thing?" I yell-whispered.

His grey-blue eyes darkened from denim to steel. "I think you're doing a fine job of that on your own."

Bennett closed the distance between us, looming over me. We stood nose to nose, mouths inches apart. Breathing the same air, close enough to kiss. I looked back up at him, refusing to show any emotion, but inwardly my stomach was pole-vaulting like it was the summer Olympics.

"Thay?" Quinn called, her voice drawing closer. "There you—"

He wrapped one hand around my lower back, caging me in, and cupped my chin with his other hand. My eyes fluttered shut as his lips captured mine, knocking the air out of my lungs and taking with it any shred of self-control I had going in.

I don't know why I parted my lips and kissed him back. Why I let him push inside my mouth, skilfully caressing my tongue with his. Nor could I explain the effect it had on me, which could only have been described as a kill switch for my brain. It was some kind of physiological reaction that circumvented my frontal lobe completely.

His fingers gently tilted my face, deepening the kiss. When his tongue swept against mine again, a sudden, unexpected electric shock of desire hit me. My knees went soft, and I clutched his shoulders with my fingertips to steady myself. A small sound of appreciation rumbled from the back of his throat as he pulled me closer.

For a brief, divine moment, nothing else existed; not my sister, not the garden, and definitely not the stupid dinner party. The only things in the world were Bennett's firm, athletic body, pressed up against my body; Bennett's strong hands, holding me firmly in place; and Bennett's delicious mouth, claiming mine. It was like drowning while breathing, flying while falling, a blessing and a curse. I hated it and I never wanted it to stop.

After some indeterminate length of time, Bennett slowly, reluctantly pulled away. Or maybe the reluctance was on my end, though I'd never admit that to him. Either way, our mouths had stayed locked together far longer than any stage kiss could have reasonably required.

He stroked my cheek with his thumb while he looked over my shoulder, scanning the garden. "They're gone," he murmured.

I nodded silently, and the truth hit me like a sledgehammer to the chest. Bennett didn't kiss me because he wanted to, he kissed me because he was playing the role of doting boyfriend—and giving an Oscar-worthy performance at that. After all, there was a reason I agreed to this crazy scheme: Bennett excelled at manipulating people, myself included.

But with our audience gone, there was no reason to continue our charade. No explanation for the way his hand lingered around the small of my back, seemingly reluctant to let go, and no excuse for my palms to remain spread flat against his chest, mapping the taut muscles beneath his impeccably tailored dress shirt.

Seconds passed and neither of us moved. The white marble fountain bubbled in the background, punctuated by the odd, faint outburst of laughter from the dining room. Our gazes locked and my heart stuttered.

Bennett smirked. "I don't think you mind our arrangement nearly as much as you claim."

"False," I said, careful to keep my voice low. "I still hate you."

"Is that so?" He released me, leaving a patch of cold behind where his hands had been. A chill ran through my body, and I bounced on the spot to warm up. In the autumn twilight, the temperature in the atrium had turned cool.

"Just like I know you hate me." To be accurate, I hated him even more now. What was he trying to prove with that remark anyway? Did he want me to *hate* kissing him? We were supposed to be on the same side, not trying to get the upper hand on one another.

Suddenly feeling vulnerable, I broke eye contact with him, and my gaze dropped to the pale apricot Juliet roses dotting the bush beside us. I couldn't believe it when my mother had mentioned the price tag—well over a million dollars for the rare floral hybrid. Now, that seemed perfectly reasonable compared to what I'd gotten myself into.

"I just find you're better in small doses." Bennett shrugged off his navy suit jacket, placing it around my bare shoulders. The satin inner lining rested against my skin, leather and warm vanilla of his cologne invading my senses again. It took me straight back to our kiss moments before and somehow increased my level of irritation with him.

I narrowed my eyes. "Don't bullshit me. You froze me out me in high school and you pretended I didn't exist in college. Specifically, you hated that we ended up at the same college." He opened his mouth, and I held up a finger to silence him. "You barely deigned to speak to me the entire time I dated Adam."

Bennett glanced down, straightening the cuffs of his shirt and meticulously rolling them up. "I wasn't aware you were so desperate for my attention. I could have penciled you in." He reached up, loosening his tie and removing it before unbuttoning the top button of his white dress shirt.

Infuriatingly, the end result was even more appealing.

"You could have started with being civil," I said. "Every time you saw me at your place in the morning, you turned around and left." Bennett had lived with Adam, and he had gone out of his way to be as hostile as humanly possible.

"I'm not a morning person," he deadpanned.

"You acted like I didn't even exist. It was rude."

My teeth set on edge, triggered by the combination of memories and his current, callous behavior. A simple apology would have gone a long way. Beneath it all, I still didn't know why he froze me out, either. But my pride wouldn't let me ask.

"I'm not sure whether you've noticed," he said, "but you're not exactly Miss Manners yourself sometimes."

It was mighty high-handed, considering the source.

I shook my head and looked away, smoothing a wrinkle in my black silk dress. As tempted as I was to try to win the argument, Bennett was known for his knife-edged tongue and for going straight for the jugular. While I had formidable emotional walls, they weren't indestructible—I wasn't sure my self-esteem could withstand the damage if we kept sparring.

Before he said anything further, I turned and inclined my head for him to follow. "Let's go back to the party."

Following our little verbal altercation, Bennett managed to get Callaghan alone, effectively throwing me to the wolves by myself. Adam was mysteriously missing, which was a positive for both our sakes, if borderline suspicious.

I drained my third glass of wine, handing it to a server passing by. As I did, Quinn strolled over, placing a hand on my arm.

"Mother and I were just talking about you," she said. Her bright violet dress cut to a deep V in the front and looked like it was straight out of the pages of Vogue. She looked about as thin as a runway model, too, if not thinner. It had been a constant trend with her lately—one that concerned me.

"Really." My eyes darted around the room, desperately searching for a tray carrying drink refills. "And why is that?"

Though, I was afraid to know the answer.

"Because we are totally onto you." Quinn gave me a knowing smile, waggling her sculpted brows.

I laughed, trying to act like I wasn't at all having an internal panic attack. The effect was more crazed than carefree. "What do you mean?"

She steered me over to a burgundy leather couch off to the side, pulling me to sit down beside her. I sank down uneasily, searching our surroundings in vain for an alcoholic beverage source.

"Bennett," she said, crossing her slender legs. "You two are so obvious."

Code Red. This is not a drill. Repeat, this is not a drill.

"We are?" My voice came out strangled.

I gripped the edge of the smooth leather seat. Our story was falling apart. Quinn knew the truth, and once we were done with this conversation, she'd tell everyone else how my relationship with Bennett was a sham. Everyone would know I'd lied, I didn't have a boyfriend, and I was undateable—and once word spread, I would stay that way forever. I would be forced to flee the city in a cloak of shame, ruined socially and forever alone.

And our mother? Our mother would have a conniption. Bad enough that this would ruin my own reputation, but it would tarnish hers right along with it. She'd never forgive me.

Quinn nodded. "Everyone can tell. We've been talking about it all evening."

Survival instincts kicked in, and I drew in a breath, steadying myself. I had to salvage this. There was no other option. Even if she had some inkling of what was going on, I could perform damage control. Bend the truth, explain away any inconsistencies, and sell the Chanel out of this charade.

She looked at me expectantly, waiting for my response.

What would Bennett do? Normally, that was the last principle I would use to guide my choices in life, but in this case, he was right— he was the perfect role model. The master manipulator himself.

I'd spent enough time with him lately to know the answer: he'd offer some vague platitude and keep the other person talking to see exactly how much they knew.

"That's interesting," I said. In a delivery from the heavens, a server passed by, and I grabbed a glass of champagne, downing half like it was the antidote to poison.

Quinn gave me a sly look. "I can't believe you thought you could pull one over on your own sister."

My heart skipped a beat or three.

"You two have been an item for way longer than you're saying." She batted my arm playfully.

Giddy relief washed over me, and I took another sip of champagne, thanking the heavens for the false alarm. Crisp bubbles with a side of relief had never tasted so good. There might be penance to pay later, and I'd gladly do it.

But on that note, *obvious*? How? Because we bickered like an old married couple? At least married couples had loved each other at one point. We didn't even have that going for us.

"Oh, well…" I shrugged. "You know how it is these days. Have to make sure they're really committed before you go public."

"Right." She nodded. "That makes sense. I did the same with Adam."

For lack of anything useful to offer, I nodded and hummed in agreement. On the other side of the room, Bennett reappeared and struck up a conversation with Charles and my mother. Charming the hell out of both of them, from what I could gather at a distance.

"I'm so glad this isn't awkward," Quinn confessed. "You were weird about it when Adam and I first started dating. I guess I should have asked you first, but I thought it would be okay since you were the one who broke up with him, and it was so long ago. You seemed to have forgotten about him completely…" she trailed off.

I didn't know what to say to that.

Maybe I was "weird" because Adam and I fell back into bed together a month before he asked her out. Having never had a one-night stand before, it was entirely out of character for me. I'd justified it to myself by reasoning that it wasn't *really* a one-night stand if he was my ex—but that didn't take the sting out of it when he blew me off the next day.

The whole ordeal left me feeling used, not to mention more than a little foolish. That's why I was too embarrassed to tell anyone. Then things went full circle four weeks later when Adam showed up on Quinn's arm at a mutual friend's party.

And proposed to her two months after that.

There's moving fast, and there's traveling at warp speed.

"But then I realized, you were probably just lonely." Quinn took a sip of her Merlot. "I'm glad that you're serious with someone too. I feel so much better about everything knowing you're happy."

I forced a smile. "I guess it all worked out."

Bennett crossed the room and came to stand in front of the

couch, shooting me a questioning look. Beneath his calm exterior, I could tell he was as emotionally exhausted as I was; it was evident in his eyes. "Are you ready to go, Thay?"

"Sure, just let me say goodbye to everyone." I stood up, quickly promising to text Quinn later, and we did a quick round of farewells around the room. Several people gave me knowing smiles, which was probably a nod to my pending 'engagement' news.

Bennett's hand landed on my lower back, gently guiding down to the door. "All good?" he asked under his breath.

"Yeah," I whispered. "She totally bought it."

As we departed, my sister shot me a sidelong look, like she thought we were about to go home and have crazy hot sex, which couldn't have been a more preposterous idea.

Sure, objectively speaking, Bennett was attractive. Especially tonight in his tailored white dress shirt with its sleeves rolled up halfway, revealing his firm, muscled forearms. And especially with the way the dim light cast shadows across his face, highlighting his strong jaw and drawing your eyes to his lips...

"What?" he asked, brow knit.

I averted my eyes and looked forward. "Uh, nothing."

Oh my God, was I just ogling him? What the hell was I doing? When it came to Bennett, the outside was never the problem; it was everything else. Clearly, the alcohol had gone to my head. It was the only possible explanation.

Well, that or the kiss.

There was only one solution: we must never kiss again.

CHAPTER FIFTEEN

Bennett

THERE'S A FIRST FOR EVERYTHING IN BUSINESS. FIRST PROJECT, first office, first business card, first time hiring someone, first time firing someone. Most first times are exciting milestones along the road to success. Well, except for firing someone—though when they deserve it, sometimes that feels pretty damn good.

But your first nasty letter from the IRS, threatening bank account seizures and legal action is a speedbump you pray you'll never hit. And I just did—doing ninety miles per hour.

"You're going to have to tell him sometime." Eric leaned back in his chair across from my desk, looking at me pointedly. He folded his fingers over his emerging potbelly, the result of stress from recently making partner at his firm.

"I will." Eventually.

For now, Ian didn't need to know. It wasn't like I was going to keep this under wraps forever; I'd tell him once I had a solution, ideally in the form of a massive cash injection.

Until then, knowing about the tax arrears—and our dire financial position—would only cause Ian unnecessary stress. As Chief

Operating Officer, his head needed to be clear to focus on oversee-ing more pressing matters, like acquiring and amalgamating the par-cel of land we'd been working on for the past year. I'd let him focus on that, while I stood on my head, trying to prevent the company from folding.

It was my fault, anyway. Or Adam's fault, if you wanted to be specific. I'd already sunk every penny to my name into this com-pany. When he'd put the screws to us two years ago, demanding a buyout, I had nothing left to draw on and no choice but to borrow from the company to pay him.

Definitely not ideal, but I figured we had enough of a buffer to survive—and we would have, except the real estate market decided to take a fucking face plant. It had been unprecedented, unforeseen, and highly unfortunate timing.

Before I knew it, our conservative projections were unrealis-tic, and our margins were shrinking faster than my balls in a cold shower. The buffer dwindled to zero, and I began using money ear-marked for specific projects for other things, trying to make it up before it was needed. Essentially, kiting within my own company.

The real estate market had since recovered, but the reality of our financial situation had not. The fallout from Adam's treachery was still haunting me.

"This seems like a fairly straightforward matter. According to them, there's a large amount of tax owing from last year." Eric scanned the sheaf of papers in his hand, identical to the ones that sat on my desk in front of me. He glanced up, eyebrows raised be-hind his black-rimmed glasses. "Unless there's more to the story. Did you request a reassessment? Are there losses that weren't ac-counted for on your return?"

"No." I wished I had a leg to stand on, but I didn't. "We owe the money."

Hopefully, Ian would understand why I kept this from him. Or maybe he would never need to know. Maybe I could somehow magically conjure the money out of thin air, get the IRS off my back, and make it all go away before anyone had to know.

Probably not.

"Okay." Eric nodded, waiting for me to continue. To explain why we hadn't paid corporate taxes for the year prior. Except I didn't have an explanation other than the ugly truth: we had been short on funds and the money went to other things. Like paying staff, so I still had a company.

"It's not like I think taxes are optional," I said. "We just fell behind, and it snowballed from there."

"That's not uncommon."

Glancing down, I re-read the details, noticing 'Bennett Charles Bradford' listed under addressees. My heart started to hammer, blood pressure spiking.

"They named me personally? What the fuck?" I stood up and began to stalk in circles in front of the window. Lately, I'd been exceeding 20,000 steps a day from stress-pacing alone.

"You're the CFO," he said. "Technically, you could be held personally responsible for the unpaid taxes. But if the corporation pays the arrears, they won't go after you to recover the funds."

I dearly hoped not, because I didn't have the funds. Contrary to what most people thought, I didn't have a big fat trust fund anymore, nor the bank account to back up my designer wardrobe. After Adam pulled the plug, I'd poured everything I had into keeping the company afloat. I was living on a prayer, leveraged to the hilt. It was downright embarrassing. Thank God for client-lawyer confidentiality.

"Look," Eric started. He drew in a breath, hesitating. "This is me putting on my Eric-your-friend hat, not lawyer-Eric talking. What's going on? The company seems to be doing well. Your projects are selling, correct?"

"Mostly," I said. "But it's been a rough couple of years. Buying out Adam ate into our operating reserves and then the low-rise condominium we wrapped up last spring didn't meet our projected price per square foot." Or my projected price per square foot, to be specific. Because those items fell under my purview, and I overshot. Significantly.

Sure, we made a profit, but barely. When you factored in the time spent and opportunity cost, it was a poor return on investment.

"Ah." Eric glanced down, making notes in his folio with his Mont Blanc. "You have a liquidity problem."

"Yes."

"Is there any way you can raise some additional funds? You know, to help get you through?"

I clamped down on the urge to snap at him. I knew he meant well, but did he really think I hadn't tried?

"Working on it."

He nodded sympathetically. "It's a tight market out there."

"It is," I agreed.

I wondered how unprofessional it would be to ask Eric for a loan. He'd recently made partner, which involved a massive firm buy-in, so he probably didn't have any cash anyway. Not to mention, it would probably be inappropriate to hit up my legal counsel for cash, even if he was my friend. No, I couldn't actually do that. But I was stretched so thin and so desperate that I didn't know what to do.

"What we want to avoid is an audit," he said. "They're a pain in the ass. They'll swoop in here and scrutinize everything from your expense accounts to what you pay for toilet paper."

Yes, I *definitely* wanted to avoid that.

"How do we make sure that doesn't happen?"

He looked at me sympathetically. "By paying them."

"And if I can't? Can I make some kind of payment arrangement like you said, give them installments?"

"We can try. They aren't always as amenable to it when you owe a large sum of money."

Well, that made zero sense. The more you owed, the harder it was to pay. I wouldn't need a fucking payment plan if I only owed a couple grand.

"Does the company have any assets it can dispose of? Real estate or other hard assets?" he asked. "Otherwise, you're in for a bumpy ride with any additional fundraising in this market."

Didn't I know it.

My phone buzzed and an appointment notification popped up on my screen.

"Shit," I muttered, looking down at the reminder. "We'll have to cut this short; I have another meeting I have to get to."

And by meeting, I meant I was going to go buy a goddamn engagement ring to continue my charade, based on some faint hope of keeping Callaghan on the hook.

I hadn't pictured myself buying an engagement ring ever, and definitely not under these circumstances. But after things spiraled out of control at the party, rumors of our impending engagement had spread like wildfire, including to my own mother—who was thrilled.

Now I understood how Thayer's fib had come back to bite her in the ass.

At any rate, everyone was expecting me to propose, and I had to follow through or risk looking like our 'relationship' wasn't solid. In order to land Callaghan, stability needed to be my middle name.

Eric nodded, pushing his chair back as he stood. "We have fifteen days to respond. Let's touch base at the end of the week to work on the statement of defense. That will give us time to finalize it before it's due."

"Okay," I said. "I'll be in touch."

But what defense did I have when I was guilty?

Stage three...metastasis to the lymph nodes...more radiation and possible surgery...

My mother reached across the table, placing a soft hand on top of my own. I blinked, snapping back to reality, and looked up to find her dark blue eyes watching me with an expression of concern.

Why was she worried about me? I should be the one worried about her. When she said her cancer had returned, I hadn't expected it to be this serious. Naively, I'd been hoping it was like before; caught early and entirely treatable.

"I haven't told Holden yet," she said. "Let me tell him when we're alone, please."

Panic crawled up my throat. I reached for my beer and took a hefty gulp, trying to swallow the ball of tension stuck in my esophagus. "Will do."

"I still have to go for more tests," she added. "But I am sure it's going to be fine. My oncologist tells us the prognosis is still very good, statistically. And you know your father's health insurance is world class."

It was true; while I resented the shit out of my uncle Richard, he provided his senior executives with top-shelf benefits, including health care coverage fit for the US President. My mother would be able to access every cutting-edge treatment available within the continental United States. The plan even covered holistic therapies like acupuncture and massage.

Still, that knowledge did little to put my mind at ease now that I knew her cancer had spread.

Moments later, my younger brother, Holden, rushed through the door of the restaurant, fresh from moot court at his law school. He leaned in and gave our mother a warm hug. Then he slid into a chair across from me, shrugging off his charcoal suit jacket.

"Alicia had an emergency at work," he said apologetically. "Client in need of an urgent root canal." His girlfriend, two years older than him, was a dentist catering to the high-end crowd. In other words, charging them through the nose for a few X-rays and tooth-scrapings. Smart gig, really. Hell of a lot more stable than what I'd decided to dive into.

"That's okay." Our mother gave him a tired smile. It hit me that she didn't look as vibrant as she usually did, only adding fuel to my bonfire of worries. "Maybe next time, she can meet Thayer."

Holden's light brown eyebrows practically hit his hairline. "Thayer?"

"His girlfriend, Holden."

The choking sensation in my throat returned, intensifying. My beer, now empty, was of no help.

"Girlfriend?" Holden looked even more confused.

"We haven't been dating long," I said, picking up the food menu to give myself something to focus on other than my brother's prying stare. The engagement ring in my suit jacket felt like it was burning a hole through the wool fabric. "But it's getting serious."

"They're talking marriage." My mother beamed over the table at me. I felt like such an asshole.

"Okay…" he muttered. Clearly, he didn't want to get into it in front of our mother, and thank God for that.

When she excused herself moments later to use the bathroom, Holden yanked my menu out of my hands, snapping it shut. He leaned over the table eyeing me like I was an enemy spy.

"Are we talking about Thayer Montgomery, Bennett? From high school? Isn't she the one who—"

Me and my big fucking mouth. And my temper…And my ego.

"Ancient history." I feigned a neutral expression, cutting him off with a wave of my hand.

He took a sip of his gin and tonic, watching me. "You're not exactly the type to forgive and forget."

I wasn't—and I hadn't. But it didn't matter right now. Our interests were mutually aligned.

"Call it personal growth," I said. "That was nine years ago. We've moved past it."

"Since when?" he demanded. "I've had to hear how much you hate her since high school. Hell, you practically made me hate her."

Okay, I may have trash talked Thayer a little in the past when I was upset about what she did. Plus, she's so damn stubborn, and she argues like it's an Olympic sport. Talk about having a smart mouth.

But her soft lips and that little sound she made when we kissed the other night were almost enough to make me forget. My cock twitched at the memory, brain immediately flipping into X-rated territory.

Fuck.

To say I wasn't handling the stress of my current situation well was an understatement, and epic sexual frustration was the cherry on top of the garbage sundae of my life. At this point, a warm breeze could get me off.

"I decided it was time to move past it," I said, picking up the new bottle of beer our server just set down. "And mom doesn't know about any of that. She likes Thayer, and we're going to keep it that way, especially with mom being sick again. Okay?"

I didn't lean into the bossy older brother role often, even as kids, so when I did, Holden knew better than to argue. Hopefully, he wouldn't manage to pry the truth out of me eventually. He could read me better than Ian, even.

Holden frowned and opened his mouth to say something. His eyes fell on our mother as she approached the table, and I shot him a warning look before he could add anything further.

"Fine," he said.

Our father was supposed to join us for dinner but didn't arrive until we were paying the bill—after Holden had already left to pick up his girlfriend at work. At least he showed up in time to drive my mother home, but I was still irked. He'd been almost entirely MIA the past few years, consumed with trying to prove himself to everyone else in the wake of his insider trading charges. Copping a plea deal like he had didn't exactly help his image, and he was hell-bent on restoring it to its previous, untarnished state. Which would never happen.

We made a slow shuffle through the restaurant, heading in the direction of the exit.

"Sorry again for being late." My father ran a hand through his salt and pepper hair, looking nearly as frazzled as I felt. Beneath his black wool dress coat, his tie hung loose around his neck. Leaning in, he gave my mom a quick kiss on the cheek as he steered her to the door. To his credit, he was a significantly better husband than father.

"Richard needed me to attend a meeting on his behalf," he added.

Of course, he did. Richard was more than happy to let my dad do all the grunt work.

"I know how it goes," I said coolly.

Coming to a stop on the curb outside, we waited for the valet to bring their car around. I was within walking distance to my apartment and glad for it, because I needed the air to clear my head.

"How are things with work, anyway?"

I tensed, trying to hide my discomfort. Was he asking to make conversation, or asking because Richard told him I'd approached him for a loan?

"Great," I lied. "Just wrapping up the next round of financing."

In a swoop of good timing, their black Mercedes sedan pulled up to the curb, and the valet hopped out, handing my father the keys. I gave my mother a hug, releasing her and trying not to worry about how frail she felt in my arms.

"I hope you bring Thayer next time," she said, giving me a warm smile that made me feel like even more of a jerk than I already did.

"I will, she just had a work commitment tonight."

The valet opened the door for her, and she turned back to look at me before sliding in. Her face lit up. "We could do dinner with her family. I'd love to catch up with Alexandra and Charles."

Guilt stabbed me in the gut. "Even better."

Between this and the ring, Thayer really was going to kill me.

And she didn't even know about Mexico yet.

CHAPTER SIXTEEN

Thayer

I F QUINN DIDN'T SHOW UP SOON, I WAS GOING TO WALK OUT of this stupid photoshoot. I could not believe I let her guilt-trip me into doing this piece for Style & Society only for her to be missing in action.

Actually, I could believe it. That was the problem.

It was twenty minutes past our scheduled start time; the makeup artist had given me a dramatic smoky eye, the hairstylist had coaxed my fine hair into a voluminous head of curls, and the stylist had poured me into a revealing, watermelon-pink dress I'd never have chosen for myself. I'd even been subjected to a round of test shots already.

The magazine's photographer, Marco, and his crew bustled around our store, adjusting lights and re-arranging furniture while Paula, the journalist covering the article, sat at the counter, going over her notes. My sister was nowhere to be found. Especially ironic when I probably looked like her more than ever.

I sank down onto the white couch in the fitting area and unlocked my phone, composing another text to her, inquiring whether she was planning to show up sometime today. I was growing slightly concerned about the fact that she hadn't even replied to my other messages. Usually, she at least provided some kind of half-assed excuse.

A split-second after I hit send, the door chimed, and Quinn rushed through the door. Her hair was in a messy bun, she was wearing head-to-toe Lululemon, and she looked like she just ran a half-marathon. Bizarre for someone generally so image conscious.

"So sorry!" She breezed by me, rosy-cheeked and breathless. Maybe there was something to my marathon theory. "My personal training appointment ran long."

Pushing to stand, I gave her a skeptical look and tried to minimize the irritation in my voice. "Long? Aren't they for set lengths of time?"

We both knew the answer, especially when it came to someone as in-demand as Curtis Graham, who had such a full roster that he didn't even take on new personal training clients anymore.

"Usually," she said, shrugging off her red down puffer and hanging it in the back closet. "But Curtis and I got carried away chatting at the end."

"Must have been some chat. You're nearly half an hour late." My annoyance shifted into concern, and I hesitated, weighing whether to pry. "You've had training sessions every day this week. Are you sure you're okay? Have you talked to Doctor Stephens lately?"

Quinn turned to face me, her expression tight. "I'm fine. Just stressed. Planning a wedding is stressful, you know, and exercise is a good stress reliever."

It was, but it was also playing with fire for a recovering exercise addict with a history of disordered eating. Doctor Stephens was Quinn's therapist, and I had a hunch that Quinn had fallen off the therapy wagon as of late. Adam probably didn't help, either; he had a strong preference for slim women and made that known. Yet another reason I couldn't stand him.

The hair and makeup crew joined us, holding up outfits while

Quinn made a face, rejecting the first few contenders. Had I realized that veto-ing was an option, I would have exercised that right myself.

She finally snagged a dress off the rack for herself, turning back to me with a nod of approval. "Apparition Boutique is letting us keep the outfits from today's shoot in exchange for the publicity. Lucky, because that totally suits you. You look gorgeous."

I glanced down, taking in the low V-neck and body-hugging lines. It was from an up-and-coming local designer. Objectively nice, but not at all my aesthetic. My wardrobe consisted entirely of neutrals; black, grey, navy, tans, the odd chocolate brown. I'd probably end up giving this frosting-pink concoction to Quinn later.

"Thanks, but it's more your style."

She tsked, shimmying into the turquoise dress she'd settled on with the stylist. "You're hot, you shouldn't try to hide it so much."

"I don't try to hide anything." It's not like I was frumpy; I still wore tailored, flattering pieces. I simply preferred a more understated look than this hot pink concoction, which was a little attention-grabbing for my taste. It was extra unfortunate because I was due to meet Bennett—along with his business partner, Ian, and his wife, plus Callaghan and his wife—for dinner after this. Thanks to Quinn's tardiness, there was no way I'd have time to go home and change or re-do my makeup. I looked like I was heading to a nightclub, not a business dinner.

The makeup artist steered Quinn into a chair and began to sponge foundation onto her face while the hairstylist got to work, taking down her hair and combing it out.

"Thayer?" Marco strolled up, camera in his hand. "We can start with you."

The photoshoot was about as unpleasant as I'd expected, especially because I was notorious for blinking in flash photos and probably required more retakes than anyone else in the history of photoshoots.

But the interview portion was blissfully brief and high-level, at least. It largely focused on Lace & Grace, our success to date, and our plans for growth in the future. Minimal personal questions, aside from one throwaway item about my marital status, where I alluded to a boyfriend. I guessed leaning into it would help maintain the charade.

And now that it was a wrap, hopefully I wouldn't have to do either again for a very, very long time.

I examined my reflection in the bathroom mirror, blending away some of the contour the makeup artist had used. While I was sure it worked in the photos, it was heavy-handed for normal life. Then I double-checked the time and confirmed that, much to my dismay, there was no conceivable way I could run home and change before Bennett arrived to pick me up. He was going to be here any minute, and I was oddly nervous for it.

My sister leaned against the doorway, her eyes gleaming with excitement. "I have a surprise," she said. "It's a good one, too."

"What is it?" I glanced at her through the mirror, trying to conceal the apprehension trickling through my body. Quinn paused dramatically before answering.

"We're doing a bachelor/bachelorette party in Mexico, all expenses paid at Las Ventanas al Paraiso. Super ritzy." She made jazz hands. "Two weeks from now."

I spun to face her in surprise, nearly smearing nude lipliner all over my cheek in the process. Our eyes locked, and Quinn smiled at me expectantly. I swallowed, fumbling for words but finding few.

"Oh, wow."

What I really meant was *oh, shit*.

"I know it's kind of short notice, but I already checked your calendar, so I know you're free that weekend."

If I had access to a time machine, I would have gone back and kicked myself for agreeing to share my electronic calendar with Quinn. It made sense at the time from a business perspective for scheduling meetings and other joint activities, but it was coming back to bite me.

"But I'm not sure Bennett—"

"Already asked him." Quinn winked at me with her long magnetic lashes. "He's free. It'll be your first trip away together, right? That'll be nice."

Oh, so Bennett knew and didn't tell me? Sounded about right.

Thanks to him, our whole fake-dating arrangement had turned into a pending fake-engagement, and now, it was about to escalate into fake hotel-room-sharing. How was that even going to work? Sharing a bathroom? Sharing a bed? One of us would be sleeping in the bathtub before it came to that.

With Millie around, there was zero hope of getting away with something like a second hotel room, either. She'd probably monitor our comings and goings using video surveillance complete with timestamp.

"Perfect." I forced a smile that was anything but happy in my reflection. Turning away, I avoided her gaze, gathering up my things off the counter and throwing them back into my makeup bag.

"Are you mad?" Quinn inclined her head, glossy lips tugging into a pout. "Don't be mad. I know you're not the biggest fan of surprises, but I asked Bennett to let me be the one to tell you."

I violently tugged the gold zipper on my makeup bag shut. I was going to get Bennett back for all of this. I didn't know when, I didn't know how, but I would.

"Not at all."

"Speak of the devil," Quinn said, glancing over her shoulder. She stepped out of the way so I could exit the bathroom. "Your *boyfriend* is here to pick you up."

Dead man walking, more like.

With a quick wave at Bennett, telling him to wait, I opened the closet and took out my grey wool coat, slipping it on. "I'll see you tomorrow," I told Quinn.

"See you," she echoed. "Have fun!"

Drawing in a breath, I straightened my shoulders and walked over to meet Bennett by the door. Our gazes met, and his eyes widened slightly, raking down my body, back up to my face, then down my body again. A tiny, nearly imperceptible smile played on his lips. His tailored navy suit hung off his frame perfectly, hinting at the sculpted muscle that I knew lay beneath.

My breath turned shallow, and my legs went unsteady, though I wasn't certain why. Maybe because I felt borderline uncomfortable in my revealing dress and dramatic makeup. Or maybe it was because he looked devastatingly handsome like usual.

Bennett placed a hand along my waist and leaned in, his lips landing on my cheek. Unprepared, I jumped slightly at the contact and a wave of warmth flooded my body in response.

"Your sister was watching," he explained, voice low. He held open the door and waited for me to go first. "You look incredible, by the way."

"You mean, I look like Quinn," I muttered as I walked past him into the bitter November chill. His silver Mercedes idled a few steps away in the dark parking lot.

"You really don't," he said gruffly. "You look like you."

Was he complimenting me or arguing with me? Both? Sometimes it was impossible to tell.

The glass door slammed behind us, and Bennett matched my strides, beating me to the car door in time to open it for me, too. The warm interior was a welcome contrast to the cold wind outside— not that it mattered, because I was practically burning up with irritation over the vacation surprise.

Bennett walked around to the driver's side and slid in beside me, placing one hand on the leather-wrapped gearshift briefly before removing it. "We should probably talk before we go to dinner."

"We absolutely should." I buckled my seatbelt and lifted my chin, leveling him with a glare. "Mexico, Bennett? Why didn't you tell me?"

Bennett sighed and raked a hand through his hair, looking straight ahead. "Quinn asked me not to tell you." He shifted in his seat, turning to face me with his dark brows knit. "If you already knew, you'd have to act like you didn't. I thought it would be easier if you didn't have another thing to pretend about."

"You could have said you were busy that weekend." I tried to sound angry, but his remorseful expression took the wind out of my sails.

"I could have, but that would have left you alone with that fucking circus in Mexico. Is that any better?"

"I guess not." As much as I hated to admit it, he wasn't entirely wrong. Aside from the obvious—and troubling—logistical issues associated with spending that much time together, I would arguably rather be with Bennett than stuck with Millie, which was the probable alternative if I attended solo. At least Bennett and I didn't have to pretend we liked each other in private.

"On that note," he said, "I went shopping like we discussed."

Bennett reached across the vehicle, and his hand nearly brushed against my thigh, my breath stilling. He popped the glovebox open and fumbled for a second, emerging with a small wooden box.

"Here." He held it out to me, looking oddly nervous.

"What is this?" But as soon as I popped open the hinged lid, the answer was evident. I stared at the contents, unblinking. My heartbeat turned so irregular that my EKG would have looked like a toddler's scribbles.

"Lab diamond," he explained.

My gaze swiveled back to him. "Lab diamond?"

"Indistinguishable from natural diamonds and significantly more affordable. I'm not exactly made of money, given the current situation."

"I wasn't complaining," I said, examining the enormous solitaire stone set in a thin pave band.

I wasn't sure whether I was more bothered by the fact that he hadn't checked with me first, or by the fact that I liked what he had picked. Though to be fair, I had never given engagement rings much thought. I wouldn't have had much input to offer beyond 'simple' or 'not gaudy.' He'd nailed that, at least.

Carefully, I slid the ring out of the holder and slipped it onto my ring finger. It fit perfectly, facets glinting in the low light of the car's interior. It was gorgeous, and I liked it a little more than I wanted to, for a number of reasons.

"How did you figure out my ring size?"

He shrugged. "I asked your sister hers."

Of course, he did, because apparently, they were conspiring against my back on a regular basis. Then it hit me: that was why she put such a weird emphasis on the word 'boyfriend' back at the store. They probably had some kind of ongoing text thread at this point, discussing Bachelor spoilers together or something.

He shifted the ignition into reverse, backing out slowly. The streetlamp illuminating the parking lot cast shadows across his face, highlighting circles under his eyes. Suddenly, he looked more tired than I had realized upon first seeing him.

"I've had a shitty week," he said, as if reading my mind. "We can think up some proposal story on the way."

"Sure." My eyes fell to the glittery stone on my left ring finger. I couldn't pinpoint what I was feeling, except to say that it was a wildly mixed range of emotions.

Then it hit me… that was the only proposal I'd ever received.

A fake proposal.

In a parking lot.

CHAPTER SEVENTEEN

Bennett

I PULLED OPEN THE HEAVY WOODEN DOOR TO LOUNGE ELEVEN martini bar, holding it for Thayer. "Ready?"

"As I'll ever be," she said. "I hope you know what you're doing."

"Always." Not the faintest fucking clue.

Ever on-brand, she breezed past me without so much as a thank you, leaving a hint of her perfume in her wake. She smelled downright edible—a blend of brown sugar, spice, and something girly I couldn't identify—which, combined with that dress she was wearing, was more than a minor problem.

Because the dress? It was something else. Bright pink, revealing a hint of thigh, and hugging her body in a subtle, teasing sort of way that made me think about what was underneath. Let's be real: I was always thinking about what was underneath Thayer's clothes.

I couldn't take my eyes off her. Hell, I couldn't think straight, which was especially dire with Callaghan due to meet us in just over an hour. With any luck, having this drink with Ian and Laura beforehand would help me get my thoughts out of the gutter and eyes back on the prize: funding.

Unfortunately, I suspected what I really needed was to get laid, but with the way things were going, that wasn't going to happen for another seventy-four days, when this arrangement ended.

But who was counting?

Blaring Top-40 music, yellowish indoor lighting, and raucous laughter greeted us as we stepped inside. Thayer's teeth sank into her bottom lip, and her pace slowed, expression clouding over.

"This is just a low-key get together over drinks and dinner," I said, jutting my chin for her to keep walking.

"Right." Thayer huffed a sardonic laugh. "Convincing your best friend and bigshot investor that we just got engaged. Totally low key."

I scanned the crowd, quickly spotting my best friend and his wife seated at a bar-height table for four. Ian was holding Laura's hand while making googly eyes at her, smitten idiot that he was. As if they'd sensed me looking at them, they both swiveled and looked at us, their eyes widening to comical proportions. I gave them a small wave, but they merely stared, apparently too stunned to wave back.

I wasn't sure what Ian expected, but Laura probably expected, well, a male version of me.

Like I'd ever be dumb enough to date someone like that.

"They're right over there." I pointed them out.

"I see them," said Thayer, starting to head in their direction. She knew Ian through mutual friends, though she didn't know him very well.

I placed a hand on her lower back as we navigated the hordes of people clustered throughout the bar. This turned out to be a bad idea because her perfect, plump ass was just a few inches below my palm. Tantalizingly close, but letting my hand creep any lower was out of the question because I wanted to avoid dismemberment.

"This is a good chance for you to get to know Laura," I told her, trying to remind myself why we were here. "It'll be more believable to Callaghan if you two seem acquainted already."

"No pressure there," Thayer muttered under her breath. She looked like she was marching to the electric chair. Maybe it added to the authenticity, though. After all, a real fiancée would probably be nervous about meeting my friends, just for radically different reasons.

"It'll be fine." The reassurance was for my own benefit as much as hers. Really, it would be fine. It had to be. Neither of us had any other options.

We squeezed through a crowded section, narrowly avoiding being plowed down by a waitress with a tray piled so high with drinks she didn't see us. Thayer nearly lost her balance, and I caught her by the elbow, steadying her.

She yanked her arm away, panic creeping into her voice. "I feel like I should have studied for this. Why didn't you give me a cheat sheet to memorize?"

"They're not going to quiz you on my sleeping habits and dick size. But it's big, by the way. Just in case they do."

"Not what I meant, but thanks for the disturbing visual." Thayer rolled her eyes. "What I meant was, at least I know Ian, but I've never met his wife. What's she like?"

"Laura's a lot like you." I reached over and took Thayer's cool, slim hand, both to reassure her and help sell our story. Two birds, one stone.

"How so?"

"She's an uptight pain in the ass."

Thayer let out a little snort of derision, elbowing me in the ribs. It tickled more than it hurt, and I flinched, choking back laughter. Ian and Laura looked over at us again, and I quickly righted my posture, forcing a straight face.

"I was kidding," I said. "Trying to lighten the mood." Mental note: next time, dodge before making smartass comment. "I meant, Laura is on the quieter side, like you. I like her just fine. I don't think she's the biggest fan of me, though."

To be more specific, Laura referred to me as the 'bad influence friend.' Like it was my fault Ian came home and threw up all over their imported limestone kitchen floor after my birthday party. I can't help it if Ian can't hold his liquor, and the barbed-wire tattoo was his idea. In fact, he wouldn't let me talk him out of it—I tried.

Thayer hummed thoughtfully. "What you're saying is, she's a great judge of character."

"I'll have you know some people find me delightful."

"And how much do you pay them to tell you that?" She tilted her chin up to me, batting her eyelashes. The look was part-doting girlfriend, part-serial killer, and somehow, entirely hot.

We took a few more steps, drawing too close to the table for me to respond any further, which was just as well—I was too distracted by my dirty thoughts to formulate any sort of clever comeback.

"Hey, guys." Ian shifted to face us. The look on his face was priceless, somewhere between bewilderment and disbelief with a dash of questioning his own sanity. I only wished I could have taken a picture. It would have made a great company Christmas card. "Nice to see you, Thayer."

"You too."

"I know you two are already acquainted, but this is Ian's wife, Laura." I pulled out a wooden stool for Thayer and she eased onto it, shrugging off her grey wool coat. "Laura, this is Thayer. Thayer, Laura."

Laura smiled warmly and waved from across the table. "Nice to meet you."

"Nice to meet you, too." Thayer tilted her head, studying Laura. "You know, you look familiar. Do you ever go to Spinfinity over on 24th?"

"Yes! The five AM class? I knew I'd seen you somewhere before."

They immediately launched into a detailed conversation about the best instructors, the recent locker room renovations, and a bunch of other things that neither Ian nor I cared about while we talked strategy for Callaghan.

Ian placed his elbows on the table and leaned forward so I could hear him over the din of the bar. "I've been doing a lot of background research on Callaghan. There's a pattern to his investing. I think we need to—"

"Oh my gosh!" Laura squealed, interrupting Ian. She reached over and smacked him on the arm in excitement. "Is that a ring I see? An engagement ring?"

Showtime.

"Sure is." Thayer held up her hand. The round stone sparkled beneath the dim lighting like there were dozens of miniature fires contained within. It was more than a little ironic that the diamond was about as legitimate as our relationship.

Laura leaned across the table to get a closer look, ooh-ing and aah-ing over the ring. She seemed thrilled with the idea of me joining the boring old-marrieds club, probably hoping that my 'bad influencing' would come to an end. "Congratulations, you guys. That's so exciting."

"It really is," Ian said. Clearing his throat, he caught my eye. He was grinning so hard it verged on a grimace. "It really, really is. Actually, would you help me get some drinks to celebrate, Bennett?"

"I'm sure the server will come by soon." I leaned back in my chair, scanning the room packed with tables and bodies. Fighting my way through the crowd again sounded less than appealing.

His smile hardened, his jaw tight. "I don't feel like waiting."

I could take a hint. When Ian's stress levels reached the breaking point, instead of getting crabby like most people, he veered over to aggressively happy. He'd forcefully insist you have a great day or cheerfully reprimand an employee for a grave error. It was unsettling and hard to interpret, like being scolded by a Sesame Street character. Right now, he had taken it to a whole new level and looked like Jack from The Shining.

"Uh, sure. What do you want, Thay?"

"Just get me the usual. Kay, babe? With a lime, please."

Babe? We were that kind of fake couple now? It didn't nauseate me as much as I'd expected. Thayer had definitely called me worse things.

"Done." I leaned in to give Thayer a peck on the cheek for the second time that evening. I didn't know what came over me, it just seemed like the proper, couple-y thing to do. When my lips landed on her incredibly smooth, soft cheek, she startled slightly, reverting to the same deer caught in headlights look she'd sported when we arrived at her mother's dinner party. I wasn't sure if it was from the kiss or at the prospect of being left alone with Laura. At any rate, she recovered quickly.

Ian and I weaved through the tables, making our way over to the bar. It was packed for a Thursday, forcing us to walk single file. Of course, I had no idea what Thayer's 'usual' was outside of coffee. I was going to have to blindly guess, and hope Thayer deemed it worthy of consumption. Why didn't she just tell me what she wanted? Women.

"Are you sure we're allowed to drink?" I asked, trailing behind Ian. "I know Laura doesn't approve of having any fun."

"You know that's not true," he said. "Just don't get wasted."

"Does that mean those tequila shots I was planning on ordering are out?"

Ian flipped me the bird over his shoulder. "Hilarious." Tequila was what he regurgitated at four AM after celebrating my 25th. He'd sworn he'd never touch Cuervo again. Good thing he had that tattoo to remind him why.

We came to a stop in front of the bar and ordered two imported beers, plus a rum and coke for Laura and a vodka soda for Thayer. Vodka soda seemed like a safe, inoffensive choice, and it did go with lime. Best I could do under the circumstances. I made sure it was top shelf because, well, Thayer.

The server disappeared to fill our order, creating a window of opportunity for Ian to grill me.

"Now that we're alone, what in the actual fuck, Bradford?" Ian kept smiling ear-to-ear as he glanced over at our dates, giving them a little wave. Thayer wasn't looking in our direction, but Laura waved back, giving a thumbs up and pointing at Thayer as if in approval.

"What?"

The bartender returned, setting our beers down on the counter next to us before disappearing again to get the rest of our order.

"Thayer?" he hissed, snatching the amber bottle off the counter. "Your fiancée?"

Should I have told him sooner? Maybe. But Ian had been at the site all week while I had been holed up in my office, trying to violate the laws of basic math to make insufficient amounts of money stretch to cover endless expenses.

When I wasn't doing that, I was either beating myself up at the gym to work off my stress or talking Holden off the edge. He wasn't coping well with the news about our mother's cancer.

"Oh, that. Yeah, we're together." I shrugged, taking a sip of my beer.

"Since *when*?" Ian fixed me with a gimlet eye. I returned his gaze evenly, expression more neutral than Switzerland. He was stellar at reading most people, but I wasn't most people.

"Since awhile." Thayer was the last person who'd do something like this, which made her the perfect accomplice.

"But—" He paused, glancing back over at Thayer and Laura, who were deep in the midst of a conversation and looked like BFFs. "You didn't think to tell me that you're getting married?!"

"I'm a private person."

"The guy who walked around naked constantly when we lived together?" Ian tilted his head back, another bout of manic laughter escaping his lips. "You're many things; private isn't one of them."

"Fine, but Thayer is. She wanted to wait to tell people, and I was respecting her wishes, as a good partner does."

Ian's cheerful mask slipped, and he gaped at me like I had sprouted three heads. "You were...Like a good...Okay..."

I waited for him to make a throwaway comment about how hot she was, or to ask what the sex was like. I'd already mentally rehearsed a thousand answers and questions. I was ready to pivot and parry on a dime.

"I guess it does make sense," he said. We gathered the drinks and made our way through the crowd back to our table. "I always knew you were into her."

What? Don't get me wrong, I could fully admit that Thayer was attractive, but her personality wasn't nearly as warm and welcoming as the pretty exterior might lead you to believe. I was still in disbelief that I'd gotten her to agree to this—and a little worried she might slip cyanide in my drink tonight as revenge. Okay, a lot worried. But I couldn't blow my cover, so I bit back the urge to correct him.

"She's always been hot." I shrugged, stepping over a stray piece of ice on the floor. "You know how it is."

He chuckled. "You used to stare at her at parties like she was the only person in the room."

No. No way. Not a chance I was drooling over Thayer like some kind of creep. Just because she was gorgeous didn't mean I stared at her. Did I?

Surely, I was more discreet than that. And either way, I wasn't into her. I could admire a luxury vehicle without wanting to take it for a test drive. Well, actually, I did want a test drive. But I didn't want to buy the damn car.

"Can it," I said under my breath as we approached where they were sitting. "I don't need Thay hearing that."

Though, it was getting harder and harder to hold onto the grudge I'd nursed against Thayer for so long. I was grappling with some highly mixed emotions lately.

On the one hand, the fallout from her betrayal had been catastrophic. Thayer was the *only* one who'd known about my father's arrest—and before I knew it, word spread through our tightly-knit town like wildfire.

After that, my family was shrouded in a veil of disgrace wherever we went. Holden was so embarrassed, he refused to go to school and failed the ninth grade, then fell into a severe depressive episode.

And my mother was so humiliated, she had quit her position on the hospital charity fundraising board, one of the things she'd cared about most.

Sometimes, I caught myself thinking it might be worth letting it go; sometimes, I wanted to wave off Thayer's betrayal, telling myself we were just kids. But trust was everything to me, and Thayer had been one of my best friends. It was a bitter pill to swallow, even if part of me wanted to.

After clearing up our bill, we headed outside for the three-block walk to the restaurant to meet Callaghan. Thayer huddled close to me, less to maintain our charade and more to share bodily warmth in the chill.

Ian pulled out his phone from his coat pocket, coming to a screeching halt on the sidewalk. "I can't believe it," he muttered, brow creased in a deep frown as he stared at the screen. "Callaghan just canceled."

"He what?" My stomach dropped like I was on a rollercoaster doing a vertical dive. "He can't do that last minute. Are you fucking kidding me?"

Thayer spun to look at me, genuine concern across her face. It almost seemed like she was invested in me pulling this off, but it was probably just her perfectionist tendencies showing through. Even faking it had to be flawless.

"Hold on. He's typing." Ian held up a hand, silencing me. The four of us huddled in silence, waiting with bated breath. After a couple of seconds, his shoulders deflated and he looked up at me, defeat across his face. "His wife had a mini-stroke."

As much as I didn't like to hear that part, at least he wasn't pulling the plug on us. "Is she okay?"

"Sounds like it, but he's not exactly angling to reschedule right now." Locking his phone, he slid it back into his pocket and scrubbed a hand across his jaw. "Understandably so. But fuck."

Fuck, indeed.

Instead of the stuffy place we had initially planned on, we opted to hit up a little Mexican joint for dinner. Everything was going fine until the topic of conversation turned to our fauxlationship. I drained the last of my beer, praying we would pass the test.

"So, Ian tells me you two have gotten serious pretty quickly." Laura looked at the two of us expectantly.

I leaned back in my chair and tried to act like I actually bought the bullshit I was about to sell. "Well, when you know, you know."

"So true." Thayer smiled back at me warmly, performing an impressively convincing impression of a doting girlfriend. I'd have believed it myself, if not for the fact that she pinched my thigh under the table as she said it.

"And when did you both know, exactly?" Ian raised his eyebrows, eyes darting back and forth between the two of us. "It seems my friend has left out a few details."

Before I could respond, Thayer jumped in. "It was when he serenaded me with Ed Sheeran while down on bended knee a few weeks ago. Acoustic guitar and everything. That's when I knew he was serious."

Like an idiot, I just nodded. What could I say to that? I couldn't even play the fucking guitar.

"Ed Sheeran?" Laura let out a snort of laughter and dropped her fork with a clang. "That's amazing. Is there a video of this?" She took a sip of ice water, still snickering.

"That's something," Ian agreed, barely keeping a straight face. His lips quirked. "Very romantic gesture."

Thayer took a sip of her lime margarita, watching me over the salted rim like a dare. "Bennett is a total romantic. He was chasing me for a long time before that, and I kept turning him down. Over and over and over again. But he didn't give up. Did you, pookie?" She booped my nose with her pointer finger.

From across the table, Ian choked on his bite of enchilada. Laura bent forward, strawberry blonde hair falling in her face as her shoulders began to shake with silent laughter.

"Sure didn't," I said, smiling through gritted teeth.

"I mean, I did have to tell him to tone down the PDA a little." Thayer set down her half-empty glass. "And we had to compromise so he was only little spoon sometimes. But after he dried his tears, we worked it out."

Little spoon? The number of times I had been any sort of spoon was a big fat zero. I felt compelled to set the record straight on that matter but knew I couldn't.

"Guess I've got my hands full now, huh?" Really, I meant it. What the hell did I get myself into?

Aside from Thayer making me out to be a sappy idiot, the rest of the night went spectacularly. Conversation flowed, laughter ensued, and we seemed to pull off behaving like a legitimate couple.

Before we headed for my car, Thayer headed for the bathroom, leaving me alone with Ian and Laura for what I assumed would be a sure-fire final interrogation.

"Not what I expected," Ian admitted. "And I mean that in a good way."

"She's lovely," said Laura, like she couldn't quite believe it. "If you divorce because she gets sick of you, can we retain custody of her instead? You know, in the settlement agreement?"

"Ha ha." I made a face at her. "Very funny."

"Who said I was kidding?"

I guess I'd overshot.

CHAPTER EIGHTEEN

Thayer

WE CRUISED DOWN THE FREEWAY IN A TENSE CLOUD OF silence while streetlights and headlights passed in a blur. From the passenger side of the car, I scanned Bennett's face, trying to gauge his level of sobriety. It was difficult to tell—three drinks later, I was more than a little tipsy myself.

"Are you sure you're okay to drive?" I asked.

Bennett kept his eyes fixed on the road. "I'm fine."

"But—"

"Unlike you, I'm not the size of Tinkerbell," he snapped. "I had two drinks over four hours, combined with tons of food. You can breathalyze me if you want. I'm sure you have one in your purse."

I didn't, but not the worst idea in the world.

"Fine," I said, mimicking his snarky tone.

Our conversation fell back into a lull. The only sound was the low whir of the heater, set to full blast from when we first got in. His silk tie, which he'd removed during dinner, now lay coiled neatly in the center console.

I reached over and turned the temperature down a few degrees, though the atmosphere was awfully chilly in the car already. Bennett's fingers were wrapped around the steering wheel like he was trying to strangle it.

"You seem a little grouchy," I observed.

"You could say that." His jaw ticked, cords in his neck tensing, but he didn't look at me. "Are we supposed to be helping each other or not?"

I blinked at him, wide-eyed with faux innocence. "Whatever do you mean?"

"We're on the same team now, remember?" He stole a glance at me, but his expression didn't shift.

"A temporary alliance. Only because my enemy's enemy is my friend." Despite that, some of those lines were growing awfully blurry. When it came to picking sides in the Bennett-Adam feud, I might have been Team Bennett. Not because I liked him, of course, but because Adam was even worse.

Bennett made a right turn onto my street, slowing down to match the residential speed limit. "Do you throw all your friends under speeding buses? I mean, come on. Ed Sheeran? Pookie?" Beneath his acerbic tone, I detected the tiniest hint of amusement, like the grudging respect you have for a worthy opponent.

I made a failed attempt to hide my smile. "Well, you did say that you wanted them to think we were crazy about each other."

"I meant crazy in love," Bennett grumbled. "Not worthy of being committed."

Maybe I overplayed my hand on that one, but I'd been irked about being blindsided with the Mexico trip—even with his somewhat endearing excuse for not telling me. Trying to make things easier for me, he claimed, but I didn't fully buy that.

It left me a with a jumble of emotions: irritation with the general situation; guilt for not believing him; and wariness telling me I shouldn't believe him. Only Bennett could invoke such wildly mixed feelings within me. It was an innate talent of his.

"What can I say?" I smoothed my hair in the reflection of the window and adjusted an errant curl. "If something is worth doing, it's worth doing right."

Bennett's body language relaxed and his lips quirked. "Does that policy extend to inside the bedroom?"

Something stirred within me—something I hadn't felt in a long time, if ever—and I did my best to ignore it.

"Do you make everything sexual?"

"You can't answer a question with a question," he said. "And yes."

"It doesn't extend to anything involving you and your deviant fantasies."

Bennett might have been acting like he was kidding, but the truth was, he was just trying to get me in bed like he did with all the other women. It was a challenge to him, a potential conquest. Though if we both knew that's all it was going in...

I crossed my legs, biting the inside of my cheek to quell the sordid line of thought. Laura was right when she said he was a bad influence.

"Not all of my fantasies are deviant. Some are merely kinky. Practically vanilla."

"Ha. I bet." I snorted and reached into my purse to retrieve my phone, desperately in need of a distraction. Multiple texts from Quinn and Lola greeted me, both of them inquiring how the night had gone. I would give Lola the real rundown at brunch tomorrow. I hadn't yet decided how or when to share the news of my 'engagement' with everyone else. That was going to require taking my new-found acting skills to a brand-new level.

The ring was gorgeous, though. I mean, if you were into diamonds. Or pretty things in general.

"Want to hear them?" His voice dropped, buttery smooth like suede.

"No."

But I'd be lying if I said I wasn't a teeny, tiny bit curious.

"Fine, you can tell me yours instead. I'm a great listener."

"Negative." Staring at the screen, I re-read the same line of text four times without comprehending it before giving up. It was impossible to focus with this line of conversation. I locked my phone, tucking it back into my bag. "Like you're one to talk about being a team player. You didn't even tell Ian? Way to drop a bomb on him."

"Trust me," Bennett said. "It was better this way."

"Catching Ian completely off guard?"

"If I had told him at work, we would have had a sixty-minute sit-down detailing how you and I got together and every development since."

Bennett eased his car into the underground parking garage of my building, making a left turn to the visitor parking stalls and pulling into the same one as last time, when he drove me home after the dinner party. We had fallen into this pattern a little too easily. It was unnerving.

In light of the tension—sexual or otherwise—between us, letting him open my door and having him standing, waiting within close proximity felt a little bit like it would be playing with fire. He killed the ignition, and I raced to unbuckle my seatbelt, opening the passenger side door before he could make around it to my side of the vehicle.

My heels echoed against the pavement as his car door slammed behind me. He caught up to me in a few easy strides, evidently walking me to my door like last time. Another potential minefield to navigate. Bennett claimed it was merely good manners and his proper upbringing, whereas I believed it was driven by ulterior motives and a plan to get in my panties.

"You'd better know what you're doing." I came to a halt and jabbed the 'up' button on the elevator with more force than necessary.

"You manage your people and let me manage mine."

"Fine," I said, because I didn't really have a choice. I caught a glimpse of my reflection in the gold-framed mirror mounted on the wall next to us, and a ripple of anxiety hit me. "I hate lying to people."

I didn't mean to say it out loud.

"You get used to it."

"I guess."

What I wanted to say was, I already lied all the time. Hid feelings I had and faked feelings I didn't. Didn't say what I meant and didn't mean what I said. It wasn't new to me and this bizarre arrangement.

But that didn't make me hate it any less.

We lapsed into silence, waiting, and I clasped my hands together, making a concerted effort not to fidget. Several tension-coated seconds later, the elevator doors sprang open, and Bennett followed me inside, stepping out of my way to let me to push the '12' button for my floor. The amount of tension within the elevator car was unparalleled. Electric energy hummed between our two bodies as we stood side by side, ascending the twelve floors. Heat crept up my body, growing with every second that passed. By the time we made it to my front door, I thought I might spontaneously combust.

I should have sent him right back down in that elevator, but I didn't.

Bennett leaned against the doorframe and folded his arms, leisurely watching me enter the key code. It took three tries before I managed to enter the four-digit sequence properly. Finally, the keypad flashed green and let out an obedient beep, granting me access.

At the same time that I looked back up, Bennett closed the distance between us. He took a step forward, followed by another, steering me around the door and pushing it shut behind him with an ominous click. Darkness surrounded us, and I fumbled behind me for the light switch, bathing the entry in a dim yellow glow.

Our eyes locked, and his expression darkened, turning smoldering. My heart went into overdrive. For a moment, neither of us moved.

Bennett leaned in, and instinctively, I did the same. Our lips met, and a flicker of desire sparked within me in response. He angled his face against mine, deepening the kiss as his tongue slipped into my mouth. It wasn't tentative or questioning. It was bossy and demanding and utterly addictive.

I needed to extinguish this fire before it grew into an inferno.

Scraping up what little self-control remained, I placed my fingertips on his shoulders and tore away from the kiss. His grip on my waist loosened, but he didn't let go.

"I thought you said you were walking me to my door to be a gentleman, not because you wanted sex."

"Can't it be both?" His eyes traveled up and down my body, and for a brief, insane moment, I wished it were his hands instead.

I took a step back, hating my traitorous hormonal impulses. "No. Besides, sex is against the rules."

"We made the rules, which means we can break them if we want to."

Theoretically true, but the rules were made so I didn't end up broken.

"Rules are rules," I said. "And rule number one: no sex."

Seeing the gigantic glaring loophole, I quickly clarified. "Or, uh—sexual activities. Of any sort. Just like the contract says. Strictly forbidden. All of that stuff. Including kissing."

"But we just broke that rule." He raised his eyebrows. "You don't seem too clear on how these rules work."

My brain was crystal clear. My body was murky as mud, working overtime to nullify the contract so I could do all kinds of foolish things. Starting with him.

"Fortunately, I'm clear on the fact that I hate you."

Bennett prowled closer, barely restrained energy radiating off his body. The corners of his mouth tugged slightly, but the heat in his gaze was a challenge.

"Prove it."

"Fine," I said. "I hate—" My breath caught as his fingers dug into my hips, yanking me up against him.

Firm muscle surrounded me, encased in masculine warmth and the distinctive woodsy vanilla of his cologne. He ducked his head and brushed his lips against my collarbone, gliding up the curve of my neck. A shiver ran down my spine, followed by a telltale cascade of goosebumps on my arms.

"Keep talking," he murmured.

"...how you kiss." *I hate it because it makes the rest of the world fade away. Because it makes me forget it's you kissing me. Or worse, because I know it's you, and I never want it to stop.*

His voice was a smile against my skin. "Is that why you kissed me back?"

"Shut up, Bennett." The words came out breathy, strained with lust and lacking any bite.

His left hand traced the side of my throat, sliding up to form a fist at the base of my hairline. He tugged at the roots of my hair, gently angling my face up to his. Liquid heat pooled between my legs in response, and I hated myself for it almost as much as I hated him.

"What else do you hate?" he asked softly.

"Your cologne."

Bennett's chest rumbled as he laughed, low and husky. "Now you're definitely lying."

"It's the truth." *I hate that you smell good all the time, even when I wish you didn't. I hate that I want to bury my nose in the crook of your neck to get a hit. I hate that your scent leaves me lightheaded in your wake.*

A sigh escaped my lips as he traced a line of kisses across my jaw, ending below my ear. With one hand protecting my head and the other still around my waist, he stepped forward, backing me up against the wall. Dark hair tumbled over his forehead as he towered over me, bracketing me with his arms.

"Anything else?"

"Too many things to list."

Bennett lowered his head and our mouths crashed together again. Lips parting, our tongues tangled in a power struggle, greedy and wanting. I caught his bottom lip between my teeth and a low growl emanated from his chest in response. His large, strong hands squeezed my breasts, tugging on the sensitive nipples through the thin fabric of my dress.

Momentum surged as we engaged in a frenzied back-and-forth, neither willing to be the first one to take things further and neither of us wanting to stop. Finally, we came up for air, breathless and lips swollen. My chest moved up and down as I watched him, trying to calm my whirling thoughts.

Bennett, on the other hand, looked perfectly composed.

He ran his hands down the sides of my ribcage, grabbing my hips. His thumbs pressed into my stomach just above my pelvic bone, dangerously close to the throbbing center between my legs. My heart thundered in my ears.

"My turn."

I glared at him. "I didn't ask you."

"Too bad." Bennett splayed his long fingers, sliding his hands back to cup my behind. "I hate those pencil skirts you always wear." He squeezed, his grip firm and demanding. I stifled a gasp as a rush of desire rippled through my body. "They make me want to hike them up and bend you over the nearest table. It's fucking torture."

"Torture suits you," I whispered. "Remind me to wear them more often."

"And that brings us to the next issue." His midnight blue eyes traveled down my face, slow and languorous, coming to focus on my lips. Reflexively, I licked my bottom lip and his pupils dilated. "Your smart mouth."

"You wish you could have my mouth."

"Absolutely." His lips tugged into a smile, eyes snapping back up to mine. "I'm sure you know what else is on that list."

He wedged a knee between my legs, pressing against me. A tiny moan escaped the back of my throat as he leaned in, hitting the perfect spot. I wasn't sure what it said about me, but in that moment, I'd let him have any part of me he wanted.

"Turn's over." I arched my back, grinding my pelvis against him. He bit his bottom lip, sucking in a ragged breath. "I hate how your body feels pressed up against mine."

Bennett leaned closer, lips barely brushing my ear. A tingle ran down my spine. "Because you know I would feel even better inside you."

God help me, I wanted to find out. I really did.

"False," I lied, scrambling to keep my mental footing. "I hate...
when you touch me." *Because I don't want you to stop.*

His gaze pinned me, and a smirk played on his edible mouth.
"We both know that isn't true."

Bennett slowly slid a hand down my hip and under my dress,
hiking up the fabric. His eyes stayed fixed to mine as he traced a
line along the sensitive skin of my inner thigh, drawing closer and
closer to between my legs. My breath snagged, willpower waning.

"Should I stop? I mean, since you hate it so much."

Silently, I shook my head no.

"You like this, don't you, Thayer?"

I gripped his bicep, nearly trembling in response to his touch.
"Maybe."

In truth, I liked it a little too much, and hated myself more
than him for it. Most of the time, I had to take matters into my own
hands—literally—with other guys. But right now, I was already
halfway there, and we were hardly even doing anything. Bennett's
psychological foreplay game was strong, I'd give him that.

His brow cocked. "Maybe?" He withdrew his hand, and I fought
the overwhelming urge to protest. "It's a yes or no question."

"I'm not going to beg."

"Neither am I." Bennett readjusted my dress, gently pulling it
back down. He reached up, caressing my lower lip with the pad of
his thumb. "But the good news is, I'm very patient."

He pressed a chaste kiss to my forehead. "See you next weekend." Releasing me, he turned and tugged the door open, letting it
fall closed behind him.

Once it clicked all the way shut, I leaned against the wall behind me, letting out a frustrated sigh.

I didn't know how much longer I could keep Bennett at arm's
length, and I didn't know what was going to happen if I couldn't.

CHAPTER NINETEEN

Thayer

WITHIN LESS THAN HALF A DAY, NEWS OF MY 'ENGAGEMENT' had spread like wildfire. Since then, I had been congratulated, celebrated, and interrogated around the clock. I had my script down pat and was practiced in offering up my engagement ring for examination while pretending to act coy about doing so.

Quinn was especially excited about this new—fake—development. After making me relay the 'proposal' story a half dozen times over the phone, she'd come to work armed with congratulatory flowers and stacks of bridal magazines, eager to bond over planning. And then she made me tell her the proposal story once more, in person.

Turns out, having a fake fiancé had granted me entrance to an exclusive club that I didn't even know existed, where other happily taken people and I exchanged self-congratulatory smiles while quietly pitying all the poor, unfortunate single people. Sometimes we'd throw in a trite comment, like, "It'll happen for her someday too," so that we could pretend that we weren't such smug and self-satisfied jerks.

Except I still was one of those single people, and sometimes, for a brief shameful moment, I seemed to get a little too comfortable in my new role and forget that important detail.

I didn't know what my damage was. I didn't even want to get married.

The minute I unlocked my door to let Lola in for girls' night, she pushed inside my condo and beckoned eagerly.

"Come on," she urged. "Let me see your ring." I held out my left hand, stone sparkling in the light, and her eyes widened. "Damn, Thay. That's some rock."

"Lab diamond."

She shrugged. "Aren't they basically the same thing? More ethical, too. At any rate, I'd have thought it was real."

Lola followed me into the living room and unscrewed the cap on the half-full bottle of Pinot Noir, filling both of our oversized glasses until the ruby liquid sloshed dangerously close to the rim. Bennett said he was the bad-influence friend of his group, and in this case, Lola was my Bennett.

A tray piled with snacks sat on the ottoman in the middle of us, stocked with tortilla chips, salsa, guacamole, bite-sized brownies, chocolate chip cookies, vegetables and dip, a cheese plate, grapes, and more. It was a little random, but desperate times called for carbohydrates.

Especially when my sister and Millie were due to arrive any minute for movie night. Quinn and I lived in the same building, which made it difficult to dodge her invitations. Not that I wanted to avoid Quinn so much as I did Millie, especially right now.

"How do you feel about your, uh, engagement?" Lola bit her lip, studying my face.

"It feels a little strange, but we didn't have much of a choice. Things sort of escalated." Again.

"Are you excited for the trip?" She rearranged herself so she was parallel to the couch, extending her long legs. Only Lola could pull off distressed boyfriend jeans and still look graceful instead of frumpy.

"Hah, no. I wish you were coming." But I was pretty sure Lola was glad she wasn't.

She tilted her head sympathetically. "At least you'll have Bennett there as a buffer."

At the mention of his name, I reached over and refilled my small plate with three more bite-sized brownies and my fourth handful of chips. Bennett was many things, but a good buffer wasn't one of them. "Bennett is half the problem."

"Not getting along?" Her amber-gold eyes studied my face. There must have been something written all over it, because her mouth fell open. "Or getting along too well?"

I groaned. "Both?"

Lola swung her legs around to face me, leaning forward with her expression rapt. "Did something happen?" Her eyes danced.

"We kissed." I swallowed a gulp of wine, followed by another, trying to hide from her behind the oversized crystal goblet.

"You…kissed."

"Yeah." Squirming, I pulled my hands into the sleeves of my grey off-the-shoulder sweatshirt, trying to hide. It wasn't enough. I tucked my knees into my body, hugging them against me.

"Not to be glib, but I kinda figured kissing came with the whole, pretending-to-be-engaged territory."

Even Lola had thought that one out better than I had.

"No," I said. "We kissed *alone*. And it wasn't just a kiss. It was—" Words evaded me, and I gestured in frustration. With a sigh, I sank down against the couch cushions.

"Hot?" she supplied, arching a brow.

"Scorching."

There had been countless kisses in the span of time between my disappointing first-ever kiss with Kevin Peele at fourteen and my anything-but-disappointing first kiss with Bennett Bradford at twenty-five. First-date kisses. Breakup kisses. Drunken kisses. Awkward kisses. Good morning kisses. Goodbye kisses. Even one bumping-into-the-furniture, tear-your-clothes-off kiss.

Obviously, I had been kissed before. But none of them compared to kissing Bennett for the first time, let alone the second. He kissed me like he knew me. Like his lips—and hands—knew exactly what I liked. How to touch me, where to touch me, and what to do to leave me wanting more. It was infuriating, obviously. No one should have that power over someone else, especially not him.

Clearly, I'd lost my mind. Or maybe that happened when I agreed to this deal in the first place. I'd sacrificed my morals to preserve my reputation, and now I was paying the price by being tempted by sin in a designer suit. But no matter how pretty the wrappings or how seductive the kisses, nothing changed the fact that Bennett should have had a big, red stop sign tattooed on his forehead. Not just for my own benefit, but as a fair warning to all womankind.

Dead End: Heartbreak Ahead.

Lola's brow creased and she looked like she wanted to say something but thought better of it. She scooped up some guacamole with a tortilla chip and shoved it in her mouth, chewing and swallowing before she spoke.

"Have you ever figured out what his issue was back in high school? Why he froze you out all of a sudden like that?"

My heart contracted painfully. "No." Avoiding her eyes, I wiped the last of the brownie crumbs off my fingers with a paper napkin.

"Why don't you ask him?"

Communicate? That was for normal, well-adjusted people. Not me, and certainly not Bennett.

"Why should I have to?" I gestured with my wine glass, burgundy liquid swaying. "I know I didn't do anything to the guy. We were friends and he completely iced me out."

Right when I needed him the most, too. Shortly before our falling out—or fight, or whatever it was—Quinn entered inpatient treatment for her eating disorder. We'd been close growing up and the abrupt separation was difficult for both of us. I felt like I was walking around without a limb. It was especially difficult given that

I was sixteen, hormonal, and not exactly the picture of emotional stability.

At the same time, my mother had been navigating a hostile divorce complete with forensic accountants, private investigators, and scandalous allegations of infidelity on both sides. She was contesting the validity of the pre-nuptial agreement while my then-stepfather was trying to have us ousted from our home he owned. Between the divorce and Quinn, my mother was at her therapist's so often, she could have collected frequent flier miles. And let's just say her medicine cabinet resembled a small pharmacy.

In the midst of all the chaos, I was having panic attacks several times a week, while trying to maintain the outward appearance of a model student and daughter—because someone in my family needed to be the functional one. Old habits must have died hard, because that dynamic persisted to this day. Quinn was the one we handled with kid gloves, and I was the one who was expected to have her life together.

"Still…" Lola trailed off. "You guys used to be friends. Now you have chemistry. It just seems like a shame not to figure out where it all went wrong."

"I'll tell you where it went wrong: him." Though it was hard to ignore the pang I felt in my gut when talking about it. Or thinking about it in general, which was why I tried not to. We were so close—until he cut me out without any warning.

"Is that why you were at the spa earlier, getting everything waxed from the neck down?" She bit into a carrot stick, narrowing her eyes.

"That has nothing to do with Bennett and everything to do with the fact that I'll be wearing a bikini on the beach soon."

There was a rap at the door, followed by four beeps in quick succession. When I'd given Quinn the code to my door, it had been intended for emergencies, but had eventually evolved into an all-access pass.

"Hi!" Quinn called from the entry, holding up a bottle of Sav

Blanc and a paper bag containing some kind of food. "I brought treats."

Millie followed behind her, both of them slipping off their shoes before they stepped into the hall. At least they knew the drill.

Lola and I readjusted ourselves, making room for the two of them on the couches. I pretended to busy myself with scrolling through the Netflix menu like it was some kind of complicated, time-intensive operation. The only problem was that three out of the four people in the room were far more interested in conversing over wine than actually watching a movie.

"What's new, Thay?" Millie's pinned held me with such precision, I felt like a deer caught in a hunter's rifle sight.

"Not much," I said. "I'm sure you've already heard the big news about Bennett and me making things official. What about you, how are things?"

Eyes still fixed on me, she picked over the array of snacks and selected only the plain vegetable and fruit options, gingerly placing them on her plate. "Oh, I won't subject you to those boring details. Tell me more about you."

"Just excited for the wedding." It seemed like a safe pivot.

Millie laughed airily, like I'd said something incredibly witty. "Which one?"

Right. I guess I was supposed to be having one of those in the near future as well.

I flashed her a broad smile. "Both, of course. Can't wait to start planning and picking out all those little details like linens and accent colors. Sounds super fun."

Beside us, Lola and Quinn fell into a conversation about potential art pieces for Quinn and Adam's new house. They'd put an offer on a white picket fence deal in the suburbs. Overhearing about it almost made me glad I was talking to Millie.

"You know, I never pegged you for the marriage type," Millie said. "Bennett either, actually. I'm pretty sure both of you swore you'd never get married."

Leaning forward, I dumped half the tray of brownies onto my plate. "I guess it just takes the right one."

"Whoever thought Bennett would be the right one?"

"Not me," I said honestly, finishing the last of my wine and wishing it was tequila.

There was a pause in our conversation, and Quinn scooted closer to me, holding out her phone. "Have I shown you pictures of the listing we put an offer on? It's amazing. Four bedrooms, three-car garage, huge yard..."

I nodded, thankful for the blessed interruption. Feigning interest, I let her show me all fifty-six listing photos and explain every selling point of the house down to its precise square footage. Quinn seemed happy so I was trying to be happy for her, even though I didn't see how Adam could make anyone truly happy.

For the rest of the evening, I tried to put Bennett out of my mind. I didn't need to see him, didn't need to speak to him, didn't even need to think about him until he picked me up for the airport in a couple of days. Despite my best efforts, however, my mind kept circling straight back to him.

Our arrangement had started with us carefully weighing kisses and measuring hugs at my mother's dinner party, trying to strike the right balance via some kind of performative relationship calculus. Now, the initial awkwardness had begun to disappear, which was both a blessing and a curse. By the end of the night with Ian and Lauren, Bennett wrapping his arm around my waist in a crowded room felt natural, and names of affection I'd never used before with anyone tumbled out of my mouth a little too easily.

But when we were alone, things did a complete 180 again. We either argued, or...did whatever we did in my entry.

This wasn't even a look-but-don't-touch situation. That, at least, would be straightforward. This was a nefarious, touch-but-not-too-much situation. And it was exhausting.

CHAPTER TWENTY

Thayer
September 11th
Grade 11

SOMETHING WAS WRONG. I HADN'T TALKED TO BENNETT IN TWO days. Not that long, objectively speaking, but an eternity for us given that we usually hung out at school between periods and texted a couple of times a day. He'd even been missing from the classes we shared together.

Not to mention, the entire school was buzzing with rumors about his father's arrest. I knew it couldn't be easy on him, and I was trying to be a good friend, but that was difficult with the way he'd gone MIA on me. How could I be there for him if he kept dodging me?

Maybe this was the guy way of coping: blocking out the world. Still, I couldn't deny it stung a little… or a lot

When I came out of AP Chemistry after fifth period, I spotted Bennett down by his locker at the end of the hall, talking to Russell Barnes. Nervousness bubbled in my belly, and I slowed my pace to a crawl, praying would Russell leave before I reached Bennett. I wanted to talk to him—and I needed to do it alone.

Unfortunately, their conversation seemed to drag on and on. I was about to make a left to head for the library instead when they exchanged a nod and Russell walked in the other direction. Bennett turned away, yanking open his locker. With his back turned to me, he pulled a history textbook out of his backpack, swapping it for another.

"Hey." I shifted my book bag on my aching shoulder; it was overloaded with hardcover textbooks. I should have made a stop at my locker too, but I'd been trying to catch Bennett all day. "Everything okay?"

Bennett turned to face me, but his expression didn't brighten like it usually did. "It's fine." He slammed his locker shut in a way that seemed to contradict what he just said.

"I texted you."

Bennett leaned a shoulder against his locker, giving me a bored look. "I know." His voice was flat, lacking all the usual warmth it had when he talked to me. He was acting so strangely that I couldn't reconcile it. Was he getting high at school again or something?

"You didn't reply," I said, stating the obvious and immediately feeling foolish for it.

"And you didn't take the hint."

The words landed like a slap. I recoiled on the spot, heat rushing to my cheeks. My breath snagged, and before I could stop it, my eyes started to well up with tears. Bennett could be mercurial sometimes, especially to other people, but he never acted like this to me.

"What's your problem?"

His square jaw ticked. It hit me then that he seemed angry about something—angry with me, but I didn't know why.

"You should know," Bennett said.

"I don't know what you're talking about."

"Right." He let out a huff of derision. "You don't even realize it."

Realize what? I wanted to press him, to figure out what he was getting at, but I was too close to breaking down in the middle of the hallway.

When I didn't respond, he shook his head and threw his bag over his shoulder. He stepped around me, heading to the biology lab for his next class without so much as a goodbye.

I remained frozen on the spot for a solid minute, caught in some combination of shock and denial. How did we go from the way things were between us at the party last weekend to this? Did Bennett change his mind about going to homecoming together? Was this his way of trying to get out of taking me? My heart sank, landing at the floor by my feet with a sad little splat.

A group of Quinn's gossipy friends walked out of the English room. Clenching my jaw, I swallowed back tears and spun on my heel, barreling for the girls' washroom around the corner. Lola was walking out as I was heading in.

"Whoa, Thay." She ducked her head, trying to catch my eye. "What's wrong?"

I brushed past her and headed to the sink furthest from the door, turning on the cold water and splashing my face. Lola followed me back into the bathroom, checking to ensure no one else was in any of the stalls. She walked up to me, offering me a paper towel.

I gently patted my blotchy face dry. "Thanks."

"What's going on?" Lola asked softly. "Did something happen with your chem exam?

I hiccupped and shook my head, biting my bottom lip. It only it was that.

"Then what is it?" she asked. "You're starting to freak me out."

What was it? If only I knew.

Avoiding meeting her eyes, I drew in a shaky breath and held it for a couple of seconds, blowing it out in a huff. My eyes were brimming with more tears dangerously close to breaking free, and I hated crying in front of other people—even Lola. I stared down at the floor, fidgeting with the sleeve of my navy uniform blazer. Lola waited patiently, gently rubbing my upper arm.

"It's Bennett," I finally managed to say. "I don't know what's gotten into him. He just completely blew me off." It was hard to admit, even to her.

Lola sighed. "Oh, Thay. He's probably just stressed with everything that's going on. You know how he can be."

"No, Lo. This was more than that. He looked at me like—" My voice started to climb, cracking along with my heart. "He hated me."

CHAPTER TWENTY-ONE

Bennett

THAYER AND I NAVIGATED THE LONG-TERM PARKING GARAGE interrupted only by the clack and rumble of our suitcases rolling along the uneven asphalt. As further proof that it is possible to argue about anything, we'd engaged in a heated disagreement about parking arrangements before even arriving.

She'd wanted to park further away and take the shuttle, while I'd insisted on parking at the more expensive lot within walking distance of the terminal. It wasn't remotely worth saving ten dollars a day when taking the shuttle required waiting in the freezing cold for the bus, cramming in with tourists and screaming children en route to Disney. I was paying, so I didn't know what it mattered to her. And since when was she so thrifty? It was rich coming from someone wearing designer sandals.

We came to a halt in front of the parkade elevator, sheltered by a delicate truce that threatened to fracture if one of us looked at the other the wrong way.

"Let's do electronic check-in." I reached over, hitting the elevator button.

Thayer's pale blue eyes widened like I'd suggested I fly the plane myself. "What? No, we have to go to the counter."

"Why? Doing it ourselves is faster." The elevator doors popped open, and I followed her inside, pushing 'G.' Thayer positioned herself arms' length away from me, facing forward.

"I don't trust those computers. Last time I did that, something went wrong."

"Did you miss your flight?"

"Worse," she said. "I got stuck with a window seat. A window seat, Bennett."

The elevator dropped sharply, taking with it my hopes of this trip going smoothly. First class for this airline only sat two across, and if Thayer was anti-window seat, that meant I would get stuck there instead. Not exactly ideal, given I was more than seven inches taller than her. Being unable to stretch out my legs in the aisle would make for a horribly cramped flight.

"What's wrong with a window seat? I thought everyone liked those." Maybe I could help her overcome this objection somehow. For my own sake.

She huffed. "For starters, it's a logistical nightmare if you need to use the bathroom, which you should need to do several times throughout the flight if you're drinking the recommended amount of water. Flying is dehydrating, you know."

Raking a hand through her long espresso-brown hair, she took a breath and continued. "Not to mention, if there's an emergency landing, you'll be one of the last ones out if you're stuck in a window seat. Which means you'll burn to death or drown depending on the nature of the emergency. Long story short, window seats equal death."

Well, that escalated quickly.

"Are you saying you're claustrophobic, or…?"

"I just like to have some freedom of movement," she snapped.

I held the elevator door for her. "Fine. Let's go check in at the counter. We have plenty of time to kill."

We entered the departures area through the revolving glass doors, checked the electronic directory, and headed up one level to the ticketing counter for Sunscape Airlines. At least with our hands occupied by luggage and no audience to convince, we didn't have to bother with our lovey-dovey act. Which was perfect, because I was pretty sure both of us felt more like strangling the other person than snuggling them.

While the escalator carried us up to level two, Thayer fidgeted with the strap of her purse, starting to look restless. She'd flown hundreds of times before; when we were kids, her family went to Europe every summer and did Christmas break in the Bahamas every winter. She regularly visited her father in France, too. Surely, she wasn't scared of flying. Then again, her window seat rant did seem to indicate otherwise. Either way, she was more tense than a presidential election recount.

The redheaded passenger service agent greeted us as we approached. "Welcome to Sunscape Airlines. Confirmation number and passports please?" Her name tag read Pamela, and her weary smile said she'd rather be anywhere but standing at this counter. Same here, Pamela, same here.

"BXZDEY," I read from my phone's electronic ticket. I pulled out my passport with our booking confirmation tucked inside, sliding it across the counter. Thayer rifled through her handbag and emerged with her passport, shoving it at me. I caught her eye and shot her a questioning look, but she quickly looked away, folding her arms against her body. To an outsider, she probably looked more like a kidnapping victim than someone headed to a ritzy beach resort.

I handed Thayer's passport to Pamela, trying unsuccessfully to flip it open and sneak a peek of her passport photo in the process. Passport photos were always hilariously bad, and I was sure hers was no exception. I was also sure that was why she'd kept it tightly shut when she gave it to me. No matter, I'd get my hands on it eventually.

"Thank you." Pamela propped open our passports and typed

rapid-fire, completing our check-in. She glanced back up, eyebrows raised. "Special occasion? Honeymoon or anniversary?"

"Just a romantic getaway." I reached over and gave Thayer a squeeze. She leaned into me, hugging me back while stepping on my toe with her foot. Hard. I poked her in the ribs in response, prompting a stifled yelp of laughter. If there was one thing she hated, it was being tickled. I'd pay for that later.

"Oh, lovely," the agent said, keys clacking. "Where are you staying?"

"Las Ventanas al Paraiso." I released Thayer, hoisting our luggage onto the weigh scale. My bag was only thirty-one pounds, but Thayer's clocked in at a whopping forty-eight pounds, nearly maxing out the fifty-pound limit. What the hell was in there?

Pamela nodded approvingly. "I've heard it's gorgeous there. My boss honeymooned there last year, and her pictures were to die for." Turning away, she bent down to put on our baggage tags, lifting them onto the conveyor belt.

"Romantic getaway?" Thayer hissed, looking up at me. I leaned closer, pretending to nuzzle her ear, which was a mistake because she smelled good enough to eat for breakfast.

"You know Quinn and company could arrive at any moment, right?" I murmured.

Thayer looked over my shoulder, scanning the terminal behind me. Her pale blue eyes snapped back to meet mine, and she opened her mouth to respond but was interrupted by the agent handing us our passports and boarding passes.

"Security is down the hall and to your left," Pamela said, flashing us a pleasant smile. "Have a safe flight."

"Thank you," we both said at the same time. But I was more concerned about my safety sitting next to Thayer than the flight itself. There was a decent chance she'd strangle me with an iPhone cord.

I moved to put the passports and tickets back into my suede duffle bag, but Thayer swooped in like a ninja and snatched her passport out of my hands before I could. She tucked it into her grey leather tote, zipping it shut.

"Don't even think about it."

"What?" I gave her an easy, lopsided grin and received a glower in return. Unfortunately, Thayer appeared to be largely immune to my charms. Well, except for whatever happened at her place the other night. I would have liked a replay of that but had no idea how to make it happen.

"You're trying to sneak a peek at my passport photo." She jutted her chin. "Don't even act like you're not."

I didn't respond because she was right. How was she on to me?

"You're snoopy," she added, like she'd read my mind for a second time. It was more than a little unnerving. What kind of witchcraft was this?

We navigated the glass-walled hallways of the airport, weaving between throngs of slower moving travelers. Which was all of them, actually, because she was traveling at an impressively fast speed for someone so much shorter than me.

"I prefer to think of it as inquisitive."

"Ha. You mean nosy." Thayer snorted, picking up the pace so we were speed-walking down the corridor, whizzing past everyone else ambling along in the same direction. Her heeled silver sandals clicked across the glossy tile flooring with each step. I couldn't think of a more impractical choice for airport footwear, but they did make her legs look great.

"Maybe you're just closed-off," I countered. "How am I supposed to play the part when you're keeping me at arms' length like you do with everyone else?"

A tiny crease appeared in her brow, disappearing almost instantly. I would have missed it if I hadn't been paying attention, but I had been. And besides that, I knew better than to go there with her. This was how she'd always been—slow to open up. It's not like it was bad, necessarily, it was just frustrating to deal with sometimes. Like right now, when something was clearly eating away at her.

I swallowed, trickle of guilt seeping into my gut. "I didn't mean—"

"I'm an open book," she said flatly. "Anything you need to know, ask away." But her speed said otherwise because she'd begun to walk even faster, practically running away from me.

"Why are you hurrying?" I asked, checking my watch as I quickened my strides to keep up. "We still have nearly three hours until we have to be at the gate."

"I'm not. This is my normal walking sp—" Thayer skidded on the glossy white tile, losing her balance and tumbling into me. I caught her elbow with one hand, steadying her. She looked back up at me, eyes wide, and a pink flush started to spread across her cheeks.

Still holding her arm, I lowered my head and caught her gaze. I rubbed her skin gently with my thumb. "Thay, just level with me. Are you a nervous flier?"

"Of course not."

"You seem awfully jittery for someone who's heading for a relaxing vacation on a white sandy beach."

Thayer hefted her carryon bag back onto her shoulder, pretending to look behind me. "I don't love flying. That's all."

"You have a fear of flying, you mean." My hand slid down to her waist, landing on the hem of her black tank top, and her posture softened a fraction.

Her blue eyes lifted to meet mine, vulnerability flashing behind them. "Call it what you want."

"Is there anything I can do to help?"

"No." She scrunched up her mouth, signature red lipstick perfectly applied even for flying at the crack of dawn. "Well…some food might help once we're past security. And a massive coffee."

"Done."

We resumed walking at a more reasonable speed and turned down the hall, sidling into the winding security lineup. It was several dozen people deep and moving ahead at a slow shuffle; we weren't the only ones trying to escape the dreary fall weather.

"Have you heard from Callaghan yet?" Thayer asked quietly.

The line moved forward, and we took a few steps, advancing in the queue. I looked over my shoulder, checking to ensure the rest of our party hadn't shown up without us noticing. Fortunately, they hadn't. It was probably too much to hope that they'd no-show altogether.

"No," I said. "We don't want to push it, given the situation."

Her teeth sank into her crimson lower lip, expression turning pensive. "I was trying to think whether I knew anyone else that you could hit up for an investment, but everyone is being tight-fisted with their money right now. I mentioned it to Lola because she works with a lot of wealthy art collectors. She said she was going to see what she could do…" Thayer trailed off, and a flicker of emotion crossed her face that I couldn't quite read. "I mean, so you crush Adam, obviously. I'd love to see him fail."

"You and me both." An unfamiliar feeling settled within me. Gratitude, maybe. Maybe even a grudging sense of trust, as difficult as that was for me to extend to her. "Thanks for trying. If you do find any leads, send them my way, and I'll give you a finders' fee."

Thayer waved me off. "You don't have to do that."

It was an industry standard, but I wasn't going to argue over it.

Security waved another handful of people ahead and we moved forward, nearly at the front of the line. I came to a stop before Thayer did and she bumped into me, immediately shuffling back two steps after our bodies made contact. The beeps and buzzes of the x-ray and wand scanners filled the silence between us.

"Do you want to grab a drink after this?" I asked. "You know, help take the edge off?"

"Drinks?" Thayer gave me a wry smile. "It's not even eight in the morning."

I elbowed her gently. "C'mon. We're on vacation."

For a moment, she looked like she was actually considering it. Getting drunk with her in the morning would be hugely entertaining, if for the surprise element alone. And it would sure take the edge off having to deal with Adam.

Her expression shifted, suddenly turning more guarded. "Thanks, but I'm going to stick to coffee for now. I have a prescription for my anxiety that I take before I fly, and I can't mix alcohol with it."

Knew it. She was afraid of flying. But I also knew better than to gloat about being right, especially when I didn't think she intended to admit that to me.

"All right," I said.

Whatever it took to get her on the plane.

CHAPTER TWENTY-TWO

Thayer

SECURITY WAS A MOST UNPLEASANT EXPERIENCE.

While Bennett sailed right through without so much as a second glance, I had the honor of being 'randomly selected' for additional screening. The TSA agent scoured every inch of both of my bags, swabbed every cosmetic item I owned, and emptied my suitcase all over the conveyor belt.

Then she went through every single item of clothing I had painstakingly folded, inspecting each one individually in front of everyone else in the security line, including my 'fiancé,' who *greatly* enjoyed the sight of my lacy black La Perla dangling from her fingers.

I mean, seriously. Did I look like a drug trafficker? I didn't even take generic pharmaceuticals.

After concluding the ordeal with the most invasive pat-down I'd ever received, we made it to Gate 32 safely on schedule. No one else with our group had arrived yet. In fact, no one was at the gate at all, probably because no one valued punctuality these days.

Bennett eyed the vacant rows of seats and raked a hand through his wavy chestnut hair, heaving a long-suffering sigh. If I made him sit here and wait for the remaining two-and-a-half hours, I'd never hear the end of it.

And maybe he had a point.

Besides, eating breakfast at a sit-down restaurant would surely be better than scrounging up something greasy from the food court. My change of heart had nothing to do with the way his face fell a little when I shot down his drink idea.

It definitely wasn't because of the attraction between us that was building by the minute, either.

Fine. That was a lie. A dangerous, delicious lie.

Just like us.

"You know what?" I said, turning to face him. "Let's go get that drink."

Bennett broke into a heart-stopping grin. "Really?"

"Just as long as they serve food, too. I don't want to end up wasted before ten."

In truth, the effect his smile had on me was a lot scarier than the idea of flying.

Aside from the lone server who greeted us at the front, the lounge side of the chain restaurant was completely deserted. Top-40 music played in the background and neon signs boasting catch-phrases blinked forlornly along the walls. It was a stark contrast from the rest of the bustling airport terminal, and I couldn't decide whether the solitude was comforting or depressing.

We walked around the L-shaped bar lined with empty stools, selecting a tall table by the window overlooking the tarmac. Bennett pulled out a metal chair for me before sliding into the one beside it. His knee brushed against mine, but neither of us pulled away. In the chill of the air conditioning, the warmth radiating off his body wasn't entirely unwelcome, not that I'd ever admit that out loud.

"Have you noticed that no one else is in here?" I asked quietly.

Bennett shrugged, grabbing two drink menus and handing one to me. "So?" His blue dress shirt was rolled up to reveal his muscular forearms, drawing my eye to them. Since when did I have a thing for forearms? It was new, but it was definitely a thing. I immediately averted my eyes, biting the inside of my cheek.

I tipped my head, leaning closer. "Does that make us alcoholics? Are we the only two lushes in this entire airport?"

"Those other travelers aren't doing it right," he said. "Morning cocktails are practically a requirement."

After settling on our orders, we watched the planes taxi to and from the gate, making idle small talk about Mexico and previous times we'd each traveled there. After our angsty make out session in my front entry the other night, I'd expected things between us to be strained when Bennett picked me up for the airport this morning. To my surprise, they weren't. Spending time with him alone was almost like picking up where we'd left off ten years ago. But with the way things suddenly soured between us back then, I wasn't convinced that was a good thing.

As the only patrons seated in the restaurant lounge, we didn't receive a lot of attention from our server, who was more interested in texting on her phone off in the corner. It took half an hour to place our order, and somehow, two rounds of drinks arrived before our food did. The good news was, one and a half Bloody Marys later, I was no longer afraid to board the plane. The bad news was, I was dangerously close to boarding Bennett instead. Somehow, the distance between our chairs had mysteriously vanished and his cologne was giving me more of a buzz than the alcohol.

Fortunately, we were in public, but it was a bad sign for my self control in the hotel room. Maybe I should make a plan to stay sober for the remainder of the weekend. Too late now, though. I had to get on the plane, and I wasn't doing it without the help of Xanax or a little liquid courage.

Liquid courage was what I needed to have this conversation, too.

I set down my fork beside the half-eaten vegetable omelet on my plate. "What are we going to do about sleeping arrangements?"

"Why, would you like to set a bedtime?" Bennett cocked a dark brow. "Maybe a curfew as well? Haven't had one since high school, but I guess I can roll with it."

"No, wise guy. I mean, where are we going to sleep?" I wasn't sure if he was deliberately being obtuse or if he was just legitimately dense, as most men tended to be.

His lips quirked. "In the bed, like at home? At least, I assume that's where you sleep. One can never be sure when it comes to you. There could be some kind of preservation chamber involved."

"You probably sleep in a coffin." I bit into my whole wheat toast menacingly, but the undercurrent of giddiness coursing through me made it impossible to keep a straight face.

"Only on weekends."

"Seriously," I said. "What if there's only one bed?"

Bennett placed an arm along the back of his stool and his fingers grazed my bare shoulder. An electric current traveled down my spine, like a circuit had been completed by the contact.

He blinked down at me, his amusement giving way to confusion. "Is this a trick question?"

"You don't think it will be weird?" Or risky—possibly in more ways than one. I had a feeling he didn't exactly sleep in flannel pajamas. And neither did I.

"We've shared a bed before," Bennett pointed out, giving me a crooked smile. "Italy trip. Sophomore year."

I groaned. "Oh, God. You're not allowed to bring that up."

"Which part?" He reached over, fluffing my hair, and warmth crept into my cheeks. "The part where you drank so much Sambuca, I had to carry you back to the hotel and sneak you into your room so the chaperones wouldn't catch us? Is that the part you're referring to? Or the part where I stayed with you because you were sick?"

"All of that," I mumbled, hiding behind my hands. A quick peek between my fingers confirmed that Bennett was enjoying this little trip down nostalgia lane a lot more than I was. To this day, black liquorice still made my stomach turn.

Plus, not all of my memories involving him were good.

"Or do you mean the next day, when you used me as a pillow for the entire six-hour bus ride to Florence because you were too hungover to function?"

Dropping my hands into my lap, I shot him a look of exasperation. "You're the one that gave the Sambuca to me."

"In my defense," he said, "I was sharing it with you. I did not realize you would be such a lightweight."

"We were fifteen. What kind of tolerance was I supposed to have?"

Then again, in retrospect, drinking at fifteen wasn't the brightest idea to begin with. But that's what happened when you had a bunch of under-supervised, over-allowanced prep school kids on a trip to Europe without their parents. I couldn't even remember whose idea it was or how we got a hold of the alcohol, but the end result was drinking in the streets, getting yelled at by a shopkeeper for being too noisy, and Millie falling into a fountain.

"Fair enough." Bennett picked up his beer, draining the last of it. "But ten years later, you're still a lightweight. Case in point: right now."

"What? I'm fine." I waved him off, but the knowing look on his face told me arguing was futile. He wasn't wrong. Two drinks on a mostly empty stomach had gone straight to my head.

His lips quirked. "Sure thing, tipsy."

"Don't act like you didn't profit off that situation. You guilt-tripped me into repaying you by helping with your English Lit term paper when we got back. It turned into me practically writing the whole thing."

"Oh, yeah." He rubbed his jawline, shaded with perfectly groomed stubble. "I got an A+. Pretty sure Mr. Anderson knew something was up, but he never could prove it."

I took Bennett's comment about my state of apparent intoxication as a reminder to eat the meal we'd come into the restaurant for, and I picked up my fork again. We lapsed into silence for a few minutes while I finished most of the omelet and all of my toast, and I couldn't help but realize how the silence wasn't stifled like it usually was when I was with other people. Much as I tried to fight it, it was comfortable—maybe even easy—to be around Bennett, in a way that made me deeply *un*easy.

"That essay talk reminded me that you still owe me a favor," I said. I'd all but forgotten about it. It was more like an insurance policy, anyway. Something to have in my back pocket. I doubted I'd take him up on it. I couldn't think of anything I'd even want.

Bennett's gaze dropped to my ring for a split-second before he caught himself. It wasn't my intention, but the reminder of our 'contract' seemed to dampen his mood.

"Have you decided what it'll be?"

"Not yet."

Another hour later, the waitress returned and passed Bennett's credit card back to him, along with the receipt. He'd slipped it to her while I was in the bathroom because he was sneaky like that. I felt bad that he insisted on paying when this wasn't meant to be a date.

"Speaking of favors," he said, slipping his Visa back into his wallet. "I did need to ask you to do something. I mean, another something."

My stomach did a somersault. Had this entire morning been a nothing but a ploy to get me to let my guard down? What did he want now?

"What's that?" I asked.

"My mother wants us to come over for brunch in a couple of weeks. Or to throw an engagement brunch for us, rather. Small and intimate supposedly, but you know how mothers get carried away. But I know I only asked you to do all of this for Callaghan. My family wasn't part of the deal. If you want, I can make up a reason to dodge it..."

"No," I said quickly. "That's fine."

"Are you sure?" His brows drew together.

"You think I'm going to bail on your sick mother? Bennett, come on."

There were lots of things I could fault him for. A laundry list of items, probably. But his soft spot for his mother wasn't one of them. With her recent relapse, I knew this had to be a delicate subject for him.

Bennett studied me for a few seconds like he was weighing how to respond.

Finally, he said, "Thanks, Thay." His throat bobbed and a glimmer of sadness crossed his face, so well-hidden I nearly missed it.

My phone buzzed on the table, screen lighting up with a text from Quinn asking whether we were finished with our meal yet. It was her third such text, but neither Bennett nor I were in a hurry to join the rest of the group. Because of Adam and Millie, obviously. Not because of anything else.

I wrote her back saying service had been painfully slow and we were still finishing our food. It was half-true. Service hadn't exactly been stellar, but we'd been done eating for over half an hour.

"Quinn is getting testy." I locked my phone and slid it into the side pocket of my bag. "We should get going."

"Probably should," Bennett agreed.

He shifted to face me, and his eyes darkened, slowly tracing my face. I froze, feeling uncomfortably seen for reasons I couldn't even explain. It was like being stripped bare in the middle of the lounge. I wondered if I ever made him feel the same way.

His warm hand landed on my shoulder and slid up to my neck, gently bracketing my jaw. A thousand unspoken words hung between us. My heart faltered for a beat before kickstarting again, rocketing into hyperdrive. Full breaths were no longer an option; I had to settle for tiny sips of air.

Beneath the table, his other hand found mine, fingers intertwining. He tilted his head, leaning in as I met him halfway. Our mouths collided, and my fingers flew to his shirt, holding on like I might lose my balance. He softly plied my mouth open, deepening the kiss. The beer he'd just finished mingled with the taste of him, stoking feelings I had been trying to restrain for weeks.

It was gentle and savoring. Less tongue, less lips, less teeth than the kiss at my place. But somehow it was more. With every sweep of his tongue, time lost all meaning, and I fell deeper and deeper into him.

We pulled apart, and I swallowed, trying to catch my breath.

"Thay?" he murmured, placing another soft kiss against my lips.

"Yeah?"

"They're paging us over the loudspeaker."

CHAPTER TWENTY-THREE

Bennett

LTHOUGH QUINN HAD US PAGED OVER THE INTERCOM, IT wasn't because we were actually late; she was just being high maintenance as per usual. Thayer was high maintenance in her own way, but it was nothing compared to her sister. Quinn would have been legitimately surprised to learn the world didn't revolve around her.

As for being interrupted, I wasn't sure whether I was annoyed or grateful. Maybe both. My head wasn't on straight lately to begin with, and that kiss hadn't helped. I needed to focus on my real priorities, like the financial fiasco known as my company.

All I could think about was the way Thayer sighed when our lips met in the restaurant, melting a little against me; the way her fingertips dug into my shirt; and the way I forgot about everything else, which had never happened with anyone before. Not to mention, whatever the hell happened at her place last week. My sanity was as stable as a house of cards, and my willpower was even shakier than that. I was used to getting what I wanted, quickly. And right now, I wanted her.

Things were volatile enough with Thayer—the last thing I should have been doing was tossing matches at it. Logically speaking, I knew that. But my lower half didn't care about logic, which was why my thoughts kept boomeranging right back to those flame-throwing scenarios.

Thayer scanned the surrounding terminal with a frantic air about her. "Is there a Starbucks around here? I didn't sleep a wink last night, and I need some coffee." She craned her neck, looking over my shoulder. "And by some, I mean an entire vat. But if I make Quinn wait any longer, I think she's going to demote me from Maid of Honor."

"You go sit down with her, and I'll grab some," I offered, jumping at the chance to escape. We still had half an hour until boarding, and I wasn't eager to face what lay ahead. "Text me if you need anything else."

"Okay, but it's my turn to pay." Thayer came to a halt and unzipped her shoulder bag, pulling out her cream pocketbook. Before she could locate any cash in her wallet, I waved her off and started to head for the shops at the other end of the hall.

"It's fine, I got it." I might have been in dire straights financially, but I wasn't that broke. Yet, anyway.

"I insist."

"This is like, ten bucks we're talking about," I said, turning back to face her. "I'm not taking your money."

She gave me a smile that was more like baring her teeth. "At least let me pay for my half, *honey*."

"We're not going halfsies on a coffee, *sweetie*."

What was this, junior high prom? A tenth-grade date?

Thayer narrowed her eyes, and I returned her gaze evenly, the two of us engaging in some weird, silent standoff in the middle of the airport terminal. Loudspeaker announcements echoed in the background. Travelers milled around us, pulling their rolling suitcases and herding rambunctious children.

"Fine, but I'll get it next time." Her lips pressed together, and she heaved a reluctant sigh. "Thank you."

Starbucks was swamped, and the line moved so slowly that I could have grown the fucking coffee beans myself, thanks to some guy three people ahead of me who ordered a boatload of custom Frappuccinos with extra whipped cream, caramel sauce, and chocolate shavings. Never understood people who wanted a milkshake at nine in the morning, but whatever. I tipped the barista extra for having to put up with that shit.

When I returned with two grande black coffees, the seating area had filled in significantly. Thayer was sitting beside Quinn, with Millie perched on the other side. Two more women I didn't recognize sat next to Millie, rounding out their group.

Adam and a few of his groomsmen were seated on the bench behind them, laughing boisterously at something on Adam's phone—drinking Frappuccinos. One of his groomsmen was the guy from the Starbucks line. Of course.

My grip on our drinks tightened as I drew closer, unsure where to sit. There seemed to be a male/female, bride/groom divide going on, but I wanted to punch the groom in the throat, which complicated matters greatly.

I walked up to Thayer and the rest of the bridal party, holding out her coffee and a bottle of water. "Sorry it took so long, line was crazy. I grabbed you a water, too."

Surprise graced her face, followed by gratitude. "Thank you."

Given that no one moved to make space for me, it was clear that my kind wasn't welcome on her bench. Reluctantly, I joined Adam and his friends on the other side of the gate, where I was introduced to Henry and Dylan, plus Louis who I was unfortunately already acquainted with. He was right below Adam on my list of Most Hated People. Almost tied, after he tried to make a move on Thayer at her mother's party.

As luck would have it, somehow, they were already wasted—and it showed. Loud, boisterous, and unruly, they fit the stereotype of obnoxious American tourists to a T. I mean, I wouldn't have minded another drink or five, but I could keep it together in public.

Spending time with them was like getting a second-hand lobotomy. An hour later, after being forced to watch some of the dumbest YouTube videos I'd ever seen and one somewhat entertaining clip of a golden retriever puppy, I heard music to my ears.

"Now boarding Sunscape Airlines flight 2535 to Cancun."

"At least it's first class," Thayer said, offering me a consoling smile.

I took her carryon from her and hoisted it into the overhead compartment beside mine. "Adam must have had some airline points to redeem," I muttered under my breath, sinking into the navy leather window seat. I'd circled back to the whole window vs. aisle topic while boarding the plane, but it was a non-starter. At least I was sitting with her and not with the bonehead bros. I suspected Quinn knew Thayer hated flying and thought her 'fiancé' would be more comforting.

Thayer sat down and nudged me with her elbow. "You have to play nice this weekend, remember?"

"It's not like he heard me."

Leaning forward, she reached into her carry-on bag stashed under the seat in front of her and pulled out a long, woven grey scarf. She unfolded it, and suddenly, it was big enough to cover our entire row.

"You brought your own blanket?"

"It's a pashmina," she said, like I should know. "Airplanes are cold. And I'm not using their blankets. God knows when they were last laundered."

This explained the gigantic oversized, overstuffed suitcase she'd brought along. Maybe she'd packed her own pillows, too. Or a mattress.

We pretended to listen while the flight attendants walked us through the usual safety spiel, and the plane began to taxi the runway, preparing for takeoff. When the engines roared to life, Thayer gripped the arm of her seat, knuckles turning white.

"I thought you weren't afraid to fly."

"I'm not," she gritted out. "I'm afraid of takeoff."

Wasn't that the same thing? Either way, it wasn't going to help either of us if she was coiled tighter than a jack-in-the-box for the whole flight. I reached over, squeezing her hand gently. She eyed it like a poisonous snake for a moment, then sighed and squeezed it back.

"Breathe," I said, rubbing the back of her hand with my thumb.

"If I wasn't breathing, I'd be dead."

"Here." I shifted my weight and placed my elbow on our shared armrest, patting my shoulder. "Just close your eyes and rest for a minute. We'll be up in the air in no time."

Thayer regarded me warily for a few seconds. "Fine." She yawned, gingerly laying her head on my shoulder. "I didn't sleep much last night. Hopefully I conk out and wake up in sunny Mexico. Or if we crash and die, at least I won't know what happened."

"Well, that's grim."

Even with half a grande coffee in her system, Thayer was asleep by time our plane hit cruising altitude. She clutched my shoulder, curled up with her shawl-blanket draped over her body. Her breaths were slow and even as her silky hair spilled down my shoulder, tickling my arm.

It felt oddly intimate, which was funny considering that she'd had her tongue in my mouth on more than one occasion recently. But I didn't mind it, either. Not that I was going to admit that to anyone else.

Adam strolled up, perching on the arm of the empty seat across the aisle from us. "She's out cold already?"

"Looks like it." I wished I were out cold too, so I didn't have to make conversation with him. Suddenly, I was glad to be in the window seat with Thayer between us. I craned my neck, searching the aisles for a flight attendant in hopes one would direct Adam back to his own seat, but sadly, there were none to be found.

His eyes scanned my face, hint of trademark smugness peeking through. "How are things going with Callaghan?"

"In progress." The middle of first class wasn't the time or place to discuss this, especially not with him. But outwardly, I didn't want him to see me sweat. It would be the equivalent of blood in the water to a shark, and I refused to be bait.

"You won't need to worry about me," he said casually. "I already secured funding elsewhere."

Son of a bitch. This was both good and bad news.

"Did you now," I murmured.

"Yup," he said. "Family helps family, right?"

Fine, I'd bite. "Richard?"

Adam cocked his head, triumph in his eyes. "Thomas."

I glanced down, pretending to check on Thayer to conceal the shock on my face. Holy shit. Thomas was Thayer and Quinn's father.

Both sisters received a generous annuity from their trust funds, but they didn't get financial help beyond that. Thayer had specifically mentioned that her mother and her husband made a rule to avoid mixing business affairs with their family life. She and Quinn had even taken out bank loans to finance a good portion of their stores.

Thomas had the money, though. Five million dollars was pocket change to him. Which brought me back to my initial skepticism about Adam's motives with Quinn.

Did Thayer know about this? If she did, would she even tell me?

No matter how much Thayer said she hated Adam, she loved her sister—and Adam's interests were intermingled with Quinn's.

"Guess that means it'll be up to the development board's approval," Adam added. "May the best project win, right?"

I gave him a bland smile. "Exactly."

All things being equal, there was no way the city would go with his project. I knew the architecture firm he'd commissioned for the development, and their designs were as tacky as he was. But all things weren't equal until I secured the funding to back our bid.

"Anyway, are you going to join us for the festivities tomorrow night?" He waggled his brows.

"What's that?" I had a sinking feeling that the bride/groom divide was going to dominate much of the weekend. We may have had our disagreements, but I'd rather stay with Thayer than Adam and his douchebro buddies. She smelled better and was infinitely easier on the eyes. Easier on the brain, too.

"Hitting up Señor Bongos in Cancun."

For the love of God. Señor Bongos was somewhere you went when you were nineteen on spring break. But we weren't nineteen, we were in our mid-twenties, which put us firmly in the 'too old for that shit' category. We would seem like old creepy dudes to all the college kids there. If Adam wanted to dance and get wasted, surely there were classier, more age-appropriate venues to do that than Señor fucking Bongo's.

Or maybe he wanted to be surrounded by college coeds. Sadly, I couldn't rule that out.

"Quinn too?" At least if the women came along, it would minimize our creep factor.

"Nah." He shook his head. "Boys' night. I don't know what their plans are. Probably the spa or some lame girly shit like that."

"Right…" The spa sounded better to me than Señor Bongos. Then again, so did a hot poker to the eye.

Though, if Adam was half as shady as I suspected, I might be able to get some dirt on him at the club—preferably in photographic form. I'd love to repay that favor.

"Are you in, or what?" He prodded. "It's my last weekend of freedom, remember? The groomsmen gotta stick together."

Thayer groaned softly, mumbling something in her sleep about matching shoes. She shifted and reached over, hugging my right arm with both of hers like a koala clinging to a tree. As a rule, I didn't like cuddling, and with anyone else, it would have made me feel claustrophobic. With her, it was kind of endearing.

I didn't want to examine the implications of that too closely.

"I don't want to wake her," I said, lowering my voice and glad for the excuse. "But we can talk at the resort later to make a plan." Or I could hide in my hotel room and drink myself into oblivion via the mini bar, which sounded like a far more appealing option.

The plane hit an air pocket and jerked suddenly, followed by a second, smaller jolt. Thayer stirred again. With a ding, the fasten seatbelt sign lit back up like a signal from the heavens above. A blonde flight attendant emerged from the galley and made her way down the aisle, checking seatbelts.

"Sir, I'm going to have to ask you to return to your seat now." She motioned to Adam's seat, over on the other side of first class. Thank God she'd appeared when she had, or he might have settled into a seat in the empty row across from us instead.

Adam rolled his eyes. "Catch you later."

Once he was safely out of the line of sight, I let out a groan, pinching the bridge of my nose. The drinks from earlier were rapidly leaving my system, sobriety rendering me painfully aware of reality.

There were so many things wrong with what Adam had just said, I didn't know where to begin. Last night of freedom? Pretty sure his freedom ended when he got a serious girlfriend. Or at least, that's what Quinn seemed to think. Though I'd heard enough rumors to believe he was sneaking around on the side. Credible sources, too.

I hated knowing that. I hated not telling Thayer even more. But she would tell Quinn and it would absolutely, positively end up in a case of 'shoot the messenger'—Thayer, myself, or both of us. Especially when I didn't have solid proof. It would be entirely my word against his, and for some bizarre reason, a lot of people considered Adam the more credible source.

Somehow, he had everyone fooled. When I was younger, I hadn't seen it myself, but he was a sociopath in a designer suit, always looking out for number one at the expense of everyone else around him. He would step on your face to get an extra nickel that he didn't even need.

In retrospect, Adam's behavior with respect to women should have tipped me off about his character. Cousin or not, I shouldn't have been surprised when he turned around and stabbed me in the back. He'd been telling me who he was the whole time; most people did.

Unless they were Thayer, in which case they didn't let anyone so much as scratch the surface.

CHAPTER TWENTY-FOUR

Thayer

THE GOOD NEWS WAS, I WOKE UP ALIVE IN MEXICO. THE BAD news was, I woke up alive in Mexico.

Even worse, I may have drooled a little on Bennett's shoulder in my sleep. He was polite enough not to mention it—which, frankly, was out of character for him.

Then there was the fact that I got tipsy and let him kiss me in the middle of the airport bar, like some kind of lust-filled teenager. Fine, I may have leaned in to kiss him too, but I'd take that to my grave. Either way, it was my second such lapse in judgement regarding Bennett. While disembarking the plane, I made a vow to stay sober for the remainder of the trip to prevent any additional mistakes.

But after enduring a fifty-minute shuttle ride to the hotel with Millie and Adam, that vow went straight out the window. Not even sunshine, palm trees, and the balmy Caribbean Sea breeze could make their company tolerable. I was dying for a margarita. Or better yet, a bottle of tequila, straight up.

Upon checking into the resort, we discovered that everyone in our group had been placed on the same floor. Everyone else opted to get drinks in the lounge while the porters brought our luggage up, but I desperately needed a breather in our room. When I mentioned my concerns about being overheard by someone while we were arguing or simply talking too loudly about things that we shouldn't, Bennett chuckled and said I needed another drink. Then I closed the elevator door on his foot. 'Accidentally,' of course.

We turned the corner and headed for room 206. Bennett stood beside me while I fumbled with the key card, adrenaline coursing through my veins. Mid-swipe, his arm brushed against mine, and my hands turned unsteady in response. The digital lock on the door flashed red, beeping at me angrily.

I swiped the card twice more, trying in vain to get it to cooperate, letting out a curse under my breath. Bennett wordlessly reached over and took the key from my fingers, gaining entry on his first try.

"After you." He held the door open for me, and I squeezed past him, into the suite. Our suite, to be precise.

It was much like the photographs online; the furnishings were clean and modern, decorated in white and shades of tan. A small loveseat and armchair sat in the living room with a wooden desk and lamp off to the side. And directly across from that was one bed. A king-sized bed, at least, but only one.

Two towel swans perched with their necks intertwined to form a heart, surrounded by crisp white bedding and a pile of decorative pillows to match. To the left of the bed was a door leading to a bathroom that looked almost as spacious as the rest of the suite. While I wasn't serious about one of us sleeping in there, I'd have gladly sacrificed the ten feet of walking space beside the bathtub to gain some breathing room in the living quarters.

My stomach bounced around in my chest like it was performing high-intensity step aerobics. One bed. Two people. It was what I'd expected, but now it was actually happening. Bennett might not have thought it was a big deal, but it was a big deal to me. Sharing a bed with him was the definition of danger. It wasn't the sleeping part that worried me; it was the possibility of other bed-related activities that had me worried.

Bennett leisurely strolled inside, and his gaze slid over to me, questioning, while I stood staring at the bed like someone who'd never seen a bed before.

"It's nice," I squeaked. "The room, I mean." Great. I could not have sounded less composed if I tried.

He snorted, slamming the door behind him. "It's small."

"We won't be in here much, anyway." The less, the better, considering the situation.

"We won't?" He set his carry-on bag on the armchair, raking his fingers through his dark tousled waves. His expression shifted into one of distaste. "That was sort of my plan. Avoid Adam and his bros as much as possible."

"You can't hide in here the whole time." I drew in a calming breath, noticing a subtle floral fragrance in the air. While researching the resort—as I always did before I stayed anywhere, because even nicer hotels weren't immune to issues like bed bugs—I read that they'd hired a world-renowned perfumer to develop a signature scent specifically for the rooms. Reportedly, it was formulated to be relaxing, but it wasn't helping me one bit.

"Fine, I'll hide at the lobby bar." Bennett smirked.

"You agreed to play along. We're both getting something out of this arrangement. Remember, *honey*?" I pulled my suitcase into the bedroom area, hoisting it on the luggage rack with an excessive amount of force. To his credit, his tendency to annoy me was helpful, because it eliminated my nervousness and replaced it with irritation.

Bennett turned away and started to hang up his shirts in the closet, voice half-muffled. "This weekend is all for you, *babe*."

Was he being serious? This entire scheme was his idea.

"I'm sorry, was pretending to like you in front of Ian and Laura not sufficient? Not to mention, plastering photos of us all over my social media to help sell your story." I crossed the room and planted my hands on my hips, glaring up at him. "Are there more dog and pony tricks you require me to perform so you don't spill my dirty laundry to the world?"

"Really?" He arched a brow, peering down at me, and suddenly, I became aware of how close I was standing to him. Too close for my own good, because I could smell his heavenly cologne, and it was going straight to my head—not to mention, other places. The slightest hint of stubble shaded his jawline, urging me to reach out and touch it. I bit my bottom lip, hoping the pain would bring me back to my senses, but it didn't.

Bennett's gaze dropped to my mouth, his eyes darkening. "If not for our arrangement, I would have told Adam to take a flying leap when he asked me to be a groomsman. Which means I just gave up four days to come here and help you."

There was an edge of frustration in his tone, and not the kind that meant he was annoyed.

"Then help." Clearing my throat, I took a step back, trying to break the spell. I side-stepped around the coffee table to put more distance between us. "And stop being such a whiner."

We began to unpack while simultaneously trying to avoid being too close to the other person. It was challenging, given the size of the room, and at one point required me to climb over the bed to avoid him.

Minutes later, Bennett's deep voice broke the silence. "What does your sister have planned for tomorrow night?"

"Huh?" I looked up from my suitcase, where I'd been sorting through clothes. Then I realized I was holding a handful of underwear—a black-and-nude lace bikini, charcoal satin boy shorts, and a frilly white thong. Bennett's mouth tugged into a wolffish grin, and I quickly shoved them beneath a pile of sundresses.

"Oh, not much," I said, fighting the heat creeping up my neck. "Quinn wanted to have a drink in here while we do our hair and makeup. Then we're heading down to meet the other girls at the lobby bar. Why?"

"Adam paid me a visit on the plane while you were asleep. He wants to go to Señor Bongos." Bennett's face was sour. I didn't blame him. From what I'd heard, Señor Bongos was a cheesy nightclub where drunken co-eds went, looking to hook up. The kind of place with deafening music, blinding strobe lights, and people vomiting in the bathrooms before they rallied and kept drinking.

Unease settled in my gut. A tiny part of me liked that idea even less than Bennett. There would be no shortage of ready and willing attractive women there. I told myself I didn't want him to derail our plan, and that was definitely part of it. But the truth was, I didn't like the thought of him with anyone else at all. It went way beyond worrying about my reputation, somewhere into 'I'd lost my ever-loving mind' territory.

I forced a laugh. "Have fun with that."

"Don't worry," he said, "I won't."

Waves lapped gently at the shore while the sun dipped closer to the horizon, painting the sky in shades of orange and pink. I slid out of my sandals, nestling them in the soft white sand before turning to recline in my lounge chair. It was almost relaxing, or it would have been if I let myself forget everything else that was going on behind the scenes, which was a Machiavellian puppet show.

Quinn sighed happily, stretching out her toned legs. She gestured at me with her half-empty mojito. "I'm so glad we got to have twin time."

"Me too." Her invitation for a one-on-one pre-dinner drink came as a surprise, especially with Millie helicoptering around. I did enjoy spending time with Quinn alone—rare as it was lately—it was just the other people in her life who made things uncomfortable.

"How are things with Bennett?"

"Great," I lied. In all honesty, I didn't have a clue. They were more like good, bad, great, awful, and everything in between. In a word, confusing. I felt him getting under my defenses a little more every time we were alone, which made me want to fortify those defenses with brick walls and steel reinforcements.

I didn't like him, didn't want to like him, didn't want things to change. But maybe they already had.

"You guys looked adorable on the plane," Quinn mused. "You were holding onto him for dear life."

That had everything to do with my fear of takeoff and nothing to do with Bennett. Or at least, that was what I was going to tell myself.

"Mmm-hmm." I forced a smile to hide the embarrassment brewing in my gut. My oversized sunglasses, which hid half my face, were a godsend.

She sighed dreamily. "I think it's sweet how you two ended up together after all these years. Especially since you were so head over heels for him back in high school."

A tsunami of sadness crashed over me, soaking me to the bone with sorrow. Quinn wasn't wrong, but it hurt to admit that even to myself. That's why I'd spent so long rewriting history in my brain, trying to convince myself I hadn't cared about Bennett nearly as much as I had. Because when I thought back on what I'd lost, and how abruptly it had happened, little hairline cracks started to form in my heart.

"Yeah," I managed to say, my chest painfully tight. "Meant to be, I guess." Clearing my throat, I tried to channel the grief into anger at Bennett. It was easier that way.

"Have you guys set a date yet?" Excitement crept into her voice, because Quinn loved nothing more than planning parties. "I can't wait to help you with all the details."

Yeah, the fifth of never. Reception to follow when hell freezes over.

"No," I said, reclining on the blue-and-white striped lounge chair. "He's pretty swamped with work right now. You know how it is. Soon, I hope."

There was a lull while I drained the last of my lime margarita, gathering up the courage to broach what I knew would be a sensitive subject. A flock of birds flew by overhead, peppering the silence with their cries. Something nagged at the back of my mind; a question I was afraid to ask but needed to know the answer to.

Reaching down, I brushed a few grains of sand off my white linen dress and tried to seem casual. "Are you, um, happy with Adam?"

"What?" Quinn shifted in her seat and turned to face me, sliding down her pink chrome aviators. Pale blue eyes stared back at me, a mirror image of my own. "Of course, I am."

"Okay," I said, a little too quickly. "I didn't mean—"

"I know Adam isn't always perfect," she interjected, tone turning defensive in a way that made it clear I was on thin ice. Leaning back in her chair, she pushed her glasses back up with a manicured finger. "But we aren't married yet. He said he takes his vows very seriously. It'll be different after the wedding."

I swallowed, debating what the morally correct response would be. Technically, Adam didn't cheat on Quinn with me. And if she was openly admitting that on some level, she'd made peace with his suspected indiscretions…what was there to be gained by telling her something that happened before she even entered the picture?

"Well, only you know your relationship." If this was anyone other than my sister, and anyone other than Adam, I liked to think I'd be honest. I liked to think I'd tell the truth: that he was a colossal douchebag and she deserved better. But given the circumstances, I only stood to look jealous or bitter or both.

If Quinn had indicated she had some doubts, maybe it would have opened the door to more honesty on my part. Maybe with the right leading questions, I could have helped her come to see the truth about Adam in a gentle way. But Quinn's immediate, knee-jerk insistence that she was happy told me she would not only would shoot the messenger, but she'd also assassinate me. That was one reason Millie and Quinn were so close: Millie was the ultimate sycophant. Quinn once didn't speak to me for a week after I gave her an honest, though nicely worded, negative opinion about a dress. She didn't take constructive criticism—or bad news—well.

"Speaking of relationships…" Quinn trailed off. "Have you ever… have you ever had your doctor look into your fertility? Just to check?"

"Uh, no." Of course, I attended my annual physicals religiously, but fertility wasn't a topic I had ever thought to broach with my gynecologist. Well, aside from making sure I had my bases covered with birth control so as to *not* be fertile.

I wasn't even sure I wanted to have children, which was a highly unpopular thing to admit as a woman. People always acted like I was some kind of evil puppy killer whenever they found out. It's not that I didn't like children, I just didn't have that deep-seated, burning desire to have one of my own. Considering the commitment it required, it seemed like something you should really, really want.

When Quinn didn't elaborate, I pressed. "Why?"

She paused, long enough for me to know something was up. "I went for a checkup a while ago because I was having all these bizarre symptoms. Weight gain, hair loss, my body temperature kept running hot and cold. I thought it was a thyroid issue, like mom had. You know, something easily fixable with a few pills. But I guess it turns out I have something called primary ovarian insufficiency?" Quinn huffed shakily. "Basically, my ovaries aren't working properly."

A tiny, hairline crack formed in my heart. Quinn had wanted to be a mother for as long as I could remember. Growing up, her baby doll was her prized possession; she carted that thing everywhere in its toy stroller, toy baby carrier, even insisted on putting the tiny toy crib beside her bed. When we got older, she began to babysit as soon as she was allowed. And when one of her good friends got pregnant unexpectedly last year, Quinn had been more than a little wistful about the whole thing. She wanted a big family—at least three kids in some enormous SUV, running around between soccer practice and ballet.

I tried to keep my voice even. "Are they sure?"

"I made them check my labs twice. Then I got a second opinion, and a third." Her voice grew thick, and I nodded, scrambling inwardly for the right thing to say, but coming up short. I reached over, gently resting a hand on her forearm.

"I'm sorry, Quinn."

She waved me off, but her face twitched like she was fighting back tears. "It's okay. I mean, I still might be able to have children. There's just no guarantee. My doctor said the sooner, the better, because it could mean years of trying or fertility treatments. And it might only be one, if I'm lucky. You know, mom tried to have more after us, and she never was able to…"

Turmoil sparked within me, immediately igniting into a five-alarm fire. Wait a minute. Was this why Quinn was with Adam? Because the clock was ticking, and she believed he was the best she could get on short notice?

"Do you think it's my fault?" Quinn asked, snapping me back to the moment. She pulled herself upright in her seat and shifted to face me. Chin down, she fidgeted with the hem of her pink sundress and wiggled her toes in the pale sand. "I'm sure all those years when I was under-eating and over-exercising had to take a toll on my body. My doctor said it isn't because of that, but I feel like they tell you that, so you don't blame yourself. I feel like I did this to myself." Her breath hitched. "I know I did."

"I'm sure your doctor would tell you the truth," I said. "Sometimes these things just happen, even if they're shitty and they don't make sense."

She gave a tiny nod, gaze still fixed on the beach at our feet. Her phone chimed inside her purse, and she leaned over, checking it. "Our reservation is in five minutes." Drawing in a breath, she let out a deep sigh. Like the flip of a switch, she shifted back into her default, face-the-world-with-a-smile mode. "We should go meet everyone."

We gathered up our belongings and slipped back into our shoes, cutting a line across the resort to the hibachi restaurant Quinn had booked for tonight. Ever the social director, she'd booked our entire weekend solid.

Our walk was quiet, both of our minds evidently clouded from our earlier conversation.

This explained so much, like the fact that Adam insisted on referring to Lace & Grace as Quinn's 'jobby.' Similar to how people call it a 'momtographer' or 'mommy blogger' to undermine a woman's perfectly legitimate career. You ever hear anyone call it a dadtographer? It was obnoxious. His master plan was to have Quinn barefoot and pregnant at home while I got stuck shouldering the load alone. Factoring in her vulnerable position, it had to be intentional. It also explained her diminishing interest in our store.

Just when I thought I couldn't hate him anymore, it soared to record-breaking heights.

As we approached the group clustered outside the restaurant, a grim realization hit me. I had to tell her about how Adam and I slept together right before they started dating. I didn't know how, I didn't know when, but I needed to—and sooner, rather than later. Problem was, I knew I would be starting World War III when I did it.

CHAPTER TWENTY-FIVE

Bennett

B ALMY EVENING AIR SURROUNDED US AS THAYER AND I EXITED the resort lounge, both of us too fatigued to make small talk. Above us, the sky was an inky black sprinkled with a handful of stars; they were far more visible here than at home with the light pollution of the city. Right now, the only source of illumination came from soft twinkle lights threaded in the tropical shrubbery lining the path.

I wouldn't say our first evening in Mexico was a total disaster, but I wouldn't say it went well, either.

There was inexplicable tension between Adam and Quinn that had manifested in passive-aggressive conversations and frosty body language, permeating the atmosphere at the table, and making things tense for everyone else. With Millie and Louis also in attendance, the net result made me want to drown myself in tequila. But I hadn't, because I still had a full night's work ahead of me, wherein I would be playing sudoku with the company's books after another payment bounced on me unexpectedly. It needed to be rectified before the bank reopened on Monday morning, which meant I had to get it done before we went to Señor Bongos tomorrow night. Much as I would have liked to use it as an excuse to bail altogether, I didn't want Adam to know I was working while on 'vacation.' It might raise a red flag and send him sniffing around.

"I'm worried about Quinn," Thayer murmured. "She's going through something difficult right now. I can't get into it, but it's tough. I feel sorry for her."

Maybe that explained the animosity between Adam and Quinn earlier. It certainly seemed to run a lot deeper than your typical, run-of-the-mill fighting that normal couples engage in. I wasn't sure whether it had to do with the money or whether Quinn even knew about her father's money. Then again, Adam was a douche. The possible sources of conflict were limitless with him.

When I realized Thayer was still waiting for me to respond. I tried to sound sympathetic but fell short, landing on a flat, "Sorry."

"Oh my God!" Thayer stopped short, both hands flying to grab hold of my arm. Her fingertips dug into my skin. "What is that?"

Some idiotic, testosterone-ridden part of me took enjoyment in her reaction; at least, the part where she grabbed me because she was scared. I came to a halt, peering down in front of us. A teeny green lizard stood in our path. It was kind of cute, actually, as far as lizards were concerned.

"I'm not a zoologist," I said, "but I think it's a gecko."

Thayer heaved a sigh of relief, peering closer at our lizard friend. A bubble of laughter escaped her cherry-red lips. "Okay, I feel silly now. It just startled me when it ran out in front of us."

"A little stressed?" I bit my tongue, fighting the urge to slip in a suggestion regarding an old, tried-and-true stress reliever: sex. Lord knew, I could have used it. It would be a win-win situation, really, but convincing her of that would be a stretch.

"You could say that."

We side-stepped the gecko, who seemed content to remain in the middle of the path. A massive bed of pink and purple flowers appeared off to the side, its tropical fragrance wafting through the air. Thayer inhaled deeply and let out another sigh, but this time it sounded weary.

We stepped into the hall leading to our room, lapsing back into silence. While Quinn was clearly weighing on Thayer's mind, I gave precisely zero fucks about her sister myself. She played a starring role in destroying my family's reputation back in high school, airing our goddamn dirty laundry through our snooty prep academy. I was convinced that Holden's lifelong struggle with major depression and suicidal ideation all funneled back to that initial incident.

Worse still, Quinn seemed utterly oblivious to the damage she caused. Self-absorbed till the end, I supposed. The fact that Quinn and I had never been close to begin with made it easier to hold it against her than it was with Thayer. That one was proving increasingly difficult.

Generally speaking, I cherished my grudges; they fueled me. If anyone told me I couldn't do something, I would do it twice and send them a picture flipping them off while I did, just to be a spiteful dick.

Not to mention, I ought to keep my eyes on the prize: securing the funding, winning the bid, and continuing my mission to annihilate Adam.

But it was easy to forget all those things when Thayer was standing beside me looking like a goddamn masterpiece. Her low-cut, flowy sundress hugged her slender frame, showing off every curve. She'd picked up a light tan at the pool earlier, and her smooth skin glowed against the crisp white fabric. Then I remembered the kiss at the airport...

"Do you have the key?" Thayer nudged me with her elbow, bringing me back to reality.

Pick your jaw up off the floor, Bradford.

I fished the room card out of my pocket and swiped us in. We both took turns washing up for bed, with Thayer allowing me to go first so I could boot up my laptop and get started. Just when I finally started to make some sense of the numbers staring back at me, the bathroom door creaked open, and Thayer padded out. My eyes stayed fixed to the spreadsheet while she passed behind me and retrieved a bottle of water from the fridge.

"Is it okay if I turn off the rest of the lights and leave this lamp on for you?" Thayer paused beside the end table, switching on the floor lamp.

When I turned away from the screen to look at her, my cock literally jumped in response. Her clingy black camisole dipped low in the front, the slightest hint of her nipples visible through the fabric. The matching shorts were tiny, and everything hugged her curves perfectly.

I must have done a poor job at concealing my reaction because her face folded into a frown, and she glanced down at her pajamas, searching for the source of the problem. I wanted to throw her down onto the bed and do unimaginably filthy things to her. *That* was the problem.

"What?" She lifted her chin, and our eyes met, which was a much-needed reminder to keep my gaze above shoulder-level. Even in my peripheral vision, the sight of her body in those skimpy pajamas was beyond distracting. I could barely remember my first name, let alone return my attention to the numbers in front of me and make sense of them any time soon. There was no blood supply running to my head.

And there was nothing I could even do about it. Fantastic.

"Nothing," I lied. "I'm just tired. "That sounds fine. I'll try not to be too loud."

Her brow pulled together. "Are you sure? You're not using work as a reason to avoid being in the bed with me, are you? I know I gave you a hard time about it earlier, but it's fine. I promise."

I wished that were the case. I really did. Unfortunately, I had more pressing matters to attend to than nursing my fragile ego.

Plus, I'd way rather have been in bed with her than stuck dealing with this.

"No, I have to untangle these figures sometime over the week-end, and I don't want to leave it till the last minute, that's all."

My eyes traced her face, and I realized it was the first time I'd ever seen her without any makeup on since our whole arrangement had started. Her skin was smooth and even, eyelashes less dramatic, bare lips a rosy pink. She looked younger in a way that reminded me of high school all over again, setting off an unfamiliar pang in my gut. Nostalgia, maybe.

I shifted in the chair and swallowed, willing the bittersweet feelings to recede.

"Do you want me to help you?" Thayer took a tentative step closer and placed a hand on the back of my chair. Her fingertips brushed my upper arm. "Sometimes a fresh set of eyes can make all the difference."

For a second, I seriously considered it. I was certain there was something I was missing, and because that's how these things tended to work, it was probably staring me right in the face. At the same time, I didn't want her to know how dire my financial situation was.

"I think I've got it handled, but thanks."

Disappointment washed over her face, subtle like she was try-ing to hide it, but detectable all the same.

"Offer stands, anyway." Thayer squeezed my shoulder and headed into the bedroom area, slipping beneath the covers before turning out the bedside lamp. The gesture of affection wasn't lost on me, and it further added to the rodeo of emotions I was trying to wrangle.

I returned my attention to the screen and made an effort to type quietly, not wanting to disturb her. Minutes passed, and I could sense that she was still awake in the darkness. Then the room took on a new type of silence and I knew she was asleep.

Guilt seeped into my brain, trickling into my consciousness like water torture—drop by drop, steady and relentless. I was an asshole. Offering to help was her olive branch, and I shoved it back in her face because of my ridiculous male pride.

There I went, backsliding again. Why did I even care about her feelings? How could I allow myself to let everything go when she'd never even apologized? The jumble of numbers in front of me made as little sense as what was going on inside my head. I could explain away the attraction piece of it. If I didn't think about the rest of it too closely, I could wave that off as a superficial desire to engage in hot, angry sex with an objectively gorgeous woman.

What I couldn't explain was everything else.

It was easier to tell myself I didn't have feelings. I sought out Thayer to avoid complications—at least, that's what I told myself. Tried to fake a relationship to avoid a real one, and now, some part of me wanted the fake one to be real. The closer we got, the more it weighed on me. The lines we'd drawn were starting to blur, and I didn't know what any of it meant.

It was quarter past nine, and I was on my third caffeinated beverage of the morning. The first two had been consumed in a frenzy twenty minutes prior.

The alarm had sounded not long after I went to bed, and Thayer slid out of bed to hit the hotel gym for an early morning workout. Who exercised on vacation? I sure as hell didn't, unless enthusiastic sex counted. Then again, I wasn't doing that either.

Thayer's voice rang out. "Bennett?"

She had returned from her gym and showered before I even got out of bed. Then she'd headed back out for breakfast with Quinn, and I'd finally started my day. Or tried to, because I was a walking zombie.

"Out here." I was sitting on the deck, nursing a coffee courtesy of room service.

I felt like shit—and looked it, based on a quick post-shower assessment. Largely because I stayed up half the night triaging emergencies like a fucking ER doctor, talking out in the hall so I didn't disturb Thayer.

First, I had to talk Ian off the ledge after he caught wind of the IRS arrears. It took significant finesse to spin that one, but eventually, I managed to convince him that it wasn't the end of the world, wasn't directly my fault, and that I hadn't so much hidden it from him as 'sheltered him' as a favor. He was still pissed when we ended the call, but it was salvageable. It would just take a lot of groveling when I returned.

The moment one fire was extinguished, another ignited, and Holden called me, completely distraught after a fight with his girlfriend. Amongst other things that were said, she accused him of being 'emotionally unavailable.' I mean, his last name was Bradford—emotionally unavailable was a given.

That situation was trickier to navigate than Ian; throw in Holden's history of anxiety and depression, our mother's cancer relapse, and my little brother was not coping well with life in general. At one point, I was questioning whether I needed to fly back home early, but I managed to talk him into sleeping in their spare bedroom and calling me in the morning. He hadn't called yet, though, and I was starting to get worried.

Thayer barreled through the living room and out onto the patio with a stack of glossy tour brochures in one hand.

"Hey, have you decided what you want to do later for an excur—oh." Her gaze landed on my torso, eyes widening. Then she quickly averted her gaze, looking up at the ceiling. "Oh, my."

Breaking news: Thayer had a thing for abs.

"Something wrong?" I locked my phone and set it aside, taking a swig of my coffee and making no effort to hide my amusement.

"You're not dressed."

I propped my legs up on the small table across from me. "Sure I am."

"Not fully dressed. It's not…proper." She stole another glance at me and looked away, shielding her line of sight using the brochures as a blinder. The breeze picked up, ruffling her long hair.

So dramatic, this one. Being undressed paled in comparison to the other improper things I wanted to do to her. But she was cute when she was rattled.

"How is this any different than when we were sitting by the pool yesterday?" Which, by the way, had been torture for me. I was certain she'd purchased the smallest string bikini on the planet.

"Because now we're alone. Go put on a shirt, please. Even McDonald's requires that."

I gestured to the glass double doors, which were propped open to the balcony. "We're not at McDonald's, we're on a beach in Mexico, and it's over ninety degrees outside."

"Turn up the air conditioning."

"Outside? Sure thing. Then I'll go put on a three-piece suit while I'm at it." I reached for my coffee cup, eyeing her over the edge of the rim while I drained the last of it.

"Would you mind?" Thayer asked, peering through her fingers. Her fake engagement ring glinted in the sunlight. "That would be great."

Suddenly, I was fully alert, and it wasn't because of my beverage. I was both annoyed and turned on, and the effect was self-perpetuating.

Pushing to stand, I walked around the other lounge chair to stand in front of her. Her scent drifted over to me and mingled with the scent of her coconut sunscreen, an incredibly appealing combination. From this angle, I could see straight down her tank top, treating me to a prime view of the tiny bikini underneath.

"No." I peered down at her, but she wouldn't meet my eyes.

Thayer's breath quickened, and she stood frozen in place, still refusing to look at me—but I was pretty sure I caught her peeking. Regardless of how we felt about each other inwardly, the superficial attraction was difficult to ignore.

A beat passed and neither of us moved, locked in one of our infamous silent standoffs.

She drew in a breath and dropped her hands, pale blue eyes taking on a dangerous gleam. "Fine."

Taking a step back into the hotel room, she planted her hands on her hips and jutted her chin defiantly. Looking me in the eye, she grabbed the hem of her white tank top and yanked it over her head, tossing it onto the floor.

I watched, transfixed. If stripping was her idea of punishment, I was absolutely game.

My grip on the mug tightened as she undid the button of her tan linen shorts, sliding them down and stepping out of them. All that remained was a small black string bikini and miles of smooth, touchable skin. Curvy hips, perfect for grabbing hold of during all kinds of naughty activities. Perfect small breasts, showcased in a halter top fastened by a single bow that would be all too easy to untie. One small tug was all that stood between me and that glorious rack.

It took every ounce of strength I had not to ogle her. Not to touch her. And it showed.

"What's the matter?" Thayer raised an eyebrow. "It's just a bikini. Like we're sitting by the pool. Right?"

I cleared my throat, but nothing could hide the rasp in my voice. "Right." Except now, we were alone.

"You won't mind if I hang out and do my hair and makeup like this, I assume." Her tongue darted out and licked her bare pink lip, eliciting another stirring below my waist.

"If you're wearing that," I said, "you can do whatever you want. Including me."

She rolled her eyes. "Pass." Spinning on her heel, she turned and marched toward the bathroom. Her hips swayed with every step, string bikini bottom showcasing her sculpted backside.

I watched her figure disappear around the corner before grabbing the stack of colorful brochures she'd abandoned on the table, sorting through the options. Ancient ruins? No. Scuba diving? Nah. A stroll through the eco-park? Maybe tomorrow.

If we weren't going to have sex, I needed some kind out outlet for all this energy and frustration coursing through my body. Something where I could chase an adrenaline rush and forget about things for a while.

My gaze landed on the bottom brochure.

Something just like that.

CHAPTER TWENTY-SIX

Thayer

I LEANED OVER THE BLACK GRANITE COUNTER, CAREFULLY wiggling my mascara wand through my lashes. In the mirror, Bennett appeared in the doorway. His biceps bulged as he folded his arms, leaning against the doorframe, and I nearly smeared blackest black all over my eyelid.

"Need something?" I asked.

His lips were folded into a sulky frown, and his eyes were dark as he watched me. In short, he looked about as frustrated as I felt. I liked to think I was hiding it better, even if I was about two seconds away from letting him tear off my bikini.

"You." Bennett pushed off the doorway and crossed the room, coming to stand in front of me.

My heart tripped and all thoughts vacated my mind. All I knew was that he was close. Too close.

I quickly screwed the cap back on my mascara, setting it aside. My eyes fixed on his throat, watching the pulse jump in the base of his neck. He reached for me, and my breath caught. His fingertips landed on my chin, tilting it up to face him.

"You said you wanted an excursion, so I picked one. Already talked to the front desk. We leave after lunch." His lips tugged into a delicious smirk that told me I was in trouble. Bennett was a thrill-seeker. Knowing him, we were probably going tequila tasting. Or to play with guns.

"You picked one?" I echoed, not even remotely trusting his judgement.

"Sure did." He held out the green and yellow brochure, intentionally poking me in the arm with the corner.

My gaze fell, followed by my stomach. No. No way.

I read and re-read the glossy brochure, scouring for alternate activities provided by the Jungle Adventure excursion company. Maybe they offered hiking, boat tours, or something else—anything else. After my third pass, it became clear my searching was in vain. Jungle Adventure offered one activity and one activity only.

With my chin still tilted down, my traitorous eyes lifted a few inches and landed on Bennett's six-pack, tracing the stacks of solid muscle that clad his torso. Grey board shorts rested low on his hips, highlighting the V chiseled into his sides, drawing my gaze even lower. My breath snagged and something inside me stirred; something I would have called attraction if it was anyone else, but it wasn't.

Bennett cleared his throat. I lifted my gaze to find him watching me expectantly, his dark blue eyes gleaming mischievously. He just busted me checking him out for the second time this morning. I needed to get some self-control. Or to start wearing sunglasses at all times. The second option was probably a safer bet.

"I don't even like getting on planes." My voice echoed through the tiled bathroom, sounding impressively level despite my stomach spinning like a carnival ride. "There is no way I'm going zip-lining. It's got to be about a thousand times riskier than flying."

I shoved the colorful pamphlet back at him. He took it from my hands, his mouth tugging in a barely concealed grin, and set it down on the speckled counter behind me.

"It's perfectly safe," he said. "About as safe as rock climbing."

Was that supposed to make me feel *better*?

"When was the last time you saw me hooked up to a belay?"

"Don't you want to try something new?"

I shook my head, letting out a little grunt that meant 'not a chance in hell.' But we both knew my resolve was already weakening.

"Come on, Thay." He bumped me with his hip and flashed me his patented, La-Perla-dropping smile in a one-two punch combination meant to knock out my objections.

Saying no was the only sensible course of action, but saying no to that face was nearly impossible, and he knew it. The fact that we were both still woefully under-clothed didn't help, either. His muscular bare chest was directly at my eye level, and it was more than a little distracting.

"It's all fun and games until someone drops to their death."

"Tell you what." He lowered his voice in a way that made me think all sorts of sordid thoughts. My eyes landed on a white terry-cloth robe hanging on the back of the door, and I strongly considered asking him to put it on. "I'll make you a deal."

The angel on my shoulder told me not to bite, but the devil on the other shoulder yanked out her pitchfork and pushed the angel off, seizing control of my mouth. "What's that?"

"If we go zip-lining and you hate it, I'll let you have the bed to yourself tonight. Hell, I'll let you have it for the rest of the trip. All three nights."

Irritation gritted at me, wearing on my threadbare patience like sandpaper. Well played, Bennett. Backing me into a corner where I either had to go zip-lining or admit that I didn't mind sleeping in the same bed with him. Too bad for him, I did mind it. I minded it very much. Especially the part where I woke up this morning with his warm chest pressed against my back and his top arm draped around my waist.

Okay, I didn't mind that part at all. And that was the problem. It took considerable willpower to drag myself out of bed this morning, and I hated myself for it. Fortunately, Bennett slept like he was six feet under. He hadn't even stirred when I slipped out of bed, which meant he was still blissfully ignorant to the fact that he spooned me for some indeterminate length of time.

"Unless you want me to sleep in the bed," he added, his grin turning suggestive.

"Not even a little," I lied.

Though, I was confident I would hate zip-lining anyway, so it was a moot point. Nothing about leaping off a perfectly sturdy tree and flying through the air attached to a thin tether sounded appealing. Especially not the part where you could die.

"It's a win for you either way, then. Either you have fun, or you get rid of me."

I eyed Bennett suspiciously. "What do you get out of this?" His offer almost seemed like a compromise, except Bennett didn't compromise—ever—which meant there had to be an ulterior motive involved.

He heaved a sigh and combed through his dark hair with his fingers, turning sheepish. "A distraction? I sure fucking need one."

I did too, just not in the form of adrenaline-seeking antics. More like, on a therapist's couch with a box of tissues handy so we could explore why I was attracted to someone I didn't even like. Make it a double session for good measure. I'd be sure to book that upon my return home.

Worse still, part of me felt strangely guilty at the thought of saying no. Even though Bennett had withheld the details from me, I knew he was facing an immense amount of pressure when it came to work and his mother's relapse. Moreover, he was shouldering much of it alone. Once in a while, his trademark self-possessed facade faltered, letting me see how much it affected him.

He shifted his weight, and his leather-vanilla cologne drifted my way, further weakening my defenses. I took a step back to distance myself, hitting the granite countertop behind me. My heart tap danced against my ribcage. He had me cornered.

"Fine." I was desperate to end this half-clothed standoff in the bathroom. It was more dangerous than zip-lining could ever be. "We can go. I hope you enjoy the couch or floor for the rest of the trip. I'll be sure to spare you a few pillows."

Because ziplining would be terrible, obviously, and then I'd be forced to evict him from the bed. Admitting I wanted anything to the contrary wasn't an option.

He winked at me and turned, strolling out of the bathroom. "Don't worry," he called over his shoulder. "I plan on having a fantastic night's sleep in that bed later. Or not sleeping, if you'd prefer. But I'll be in the bed either way."

Like a ping pong ball, I'd gone from attraction to sympathy to annoyance in a matter of seconds. I'd never felt so conflicted toward someone in my life.

As luck would have it, we ran into everyone else having lunch at the tiki bar beside the beach. Before you could say 'bad idea,' our excursion had expanded to include the entire bridal party. I was a little surprised Quinn was up for it, but once Adam pounced on the idea, maybe she felt like she had to join.

For the entire thirty-minute shuttle ride, unspoken tension lingered between Quinn and Adam. Adam acted like the douche that he was. Millie kept making eyes at Bennett like I wasn't even there. Louis kept making eyes at me like Bennett wasn't even there. And Bennett looked like he wanted to strangle both Adam and Louis with his bare hands.

By the end, I was actually eager to get off the bus. Falling to my death was a more appealing alternative.

Our tour guides quickly ran us through a safety orientation and what to expect. Then they broke us into two groups and directed us to our respective stations to suit up with safety gear, pairing Adam and Quinn with the others, and leaving me and Bennett with Millie and Louis.

"Bennett, can you help me clip this harness?" Millie pouted, batting her lashes at him. "I think it's stuck."

Despite our entire relationship's sham status, it irked me. Fake fiancé or not, he was still mine as far as everyone else was concerned. Louis's eyes bounced between the three of us in amusement, probably hoping it would spark a fight. Bennett shot an uneasy look in my direction.

"I can help you," I offered, making a point to sound sickeningly sweet. Everyone knew I was never that nice, which got my point across perfectly. Annoyance flashed across her face, matching the way I felt inside.

Stepping closer, I grabbed hold of the clip on Millie's harness and fastened it for her quickly. "There." I patted her shoulder, giving her a fake smile. "I know those things can be tricky for some people."

Once we were suited up, we held back and let Millie and Louis lead the way along the narrow path to the first platform.

"Still think this was a good idea?" I muttered under my breath.

Bennett stepped closer to me, throwing an arm around my shoulder specifically to annoy me. Or to seduce me. Either way, it was working. "You're the one who told them where we were going."

"What did you want me to do, lie?"

"Yes," he hissed.

Inside his pocket, his phone vibrated. He withdrew his arm, stepping away from me before checking his screen. Ever so slightly, he tilted the phone away from me as we continued to walk along the path. I bristled. Of course. I shouldn't have been surprised.

He exchanged a few texts with whoever was on the other end, completely ignoring my presence. After several more minutes of walking in silence, my patience ran out. It was a Saturday, and I was pretty sure this wasn't work-related.

"Really?"

His gaze flicked up to mine, brow creased. "What?"

"Tell me you aren't texting with another woman right now."

"I'm not," he said quietly, his tone taking on a knife edge. There was an unfamiliar hardness behind his eyes. "It's Holden. He's been having a hard time."

Irritation dissolved into guilt. Maybe I shouldn't have assumed the worst, but could you blame me? Bennett didn't exactly have a stellar track record with women.

"Oh," I whispered. "I'm sorry."

"Yeah," was all he said.

I tried to hate zip-lining. I wanted to hate zip-lining. And I really, really wanted Bennett to be wrong. Unfortunately, he won—again.

While stepping off the platform for the first time was legitimately terrifying, by mid-descent, I was enjoying the view, and as much as I hated to admit it, having fun. In fact, I wasn't going to admit it, but Bennett had gone first and was already waiting for me on the other side. He caught me smiling as I sailed to the platform.

He even took a picture for proof.

Sneaky bastard.

Despite that, a blanket of unease hung between us ever since the text incident, following us all the way home on the shuttle. The emotional tug-of-war was starting to take a toll on my sanity. Sometimes he softened toward me, other times he withdrew and acted like he resented the fact that I existed.

And clearly, neither of us trusted each other.

We showered and changed back at the room, engaging in polite, stifled talk only when necessary. By the time we were due to meet everyone for dinner, the formality between us was too much to bear. Between my pale blue maxi-dress and his light blue dress shirt, we had accidentally coordinated our outfits. Outwardly, we looked the part, but we wouldn't be convincing anyone while acting this way.

I caught hold of his arm before we strolled into the seafood restaurant, bringing us to a stop. "Hey," I said. "I'm sorry about earlier. I shouldn't have assumed…"

Bennett turned to face me. "It's fine." But his face said otherwise because his jaw was wound more tightly than the zip-line earlier.

"I didn't mean to jump to conclusions."

He huffed. "I just thought you might realize by now that—"

High heels clicked on the path behind us, and a feminine voice rang out. "Bennett? Oh my God, is that you?"

We both looked to the left to find a pretty blonde in a gauzy, bright orange dress sauntering toward us. Her eyes were glued to Bennett, face lit up like she'd seen a long-lost friend. The two other women she was with lingered by a nearby flowerbed, waiting at a distance.

"Oh, hey…" Bennett forced a smile that looked more like a grimace. I'd never seen him look so uneasy. He was completely off his game. It took me a second to figure out why, but then it hit me head on: he didn't remember her name. And he'd definitely, definitely slept with her.

I half-wished a coconut would drop out of the tree above us and bonk him on the head.

"Small world, huh?" she cooed. "Can't believe we ran into each other here."

"Totally," he agreed, wrapping an arm around my waist like it would somehow help his predicament.

The girl blinked at him expectantly, waiting for an introduction. For him to say something. For him to do something. Several blinks later, the awkwardness grew to the point where it began to give me second-hand embarrassment.

"I'm Thayer." I extended my hand to her. "Bennett's fiancée. Sorry about him, he's had a little bit too much tequila already."

Her bright coral lips parted into a smile, and she giggled. "Sounds like he hasn't changed one bit. I'm Nina."

Bennett snapped out of his stupor and managed to engage in some small talk, though it was clear he didn't remember who this woman was. On the one hand, I tried not to judge people for what they did in the bedroom; it's not like I was a virgin. On the other, I could have written a list of first and last names of everyone I'd been with, along with identifying details like their birthdays, addresses, and parents' names.

"Oh dear. Would you look at the time?" I said, glancing at my watch. "We have to get inside or they're going to give away our table. It was so lovely to meet you, Nina."

With a wave in her direction, I steered Bennett back to the doors of the restaurant while the scaffolding holding up my hopes came crashing down around my feet. Hope I didn't want to have in the first place. In its wake, all of my doubts multiplied exponentially, branching off to spawn additional doubts of their own.

I'd been beating myself up for being off base with the text, when I wasn't that off base after all. Not to mention, I had been about one make out session away from letting Bennett get into my Agent Provocateur panties. What the hell was I thinking?

Bennett held the door open for me and followed behind, striding quickly to catch up. "That isn't—that was a long time ago. Like four years ago."

"Yup." I didn't look at him, coming to a halt at the empty hostess station and waiting for them to return. The restaurant had two rooms, and I couldn't see the rest of our group.

"Thayer."

Where was the hostess? This was a four-and-a-half-star resort. The service was supposed to be prompt.

"Look at me." He grabbed my hand, stepping into my line of sight. I complied, pointedly looking at the pearly button on his shirt at eye level. He didn't say *where* to look.

"I know that looks bad," he said. "But it was a long time ago. I'd just graduated, I was working eighty-hour weeks, and I was partying lots to blow off steam."

"You don't have to explain it to me." It wasn't like I had a right to be upset about something he did in the past. Or about what he did now, even. This tangled web of lies we'd woven wasn't real.

Before he could say anything further, the hostess sashayed up and grabbed a stack of menus, greeting us with a smile. Neither of us spoke as she led us to our table in the back, Bennett's fingers were still interlaced in mine, but it didn't have the same effect it had before. Now I knew it was just for show—and it had to stay that way, because I wasn't in the habit of making bad decisions.

Running into Bennett's past solidified what I already knew: he was a terrible emotional investment, and I wasn't going to let myself end up like Nina.

CHAPTER TWENTY-SEVEN

Bennett

BASS ASSAULTED MY EAR DRUMS, PRACTICALLY RATTLING MY teeth. A vague stench of stale sweat hung in the air. Blinding strobe lights flashed in the dark as smoke poured out of machines around the corners of the dance floor. And with every second step I took, the floor was suspiciously sticky.

The day had taken a steady downward trajectory. First, I failed to make a move on Thayer in the bathroom this morning when I had the chance. Her face had 'kiss me' written all over it. Actually, it had 'fuck me' written all over it, but I did neither because I was an idiot. An idiot who choked. Because Thayer had some kind of detrimental effect on my ability to perform basic cognitive functions, like thinking and forming coherent sentences.

And after what happened with Nina before dinner tonight, I'd probably never have another opening again. That run-in was the kiss of death. Like the flip of a switch, Thayer had gone straight back into ice queen mode. Sure, she'd played the part during our meal with everyone, but I could tell the difference between when she was faking it and being genuine with me, and she had been firmly in the former camp. After chipping away at her walls over the past couple of days, the sudden reversal was more than a little frustrating…in several ways.

Now I was trapped in a bad cheesy movie where the dude bros surrounding me were twenty-five going on fifteen, and they were doing shots of cheap tequila while ogling women who were still in college. At least, I hoped the women were that old. I couldn't say for sure.

I'd wasted all evening watching Adam engage in borderline inappropriate behavior without doing anything I could use as blackmail material. It was too noisy to record any of the sexually suggestive comments he'd made, and while Quinn would probably frown upon him dirty dancing with other women, he hadn't done much more than that. I needed something solid, like a kiss I could capture on camera, and I didn't get it. Even so, I'd seen enough to be confident Adam didn't behave nearly as well when I wasn't around. But without hard evidence, I wasn't going to bother going down that path.

"Have you submitted your final plans to the city yet?" Adam leaned closer, practically yelling into my ear, but he was still barely audible over the DJ announcing the next song.

At this point, he was treating me like an old pal instead of a business competitor. This was by design. I'd pretended to forgive my sorry excuse for a family member for two reasons: the obvious one being my deal with Thayer and my ultimate end goal of closing Callaghan, who'd finally rescheduled for dinner upon our return.

But making nice with Adam provided the secondary benefit of the whole, 'keeping your enemies close' thing. The drunker he got, the greater the chances of something useful slipping—and he was pretty drunk.

No harm in leading him a little bit astray.

"Not yet," I lied. "Ran into some structural problems with the design." We'd submitted the plans three weeks ago, and they were in review with the planning and development department, but Adam had no way of verifying that information. That's why he was asking. He was as cutthroat as I was, he just wasn't smart enough to be sneaky about it.

Plus, he was overconfident at the best of times and letting him think we were experiencing difficulties would feed into that. Cocky tended to equal careless, in his case, and a careless mistake would be a good thing for me.

He nodded. I could practically see the gears turning in his brain, albeit slowly just like him. "Muller Engineering?"

"Yeah." Another lie. The last thing I needed was this asshole knowing who our subcontractors were.

"I'm sure you'll sort it out. You always seem to rise from the dead." A smug smirk played on his lips, sending off alarm bells in my head. His statement was odd, given this was the first time I'd ever been in such dire straits. Unless he knew how badly his departure had harmed Flux. Either way, something was off. I made a note to dig into the books again when I had the chance. My gut said I was missing something; I just didn't know what it was yet.

Adam tipped his beer bottle toward mine, clinking the necks together. "May the best project win."

"I'm sure it will." In other words—mine.

I pulled out my phone, pretending to read a message while checking the time instead. Only twenty-two minutes had passed since I last looked. I had tolerated a few hours of this shit, but I was at my breaking point. I wasn't sure what Thayer and the girls were up to, but I'd rather go back to the room alone than stay here any longer. Maybe take matters into my own hands while I was at it, since I obviously wouldn't be getting laid any time soon.

"I'm going to take off." I clapped Adam on the back with a little more force than was friendly, wishing it was an uppercut to the jaw instead. Thanks to his booze-addled brain, he didn't seem to notice.

"So early?" He gestured to the group of barely clothed women gathered around us as if they represented a reason to stick around. But if anything, it was the opposite. I wasn't dumb enough to hook up with someone else and botch this entire deal—least of all in front of Adam. There was also the fact that the only woman I was interested in fucking was back at the resort, even if she had zero interest in that happening.

Then again, Thayer had looked about as happy as I was at the prospect of me hitting this club tonight. I wanted to say it's because she cared on a deeper level and felt sorry for me, but I suspected it was merely that she didn't trust me not to screw things up.

Louis made a face. "Come on, man. It's not even midnight."

Yeah, and he was hoping I *would* stay and screw things up. Louis wasn't exactly on board the Thayer-Bennett ship.

"Getting a headache," I told them. Figuratively speaking, this was true. I had ninety-nine problems, and Adam was only one of them. I had something more important to deal with.

The half-hour cab ride back to the resort flew by in the blink of an eye. I was lost in my thoughts, consumed with trying to decipher the situation with Thayer. Just when I would think I had her figured out, something else would happen and send me straight back to square one. We were alternating between abiding by the agreement and pretending it didn't exist. It was like playing snakes and ladders on steroids.

Instead of heading back to our room like I'd intended, I made a detour at the last minute and cut across the resort to see if the bridal party was still at the tiki bar. I didn't know when I'd become 'that guy'—inserting myself into a girls' night out like some clingy boyfriend—but the hot/cold, push/pull dynamic was gnawing at me relentlessly, like a splinter stuck under my skin.

And while Thayer might be pissed about me crashing the party, she was already unhappy with me, so it's not like I had much to lose. Plus, I didn't give a flying fuck about what Quinn and her friends thought.

A few minutes later, I stepped into the open-air bar. Fans breezed overhead in the raised ceiling while I passed the hallway that led to the bathrooms, pausing to scan the array of tables. As I came to a halt, someone turned the corner and plowed into my shoulder.

Someone half my size. Someone who smelled like heaven, mixed with brown sugar and coconut-scented sunscreen.

Thayer.

The instant I saw her, my reaction was immediate; visceral. A rush that I couldn't even put into words.

If it hadn't been for this moment, I might have thought I was broken. Because every other attractive woman I had laid eyes on all evening had elicited exactly zero response from me. Not interest, not curiosity, not even appreciation. But this one blew me away.

It was a good news, bad news scenario. The good being that I wasn't broken, the bad being that I was in way too fucking deep and there was a decent chance I was the only one.

Thayer's glossy lips parted slightly as she looked up at me, wide-eyed with surprise. Our gazes locked, and I felt a smile tug at my lips, impossible to fight. She blinked slowly, returning my smile, and cautious hope took root within me. Then she seemed to remember what happened earlier, and her half-smile faded, crushing my hopes with it.

If I couldn't get past her walls for more than a millisecond, I was about to make an epic fool out of myself.

"Bennett." She took a step back, smoothing her long hair. "What are you doing here?"

"Thanks for the warm reception," I said dryly. The fool outcome was looking more and more likely. Too late now, though. I was already here, and unfortunately for us both, I had tunnel vision once I had my mind set on something. I was going to see this through no matter how badly it might go.

"That's not what I meant." Her tone softened. "I just thought all the guys were still at the bar."

"They are."

From across the bar, Quinn and the rest of her friends broke out into a fit of hysterical laughter. None of them had noticed us talking, which afforded us some small degree of privacy.

Thayer stole a glance in their direction before returning her attention to me. She adjusted the strap of her light blue dress and lowered her voice, worry across her face. "Is something wrong? Why did you leave?"

"Several reasons." Taking a chance, I reached over and placed a hand on her waist. Her posture softened, leaning into me. "Mostly you."

Thayer's brow creased. "Me?"

"We need to talk."

I didn't know what I was going to say, exactly. All I knew was, I was fucked. Because the instant I saw her tonight, something deep inside of me said, 'mine.' Then my brain kicked in and said, 'you wish.' Now I was on a mission to do something about that or go down in flames trying.

Her teeth snagged her lower lip. "I can't just leave."

"Sure, you can. You can blame me. Everyone will believe that."

Before she could protest, I steered her through the room, back over to their table. By the time we made it over there, she seemed to have gathered her wits again.

"Look who I found," Thayer said, gesturing to me. All the heads at the table turned and their eyes landed on us, curiosity ill-concealed.

"Did the guys come back with you?" Quinn's voice was so hopeful that it almost stabbed at my cold, dead heart. Almost.

"Not yet," I said. "I don't think they'll be too late, though." Who knew if that was true, it just seemed like it would wrap up this conversion in a tidy little bow, so I could get the hell out of here.

"Is my fiancé behaving?" Quinn asked in a kidding-but-not-really tone.

I was certain she knew more about Adam's antics than she let on, and I was less convinced than ever that she had a clue about her father's investment in Adam's company. How to best leverage those facts to my advantage was still unclear, however.

"As much as can be expected." I grinned like I was joking, but it was clear neither of us were. "Speaking of behaving, do you mind if I borrow my fiancée? We had a little tiff earlier, and I have some groveling to do."

Millie threw some heavy-duty side-eye in our direction. Quinn made an 'aww' face, mirrored by her other two friends.

And Thayer looked like she was going to go drown me in the ocean.

CHAPTER TWENTY-EIGHT

Thayer

BENNETT SLID AN ARM AROUND MY TORSO AND TUCKED MY body against him. His large hand locked into place above my hip, fingers splaying against the thin fabric of my light blue sundress. Warmth flooded my body from head to toe.

"Have a nice evening, ladies." He lobbed another devastatingly charming smile in their direction and turned us ninety degrees, beginning to pull me away from the table. I wanted to be annoyed—should have been annoyed—but my body had other ideas.

"See you in the morning for brunch," I called over my shoulder. Quinn cheerfully echoed my sentiment, but not everyone was as enthusiastic in their reply—namely Millie, whose laser-like stare practically burned a hole in the back of my head.

Taking smooth, determined strides, Bennett steered us through the lounge and toward the door like a man on a mission. Only, I had no idea what his mission was.

"What are you doing?" I asked under my breath.

"Like I said," he repeated, "we need to talk."

A non-answer answer, but it was typical for him to be infuriatingly vague.

"About what?"

His gaze cut over to me, dark brow lowered. "Not here."

Maneuvering around tables, I matched Bennett's brisk pace while my brain scrambled to find an explanation, coming up empty-handed. I hadn't expected him to come back from the club early, let alone drag me out of the tiki bar like it was on fire. Especially not after I'd given him the cold shoulder all evening.

My stomach skydived, confusion giving way to apprehension. Was that why he came back? To initiate another petty squabble? And if so, would it be a real argument or a re-enactment of our weird, scantily clad standoff in the hotel bathroom?

Lately, I couldn't tell whether we were fighting or flirting. If anything, it was a paradoxical blend of both—hate-flirting, which had nearly escalated past the flirting stage on more than one occasion recently.

I was both relieved and dismayed that it hadn't.

Pressed up against his towering frame, I drew in a steadying breath, but I was still hopelessly off balance. Being caught in his orbit had a destabilizing effect, like gravity drawing me directly and inescapably toward him.

Then I reminded myself of the gigantic scarlet billboard that had appeared earlier today, warning me to steer clear of this man in bold-letter print. Nina's appearance was a wakeup call from the universe, trying to shove me out of dangerous territory and back onto the straight and narrow.

A little late for that now, though. I was firmly in dangerous territory and firmly enjoying it. It was easier to keep Bennett at arms' length when he wasn't literally at arms' length—like right now, with his firm muscle caging me in from the left and his possessive hold on me from the right, I didn't stand a chance.

We stepped outside, greeted by warm, humid air and the faint crashing of waves against the shore. A couple hanging lanterns glowed against the darkness, their cones of golden light casting long shadows against the pavement. I took a step to my right, moving to take the path that led back to our hotel room, but Bennett tugged me in the other direction, leading us down a small set of stairs to the beach.

White moonlight cast down on the water along the shore, reflecting off the surface. The heels of my shoes sank into the sand, and I came to a stop, slipping them off. Bending down, I picked up my sandals with one hand while Bennett's hand lingered on my bare shoulder, evidently unwilling to let go.

"Where are we going?" I glanced up at him questioningly.

"Shortcut back to the room." He jutted his chin at some indeterminate point off in the distance. "It's faster to go down to the fitness center and cut across."

I stood back up, and his hand found the curve of my waist again. My heart fluttered in response, tapping Morse code against the wall of my chest.

"Why are you in such a hurry?"

He nudged me along with his elbow. "This is not a public conversation."

Nervousness bubbled up within me like a bottle of shaken Dom Pérignon. What did that even mean? Aside from us, the beach was deserted, not exactly what I'd call public.

A glimpse in his direction revealed little. Beneath the pale moonlight, his strong jaw was set and his dark eyes were determined, but his expression was otherwise unreadable.

With minimal conversation aside from Bennett's one- and two-word directions, we resumed walking and reached the building that housed our hotel room in less than half the time I'd expected. He'd been right about the shortcut, at least.

Without missing a beat, Bennett pulled out his key card and swiped it, shoving open the door and placing a hand along the small of my back to usher me inside. I brushed past him, trying to pretend like I wasn't nearly as fazed as I was—but my heart was drumming against my ribcage so violently I thought it might crack.

I set down my metallic sandals next to the mirrored closet, using the opportunity to quickly check my reflection. My makeup was intact, hair still in loose waves, and I didn't look nearly as nervous as I felt. Then I made the mistake of looking at him through the mirror and my nerves shot through the roof like a bottle of champagne being uncorked. Tall, dark, and devastating. He was intimidation in human form, especially with this newfound intensity I couldn't interpret.

Bennett shut the hotel room door behind him, locking the deadbolt, and in a heartbeat, he was standing in front of me. I lifted my chin to find a stern frown across his handsome face. Unfortunately, stern was a good look on him. My 'straight and narrow' plan went right out the window—the crooked path was far, far more appealing.

My mouth went dry, along with my reserve of willpower. "What—"

Bennett shook his head almost imperceptibly and took a step forward, into my space. I stepped back and he walked me a few more paces backward until we were standing in the small kitchenette. He picked me up, effortlessly hoisting me onto the glossy granite surface. I drew in a breath as the cold stone seeped through the flimsy material of my dress, chilling the back of my thighs.

He leaned in so we were eye to eye, and his hands landed on either side of the counter, pinning me in. Our gazes locked as he studied me, his tongue skimming along his bottom teeth as if in thought, pausing before he spoke.

"You're upset with me," he said.

"No." I was lots of things, that just wasn't one of them. Insane, possibly. Yes—definitely insane, because right now I could not tear my eyes away from his full lips. Could not stop wishing those strong hands were on my body again. Could not stop imagining his mouth against mine, fingers tangled in my hair...

Could not even formulate a multi-syllable response, apparently. Bennett raised his eyebrows pointedly. "Yes."

"I'm not."

Scared of him and whatever I was feeling? Absolutely.

Upset with myself for developing feelings for the wrong person? Maybe.

But upset with *him*? Technically, I wasn't.

His gaze darkened. "You keep telling yourself that, but I'm not buying it. I'm not moving until you talk to me, and I've got all night."

"Guess you'll be standing here for a while, then."

"Are you upset because of what happened with Nina?" He tilted his head, and his eyes slowly traced my face, methodical and probing, assessing me in a way that made me feel naked while fully clothed. I clenched my jaw and tried not to visibly react, but I knew it was futile; I'd never successfully lied to Bennett before. I sure as hell wasn't going to magically start now.

"Of course not," I said, using considerable effort to keep my voice even. "Why would I be?"

A ghost of a smirk played on his lips "Are you jealous?"

"Jealous of someone you forgot? No, Bennett. Quite the opposite."

And just like that, I had revealed too much. I clamped my mouth shut, but I couldn't take back what I'd said.

His breath caught. "You don't actually think—" He reached up, gently tracing along my jawline with his fingers. A shiver of pleasure ran down my spine at the contact. "Thay."

"What?" I whispered.

"I could never forget you."

Something bittersweet washed over me, tugging at my heart like nostalgia mixed with hope. I closed my eyes and shrugged, at a loss for what to say. I was expecting aggressive Bennett, or joking-around Bennett. I didn't know what to do with this new, sincere version.

His thumb skimmed my cheek, moving to trace my lower lip. Somehow, the softness of his touch demolished the walls around my heart like a wrecking ball, rendering me more vulnerable than ever. And I hated it.

"Why do you think I'm here?" he asked softly.

I peeked up at him. "To spy on Adam?"

"Fringe benefit," Bennett admitted, lips quirking into a grim smile. "But that isn't the real reason, and I think you know it."

Part of me wanted to believe him, but another part of me was too scared to allow myself to take that leap of faith. I had too many questions, too many things I wanted to ask but couldn't seem to say. My brain had ceased operations, solely guided by the cascade of hormones coursing through my veins.

Survival instincts took one last swing, flailing desperately, but I knew it was a strike before I even spoke.

"We hate each other, remember?"

His expression sobered, and he tilted my chin up to face him. "I never said I hated you. Not once."

Bennett ducked closer, and his mouth hovered inches away from mine, breath warm against my lips. His other hand wrapped around my lower back, holding me in place. My hands flew to his bare forearms, holding on as if for balance while desire coiled between my legs. I was past the point of no return. I couldn't even see it.

CHAPTER TWENTY-NINE

Thayer

OUR INHALES AND EXHALES MINGLED IN THE SILENCE OF THE hotel room, rushes of air crashing together like waves against a shore.

Electricity buzzed between us as Bennett brushed the tip of his nose against mine, barely grazing the skin. My stomach fluttered with anticipation, and my breath stilled, eyelids drifting shut. He paused for a heartbeat before pulling away again.

Confusion washed over me, and I blinked slowly, bringing him back into focus. His blue-grey eyes swept across my face and tenderness flashed behind them, cutting straight through my emotional armor. It was like being seen for the first time, excruciating and exhilarating all at once, and it took every ounce of strength I had not to turn away.

He cupped my chin, his touch gentle but firm. "Are you okay?"

I swallowed, fighting to regain my self-restraint, but it was a lost cause. With a single look from him, every wall I'd built around myself had collapsed, crumbling to dust.

"I'm fine." Other than my trembling hands, thundering pulse, and fully exposed heart.

Bennett's mouth tugged into a knowing smile, like I'd said more than I actually had. "You're not breathing, Thay."

He was right—I wasn't. My lungs sucked in a gulp of air at the reminder and my respiration resumed a steady pattern that was more compatible with sustaining life.

"Yes I am." Now, at least.

"You're nervous." His hand on my back moved in slow, easy circles over the thin fabric of my dress, warming the skin beneath.

Nervous was one way of putting it. Because in addition to the innumerable breaches of the contract between us, I'd broken an even more important rule of my own: I'd let him in. Not just a little bit, either. Fully. He'd bypassed my defenses and gotten right to the core of who I was. To the soft, squishy, sensitive parts; the parts that needed protection most.

Now I was adrift in an inflatable lifeboat, completely at his mercy while I floundered in the middle of the ocean without a way to get back to solid ground. I didn't know whether he was going to rescue me or drag me under—didn't know whether he was a ruthless pirate or benevolent captain—but I wanted to find out.

I needed to find out.

When I failed to respond, his dark eyebrows pulled together, questioning. I snagged my bottom lip between my teeth, releasing it and offering the only answer I had.

"Not in a bad way."

Bennett nodded, a low hum rumbling in his chest. He reached up and gently tucked a strand of hair behind my ear, the effect strangely calming. "It's just me," he said. "Us."

"It's the good kind of nervous," I insisted. "The 'waiting for you to kiss me again' kind."

My mouth snapped shut. Part of me wanted to die for saying that; the other part was too busy swooning over the wolffish smile it had awarded me.

His eyes danced. "Done."

Tipping his head, his lips claimed mine, gently plying them apart and setting off a cascade of fireworks throughout my body. His large hand pressed into the curve of my back, steadying me and leaving me off-balance all at once. I let out a blissful sigh as his tongue swept against mine, tasting the bitterness of beer and sourness of lime. All my doubts faded into the background, instantly forgotten.

Our mouths moved together, slowly savoring; tasting; teasing. Making up for lost time like our lives depended on it. I'd missed kissing him. Why weren't we doing this all along? Some part of my brain knew the answer to that question, but the rest of me didn't care. It was heaven and hell combined, a blissful moment I never wanted to end but knew had to stop eventually.

Bennett captured my lower lip between his teeth, gently tugging before letting it go. I seized his bottom lip in return, nipping at it as he let out a low groan. Back and forth, we engaged in a delicious give and take until we finally broke apart, the two of us winded and in desperate need of air. At this point, oxygen deprivation seemed like it was par for the course around him.

"Holy shit." Bennett leaned his forehead against mine, trying to catch his breath. My hand pressed against his chest and his heart pounded against my palm.

"This definitely violates the agreement," I murmured.

"Fuck the agreement." His grip on me tightened and his mouth crashed against mine, knocking all the air out of my lungs again. This kiss was insistent—bossy and demanding. His tongue pushed into my mouth, deepening into a toe-curling kiss that made desire coil within my belly in response.

His strong hands slid down the sides of my torso, digging into my hips and holding me in place. I melted in response to the heat of his body against mine, clutching his bare forearms. Every point of contact between our bodies was charged with magnetism, every touch from him stoking the glimmer of yearning within me until it grew into an inferno.

Liquid heat pooled between my legs, want spiraling into need. It was sensory overload on every level—the taste of his mouth; the firmness of his muscles; his low, masculine sounds; undeniable lust across his face; and the heady, intoxicating alchemy of his cologne.

I drew in a breath as his fingers found the hem of my dress, slowly inching it up until the thin fabric was bunched up around my hips and my upper legs were completely bare. Bennett's warm palms landed on my thighs, parting them to him. His gaze dropped to the scrap of lace between my legs, which served more as a window dressing than any sort of coverage. I was on full display down below—all of me.

His irises darkened, turning midnight blue, and he uttered a low, feral growl of satisfaction. "Jesus, you're perfect."

Grabbing my backside, he yanked my body to the edge of the counter so that I was nearly teetering off, forced to hold onto him for balance. Our mouths came together again, and his hands dug into my flesh, picking me up off the counter and pulling me against his firm body. If there were any lingering questions as to why he'd dragged me back to the hotel room so quickly, the rock-hard erection grinding against me was my answer.

A breathy moan escaped from the back of my throat, reverberating against his lips. He lifted me again, connecting with the perfect spot through my underwear, earning another needy noise from me in response.

"I love when you make noises like that," he murmured, dragging his lips across my jaw. "Can't wait to see how loud I can make you."

A garbled sound of agreement was all I could manage. After a few more teasing thrusts, Bennett placed me back down on the stone surface. His fingers crept up my inner thigh, drawing torturously close to my center. He tugged aside my underwear, and his fingers slid against me, triggering an explosion between my legs.

"Oh." I sucked in a breath, my fingertips digging into his muscular biceps. I'd always prided myself on having stellar self-control—on having superior self-discipline, the ability to stick to a schedule, and for exercising moderation in all things. But the one thing I couldn't moderate was Bennett. The more I got, the more I wanted, and right now I wanted all of him.

"That night at your place…" he trailed off, sinking one finger inside me. Another finger followed, gliding through my slick folds and curling to stroke my G-spot. I gasped at the fullness as pleasure shot through my core, my legs jolting in response.

"What about it?"

"Did you touch yourself like this after I left?" Bennett's teeth sank into my earlobe. "While you were thinking about me?"

His thumb grazed my swollen bundle of nerves, and everything turned hazy, my back arching in response. I whimpered, lost in the sensation and unable to speak. There was no denying I'd entertained fantasies about him. Highly detailed, graphic fantasies just like this. I'd fantasized about him in my bed; I'd fantasized about him in my shower; I'd even fantasized about him on my couch. My fantasies were good—satisfying even, thanks to the assistance of battery-operated technology—but the real thing was better.

That's what made this so dangerous. Now that I'd crossed that line, it would be impossible to return to the other side. Somehow, I knew this was a one-way trip. I was hooked.

"Did you?" he pressed, circling his thumb against me again.

I let out another involuntary whimper. "Y-Yes." My cheeks heated at the admission. "Did you?"

Bennett laughed huskily. "Every goddamn day."

"You fantasize about me?" Of course, I did have some idea—I'd seen the way he looked at me in a bikini. But hearing him say it was like pouring gasoline on a bonfire. There was something incredibly arousing about knowing I was wanted like that.

"All the time." His fingers stroked me again, and I yelped, an approaching orgasm pressing in on me from all sides. He slowed down, teasing me without giving me release. It was such divine torture that I couldn't decide if I wanted to kiss him or kill them. "Want to know what I was thinking about earlier?"

I writhed against him greedily. "What?"

"I was thinking about my face between your legs. Followed by my cock." The words nearly took me over the edge, and I cried out in protest as he withdrew his fingers from me, slipping them into his mouth and sucking my juices off before removing them again. A wicked grin spread across his face. "See? I knew you would taste amazing."

Frustration of all kinds slammed into me. "You said you wouldn't have sex with me even if I begged you."

His grin was both devilish and devastating. "That was a lie, obviously." He gripped the base of my throat with his free hand, sliding up the side to fist the roots of my hair. Teeth scraped my bare skin at the juncture where my neck and shoulder met, and I groaned, arching my neck to urge him on. "A dirty, filthy lie."

"I should make you pay for that."

Bennett chuckled. "I'll beg right now if you want me to. But I think we can both agree there are better things I could do with my mouth." He pressed an open-mouthed kiss below my ear, sucking hard; hard enough that I knew he'd leave a mark, but I didn't mind. "What do you think, Thay? Should I fuck you with my tongue before making you come while I'm inside you?"

I hummed in agreement, sliding my palms down his sculpted shoulders. "Yes to both."

"First, I need to see you. All of you." He tugged at the zipper of my dress, splitting it apart and pulling the straps off my shoulders to bare my upper half.

I shimmied out of the loose fabric and kicked it aside, onto the floor. Suddenly, I was left in nothing but very expensive, very skimpy lace. I may have ransacked our store's new arrivals in preparation for the trip. You know, because wearing nice underwear is important in case of a zip-lining accident.

Fine. Agent Provocateur had one purpose and one purpose only: to be removed by someone like him.

Bennett's gaze dragged down my body, eyes widening at first

and then growing hooded. His fingers traced the lace-trimmed edges of my balconette bra, leaving a trail of goosebumps along my skin.

"You're a goddamn masterpiece." His voice was husky, strained with desire.

I began to unbutton his dress shirt, working my way down one button at a time, but he was too focused on me to notice. Letting out a low hum, his palms curved down my ribcage. He drank me in like I was water and he was dying of thirst. With anyone else, I would have felt too exposed—like I was on display. But the expression on his face was best described as awe.

After finishing with his shirt, I unfastened his pants and he shrugged out of both, eyes glued to me the entire time. I seized the opportunity to ogle the smooth stacks of muscle that greeted me, along with pair of black boxer briefs that hugged everything. And I do mean everything.

After another second, Bennett's eyes lifted to mine. His look of reverence shifted into wicked determination, corner of his mouth lifting. "I'm going to fuck you until you don't remember your own name."

Sliding one finger beneath the waistband to my thong, he skimmed my lower stomach beneath the gossamer-thin fabric. My body ached, desperate for him to continue lower and finish what he'd started.

"Should I keep going?" Bennett ducked his head, and his lips grazed the curve of my breast, nimble fingers making quick work of the clasp behind my back. In a flash, my bra disappeared, and he drew one nipple into his mouth, palming my other breast with his hand. He stole a glance up at me, brow cocked. "Or should I stop?"

The thought of stopping was nearly as bad as death. "Don't stop."

He tsked. "That wasn't one of the options." Moving lower and kneeling before me, he nipped at my hipbone, immediately lathing the spot he'd bitten with soft kisses.

"Keep going," I said. "Please."

Bennett smiled against my skin, smoothing his hands down my legs. "That's my girl."

And with those words, I was a goner. I had completely and irrevocably given him a piece of my heart.

Reaching up, he hooked his fingers under the delicate straps of my underwear and gently slid them down past my feet, tossing them aside onto the counter. Then he placed my left leg over his shoulder, exposing me to him before planting a trail of soft kisses along my upper legs.

I leaned my head against the cupboards behind me, and my fingers sank into his silky hair, tugging. He licked and sucked the delicate skin of my inner thighs, moving close to where I was desperate for him before retreating again, teasing me over and over.

With every circle he traced, he got a little bit closer without giving me what I wanted; what I needed. His mouth landed on the crease of my inner leg, drawing a whimper of frustration from me. "Bennett."

Finally, his tongue landed where I was heated and aching, mouth closing around me. Pleasure spiked, nearly causing me to come on the spot. I drew in a sharp breath and jerked against him involuntarily. "Oh God."

My back arched, my body begging for more as his fingers thrust inside me, working in synchronization with his mouth. With determined sweeps of his tongue and encouraging sounds, he began to devour me.

It was only a matter of seconds before everything grew fuzzy again and tension started to coil within me, pressure building. His tongue flicked against me again and I saw stars.

"There," I begged, moving my hips.

Bennett let out a low sound of agreement, sucking my clit gently and sliding a third finger inside me, creating a divine sense of fullness. The combination of sensations internally and externally was almost too much for me to handle. Heat flooded my body and a thin sheen formed at my hairline, breath turning into tiny, needy pants.

"I'm—" I broke off, unable to finish my sentence, and my words slurred into an appreciative moan. I trembled beneath him, unraveling bit by bit as I approached the precipice, then suddenly everything exploded in a burst of bright, white light.

More sounds escaped from me as Bennett kept working me mercilessly, wringing every last quiver from my body until I was too sensitive to continue. Just as I was about to push him away, he relented and released me, pulling his fingers out and planting a final open-mouthed kiss between my legs.

He slowly kissed his way back up my body, starting with the tops of my thighs and moving up to my hips. Moving higher, his lips grazed along my stomach, breasts, and neck. By the time he reached my lips, I'd almost caught my breath—but not quite. Full sentences weren't an option yet.

Bennett's lips quirked, pulling into a crooked half-grin that said he knew exactly how I was feeling. "How are you doing, beautiful?"

"Can't talk, still recovering." I shook my head, leaning my forehead against his broad, bare shoulder. His hands smoothed down my arms, soothing and protective, coming to wrap me in an embrace. My brain gradually started to reboot, though I couldn't have trusted my legs to hold me upright if my life depended on it.

A few more seconds passed, and my heart rate normalized, breathing slowly started to return to normal. When I lifted my head, he ducked closer and kissed me softly, stroking my hair.

"You sound fucking hot when you're moaning my name," he murmured. His rough tone and dirty words contrasted with his gentle touch. "Bet it's going to sound even better with my cock buried inside your pussy."

My fatigue of moments ago vanished, replaced with the intense desire for exactly that. All I wanted was to have his skin pressed up against my skin, our bodies joined together.

"Let's find out." I wiggled my hips against him, bare entrance rubbing against the bulge in his boxer briefs. Bennett leaned his head back and groaned, thrusting against me.

"Hang on," he said, voice strained. "I have condoms in my suitcase."

I glanced over at his luggage in the bedroom area, fifteen feet away, then gave him a helpless look. "Not sure I can walk. You did a number on me." While parts of me had recovered, that definitely wasn't on the table yet. Even sitting down, I could tell my legs were jelly.

A look of self-satisfaction crossed his face. "I got you." His hands slid under my thighs, and he picked me up, wrapping my legs around his waist. There was a tenderness in the way he handled me that made my heart swell. Mouth claiming mine, he walked me over to the bed and eased me down onto the mattress, caging me beneath his frame.

He reluctantly pulled away, studying me with a sulky frown. "It's too hard to stop kissing you." Immediately, he leveled me with another, crushing kiss while his hands explored all over my body. I writhed against him, tugging down his boxer briefs while he helped me pull them all the way down.

"I should..." Bennett's expression was torn. The two of us fully naked was too much temptation for either of us to handle. He rolled away from me and pushed to stand, fumbling around in his suitcase before emerging with a box.

Miles of smooth, muscular male backside faced me. So firm and inviting that I had the strangest desire to sink my teeth or nails into him, or maybe both.

Suddenly aware of my own exposed state, I pulled the top sheet free and artfully draped it over my body. Then I propped myself up on one elbow, reveling in the view, giving him a wry smile. "An entire box? Aren't you prepared."

Bennett tore the cardboard open, shooting me a cocky smile over his shoulder. He grabbed a handful of foil squares and walked over, tossing them on the nightstand. "Oh, I'm a fucking Boy Scout."

CHAPTER THIRTY

Bennett

MERELY KISSING SOMEONE SHOULDN'T LEAVE A GROWN-ASS man winded and wanting for words. Yet embarrassingly, that's exactly what happened the first time I kissed Thayer—though I liked to think I hid it well.

It set off some alarm bells inside my head, but I wrote off that first kiss as a fluke. The product of pent-up sexual frustration, superficial attraction, and my fondness for a challenge. Because if there was one thing I liked, it was winning.

But the second time we kissed at her place, it happened again; same explosive chemistry, same dumbfounding effect on my brain. At that point, I started to think I might be in trouble.

And the third time we kissed at the airport bar, I knew I was fucked. It was undeniable confirmation that I was feeling things beyond the physical. Things I didn't know how to label, how to process, or how to express. Other than, well, doing the obvious with the hottest woman alive, who was naked and waiting for me in bed.

I tugged the bedsheet free and slipped in beside Thayer, mattress sinking beneath my weight. Lying on my side to face her, my gaze dropped to her half-hidden breasts, tracing the swells of her cleavage, before dipping even lower to the slight outline of her nipples visible through the white sheet.

Thayer slid her slender, smooth calf between my legs, intertwining our lower halves. A contented warmth gleamed in her eyes. Her long hair was tangled, cheeks flushed pink, and her red lipstick was notably absent, rubbed off by yours truly. Probably all over my face, come to think of it, not that I cared at the moment.

She glanced at the handful of foil wrappers scattered on the wooden nightstand. Then she turned back to me, narrowing her eyes, but the tug of her lips gave her away. "You knew I was going to have sex with you."

Knew? No. Prayed? Yes. Made an offering to the gods? Possibly.

"I had a hunch it might be on the table." I slid my palm down the curve of her bare waist and my cock twitched, so stiff it verged on painful. At this rate, I'd be lucky if I didn't end up in a Mexican ER later, seeking treatment for a prolonged erection, no little blue pill necessary.

Her kiss-swollen lips tugged. "Cocky bastard." Maybe I did possess a little more hubris than usual. Probably because minutes ago, she was moaning my name loud enough for half the hotel complex to hear. There wouldn't be any concerns about people buying our relationship after that. Only problem was, I was starting to buy it too.

I ducked in closer for another kiss. Our mouths met again, and heat spread through my body, sparked by the contact and fueled by desperate want. My tongue swept against her bottom lip, gently plying to deepen the kiss. Thayer made a little 'uh-uh' sound and smiled against my mouth teasingly, refusing to grant me access. Her hand wrapped around the base of my shaft, and a low groan escaped from the back of my throat.

"You're killing me." I leaned my forehead against hers, which was equally feverish pressed up against mine. The air conditioning was set to sixty-eight degrees, but between our body heat, the room felt like it was well over one hundred.

Her laugh was low, seductive. "That's sort of the point."

My hand slid up her ribcage, palming her supple breast and squeezing. Her lips parted slightly, like the playing field had suddenly leveled. Then she stroked me again and it tilted sharply back in her favor. I'd never been much of a hand job guy, but if I let her get too carried away, I might not make it past that tonight. My ego would never, ever live that down. Nor would other parts of me.

"You're such a tease."

Thayer leaned in and kissed me softly, pulling away before I had the chance to kiss her back. "You like it."

She was right. I did—a little too much. I pinched her pink nipple between my finger and thumb. It hardened beneath my fingers, her lips parting to draw in a soft gasp in response. Checkmate. My tongue slipped inside, tangling with hers. Her grip on me tightened and our kiss turned wild and needy.

My fingers skimmed down her torso and between her legs, sliding against her warm, wet center. Thayer's hips circled in response, grinding against me. I kept teasing her, and she kept giving it right back to me, hand moving up and down in a perfect rhythm until I was one stroke away from needing to calculate baseball statistics inside my head. All I could think about was being buried inside of her.

We broke apart, short of breath and frustrated in the best possible way. The scent of her perfume filled the air between us, beckoning in a way that made me want to bury my face in every inch of her skin all over again. I could gladly have her for breakfast, lunch, and dinner.

"Do you have any idea what you do to me?" I asked, gently cradling her jaw.

Her eyelids were hooded, eyes smoky with desire. "I think I have some idea. But maybe you should tell me, just in case."

"You drive me crazy." My mouth landed on her jawline, nibbling and sucking the smooth, soft skin. She arched her neck, fingers tugging at my hair while I continued to lavish kisses on the spot beneath her ear. "I want you more than I've wanted anything in my entire life."

There was something scary about admitting that, but it was freeing at the same time.

"I want you too," she murmured.

Leaning over, I grabbed a condom off the nightstand and tore the wrapper open. She watched expectantly as I unrolled it, trying to conceal my unsteady hands from all the adrenaline. It wasn't exactly the first time I was doing this, but it sure as hell looked like it.

My hands gripped her thighs, spreading them open and hungrily taking in the sight of the small, trimmed patch of hair, and the tiny birthmark on her inner thigh that I'd already memorized. I kneeled between her legs, and when she gazed back up at me, lush lips parted and expression soft, the strangest sense of déjà vu barreled into me like a freight train.

Only, we'd never been here like this before.

I lowered to hover above her, biceps tensing as my elbows pinned her in beneath me. The head of my cock barely grazed her entrance. Thayer let out a cross between a whimper and a moan, digging her fingertips into my ass and trying to pull me into her. It was torture, delicious torture. I had to channel every shred of willpower I had to stop myself from slamming inside.

She blinked up at me, lush lips parted slightly. I pushed against her again, giving less than an inch before pulling away.

"Tell me what you want," I said.

While I said I'd get Thayer to break the no-sex rule, part of me didn't think she actually would. And I definitely didn't expect it to be anything more than sex, yet what was going on between us right now felt like a hell of a lot more than that. I didn't do relationships, and as far as I knew, Thayer didn't do casual sex, which meant that both of us had precisely zero clue what the hell was happening. I was too caught up in the moment to think that far ahead, though.

"You know what I want." She squirmed beneath me and circled

her hips, rubbing her pussy against the head of my shaft. My dick silently cursed at me for not taking the bait.

"Yeah." I smirked, fisting my cock and lingering at her entrance. "But I want to hear you say it."

Thayer blinked up at me through her dark lashes. "Fuck me before I change my mind."

"I like when you're bossy." Good thing too, because it happened a lot.

My lips captured hers, tumbling into a ravenous kiss. She made an impatient sound, tugging at me again to draw me closer. I slid into her as she did, and she moaned into my mouth, a low grumble echoing in my chest in response.

It was like going from black and white to seeing color for the first time; addictive and incomparable. I pulled back and slammed all the way in, deeper than before, filling every inch of her. Her walls clamped down around me, and a shiver of pleasure ran through my body, telling me I could stay buried inside her forever and die happily.

We fell into a steady rhythm, her hips rolling against me with every thrust. I reached down, rubbing her with my thumb in rhythm with each slow, languorous movement. She looked back up at me, eyelids heavy and eyes glassy.

Her eyes focused on me with such a look of vulnerability it went straight to my heart, tugging in an unfamiliar way. Pretty sure I'd never made so much eye contact during sex in my entire life. Sex and intimacy were two different things—things I kept intentionally separate by avoiding the latter completely—but this was definitely both.

I rocked into her again, watching her beneath me. "Fuck, Thay. You feel even better than I imagined."

She inhaled sharply, a flush across her cheeks. A tingling ignited at the base of my spine, threatening to send me over the edge. It was all too apparent that I had some serious delusions of grandeur with respect to how this was going to go down.

In my head, I pictured a marathon sex fest; multiple positions, multiple orgasms for her, you name it. But now that I was buried inside her to the hilt, I'd be lucky if I got her off again before I lost control. Good thing we had all night, because I was definitely going to want a repeat performance. Might need one, too, for pride's sake.

Her body tensed, fingers digging in. Careful not to change my rhythm, I snagged her earlobe between my teeth. Having her come all over my tongue was hot as fuck, but I wanted—no, I needed—to watch her face this time.

"I know you can come again for me," I said, lowering my voice as I tilted my hips. "Come on my cock."

Thayer shivered, and her palms slid down my back, holding onto me. For a moment, my own impeding orgasm receded slightly, and I lost myself in watching her. Her jagged, uneven breaths; dewy skin; hair spread against the pillow.

"I…Oh, God. There." She leaned into the pillow, sliding her left leg higher, past my waist. I grabbed her calf and hooked it over my shoulder. Her nails dug into my arm. "Bennett."

Hearing her moan my name like that destroyed what little willpower I had left. Once she started to unravel beneath me, I gave in and let myself follow right behind her with a growl.

"Fuck." After what amounted to edging myself around her for the last month, I came harder than I ever had before. For what was seconds or minutes or an eternity, the only thing that existed in the world was our bodies wrapped together, Thayer begging me not to stop.

Reality slowly faded back in, leaving us both sweaty and exhausted. I lowered my temple to hers, resting without crushing her small frame.

"Goddamn." My heart pounded like a bass drum against the wall of my chest. For someone who considered himself to be in great physical condition, I was embarrassingly tapped out.

She giggled. "You could say that again."

Turning my head, I kissed her, and my fingers sank into her

hairline, gently fluffing her hair before trailing down her face and tracing her bottom lip. Thayer gave me a tired smile, leaning into my hand affectionately. She looked a little wrecked, and I loved knowing I was the one responsible for the destruction.

Her fingers traced the stubble along my jaw. "I never would have pegged you for the cuddling type."

"Only with you," I said, stroking her cheek. I knew I'd have to get up eventually, but I wasn't in a hurry.

"Bet you say that to all the women."

My hand stilled, tilting her face to mine. "Not even close."

I should have seen it coming—and maybe I did, subconsciously. But old habits are hard to break, and like everyone else in my family, I had a PhD in Denial. I'd spent twenty-five years keeping up appearances, looking the other way to further my own interests, and ignoring inconvenient details.

What's more, I'd made a second job out of avoiding those pesky things known as emotions. Emotions make you vulnerable, and what's another word for vulnerable? Weak. Looks like I just found my Achilles heel.

After cleaning up, I lounged against the headboard while I waited for Thayer to emerge from the bathroom. The door swung open to reveal her in a skimpy black satin robe tied at the waist, and I had the immediate urge to tear it right off of her.

She walked back out of the bathroom and turned to face her suitcase, sifting through her clothes. I sat up, abs flexing as I planted my elbows on my bent knees. The sheet hung dangerously low around my hips.

"Don't you dare," I said.

"Don't I dare what?" Thayer froze and pivoted to face me. Her eyes dropped to my torso, widening.

"Don't you dare get dressed."

She chewed on her bottom lip uncertainly, studying me fully naked in the bed.

"For the record, there's a no-clothing and no-cover-ups rule in this bed from here on out." I paused. "Or maybe in this room. Yeah, let's go with that."

Thayer huffed a laugh, but she padded over to the side of the bed. I swung my legs over to sit facing her. Her eyes fell to the noticeable bulge tenting the white sheet covering my lap, mouth forming a tiny O. I gently grabbed her wrist, tugging her down to straddle my waist and gripping her perfect ass.

Her hair tumbled around us like a curtain, lips tipping into a grin. "Are you trying to seduce me again?"

"I should have told you not to expect much sleep."

Sun prodded at my eyes, urging me awake. I squinted and the room came into focus. But when I went to slide out of bed, the events of the night before came rushing back to me—along with the realization that Thayer was wrapped around my body, still sound asleep.

Pausing, I studied her features. Her dark eyelashes nearly dusted her cheeks, full lips formed in a subtle pout while she slept. It was hard to tear my eyes away from her, as creepy as that felt. I still didn't know what any of this meant, but I did know my usual strings-free approach wasn't going to work. Not with Thayer.

She let out a soft, sleepy groan, shifting against me. A wave of guilt washed over me, because I didn't want to disturb her. In fact, I would have much rather gone back to sleep with her and forgotten about life for awhile. But I had a shit ton of work to do.

That is, if I could get my brain to cooperate after a night of broken sleep. After going at it twice in a row, we'd crashed quickly, only to wake up in the wee hours of the morning for another round. Now it was just past nine, and almost comically, my body was ready for round four. Or one part was, anyway. The rest of me was sleep-deprived and desperate for caffeine and food.

I carefully eased out of bed and took a shower, making a point to move quietly around the bathroom as I did. Then I wrote her a quick note in case she woke up while I was gone, and headed downstairs for coffee, preferably in the form of a gigantic vat.

By the time I got back from the café downstairs with two extra-large coffees in hand, the bed was empty, and Thayer was in the shower, which allowed me the chance to boot up my laptop and try to make sense of the company's year-end. Something about the numbers still wasn't adding up, though.

I'd just pulled up the previous year when Thayer padded out of the bathroom and gave me a nervous smile, toweling off her hair. "Hi."

When our gazes locked, the mood instantly shifted. There it was again, the vulnerability that tended to rear its head unexpectedly. Only it was multiplied exponentially right now, and I think both of us sensed it.

"Hey." I pushed to stand, crossing the room to her. My hands landed around her waist, underneath her thin white tank top. For a heartbeat, neither of us spoke. It wasn't awkward, exactly, more like tentative.

Tilting my head, I leaned in to kiss her and she looped her arms around my neck, drawing me closer. I backed up a step, bringing her with me as I leaned against the dresser. "Last night…" I started, unsure of where I was going with the sentence.

Her face faltered, gaze cutting away from me. Tension shot through her body, and she stiffened beneath my hands. "It's just sex, right? Doesn't have to mean anything."

It was a figurative kick to the balls, but I was pretty sure it was coming from behind those goddamn ten-foot fortified walls she always tried to put up. As frustrating as it was, at least I could usually identify it by now.

"It meant something to me," I admitted. The five scariest words I'd ever uttered.

She studied me with her brows drawn together, uncertainty shining behind her pale blue eyes. "It did?"

"Of course." I wanted to say more, but I was completely in over my head. Moreover, she looked like she was a couple of wrong words away from fleeing the hotel room. Maybe less was better for now.

Thayer drew in a slow, deep breath, releasing it in an audible sigh. "Okay. Um, me too. I just…I don't know what any of it means?"

I didn't, either.

"Maybe we don't need to know. As long as we're on the same page." Whatever that was.

"Yeah." The tension she was holding eased, and she leaned into my chest, warmth of her body radiating against mine.

We stayed like that for a few moments, soaking in the closeness of each other. She smelled so good straight out of the shower that it almost drove me wild. No perfume was involved, so it must have been pheromones.

"But on a totally unrelated note," I said, reluctant to ruin the moment but desperate enough to ask. "Can you help me with something before we go?"

Almost an hour later, and long overdue for brunch, Thayer and I were still camped out at the kitchen table in our hotel room. She was now privy to the good, the bad, and the ugly inner workings of Flux's financial statements. Letting her see the mess of my professional life meant my ego had taken a beating in the process, but at least it was out in the open. It felt slightly liberating. I just hoped she wasn't about to run for the hills—or be completely turned off.

She scrunched up her mouth, staring at the screen for a beat, then her gaze slid over to me. "Adam really screwed you, huh?" There was a heavy undertone of anger in her voice.

"Is it that obvious?" Then again, Thayer wasn't one to miss details.

"You must be so stressed out." Her tone softened and she placed her cool hand on my bare knee in a way that was meant to be comforting but had a slightly different effect. "Little bit." We both knew that was a drastic understatement. "Hopefully, this is the home stretch before I lock down Callaghan and Flux has some operating capital again."

"Speaking of operating capital, I did notice…" She removed her tortoiseshell glasses and pinched the bridge of her nose, hesitating like she wanted to say something but was afraid to.

I leaned over the table, trying to see what she'd been looking at specifically. "What?" "This numbered company here." Her perfectly manicured fingernail rapped the laptop screen. "Don't you think the transactions associated with it look strange?" She scrolled with the mouse, tracing a pattern with her other hand.

"I had, but they weren't for large amounts of money, so I'd filed it under 'I have bigger problems' and had promptly forgotten about it."

"But did you also notice…" Thayer frowned. "They stop when Adam left the company."

CHAPTER THIRTY-ONE

Thayer

DUE TO A MISCOMMUNICATION—OR POSSIBLY MISPRONUNCI-ation on our part—with a cab driver, Bennett and I ended up three blocks from our destination in downtown Playa del Carmen, where we were due to meet Quinn and the rest of the group for brunch. Fortunately, or unfortunately, they'd been running late too, which meant we would still be subjected to a full-length meal with Adam, Millie, and Louis

Late morning sun blasted down on my shoulders, almost unbearably hot even in my gauzy white sundress. The streets around us bustled with action; cars blaring their horns, pedestrians risking their lives by darting out in front of them, and street vendors shouting to be heard over it all. But the chaos around us paled in comparison to the turmoil of thoughts, emotions, and questions inside my head. Our dynamic was mired with tension and uncertainty. More intimate in a way, but distant in another.

Complicating matters was the fact that part of Bennett's mind was somewhere else—understandably so. He was notoriously impulsive, verging on hot-headed with the right provocation. He'd always been that way, from the time he told off a teacher in the fifth grade, to the time he punched a guy in the face for groping me without permission at a party sophomore year.

I wasn't sure how I had expected him to react to the revelation that Adam had been siphoning funds from their company, but I definitely hadn't expected a total non-reaction. An eerie veneer of calm had settled over him, and he'd stared at the screen blankly for a good minute or two. Finally, he'd frowned and said he'd take care of it when he got back home. I didn't know what 'take care of it' meant. Judging by the homicidal look on his face now, I was a little afraid to find out.

A drunken tourist stumbled in our direction, his gait unsteady and sweaty face flushed. Bennett's broad hand wrapped around my lower hip, pulling me out of his path. He let his fingers slide lower, nearly brushing my backside with each step I took.

"You're taking some liberties with the hand placement there," I said teasingly, trying to lighten the mood.

His jaw ticked, cords in his neck tensing beneath the collar of his white linen shirt. "It's either keep my hands occupied or have them end up around Adam's throat when I see him."

Guilt settled in the pit of my stomach. The wound was so fresh it was still oozing blood, and now Bennett was about to sit through a meal with his assailant because of me.

I stole another glance at him, but he didn't meet my gaze. "I'm sorry."

"For what? All you did was show me what was right in front of my face." Bennett scrubbed his free hand across his stubbled jawline. "On some level, I think already knew. Maybe I just didn't want to see it. Didn't want to believe…" He huffed a sound of disgust, his gaze fixed ahead.

"That he'd do that to you?" I finished. "That's understandable. No one wants to think the worst like that, even when it comes to someone like him."

Adam looking out for his best interests wasn't exactly news, but even I hadn't expected him to stoop to theft. He'd been clever about it, too; taking small amounts frequently over a long period of time, carefully disguising them to look like vendor payments. Each transaction was small enough not to draw notice or cause alarm, but the total amount added up to be enough to damage the company's bottom line.

Bennett shook his head. "No. That I missed it back then. That's on me."

"You trusted your business partner like anyone would, and he took advantage of that. He's the one in the wrong."

"And I'm the sucker."

I wanted to argue that point, but I could tell Bennett's mind was set. He needed more time to process what had happened and pushing it wouldn't help. Neither would suffering through a meal with the entire bridal party, including the white-collar criminal himself, but Bennett had insisted we keep our plans to meet them for brunch. He didn't want to cause suspicion on any level, whether it was casting doubt on our own relationship status or letting Adam know he was on to him.

Good thing we were experienced in pretending. Which brought me to another issue: our very-much-not-pretend night filled with earth-shattering sex—and the fact that I wanted it to happen again.

I felt like I belonged in a billboard for a drug PSA that read, "One time can get you hooked." Like an addiction in the making, one that I already didn't want to quit.

A group of pedestrians began to cross, and we stepped off the curb along with them, weaving through the crowd. Finally, we made our way onto fifth avenue, the main tourist hub of the area, and the restaurant came into view one block over.

"I don't think Adam likes seeing us together," Bennett mused, almost as if to himself instead of me.

"Well, he probably finds it awkward being around you after what he did."

"Adam isn't self-aware enough for that," he said. "He's jealous. It's obvious."

"What?" I scoffed. "That's crazy."

A glimmer of amusement pierced the clouds of Bennett's stormy expression. "You mean you haven't noticed? C'mon, Thay."

I knew better than anyone that Adam had a jealous, possessive side to his personality. When we were together, he constantly accused me of flirting, when I wasn't, and then I would catch him doing that very thing. Projection, I supposed. That was one reason, among many, I didn't like him with Quinn—not envy, like everyone else had seemed to think.

What I didn't know was whether Adam was the same way with Quinn as he'd been with me or if he'd evolved past his Neanderthal mentality since then. I hadn't asked. I wasn't sure I wanted to know the answer. Either it meant my sister was also being treated poorly, or I was uniquely deserving of such treatment. Neither answer was comforting.

And this discussion was an unpleasant reminder of my biggest mistake of all: foolishly falling into bed with Adam several months ago. But how was I to know Adam would turn around and embark on a whirlwind courtship with my sister, propose almost instantly, and push for a quick wedding? Prickly heat crept up my chest, and I swallowed, trying to push it back down.

I zoned back into my conversation with Bennett. "As a general rule," I said, "I try to ignore Adam as much as possible."

"Always a solid policy," he muttered.

We stepped up to the glass double doors of the restaurant, framed by two enormous potted plants. Instead of opening the door for me, Bennett pivoted to face me, both hands grabbing hold of my waist. Whatever was on his mind moments ago had clearly been pushed aside, because the look he was giving me now was nothing short of sinful.

"Just so we're clear…" His grip tightened on me, and he leaned closer, lips brushing the shell of my ear before he continued, "you're mine later."

I blinked slowly, a shiver of pleasure running down my spine. The instantaneous effect he had on my body was more than a little unsettling. He was able to bypass the warmup stage entirely, taking me from zero to sixty with a simple touch or a heated gaze.

"Is that a promise?"

His mouth tugged into a lopsided smile that made me so unsteady, it was like the pavement beneath my feet had turned to a trampoline. "It's an order."

He released his hold on me and pulled open the door, placing a hand along my lower back to usher me through first. My fingers raked through my hair, suddenly self-conscious, but it had nothing to do with how I looked and everything to do with how I felt.

When I lost my virginity senior year, I spent the following days convinced that somehow, 'I had sex' was written all over my face, and with a simple look, my mother would be able to tell.

I was wrong, of course, but just like back then, I couldn't shake the feeling that the message 'I had sex last night' was written plastered across my face like a billboard. Or in this case, 'freaky hot sex.' The hickey Bennett left on my neck didn't exactly help, either; concealer only covered so much. I didn't know why I felt self-conscious about it in the first place, considering everyone else thought that was what we'd been doing all along.

If I was being honest, deep down I knew it was less about feeling exposed to everyone else and more about feeling exposed to Bennett—in every sense of the word.

Because the universe was conspiring against me, Bennett and I ended up seated at the end of the long rectangular table, down by Adam and Quinn. Service at the restaurant was unbearably slow, verging on nonexistent, but the drinks were strong and that made it marginally more bearable.

By the time our food finally arrived, two margaritas later, Quinn was in the midst of a heated debate with Millie regarding the merits of tall versus short table centerpieces. Quinn was firmly on team tall, while Millie was arguing the benefits of short. It was about as interesting as it sounded. Bennett had given up on hopes of our server returning and sobriety was not an option.

"Does anyone else need anything?" He pushed back his chair to stand and surveyed the table, questioning. His eyes landed on Quinn's empty water glass. "Quinn, do you need a drink? Want what Thay's having?"

Something flashed across her face. "Er… thanks, but no. I had too many last night."

Obviously, I could tell when Quinn was lying just by looking at her. But I didn't need to, because I was with her last night and she was as sober as a nun. I thought she'd been drinking, but maybe her rum and Diet Cokes had just been Diet Coke. An inkling of suspicion crept into my mind, bleeding into the rest of my thoughts. Why wasn't she drinking? Was there a chance she could be pregnant after all? She did say they were trying.

Bennett ventured over to the bar for our refills. Quinn avoided my prying stare and resumed her conversation with Millie, leaving me alone with Adam.

"So, Thayer." Adam rested an ankle on his knees, eyes glinting darkly. "Bennett, huh?"

"What about him?" I asked blandly, watching Bennett lean over the counter to order and praying the bartender would make it snappy.

Adam glanced over at Quinn, who was gesturing animatedly to Millie. Emboldened by the fact that no one else was listening, he leaned closer. "It's an unexpected pairing, you have to admit."

Anger started to simmer in my gut, rapidly heating to a low boil. For some reason—maybe he'd taken up recreational drugs or was nursing a recent head injury—Adam seemed to think this was his business. Even four years later, while engaged to someone else.

Our slip up a few months ago certainly didn't give him any excuse to be territorial, especially not when he was engaged to someone else almost instantly afterward. Not just anyone else, either. My sister. I wanted to grab her left hand and slap him in the face with it, ring side first.

When I didn't reply, Adam pressed, "Quite the odd couple, don't you think?"

Bennett strolled back to the table, our drinks in hand. He set down my lime margarita gently and then slammed his own tumbler down with a bang, pulling out his seat and sliding in beside me. Clearly, he'd overheard some of the exchange, because an air of menace radiated from him. I didn't need to look to know he was shooting daggers at Adam with his eyes.

"Well, you know what they say." I smiled brightly, putting my hand on Bennett's knee so he wouldn't kick Adam under the table. "Opposites attract."

Adam's eyes snapped over to Bennett. "Or implode."

In my peripheral vision, Bennett's nostrils flared. But instead of firing back, he rolled his shoulders and slung his arm around the back of my chair, gently rubbing my upper arm with his hand. The possessive-slash-protective vibe did something to me on a primal level that definitely wasn't helping me keep the 'just had sex' look off my face.

"Oh, I don't know about that. I think we'll go the distance, don't you, Thay?" Leaning closer, he kissed the top of my head. It was unexpected, and kind of nice. "Turns out, she's always had a little thing for yours truly."

Well, that part wasn't so nice. Why make me out to be a lovestruck stalker in this situation? Egotistical bastard.

"Really." Adam stabbed his enchilada, sawing it viciously with his serrated knife.

"It's true." I suppressed a nervous laugh, prompted by a mixture of irritation, low-grade panic, and Bennett's effect on my brain. Hopefully, everyone would assume I was giddy with infatuation.

"She's carried a torch for me since the third grade," Bennett added.

I nearly choked on my mouthful of lime margarita. In his dreams, but I couldn't say that out loud. Instead, I was forced to offer some kind of substantiating information on the fly.

"He gave me the biggest valentine in the class. It said, You're Turtle-y Awesome. That was it," I said. "I was a goner."

Adam blinked in disbelief, voice dripping with disdain. "That was it?" He couldn't be bothered to celebrate Valentine's Day as an adult, let alone as a child.

"Why is this the first time I'm hearing this?" Quinn squealed, leaning over the table. Her glossy pink lips tugged into a puppy dog pout. "That's freaking adorable."

Bennett looked thoughtful for a moment, an easy smile forming on his lips. "Oh yeah. I remember giving you that. You gave me a big pink heart. It might even still be at my parents' place."

Telltale warmth laced my cheeks, and I took three gulps of ice water while fighting the urge to crawl under the table. I turned my attention to my plate of fish tacos, pretending to be ravenous.

Instead of inventing a made-up story—like a normal person would, to support their made-up relationship—I'd gone and used a real memory. One that Bennett remembered, too. With his enormous ego, he'd think that I had secretly been in love with him our entire lives.

That was absolutely not the case. At least, I didn't think it was. I was pretty sure it wasn't. Mostly.

We would never speak of the turtle valentine again. Hell, we'd never mention Valentine's Day again, either. Or turtles. Or hearts. Or stationary. Maybe forget holidays altogether and pretend they didn't exist, for good measure.

After another hour of stilted chatter, I literally flagged down the server and requested the bill, adding her a telepathic 'PS' that I'd tip triple if she made it quick.

Quinn had moved down to sit with her other friends. Louis seized the opportunity to slide into Quinn's vacant seat, using his job as a commercial realtor as a conversation starter—even though I wasn't in the market for additional commercial space. And Millie was pretending to reminisce about the good old days while attempting to flirt with Bennett. Bennett was about as receptive as a piece of cardboard.

"Speaking of old times," Millie said, her thin lips forming a sly smile. "Do you remember senior prom?"

"Not really," Bennett said, biting into a leftover tortilla chip with obvious disinterest.

"Oh, come on," she insisted. "When everyone in our group danced to that song by the Silver Devils…"

I tuned her out, my attention back to Louis. "We should go for coffee next time I'm in that part of town," he finished saying.

"Did you not see the ring," Bennett interrupted dryly, leaning closer and gesturing to my left hand, "or do you just not care?"

Louis opened his mouth to respond. Like an angel sent from above, our server materialized out of thin air with the bill at that very moment—apparently motivated to be prompt now that payment was due.

Adam placed one finger on the black leather folio, making a show of sliding it across the table over to the two of us. "Your turn to treat, cuz."

Bennett's gaze swung in Adam's direction, and he cocked a brow. "Pardon me?"

"We're taking turns this weekend. Louis got the drinks at the club. You're up." Adam nodded to the bill. A thinly veiled dare lay beneath his words.

"Right," Bennett said. There was a split-second of hesitation before he pulled out his Visa, sliding it to the waitress. Then I caught sight of the bill, and my body tensed like a steel trap. We'd racked up a sum in the four digits. My intuition was rarely wrong, and I had a bad feeling about this. From Bennett's stiff posture, I could tell he did, too.

Moments later, the server returned with an apologetic look on her face. "I'm sorry, sir. There is an… uh, issue with your card." She handed the piece of plastic back to Bennett, who clearly didn't have any idea what to do. Adam watched, hawk-like, and my instincts kicked in. I snatched the card out of Bennett's hands before he could react, glancing down briefly and feigning recognition.

"Honey." I swatted him on the arm. "I told you that credit card was about to expire three weeks ago. Remember?"

Confusion flickered across his face, vanishing as quickly as it had appeared. "Oh shit," he said. "That's right, you did."

Reaching into my purse, I pulled out my wallet, quickly selecting a credit card at random and handing it to the server. "Put it on my card, please." I turned back to the rest of the table and rolled my eyes. "I swear, this man works too much for his own good."

Bennett laughed easily, slipping back into his usual unflappable facade. "I guess it's a good thing I have you." He reached down, gently squeezing my thigh. Butterfly wings fluttered against my ribcage, and the combination of his touch and those words had a much bigger effect on me than I knew they should.

CHAPTER THIRTY-TWO

Thayer

THE MINUTE WE STEPPED OUT OF THE RESTAURANT, AN EAR-splitting crack of thunder echoed, and the sky opened up, drenching the streets like a bucket of water turned upside down. I told Bennett it was a bad omen; he laughed and waved me off, blaming it on the tail end of hurricane season—but he didn't know what I knew.

Torrential rain poured down as our cab sped back to the resort, traveling down the highway at an alarming speed given the poor road conditions. Quinn and the rest of the girls had stayed behind to shop, but I begged off due to a lack of sleep that had left me dizzy with fatigue. After an afternoon nap, I was going to meet them in Quinn's room for drinks... not that she was drinking. Why wasn't she drinking?

Bennett's deep voice jolted me back to reality, interrupting my train of thought just as it started to go off the rails. "Are you upset about having to cover the bill?"

"What?" I croaked, turning away from the window to face him. His tanned arm was slung around my shoulders, tucking me into him like two pieces of a puzzle, but even the comforting weight of his body wrapped around mine wasn't enough to stop the spin cycle in my brain. "No, not at all."

"Are you sure? I'll pay you back once I move some money around." He regarded me with a mixture of concern and apprehension—the subtext being, he thought I actually cared about his credit card balance. I'd have been offended, had I possessed the adequate mental bandwidth.

"I promise, Bennett. It isn't that. It's just…" My throat snapped shut like a vise, cutting off the words. I drew in a gulp of air, but it felt like all the oxygen had been sucked out of the vehicle. Bennett's frown deepened as he watched me, waiting for me to finish the sentence. "I noticed that Quinn wasn't drinking," I explained.

"So?" He shrugged, pulling me closer. I nestled against his shirt and turned my face toward him slightly, inhaling the heavenly scent of rain mixed with his cologne. "She's probably hungover."

If only that was the reason. I rubbed the band of my engagement ring with the pad of my thumb, caressing the smooth polished metal. It was nervous habit I'd picked up at some point on this bizarre journey—a habit I would have to break eventually, which was just another bullet point on my itemized list of problems.

The cab pulled through the wrought iron gates leading to the resort complex, slowly winding along the driveway lined with manicured bushes and colorful arrays of tropical flowers.

"Still want to take a nap when we get back?" Bennett's other hand slid from my knee, up to my bare thigh, and his long fingers toyed with the lace-trimmed hem of my sundress. A flicker of desire sparked my core, stoking with every small movement he made, but I made an effort to keep my face impassive.

"Why, what did you have in mind?"

He reached up and tugged affectionately at the damp ends of my hair. Ducking his head, he lowered his voice to a velvety hush. "Since we're already wet, we should put that shower bench to good use."

"We'll see." It was a lie; I didn't even know what he meant, and I still wanted it.

The remainder of the trip flew by in a lust-filled, hormone-fueled blur. I was flying so high that Millie and Adam's presence barely even fazed me. Before I knew it, we'd arrived back home—but everything had changed.

After two more days of very little sleep, lots of sex, and rapidly growing feelings, I was deeper in than I'd ever been before and even less eager to broach the 'what are we doing' subject. Sure, Bennett had whispered sweet nothings in my ear in and out of the bedroom all weekend long, but I still didn't know what any of it meant, and I was fairly certain I was headed for heartache. His track record spoke for itself.

Despite that, the weak part of me was content to enjoy this state of ignorant bliss while it lasted. And by weak part, I meant the part between my legs. Okay, fine. It wasn't fair to blame it on that. My stupid, traitorous heart was the one driving the bus—and my heart was drunk on him. That was what made it so scary.

Bennett walked me to my front door, and we lingered outside, engaging in the longest goodbye in the history of humankind while I prayed none of my neighbors would walk by and see us making out like teenagers in the hall.

His fingers raked through his hair, cocky post-kiss grin turning sheepish. "I wish I could see you sooner, Thay, but I'm going to be swamped all week. I have to head straight into the office from here to catch up on work. Plus, with what you found…" His smile faded, and his lips pulled into a terse frown. "I have to do some more digging, and I have to do it myself. I can't risk letting a forensic auditor poke around in the books. For several reasons."

"It's okay," I said, only half-meaning it. "It's only a couple of days, and I have a ton to catch up on, too."

Not only did I need to prepare for our grand opening of our third location three months from now, but I also needed to find a way to talk to Quinn about Adam and our father's investment in his company. I had to find an approach that would minimize the fallout. Only, I was fairly certain there wasn't one. It was going to be a disaster.

The rational part of me also knew some time apart from Bennett would be good. It might give me a chance to catch my breath, clear my head. Maybe I could consider it a detox period, like an addict going cold turkey. Except I'd be right back at square one this Friday, when we were supposed to have dinner at Bennett's place to strategize before seeing Callaghan for dinner the following evening. I was pretty sure "strategize" was code for something else, especially since we didn't exactly need to plan or practice the relationship side of things lately. That was coming all too naturally.

Bennett walked me a few steps back until I was pressed up against my front door, leveling me with another scorching kiss before slowly, reluctantly pulling away. With every other man I'd been involved with, I was eager—verging on desperate—for a break after a single night of shared sleeping accommodations. But right now, I felt a different sort of desperation entirely, because I didn't want him to leave.

"I should go," he murmured, brushing his lips against mine.

"Okay."

He groaned, tightening his grip on my waist. "But I don't want to."

I laughed. "I'll see you in three days."

CHAPTER THIRTY-THREE

Thayer

ETWEEN WAKING UP TO A GOOD MORNING TEXT FROM Bennett and attending a seven AM spin class with Lola, my Friday morning got off to a strong start. Then it promptly crashed and burned when, one hour before the store's opening, I inadvertently started a war with Quinn in the midst of our weekly inventory replenishment. TGIF, indeed.

"Of course, I knew." Quinn squared her shoulders and jutted her chin, a mirror image of our mother's 'I've never been wrong in my life' stance—her fighting stance. She was fury in a fuchsia shift dress.

I set down a box of satin nightgowns, dusting off my hands. "You knew that our father gave your fiancé five million dollars?"

On the second last night of our trip, I'd confessed to Bennett that I was worried Quinn was pregnant. In turn, he'd informed me that Adam's big fish investor was none other than my beloved father. This triggered a full-blown panic attack, where I became convinced that I was literally dying, complete with hyperventilation and tunnel vision in the middle of the beach. Bennett spent half an hour patiently talking me down.

Once I was off the ledge, I'd vowed to talk to Quinn about it in a calm, non-threatening manner upon our return home. Or vowed that I would try to, anyway, because Quinn perceived all forms of confrontation as threatening and was terrible at staying calm. Case in point: this entire conversation.

Quinn flounced over to the other side of the room and examined the boxes of new inventory, making a point to avoid my prying gaze. "Daddy didn't give it to Adam." She sliced open a box, voice taking on a shrill edge over the ripping sound. "He invested it with him."

"And you knew but didn't tell me."

Her posture deflated slightly, and she paused, mid-cut. "I didn't know it was a done deal, but I knew they were talking. I was the one who suggested it."

My stomach lurched, disbelief mingling with a faint sense of anger that I knew wasn't fully justified but couldn't seem to quell. At this point, I was confident Adam's intentions with my sister weren't good, but it was even more frustrating to see Quinn do his dirty work for him.

"Why?" My tone came out harsher than I'd intended. Unfortunately, when it came to my sister, it was the execution that mattered and not the intent.

She glanced up from the handful of pink and purple Hanky Panky thongs she was sorting, raising a slender eyebrow. "Because I love him? You'd do the same thing for Bennett in a heartbeat."

Would I? I honestly didn't know.

"This is a bad idea, Quinn. What if the investment goes south?"

"We're all adults," she said. "Daddy knows investments carry risk."

"But don't you think there is a chance that Adam's..." *Using you.*

Instead of finishing my sentence, I seized the mug of lukewarm coffee on my desk, draining it to stop myself from saying something I'd regret. The only way to get through to her was the indirect route. I had to provide enough evidence for her to see the truth for herself. Difficult when she was determined to squeeze her eyes shut to avoid it.

Quinn's tone was laced with acid. "What? What is Adam doing?"

"Why haven't you been drinking?" I asked, spinning around to face her, still clutching the empty mug. "Are you pregnant?"

The question I had been agonizing over for the past week hung in the air. I'd been watching her like a hawk, but I couldn't tell. She was still drinking copious amounts of coffee, still working out like a maniac, and she'd eaten raw sushi for lunch yesterday.

Quinn stiffened, posture turning ramrod straight. "No. At least, not yet. But I'm trying to be as healthy as possible just in case."

"Quinn." I shook my head, half-wishing I could shake some sense into her. "Don't you think you're rushing things?"

Not to mention, she was still teetering on being worryingly thin. I was by no means a fertility expert, but I suspected a few extra pounds would probably help. Then again, her getting pregnant wasn't exactly the best idea in the first place. I was sure Adam was playing the long game with her, and I didn't want her to be tied to him permanently when things fell apart.

"Not all of us have the luxury of time," she snapped. "And some of us actually want a family."

Resentment coated her words, the implication clear. On some level, I understood where she was coming from. It wasn't fair; health impacts aside, the loss of fertility wouldn't cut me nearly as deeply as it did her. At best, I was on the fence about having children, leaning heavily toward not.

"I just want to make sure you don't get hurt," I said.

"I'm perfectly fine."

"But—" the syllables formed a traffic jam in my throat.

"I'm fine," Quinn repeated. She made a show of turning to look at the clock on the wall. "It's almost ten. I have to go refresh the displays up front before customers start to arrive." Box in hand, she barreled by me and let the office door slam behind her, leaving me holding the words I should have said.

Two hours later, Quinn and I had reached a frosty truce, forced to interact for the sake of maintaining a functional company. Hostility lurked beneath our civil words, and I remained tucked away in the back office, occupying myself with sales and expense reports in order to avoid further interaction.

Beside the keyboard, my phone lit up.

Lola: Are we still on for brunch tomorrow?

Thayer: Always. Can't wait.

Lola: And you're going to give me the scoop about your trip, right?

Lola: RIGHT?

Thayer: Of course.

Lola knew me well enough to know something was definitely up. I hadn't gotten into details with her over text, because frankly, it felt weird to. Spilling about what happened with Bennett would be hard enough in person. I wasn't the type to dish about what I did in the bedroom. Or the shower. Or the kitchenette.

Over the security intercom, the entry chime sounded, and a muffled male voice greeted Quinn. It was impossible to discern his identity through the solid wood office door, but I had a strong hunch it was Adam. My grip on the wireless mouse tightened, and I returned my attention to the spreadsheet in front of me, adjusting the budget for our grand opening to reflect the catering quote. Six hours to go before I could leave this problem with Quinn behind— throwing myself headfirst into another.

Lola: Just give me a little teaser. On a scale of 1 to Sex God, how was it?

Thayer: We're going to need some mimosas for this conversation.

Lola: Sex God it is. I knew it. Love this for you.

I bit my inner cheek, stuffing down the sordid flashbacks that had started to swirl inside my brain. Before I could compose a reply, the office door swung open, revealing none other than Mr. Sex God himself.

My phone slipped out of my fingers, landing on the floor with a clatter.

"Bennett," I said, a little too brightly. "Hi."

He sauntered into the room holding a red holiday-themed Starbucks cup in one hand and closed the door behind him with the air of someone who owned the place. Leaning forward, I kept my gaze fixed to him while I fished around for my phone underneath the desk. For someone who'd reportedly had a rough week according to our frequent texts, he didn't look like it. His navy suit was immaculate, dark hair freshly trimmed, and his presence was as disarming as ever.

Our eyes locked, and I almost dropped my phone again.

"Did I interrupt something?" Bennett nodded at my hand.

"No, I—" Glancing down, I locked my screen to conceal Lola's text thread. The last thing I needed was Bennett seeing that sex god confirmation, though it's not like he didn't know already. It was obvious from the way my body reacted to his touch. And his tongue. And, well, his other body parts.

I pushed my rolling desk chair back and stood up, smoothing my charcoal grey shift dress. Had I known he was coming, I would have at least retouched my makeup. Why did I feel so self-conscious? He'd already seen me naked in more ways than one.

"Is everything okay?" I asked.

"Everything's fine. Can't I bring you a coffee?" His mouth tugged in a way that told me his impromptu visit had zero to do with the hot beverage in his hand.

My heart strummed in my chest. "Is that why you're here?"

"Fuck no." Bennett abandoned the cardboard cup on the corner of my desk, stepping around it to stand in front of me. His large hands wrapped around mine, thumbs stroking the backs of my hands. "I missed you."

"Careful, or I might start to think you like me."

His expression sobered, and he released my hands, pulling me closer. "I more than like you."

My brain didn't know how to react to that. It didn't have much time to try, because his lips claimed mine, and my ability to think completely vanished. He drew in a breath, pushing deeper into my mouth, and my fingers sank into his hair, tugging and mussing the perfect waves. His mint-tinted tongue brushed against mine again, and the kiss turned all-consuming.

In a flash, he shrugged out of his suit jacket, abandoning it on the desk chair beside us. His fingers slid past my hips and landed on my bare thighs, slowly inching my dress higher. I began to fall under his spell, until the possibility of imminent nudity in the middle of my office brought me back to reality.

"There's a security camera in here." I pointed behind him to the glossy dome embedded in the ceiling.

Bennett didn't even turn to look. "So?" His gaze stayed pinned to me, heated and predatory, eliciting a throb of desire between my thighs.

"You might be into exhibitionism, but I don't want to give the monitoring center at United Security an eyeful."

He surveyed the office methodically, and his eyes landed on the open door to the powder room. Roguishness dawned across his face. "There's no camera in there."

"True, but—" Before I could finish saying, 'Quinn is right in the other room,' Bennett was already steering me through the doorway. He flipped on the lights on his way past and locked the handle, securing us in the sky-blue painted powder room under soft white fluorescent lighting. I was sure I'd think back on this encounter every time I came in here, which was probably one of his goals.

"What about my coffee?" I teased.

He reached down and rolled his shirt sleeves up, exposing his forearms. "Looks like you'll be drinking it cold."

Bennett nudged my thighs apart with his knee, hiking up my dress. My teeth sank into my bottom lip, cheeks heating. His expression darkened and his muscular thigh pressed between my legs, pinning me against the sink. When he dug in again, my pelvis swayed in response to the blissful sensation it created, greedily seeking more.

He cradled the back of my head, and our mouths came together again, but this time his lips moved gently against mine, questioning. I kissed him back, and he gripped me tighter, the possessiveness of his hold on me demolishing the last of my objections. Doing this was utterly insane, but I didn't care.

His hands smoothed up my back, tugging the zipper to my dress down. It split open and pooled around my feet, leaving me in nothing but a lace-trimmed burgundy bra, matching thong underwear, and my black pumps. A chill settled across my skin and anticipation grew between my thighs.

Bennett spun me around and planted my hands on the edge of the porcelain sink, meeting my gaze in the mirror with a wicked grin.

"Look at you," he said. "You're fucking flawless."

I watched in the reflection as his broad hand slid up my ribcage, cupping my breast and squeezing. His other hand trailed down my stomach, past the waistband of my underwear, dipping between my legs where I was already heated and aching for him. My hips swiveled against his hand, and I sucked in a breath. Bennett let out a low groan, hard length pressing into me from behind.

"You're so wet." His lips clamped onto the junction between my shoulder and my neck, sucking hard enough that I was certain he'd leave behind a mark. He released the skin, bringing his lips to the shell of my ear. "Can I fuck you in here?"

"Y-yes." Pleasure rippled through my core again.

A deep chuckle reverberated in his chest. "Knew you had a naughty side."

My breath hitched as Bennett hooked his thumbs around the

waistband of my lace thong, tugging it all the way down. He kneeled to help me step out of it, carefully lifting my feet one at a time so I didn't trip in my heels. The tenderness to his actions was a sharp contrast to his dirty talk just moments ago.

He smoothed his hands up my body and his teeth gently sank into the curve of my behind. I startled and he laughed softly, standing back up. His lips landed on my bare shoulder to claim the same spot as before, and heat unfurled between my legs. I leaned against him, wrapping my hand around his neck to pull him closer.

He removed his hands from my body, leaving my skin cold in their wake, and my heart skittered in anticipation. I couldn't see what he was doing in the mirror, but I could hear his belt clanging, followed by the rip of the foil wrapper. He grabbed my hips and yanked me closer, nudging up against my entrance, and we both let out a breathy moan as he plunged inside of me.

Overwhelming pleasure of him filling me mingled with intense relief, like three days apart had been three years. His sculpted forearm wrapped around my stomach, protecting me from the square edge of the sink while he rubbed my clit with each thrust. Ecstasy echoed through my body, every thrust perfectly timed with the movement of his skilled fingers.

The front door chimed, alerting us to someone entering the store. I stiffened and the spell broke, taking my looming orgasm with it. While Quinn was up front to handle any customers or deliveries, that didn't change the fact that I was locked in the bathroom, getting railed at ten o'clock in the morning.

Super professional.

Bennett slowed his rhythm, sensing my unease. He pushed my hair aside and pressed a gentle kiss below my ear. "Don't worry, Thay. We can be quiet."

His fingertips circled my swollen bud of nerves, flooding my core with another wave of bliss. Some of my misgivings faded into the background and I leaned against him, beginning to relax. He tilted his hips, resuming a faster pace that rendered me dizzy with pleasure. A breathy moan escaped my lips, echoing off the walls, and I tensed again.

"I can't"—I gasped as he slammed into me, bringing me dangerously close to the edge—"be quiet."

He clamped his warm, rough palm over my mouth, and my eyes widened, surprise flickering through me. With anyone else, I would have balked, but with Bennett, it was unexpectedly reassuring. His grip was gentle yet secure, dominant in a way that made me feel safe giving up control.

His warm breath grazed my cheek. "Tap my hand twice if you want me to stop, okay?"

I nodded, making a smothered sound of agreement. He slowly pulled back and sank inside me, deeper than before. My eyes rolled back, and I let out a desperate whimper, thankful for the sound barrier.

With each wave of movement, he hit places I hadn't even known existed, bringing me to new heights of pleasure I hadn't thought possible. As I approached the point of no return, an overwhelming wave of emotion and sensation hit me all at once, and my eyes clenched shut.

"Eyes on me, beautiful." Bennett nipped at my neck, his teeth sinking in just hard enough to sting.

Our gazes met in the mirror while he continued to claim my body mercilessly. He held me in place, watching me arch against him. I'd never let someone else have so much power over me before, sexually or otherwise, but something about it was incredibly arousing.

He slammed into me again, earning a muffled cry against his palm as I teetered right on the edge.

"You're close, aren't you?" His voice husky, rich like coffee and twice as addictive.

I silently pleaded with his reflection for release. "Mmhmm."

He removed his hand from my mouth and bracketed my jaw, turning my face to his and clamping his lips over mine. With his next thrust, his rough kiss captured my needy sounds, and he let out a rumble of appreciation. I surrendered to the sensation building in my core, letting him take me over the brink. Reality vanished, and with a desperate cry, I fell into him, trembling as swells of pleasure wracked my entire body.

I was just starting to float back to reality when, with a few more thrusts, Bennett's body tensed, and he stiffened, letting out a low groan. He stilled, and his arms slid around my waist, wrapping me in a reverse bear hug. I nestled against him, feeling the steady rise and fall of his chest. Even with the mind-melting orgasm he'd just given me, the way he was holding me was ten times more euphoric.

"Fuck." The word was a satisfied sigh across his lips. He rested his cheek against mine. "Thay…"

Unsure how to respond, I waited for him to finish, but he didn't. Silence enveloped us while his heartbeat drummed against my back like it was tapping out a message in Morse code. I closed my eyes, wondering what his heart was saying; wondering if it matched mine.

With a heavy exhale, his breaths turned more regular, and his heartbeat slowed, but his hold on me didn't falter. He nuzzled my neck, planting a soft kiss on my collarbone. "We should have coffee breaks together more often."

My eyes fluttered back open to find him looking at me in the mirror with a mixture of affection and playfulness.

"Maybe I should come to you next time," I said. "Create a scene at your workplace for a change."

"Please do." A low growl rumbled in the base of his throat. "I'll park your ass on my desk, spread your legs, and call it a business lunch."

Bennett squeezed me and kissed my cheek before pulling out and disposing of the condom, leaving me alone. Another glance in the mirror confirmed I was still pink-cheeked and clearly post-coital. I got dressed and tried to perform damage control on my hair and makeup, with little success.

I reopened the bathroom door to find him tugging down his

shirt sleeves, refastening the cuffs. He glanced up at me, dark hair tumbling over his forehead.

"You're still coming over later, right?" He ran a hand through his messy locks, effortlessly smoothing them back into place. Unlike him, I was still sporting undeniable sex hair. Without a curling iron or brush, I could only do so much.

"You want me to?" Suddenly feeling uncertain, I stepped closer and came to stand in front of him.

"Of course." His fingers circled my wrist, and he tugged gently, pulling me into him. He wrapped his arms around me, tracing his nose along my cheek. A tiny thrill ran down my spine. "And you're staying over, right?"

"Right," I said, still breathless. We hadn't discussed that part when we'd made plans. But while I was basking in the post-orgasm glow, riding an oxytocin high, it sounded perfect.

"Good." Bennett leaned his forehead against mine for a beat before pulling back, brushing his lips along my temple. Then he nodded to my desk, where a stray MBA program brochure lay on the counter. More evidence I wasn't thinking clearly when he stopped by, or else I would have hidden it when I saw him. "Are you thinking of going back to school, Thay?"

I gave a small shrug. "Maybe."

With Adam's recent reappearance in my life, it was harder than ever to ignore the fact that I'd graduated college nearly five years ago and still hadn't executed the biggest item on my five-year-plan. Not to mention, I was concerned about the future of Lace & Grace. If Quinn bailed on me to become a stay-at-home-mother, I didn't think I could manage the business alone.

Yet for some reason, I felt guilty at the prospect of deserting her—even though that had been our plan all along.

"If you want to do it, you should go for it," he said softly. His dark blue eyes searched mt face, gleaming with tenderness. "Don't let Quinn stop you."

"Still thinking about it." Working up the courage, more like.

He nodded like he knew not to push and gave me another quick kiss on the lips before releasing me. "See you tonight."

Bennett strolled out looking the same way he did when he walked in. Calm, composed, and completely put together. Not a single hair out of place.

I looked…well, like I'd just been bent over a sink.

For the rest of the morning, I caught myself zoning out and thinking about Bennett when I should have been focusing on work. It was becoming a serious issue. I'd never made so many errors in Excel in my entire life. This infatuation I was harboring was legitimately like being on drugs. Or at least, what I assumed doing drugs would be like, having zero firsthand experience.

"Earth to Thayer." My sister tapped the desk with a petal-pink fingernail, but her tone was gentle. Her mood swings were unpredictable lately, and things had seemingly thawed between us compared to earlier.

"Sorry, what was that?" I glanced up and spun my chair to face her.

"As I was saying, we had a bridal party come in while you were, um…on your break. They dropped over a grand."

"Sounds like you did a great job selling them." To her credit, Quinn was fantastic with people, which translated into being a great salesperson. She was the main reason our revenues had increased steadily year after year, even when the retail sector wasn't growing at the same rate.

"I sure did." Quinn eyed me, her hot pink lips quirking with amusement. "And don't worry, I turned up the music in the floor area."

Oh, God.

I swiveled my chair, turning back to face the monitors. "I'm going to finish working on these numbers."

"Okay. I'm running out for a coffee. I'd bring you one, but I think Bennett already did." Quinn headed for the door, beige Jimmy

Choos clicking on the hardwood. She paused with one hand on the doorknob and turned back to face me. "I'm not judging you, Thay. I think it's sweet."

"Sweet?" That was a generous way to describe a mid-morning quickie in the office.

"You know…" She gestured to me with a knowing smile. "Seeing you in love. I don't think I ever have."

My stomach fluttered. "We're never talking about this again."

I wasn't in love with Bennett.

Was I?

CHAPTER THIRTY-FOUR

Bennett

A HALF-EMPTY BOTTLE OF MALBEC SAT NEXT TO US ON THE end table while Thayer snuggled up beneath a fuzzy blanket next to me on the couch, ice-cold bare feet nestled next to mine. For the life of me, I'd never understand how she was always freezing. In contrast, I was always warm, if not verging on uncomfortably hot. I guess we evened out, which was true in a lot of ways.

She arched her neck and leaned against me with a sigh while I stroked her silky hair absentmindedly. We were half-watching a recently released drama on Netflix, but we'd both already seen it before, so it was more like background noise to our idle chatter. I didn't know when I turned into the 'stay in and watch a movie on a Friday in our lounge clothes' type of guy, but as it turned out, I liked it. A lot more than I had expected.

The movie credits began, and Thayer spoke up.

"How's your mom doing?" She shifted and looked up at me, tone hushed. There was a pang in my gut, both from the topic and from the care shining in her eyes as she asked.

"She seems to be responding to treatment so far," I said. "Long road ahead still, though."

"I bet." She traced the rim of her wineglass with a slender finger. "And she's still planning that party for us. I feel like I should help, especially now that my mother got involved and it's ballooned into this big event."

Unsurprisingly, once our mothers connected, what had started as a casual Sunday morning brunch had morphed into a semi-formal Saturday evening cocktail party. My mother didn't seem to mind, though, and she was enjoying planning. Maybe it was a good distraction.

"Don't feel bad," I told her. "My mom loves planning events." I wished she'd go back to volunteering on the hospital charity board. She claimed she was still too embarrassed after my father's scandal, even though most of the other board members from that time had since moved on. Personally, I said fuck anyone who judged something like that, but unfortunately, my mother didn't have nearly as thick of a skin as I did.

Thayer sat up and refilled both of our glasses, looking thoughtful. "Well..." she trailed off, "hopefully my mother doesn't drive her too crazy. She can be a lot to take sometimes."

"I think it's a good distraction. It gives her something else to focus on besides chemo."

Of course, neither of us wanted to address the fact that this party was to celebrate our farce of an engagement. Our relationship had begun with an expiration date, but that wasn't all this was anymore, was it? Otherwise, what were we doing here at my place? There was no one here, nothing to prove. There was something real between us, even if we were both too afraid to broach it.

Thayer inclined her head, eyes raking over my face. "Are you worried about tomorrow?"

Why would I be worried? Closing the deal was only make or break. The difference between success and insolvency. Maybe I was being a tad dramatic. It's not like Flux would go bankrupt tomorrow if this fell through. We'd simply bleed out slowly while limping our way to an agonizing and publicly humiliating death. No big deal.

But I didn't particularly want to admit the full extent of my worries to Thayer.

"Callaghan is ninety percent of the way there," I said. "Or eighty percent, at least. All he needs is a little reassurance that he's in good hands."

Something popped into my mind from out of nowhere. Something that had been nagging at the back of my mind for ages. Maybe it wasn't my business. Hell, it definitely wasn't my business. But that had never stopped me before.

"Forget about work." I shifted, turning to face her on the couch. "Let's do a question for a question." We hadn't done this since high school, around the time that things between us had started to change and free-for-all questions began to carry too much risk.

Thayer scrunched up her mouth and her pale blue eyes darted around the room before landing back on me. She tucked a lock of dark hair behind her ear; a nervous tell of hers. "That sounds dangerous."

"I won't ask anything I don't want to know."

"That's what I'm afraid of."

I ignored her protest, which was usually the best way to overcome her objections. "What happened with Pierce Cunningham? I'm told you humiliated him wonderfully. After whatever you said to him, he unloaded that Benz faster than he shorts stocks." Somehow, I took a little too much enjoyment in knowing that last part. I liked being one of the few people who got behind Thayer's walls. Plus, it made it marginally less terrifying that I had let her get past mine.

Thayer shot me a look that could wilt a plant at thirty feet, much like the look I imagined Pierce had received. "He should have been embarrassed. There was a used condom on the passenger side floor of his car when he picked me up. It was disgusting, and I said as much."

"Ah." Well, that wasn't so unreasonable on her part. In fact, that was understandable. But now I was even more curious whether the other things I'd heard were true or if they had also been distorted. Often, the rumor mill—specifically, Millie—twisted stories.

"What about Abbot?" I asked. "Everyone thinks you tore his heart out on his birthday."

That particular rumor grew more and more salacious each time I heard it. According to the first version, Thayer gave him the old, 'it's not me, it's you' routine. A couple weeks later, the story had morphed into a dramatic tale where Thayer slapped him and dumped a Grey Goose martini over his head in the middle of the restaurant. The second version didn't ring true. Thayer was too practical to waste good vodka.

She grimaced and looked away, toying with the black satin tie of her pajama pants. "He wanted to move in together."

Huh. Will Abbot was, well, a lot like me. Or the version of myself I was a few months ago, at least. Enjoying the benefits of being young and conventionally attractive by banging his way across town. He wasn't exactly known for being a fan of monogamy, which meant he must have been crazy about Thayer. It bothered me, even though I knew it shouldn't.

My hold on her thigh tightened. "I didn't know you two were serious." I tried to sound casual and failed.

"That's the thing," Thayer said, seemingly oblivious. "We weren't. We had dated for maybe a month, tops, and all of a sudden, he took me out to dinner and asked me to move in with him. On his *birthday*. It was awful. I didn't want to say no, but I couldn't say yes. I tried to be nice about it, or as nice as you can be when you're breaking it off."

"Poor chump. I'll give you the benefit of the doubt on the Crosby rumors."

Thayer made a sour face. "He tried to pull up my skirt under the table at Culina on our first date. Wouldn't take no for an answer. It was leave or stab him with a seafood fork."

Wish I hadn't asked that, because now I had the urge to find him and stab him myself. Crosby was tall, broad, and twice Thayer's size. The scenario she was describing did something dangerous to my blood pressure. If I ever saw him again…

"Wait a minute." She swatted my arm. "Why am I giving you my life story? It's your turn."

"Ask away."

Everything was fair game, with the lone exception of the unspoken elephant in the room. I didn't want to get into that with her now—or ever. After Mexico, I'd decided to put it to bed and move past it. It didn't matter anymore.

Thayer sat up and criss-crossed her long legs, clad in grey-and-black plaid pajama pants. My breath caught in my throat while I waited for her to speak, hoping for anything but that.

"Have you ever had a girlfriend?"

Or that.

"Like someone I dated for a while?" I clarified. Even then, the answer was no unless I was being extremely generous with the definition of "dated" or broad with the interpretation of "a while". With the exception of Thayer, I tended to lose interest quickly.

"A girlfriend," she repeated. "A real relationship. Someone who met your parents, that kind of thing."

"Uh…no," I admitted. "No one that meets those criteria."

"Oh." Her expression stayed neutral, but something flashed behind her eyes. While she was working hard to hide it, I could tell she was more than mildly horrified by this disclosure. She reached over and tugged her on her black knit cardigan before continuing. "Next question. What actually happened with Adam?"

I regretted starting this game.

"He pulled the plug without any warning at a highly volatile time for the company, leaving me left scrambling for cash to buy him out." AKA, he screwed me.

"I know that part," she said patiently, "but why? You must have worked well together at one point for Flux to go as far as it did.

Millie said the split was acrimonious, so I'm curious about the history there. Did something happen with you two?"

"Well…" I ran a hand through my hair, trying to formulate a response that didn't paint me in a negative light. There was fault on both sides, if I was being brutally honest—and I did want to be honest with her. "It wasn't a good match. We both wanted to run the show, which meant we butted heads a lot. Ian is a lot more chill, which means we work better together. I guess in some ways, Adam and I are too much alike."

She shook her head. "You're nothing like Adam."

"Why did you date him, anyway?" I asked, as the green-eyed monster that had been tugging against its leash for weeks finally broke free.

Those rumors about other guys she'd dated may have annoyed me, but remembering her with Adam made me homicidal. Seeing it for myself had been even worse. I was in peak physical shape the whole time they dated, because it was either to channel my rage into lifting heavy weights or risk throwing one at Adam's head. Worst part was, I knew I had no reason to feel that way or claim to her, which meant I couldn't even hold it against him. And I hadn't.

But now that I thought back on it, I was sure Adam knew exactly what he was doing. He might have been a prick, but he was also highly observant. You had to be, in order to be as good at fucking people over as he was.

Thayer looked away, pursing her lips, and her shoulders heaved with a sigh. "This is embarrassing to admit, but I think I just wanted a boyfriend. First and last time I ever did that. He's living proof that it's better to be alone than to settle." She paused. "You know, your questions all seem to have a common theme. Are you jealous?"

"No," I insisted, but it didn't sound convincing even to my own ears. Guess she hadn't missed my not-so-subtle reactions after all.

"Uh-huh." Her mouth tugged into a smug, sexy smirk. There was probably something fundamentally flawed about the fact that

I loved it when she gave me a hard time. Still, it didn't change the fact that I did.

"Fine," I said. "Maybe I don't like picturing you with anyone else."

She blinked and her lips parted in surprise. The implications of what I'd admitted hung in the air. On the coffee table in front of us, my phone lit up with a text.

"Sorry," I said, reaching for it. "I need to make sure it's not Holden. We were texting earlier." More specifically, I was trying to convince him to restart weekly therapy sessions.

When my eyes dropped to read the message, my heart sank like a block of concrete in the Hudson River. Of course. The most inappropriate message with the most inopportune timing ever.

Thayer's gaze drifted to the screen, and she swallowed audibly. Her small frame stiffened against mine. "That's not Holden."

"That's someone I haven't spoken to in a long time." I offered the phone to her so she could read the whole message. There was nothing to hide; while receiving a booty call invitation wasn't a great look for me, Phoebe's message referenced this past summer, making it clear that we hadn't seen each other in several months. "See?"

Thayer eyed the phone warily, reluctantly taking it from me and skimming the message. She slid the phone back into my hands, but she still radiated uneasiness. Sometimes, I felt like I was one wrong remark away from blowing things up permanently. I didn't know if changing that would take time, or if there was something more she needed from me. I'd already opened up more than I ever thought possible, and she wasn't the only one who was a little scared.

"Define long," she said.

"Well before Starbucks, Thay."

She studied me, worrying her bottom lip. "Have you violated our agreement at all? Be honest."

Pretty sure we'd ripped our agreement to shreds between all the things we'd done, but I hadn't violated it in the ways she was worried about.

"We had sex, so I think you know I did." But my attempt at a joke fell flat, and the tension in her body didn't dissipate.

"I meant in any other ways," she said, reaching for her glass of Malbec. "Even early on."

"No," I said honestly. "Have you?"

Thayer winced, mid-sip. "Maybe."

What? Now it was my turn to sweat—and it showed. I fumbled for my own wine glass and threw half of its contents back in one gulp.

"Oh my God, no." Her hand flew to her mouth, and she laughed softly. "Not like that, Bennett. I haven't slept with anyone. Who do you think you're dealing with? But I may have let our arrangement slip to Lola over brunch."

Oh. Well, that was far better than her sleeping with someone else behind my back, but hopefully Lola knew how to keep her mouth shut better than Quinn or Millie.

"How much does Lola know?" I asked, trying not to sound as terse as I felt.

"Um…" Thayer pursed her lips thoughtfully. She reached over, and her fingers landed on my sweatpants-clad thigh, slowly inching higher. And higher. My cock stirred, even though this would make round three for us today.

While I should have been tired, I had way more stamina than normal when it came to her. Until now, I'd never understood what my friends meant when they had said that sex was better with someone you cared about. But that wasn't the only thing that surprised me; it was how much I liked having her around in other ways, too. Even without sex, I'd have happily been around her all the time. It was a new feeling for me, and I didn't know what to make of it.

"Are you trying to cop a feel to distract me?" I asked.

She shot me a sidelong glance, batting her eyelashes. "Is it working?"

"I think you know it is."

Thayer squealed as I turned and grabbed her by the waist, pulling her on top of me. Her thighs straddled mine, pelvis rubbing against my half-erection that was rapidly growing harder by the second.

My hands cupped her behind, fingers digging into her phenomenal ass. "Now, none of that Ed Sheeran shit tomorrow, or I'll spank you so hard you can't walk later."

Thayer arched a brow and leaned in, brushing her lips against mine. Her long hair fell in a curtain around us, the clean, herbal scent of her shampoo drifting in the air. "Is that supposed to be a deterrent or an incentive?"

The next morning, Thayer and I enjoyed a nice, leisurely breakfast in bed. And by that, I mean we stayed in bed, and she was breakfast. Unfortunately, she had to leave after to meet Lola for brunch while my presence was required at Flux for an alleged 'emergency' per Ian.

Spoiler alert: it was not an emergency.

"You have got to be fucking kidding me." I leaned over Ian's wooden desk, fighting the urge to throw something. Ian had lots of kitschy knick-knacks to choose from. It would have been remarkably satisfying to break a window with one of them. Instead, I snagged a pencil from his pen cup and snapped it in two.

"It's not illegal to overcharge someone." Ian leaned his elbows on his desk, and placed his head in his hands, fingers tugging at his hair. "At least, not in this context."

Disbelief bowled into me. "You're telling me that Adam ripped us off by marking up services by five hundred percent, and there's nothing we can do about it."

When Ian summoned me to the office on a Saturday morning, I'd been expecting a bombshell. Some kind of earth-shaking revelation that would enable me to destroy Adam once and for all. All I got was a big, fat dud. Ian's 'urgent' news was that he'd looked into the companies Thayer and I had flagged for possible associations with Adam, but they all seemed legitimate, at least on the surface.

Beneath the surface, was no doubt, a tangled web of legal shields, but we didn't have the time or resources to unearth them.

"It's not a crime for someone to overpay you," he reiterated, staring at the desk. "Much as I wish it was."

"But he vetted the vendor. He *was* the vendor."

That shady fucker colluded with one of his friends and charged us through the nose for online advertising, among other services. Over-billing was much harder to act on than straight-up theft; it was basically impossible.

How the funds had been funneled back to Adam and AM Developments, I hadn't yet determined, but I was confident at least a portion had been. I doubted the IRS was aware of it, either. Bringing that to their attention via anonymous tip was at the top of my to-do list. If they were up my ass, Adam might as well enjoy a rectal exam, too.

"It's a conflict of interest at best, and good luck pursuing that. He's not on the board or employed by the company anymore, which would be the usual means of recourse."

"I will find some recourse," I said evenly. "Wait and see."

"I've retained a PI to look into him. The most morally grey one I could find without actually breaking the law by hiring him. I'm not entirely confident about that last part, either." Ian looked at me from over the rim of his stainless-steel travel mug, expression grim.

"Perfect." I was certain there would be skeletons if we found the right closet.

"How are things with Thayer, anyway? You guys have a nice night in?"

Ian was playing me, and it was working, because it was difficult to stay angry about Adam and think about her at the same time.

"We did." Night, morning, you name it. All over my apartment. Though if I was being honest, it was way more than that.

Lately, my phone had been inundated with messages from my friends—and several women—wondering why I had dropped off the face of the planet. I guess I had, over the past month, though I'd been too preoccupied to notice. But rather than missing it like I would have expected, I'd come to realize that making dinner and a watching movie with Thay was infinitely more enjoyable than going to some new club like I would have before.

"Good," Ian said. "You do seem calmer."

That was a diplomatic way of putting it. If not for her, there would have been a chair through the window right now.

But instead, I just shrugged and entered the pin to my laptop on his desk, drumming my fingers as I waited for it to load. Despite what Ian said, I wasn't letting this Adam thing go. I would find a way to make him pay. With interest.

"Do you think you're ready for tonight?" A hint of uncertainty betrayed Ian's otherwise neutral expression from across my desk.

"We've got this in the bag," I said, double clicking to open the notes I'd compiled to prepare for this evening. "We'll close him, get the money, and win the bid." The last part was basically a given; Ian had connections in the planning department, and our project was the front-runner by far. We just had to come up with the cash to make it a reality.

"If you say so," he said.

"I know so."

CHAPTER THIRTY-FIVE

Thayer
September 8th
Grade 11

"**Y**OU KNOW THE LEAD FOR THE SCHOOL PLAY IS GOING TO GO to Vivienne again, she's such a teachers' pet..." Millie prattled on. I had just left AP Bio and if she didn't stop pumping nonsense into my already overflowing brain, my head was going to explode and splatter all over the pavement.

"By the way, did I tell you I met Bennett's cousin, Adam?" Millie asked me. "He's super hot. I'm going to see him at Model UN tonight."

"Awesome," I murmured. I wish Quinn was here. She was almost finished with her inpatient program at the Childrens' Hospital Eating Disorder Clinic. I couldn't wait for her to be back at school.

"Speaking of Bennett, what's going on with you two?

My mouth went dry. "What do you mean?"

"He asked you to homecoming, right?" Millie watched me intently, waiting for a reaction. I knew she'd always liked Bennett. Her questioning wasn't coming from a friendly place, even if she was working hard to make it seem that way.

"Yeah, we're going together."

"As friends," she said pointedly, "or as a date?"

If only I'd had the guts to ask him that myself. First, he refused to kiss me during 7 Minutes in Heaven, and then he asked me to homecoming. Consider me confused.

Speaking of Bennett. My eyes landed on him leaning against the brick wall beside the parking lot, phone in one hand, and something else in the other. What on earth was he doing? He knew better than that.

Millie nudged me gently. "Thayer?"

My attention turned back to her, patience vanishing. "Sorry, Millie. I have to go."

"But—"

"I'll catch up with you later." I turned and cut across the parking lot, striding up to Bennett. My homecoming date was breaking about seven different rules in the school's handbook. If he wasn't careful, he wouldn't be attending our school much longer.

"Have you lost your mind?" I demanded.

Bennett exhaled a cloud of smoke. "Not recently."

I snatched the joint from his hands and grabbed his sleeve, yanking him around the corner out of sight. "What the hell is this?" Bennett didn't smoke—cigarettes or otherwise. And he definitely wasn't foolish enough to do it on school grounds, where they had a zero-tolerance policy.

"What does it look like?" He gave me an unimpressed look. "Do you want a hit, or can I have it back?"

"You're going to get expelled," I hissed, stubbing out the glowing end against the red brick.

He reached over and snatched it out of my hands. "So?"

"So?" I gestured. "So? What's going on?" His tie was loosened, uniform dress shirt wrinkled, and he was a disheveled mess. Bennett never looked like this—ever.

"Let me guess," he said. "You're going to give me a speech about how if I get expelled, I'll never get into a good college. And without a good college, I won't be able to get a good job."

"Well, yeah." That was exactly what I was about to say. That was how we'd been raised; eyes on the prize, stay in line, and you'll get the golden ticket eventually.

Bennett snorted. "What's the end goal there, exactly? So I can work my life away, only to get accused of some 'white collar crime' bullshit like my dad?"

A group of students came out the side doors, chatting loudly. We paused, waiting for them to continue through the parking lot until they were out of earshot.

"Bennett," I whispered, touching his arm. "What happened?"

"It seems my dear old dad was skirting the law and got caught." His jaw worked. "And by caught, I mean he got arrested last night."

CHAPTER THIRTY-SIX

Bennett

AN HOUR INTO DINNER AND SEVERAL DRINKS DEEP, everything was going smoothly. Ian had miraculously secured reservations for a private room at MRKT, a highly sought-after local farm-to-table restaurant. Callaghan was slowly warming up to me, even if it was practically requiring backflips and significant self-censoring on my part. And Thayer was charming the pants off Laura and Callaghan's wife, Lenora. I couldn't have chosen a better fake fiancée if I tried.

Callaghan watched the three women talking for a moment before turning back to me.

"Alexandra invited me to your engagement party on the eighteenth," he said. "She told me she's hosting it with your mother."

Once Thayer's mother, Alexandra, entered the picture, our mothers had collectively gotten out of hand. The guest list for our party had tripled, it had been bumped a week later, and the time had moved into the evening. In other words, what was supposed to be a low-key brunch was now a full-on semi-formal soiree. The only thing that hadn't changed was the venue; it was still being hosted at my parents' house, like my mother wanted.

"Looking forward to it," I said. Low-level guilt hummed in the back of my mind like static interference. I hated lying to my mother, but I hated the idea of her watching me go bankrupt even more.

Callaghan cut off another bite of his steak, glancing up at me. "Have you set a date for the nuptials?"

"Just nailing down a date now. We're thinking early summer." I'd rehearsed some of these lies in my head so many times that they sounded shockingly natural at this point.

Ian cocked his head thoughtfully. "Did you pick a venue?"

Well-meaning bastard. No, Ian, we hadn't chosen a venue for our non-existent wedding. We hadn't even talked about what was going to happen in a few weeks—after Callaghan, after Quinn and Adam's wedding, after all of our reasons for faking it disappeared.

I wish I could have let Ian in on the truth, like Thayer had with Lola, but Ian was a shitty liar. It was too risky.

"We have a few contenders in mind, but we haven't decided yet," I said. "I'm leaving it up to Thayer. Whatever will make her happy."

Callaghan nodded. "Smart man."

"Honey," Lenora called over. "Thayer was telling me they were looking at having their wedding ceremony at that old, converted barn. You know, the one on the way to our acreage." Barn? What barn? I had no idea what or where this barn was, so I sure as hell hoped someone wasn't about to ask me for details.

I leaned over, catching Thayer's eye, and brushed my foot against hers under the table. "That sounds great, Thay. I can't wait for you to take me there so we can check it out together."

"Of course." She gave me a wistful smile, like she was actually looking forward to doing that. "Bennett's been working a lot lately, so I've been checking out venues with Quinn instead. But we'll make the final decision together, right, hon?"

"Always," I said.

Bullet dodged. For now.

Another hour later, we were wrapping up dessert with Callaghan all but officially sold. It was so close I could feel it. It helped that Adam wasn't here to get in the way for once.

Ian set down his fork, swallowing a bite of flourless chocolate torte. "We can have you come by this week to sign all the paperwork."

My adrenaline spiked, and I ceased breathing. *Come on...*

Callaghan dabbed his mouth with the white linen napkin. "Actually, we're going on a quick getaway to Turks and Caicos. Just for ten days. But we'll be back late next Friday, so let's sign the papers the following Saturday at Bennett and Thayer's engagement party. We can get it out of the way early in the evening."

I'd have strongly preferred to 'get it out of the way' now, but it was something. Basically as good as done. I hoped.

"That sounds great," I told him.

Thayer offered a gracious smile. "We can't wait to see you there."

After clearing up the bill with Ian, Thayer and I headed into the parking lot, fingers intertwined. I was flying high with no hope of coming down any time soon. Winning over Callaghan was great. But in the immediate future, I only had one thing on my agenda: her.

We came to stand in front of the passenger side door to my black BMW coupe, lit only by the dim glow of the nearby streetlight. Thayer's eyes dropped to my mouth before lifting back up to meet my eyes, and she gave me a tiny, almost imperceptible smile. By now, I knew exactly what that smile meant.

Leaning in, I brought my mouth down to hers. When our lips connected, she let out a little sigh and parted her lips, granting me access. Our tongues brushed together in a wine-tinted kiss, and everything else around us started to fade away. Somewhere in the distance, a car door slammed, and we pulled apart, suddenly remembering where we were.

"Not going to lie," I said, nuzzling the top of Thayer's head and breathing in the clean, familiar scent of her shampoo. "I was a little disappointed you didn't mention Ed Sheeran." I pushed her up against the car door, my hands pinning her narrow waist beneath her wool peacoat.

Thayer laughed softly, turning to bury her face in my chest. Her arms wrapped around my torso, hugging me against her. "That went perfectly, though. You did it."

"We did it." Reaching down, I tilted her face up to mine, taking in her features in the half-light. Her tongue darted out, moistening her full bottom lip. God, I loved those lips. "Now I'm going to do you."

She drew in a soft inhale, voice turning breathy. "Oh, yeah?"

"Yeah." My fingers walked up her bare thigh, pausing when they reached the hemline of her little black dress. Her pupils dilated as I slid one finger beneath the fabric. I traced back and forth against her bare skin, feeling goosebumps pop up in response. "What color are your panties?" I was always curious, because I hadn't seen a repeat set of lingerie on her yet. Perk of her job, I suppose.

"Black," she said. "Lace. They're new, and they're very, very tiny."

All the blood vacated my brain with a whoosh, going straight to my other head. I removed my hand from beneath her dress and grabbed the handle, opening the car door for her. "We'd better get out of here before we're not allowed back." If she didn't get in the vehicle, I was going to do something indecent to her in the middle of the parking lot.

After closing her door, I walked around to the driver's side and started the engine, easing out of the parking stall. I signaled and pulled onto the street, thoughts circling straight back to what I was going to do when we got back to her place. It was a pity the local freeway didn't have an unrestricted speed limit like the Autobahn so I could make the trip home that much faster. Getting arrested for reckless driving would be a definite mood-killer.

"Speaking of your underwear," I said, "I'm going to tear them off the minute we walk through the door."

Thayer raised an eyebrow. "You wreck them, you pay for them."

"Money well spent. What should I do to you after that? Should I fuck you against your front door, or should I push you against the wall and go down on you first?" In the dim light, I could see her squirm slightly as a pink flush spread across her cheeks. I loved talking dirty to Thayer. Seeing her get worked up because of me was a massive turn-on. And when she got a little dirty back, it was even better.

"I like the second one." Thayer reached over, slowly stroking my thigh. My cock silently begged for her to move a little higher and to the left, but she didn't. "What else?"

What wasn't I going to do? At this point, I was going to keep her up until dawn working my way down the list. Her neighbors might not be too pleased, but too bad. That's what earplugs are for.

"For round two, I'm going to pin your wrists over your head and—" I stopped short when Thayer removed her hand from my leg. In my peripheral vision, she hiked up the hem of her dress and shifted in her seat, reaching beneath her legs. My cock twitched, breath stilling. Was she… no. Was she taking off her underwear?

"What are you doing?" I murmured, stealing a glance at her.

Thayer batted her eyelashes at me. "Nothing." Reaching over, she placed the tiny, delicate scrap of black lace in the center console, laying it directly on top of my cellphone—a visual reminder that she was bare beneath her dress. "You were saying?"

My grip tightened around the steering wheel. "I'm going to…"

"Going to what?" Her fingers slid up her bare inner thigh, inching higher and higher.

My gaze darted over to her again briefly before returning to the task at hand: driving. Or trying to, at least.

"Bend you over my bed," I continued.

She leaned back in the passenger seat and her fingers curled, disappearing beneath the hem of her dress. "Mmm…" Her moan was low and throaty, practically vibrating against my dick. Thayer's eyes drifted shut and her hand moved beneath her dress again. While I couldn't quite see what she was doing, I knew—and it was torture. With Thayer pleasuring herself next to me, it was impossible to think straight, let alone safely operate heavy machinery.

"Then what?" her voice was husky. "Keep talking so I can pretend you're the one touching me."

Fuck me. I wasn't going to get us home in one piece.

"Are you trying to get us into an accident?" I rasped, steering the car back into the right-hand lane from where it had started to drift onto the shoulder. Maybe there was a rest stop coming up where I could pull over and could rail her.

"What do you mean?" Thayer opened her eyes, giving me a pouty little frown. "You're the one talking dirty. You don't want me to react?"

"I want you, all right. I want to fuck you until I feel your pussy clench around my cock."

"Yes, please." She stroked herself again and drew in a jagged breath, arching her back against the leather seat. I reached over and placed my hand over top of hers, feeling her fingers plunge inside her pussy. Instant blue balls. I withdrew my hand and shifted in my seat, readjusting myself, but it was impossible to get comfortable.

We passed a roadside sign indicating we had twenty-one miles until her exit. I was looking at a minimum of more than twenty more minutes until we got to her place, even if I disregarded the speed limit. Probably closer to thirty, factoring in traffic lights and construction. Unacceptable. My manhood would fall off before then.

Fortunately, the next exit was a great alternative.

"You want to play like that? Fine." I signaled and made a sharp left, pulling onto a single-lane side road paved with gravel. My blue-white LED headlights cut into the inky darkness, and the rough surface rumbled noisily beneath my tires, small rocks pinging off the car's exterior.

"Where are we going?" Thayer asked.

"We're taking a little detour." I needed her naked, now. Needed her skin against mine, needed to be buried inside her, needed her moaning my name in my ear.

She broke into a curious smile. "Why?"

"Because we're half an hour from your place, and I can't wait that long."

CHAPTER THIRTY-SEVEN

Thayer

BENNETT EASED HIS CAR DOWN THE NARROW GRAVEL LANE, carefully navigating a series of curves and small hills, kicking up a cloud of dust in our wake. He slowed to a stop where the road came to an end and shifted the car into park, killing the ignition. We were far enough out of the city that the only light came from the half moon, casting his strong features in shadows.

Curiosity piqued, I surveyed our surroundings through the window but found only tall, mature trees and utter darkness. "Um... where are we?" I asked. "Are you sure we aren't trespassing?"

"Ian and Laura closed on this land last week." Bennett unfastened his seatbelt and released it, letting it hit the door panel with a clang. The power seat controls hummed as he moved his seat away from the steering wheel, reclining it slightly. "Couple acres. They're going to build on it, but right now, it's vacant. And completely isolated."

He shrugged out of his suit jacket, tossing it into the backseat, and I watched, mesmerized, as he deftly rolled up his shirt sleeves.

In the sliver of pale moonlight, the veins in his exposed forearms did something to my brain—and other parts of my body.

When he turned to face me, the hunger in his expression was evident even in the dark interior. He inclined his head, beckoning me with one hand. "Get over here."

In the silence of the vehicle cabin, his voice was deep and commanding, the order utterly impossible to resist. A thrill ran through my body, like plunging downhill on a rollercoaster. I'd never had car sex before. I wasn't one to be reckless—which decisively ruled out all forms of exhibitionism—but in this case, I trusted him.

His eyes stayed fixed on me, jaw tensed, while I hiked up my dress and crawled over the middle console. It was difficult to make the process appear graceful, but the spellbound look on his face told me that he didn't care. I started to lower myself to straddle him in the driver's seat, but the bottom of my dress dug into my thighs, restricting my range of movement.

"*Now,*" Bennett growled. He hooked his fingers beneath the hem of my dress and slid it higher, giving me space to spread my legs wider. Then he grabbed me by the waist and yanked me down against him, eliciting a soft gasp from my lips. Without underwear, my bare center pressed directly against the fabric covering his erection. I swiveled my hips, and a sound of appreciation rumbled in the back of his throat in response.

"Now who's bossy?" I asked.

"You knew exactly what you were doing." His palm connected with the curve of my behind. A loud smack punctuated the air, and I let out a yelp, more out of surprise than pain. He rubbed the spot he'd just spanked, squeezing it.

"You started it."

His hand slid up the back of my neck, gripping the roots of my hair. "Glad I did." He nipped at my jawline. "That was fucking hot."

Bennett tilted my face toward his and his lips crushed mine. When our tongues brushed together, my fingertips dug into his shoulders, toes curling with pleasure. He wrapped an arm around my waist and held me against him, devouring me. It was dominant, demanding, and rendered me completely drunk with desire. I'd have failed a Bennett breathalyzer on the spot.

I unfastened the top buttons of his dress shirt, working my way down until the crisp cotton fell open, and he tugged it off, tossing it aside. My hands glided down his bare chest, exploring the stacks of muscle beneath his perfect, taut skin. Liquid heat pooled between my legs, a need for him sparking into a flame. I had never craved someone the way I did with him, and I wasn't sure I'd ever get used to it.

My breath stilled as Bennett slowly trailed his fingers along my back, his touch deliberate and full of sinful promises. When he landed on the zipper of my dress, he paused and smiled against my lips, sending a flutter through my belly. In a flash, I was left in nothing but my lacy black demi-cup bra. A fire ignited behind his eyes as they raked down my body, lingering on my breasts like he was trying to memorize every peak and every valley.

"Let's get this out of the way, too," he said. Reaching behind me, he deftly unfastened the band of my bra and removed it in one swift motion. Cool air hit my nipples, and they tightened. He caressed the pebbled buds with his thumbs, letting out a deep, rumbly groan when they hardened even more beneath his touch. Something about his gaze was reverent, like he was cherishing every inch of my skin.

"How are you so perfect?" He lifted his chin to look at me, expression almost pained.

"I'm not."

"Trust me," he said. "You are."

His hands slid under my thighs, gripping, while my skin hummed beneath his touch. He hoisted me up slightly and leaned in, dark hair tumbling over his forehead as he grazed my sensitive nipple with his teeth. An electric shock of pleasure shot through me, hips rocking. A needy whimper escaped my lips, and his hold on my thighs tightened in response to the sound.

Bennett swirled his tongue around my nipple, teasing me with torturous precision. My head rolled back, and my fingers sank into his hair, silently urging him on. Another rush of heat flooded my body, a desperate need for more of him everywhere, all over me.

I was nearly delirious with need when he pulled back, lifting his chin to look up at me. He watched my face as he yanked me down against him, lifting his hips to meet me halfway. His rock-hard erection hit the perfect spot between my legs, and my pelvis tilted, grinding against him instinctively in response. The heavenly friction between our bodies was both a relief and a tease, so close yet so far from what we both craved.

"Thay," Bennett growled, leaning back against the leather seat. "You're going to be my undoing."

I could have said the same about him. Before, I'd always been take-it-or-leave it when it came to sex. Dry spells didn't bother me— and I'd had lots of them, by choice. But with Bennett, it was completely different. By the time I tugged open his belt buckle, I was so intoxicated with lust that it was like unwrapping a present.

He wasted no time sliding out of his pants, taking off his black boxer briefs at the same time. Then he pulled me closer and positioned us so I was straddling him again, only this time we were both naked. My breasts brushed his bare chest while I rested my hands on his shoulders, hyperaware of every junction where our skin touched. His thick shaft pressed against my lower stomach, but the expression on his face was more tender than lustful.

We lingered, looking at each other in the dark for a couple of heartbeats, neither of us saying anything. Bennett smoothed his palms along the sides of my ribcage and squeezed me. He brought one hand up to cup my face, tracing my lower lip with the pad of his thumb.

His mouth tugged into an affectionate grin. "Hi, beautiful."

"Hi," I whispered, running my fingertips along the groomed stubble that shaded his jaw.

Something about the moment felt precious, unlike anything I'd ever experienced. But there was a hint of bitterness beneath the candy-coated shell, a silent understanding that the clock was ticking, and sooner or later, we'd have to face reality. If not ending this, then owning up to things we were both afraid to admit.

For a moment, it looked like he was about to say something, but he didn't. He wrapped his hand around the back of my neck, bringing my mouth to his for a gentle kiss instead.

"Let me grab a condom," Bennett murmured. "There are some in my overnight bag." He leaned back and reached behind him into the backseat, rummaging around blindly for a moment before emerging with a foil wrapper. In one smooth movement, he tore it open, and I leaned back against the steering wheel behind me to give him space while he furrowed his brow, unrolling it over his length.

He glanced back up at me and his large hands splayed possessively against my hips, guiding me as I sank down. I took him in slowly, relishing the sensation of him stretching me. It was intoxicating and addictive, like our bodies were made to be joined together.

"Oh, God," I whimpered. I started to rock back and forth and my grip on his shoulders tightened, his hold on me following suit. Our pace quickened, turning desperate and heated. An overwhelming wave of pleasure started to build within my core, and my eyelids drifted shut as the sensation started to overtake me.

His fingers dug into my hips, slowing me down. "Look at me."

I slowed down, reopening my eyes, and when our gazes locked, his expression softened. Something unspoken clicked into place between us. It was the most intimate experience I'd had in my entire life.

"There you are," he said, flattening his palm against the small of my back.

Our lips came together, and his tongue swept against my bottom lip, easing into my mouth. I sank down, taking him even deeper than before, and we both drew in a shaky breath. When I lifted myself up again, Bennett reached between us and pressed his thumb against my sensitive bundle of nerves, sending a rush of white-hot pleasure through my center.

We found a blissful, lazy pace, savoring each other. He watched me, eyes hooded, stroking my center in perfect rhythm with me riding him. Heat rushed to my face; a telltale sign I was almost at the peak. Bennett grabbed my waist to lift me up and slammed into me from below, hitting a spot that made me see stars. My breath caught, walls clenching around him. Even with me on top, he was now completely in control.

"That's it, baby." He flexed his hips, hitting the same, euphoric spot again. "Come for me."

Everything exploded in a ball of bright, shimmering light, and I moaned against his mouth, nails digging into his bare shoulders. Wave after wave of pleasure flooded my body, overtaking me. A chorus of pleas escaped my lips, crying out his name and begging him not to stop.

"Thay." Bennett groaned, gripping me tightly as he jerked with one final, brutal thrust. I felt him throb inside me with release while the rest of his body stilled.

After a couple of seconds, he let out a sated sigh and wrapped his arms around me. He brushed my neck with his lips, rubbing small circles along my lower back. Limp with exhaustion, I rested my forehead on his shoulder and breathed in his comforting scent, smoothing my palms down his sculpted upper arms. It was like reading a map I knew by heart; every inch of his body had grown familiar to me, from the shape of his biceps to the way our bodies felt tangled together.

Unspoken words lingered between us, but I wasn't sure we'd both say the same thing.

We stayed suspended in a bubble of quiet, comfortable intimacy, until our heart rates gradually slowed, breathing returning to normal. But inwardly, I felt nothing like normal—he'd taken a piece of my heart somewhere along the way, and I wasn't even sure he realized it.

CHAPTER THIRTY-EIGHT

Bennett

NOTHING LIKE GETTING AN EMAIL FROM YOUR LAWYER ABOUT the IRS before ten AM to ruin your Monday morning.

I leaned over my desk, rubbing my temples while I re-read the body of Eric's message. According to Eric, the IRS was 'amenable' to an installment plan—with steep interest, of course, because why not twist the debt-ridden knife? While it was still good news in theory, they wanted an answer right away. Problem was, I didn't have an answer. Until I had Callaghan locked down, I couldn't safely guarantee I'd be able to adhere to a payment schedule, and failing to uphold my end of the bargain would put me in even worse standing with them.

Twelve days. I just needed to get through twelve more days, survive my fake engagement party, get Callaghan's signature on those papers, and then my problems would be over. Well, almost over; there was still the matter of securing the bid with the city, but Ian was adamant that he had that in the bag. He'd been all but promised it by the head of the planning department. It was a no-brainer, anyway; Flux's project was superior to AM Developments' in every way.

I picked up my freshly refilled mug of coffee, praying the caffeine would somehow kickstart my brain, and then I stared at the monitor, debating how to reply to Eric. Maybe we could begin to negotiate the specifics of the agreement and drag it out as much as possible, thereby buying me some time to make sure I had the money lined up. I didn't want to flat-out tell my lawyer that was my strategy, though. It didn't seem like it was entirely ethical.

The door to my office swung open, unsolicited, and I glanced up to find my least favorite person in the world standing in my doorway. There was no good time for an impromptu visit from Satan's understudy, but I was especially displeased at the intrusion before I'd even had time to finish my second coffee of the day.

My blood pressure tripled as Adam swaggered in without an invitation, wearing an expensive-looking navy designer suit and a shit-eating grin that told me my morning was about to go even more sideways. Seizing hold of the mouse, I saved my email draft and closed it in case he somehow caught a look at my screen.

"Hey, cuz." He rapped his knuckles against my desk.

"Who let you in?" I asked, trying to seem indifferent instead of irritated.

Although we had tried to minimize the fallout for the sake of maintaining a professional work environment, Flux's staff were more than aware of the negative circumstances surrounding Adam's departure from the company. Anyone employed by me should have known better to give him free reign of our floor. Not only was he an annoying asshole, but he also could have been trying to engage in corporate espionage.

Adam snagged my favorite Mont Blanc pen off my desk, twirling it between his fingers. "Your receptionist, Janine. She always had a thing for me. Applied for a job with AM awhile back, actually, but I'd already filled the position with this hot blonde named Trisha."

Note to self: Fire Janine.

"But enough about me," he said. "Let's talk about you for a minute. How are things with Thayer?"

"Great." I resisted the urge to throw my coffee at him. As tempting as it was, it would have been a terrible waste of a premium Kona blend.

Adam clucked his tongue. "Think they'll stay that way if you lose the bid?"

"I'm not even a little bit worried about that." A half-truth; I wasn't a little worried, I was a lot worried. Being broke—and possibly, unemployed—wasn't exactly an appealing attribute in a grown man. Plus, I didn't want it to look like I was pulling an Adam and pursuing Thayer for her money.

"I could buy you out," he offered, setting the pen on my desk without putting it back where it belonged. "We could roll Flux under the umbrella of AM Developments."

My grip on the mug tightened to the point where I thought it might shatter. "A merger?" I shot him a look of disbelief, because his offer was as insulting as it was delusional. "Hard pass."

Adam sank into the guest chair across from my desk. I reopened my email and composed a message to my assistant, Shane, directing him to terminate Janine with two weeks' severance. Then I requested that he place security on standby in case they needed to escort my current 'guest' out of the building. Adam craned his neck, trying to catch a glimpse of my screen, and I hit send before he could read the message, exiting the email program.

"Let's be honest, Bradford. We both know it would be a bailout," Adam said, leaning back in his chair again. "Flux is circling the drain. But it does have a few properties of value, so I'd keep those and let you stay on as project manager. You know, out of the kindness of my heart."

Not in this lifetime. I would move back in with my parents before I lowered myself to working for Adam, and I had no intention of doing that anytime soon, either.

When Adam saw the disgusted look on my face, his smugness factor shot through the stratosphere. I made a conscious effort to neutralize my expression. While he was annoying the shit out of me, I didn't want to give him the satisfaction of letting that show.

"Don't be proud, Bennett. The optics are better for you than declaring bankruptcy."

"Good thing I don't plan to go bankrupt."

"Speaking of optics, the timing of your relationship is interesting." He folded an ankle over his knee, gaze zeroing in on my face. "Didn't you say you'd rather eat glass than get married?"

I had said that, along with various other disparaging comments regarding marriage, like the fact that I thought it was a one-way ticket to boredom and a dead bedroom. In retrospect, my stance seemed a little extreme, but now wasn't the time to examine my change of heart on that subject. I couldn't afford to engage in am impromptu navel-gazing session with Adam sitting in front of me.

I shrugged, taking a sip of my coffee. "People change."

"Indeed," Adam mused. "You sure seem to have changed in the nick of time."

"What are you trying to say?" Funny that he was trying to imply something about my reasons for being with Thayer when he was the king of ulterior motives himself.

Then again, Adam wasn't wrong. At least, not about how it started.

"Nothing," he said innocently. "It's just interesting, that's all."

"Circling back to the point," I said. "I'm not interested in your offer. I have several meetings on my agenda this morning, so perhaps Janine can show you out." I pointed to the door.

"Don't say I didn't warn you when you lose the bid."

My jaw clenched. "What do you mean, *when*?"

Way to take the bait, Bradford.

Adam pushed to stand. "You haven't heard? The city is going to accept my bid." He gave me a faux sympathetic look. "Of course, that's not public information yet. I guess you wouldn't know, since you don't have the same connections I do. But you'll see for yourself soon enough."

The edges of my vision started to turn grey as he turned and sauntered over to my door, lingering in the threshold. "Don't worry," he said. "You'll always have a job waiting for you at AM Developments. That's what family is for, right?"

Before I could respond, Adam disappeared down the hall. Which was just as well, because the only response I could formulate was a string of insults and profanity.

The door clicked shut behind him, encasing me in a silent tomb of misery. Worries whirled through my mind, picking up additional fears like debris, forming an F5 tornado of panic. I was fucked. Utterly fucked. I was going to go down in flames while Thayer witnessed the whole thing.

Not ten minutes later, after I'd finally crafted a sufficiently vague email to Eric, my door swung open again. If it was Adam again, I was going to throw my Flux-logoed coffee cup at his oversized head. Instead, I looked up from the computer to find Ian holding a sheaf of papers in one hand, his expression tight and sandy hair disheveled.

He stalked into the room and flopped into the chair across from me. Frowning, he stared at the floor in front of him and drew in a long inhale, holding it for a couple of seconds before exhaling loudly.

"Are you okay?" I asked. Maybe this was some kind of marital thing, not even related to business. Of course, I didn't want that to be the case, but my sanity couldn't withstand another Flux-related fire, either.

Ian's gaze rocketed over to me and the look in his eyes said it all. "I've been informed that we're going to lose the bid," he said. "I wanted to prepare you."

A lead weight formed in my stomach. I swallowed the last of my coffee, but suddenly the smooth blend tasted bitter.

"Funny," I muttered, setting down the empty mug. "Adam just came here to tell me the same thing."

"He did?" With Ian's office tucked away in a corner, he was blissfully unaware of most office comings and goings.

"Janine let him in. I guess he didn't grace you with his presence on the way out." I stood up and began to pace near the window, leather Oxfords clicking on the glossy tile. Tiny flakes of snow whirled in the air outside, and the grey overcast sky was as bleak as my mood. "By the way, Janine won't be with us much longer."

When he didn't say anything more, I turned back to face him. His expression was grim, much like our situation. We were on a crash course and there was no time to swerve.

"Why are we going to lose the bid? How do you even know?" I asked, trying to keep my voice from climbing. I was frustrated with the situation, not with Ian. "You told me you had this in the bag with your connections in the planning department."

"I did," he snapped. "Until the mayor pulled rank."

I turned back to face him. "The mayor? What the fuck?" Maybe I should leave the office after this to go throw around heavy things at the gym. It was that, or start throwing the furniture. I hadn't broken a chair in a while, and I wanted to keep it that way.

"Strange, right? It doesn't make sense. Why would the mayor overrule the planning and development board? He never interferes with administrative matters like that."

"Adam doesn't have any connections to the Mayor that I know of," I mused. Emphasis, that I knew of. But my cousin was nothing if not sneaky. "Nor does Richard."

"I have that private investigator looking into Adam. So far, it's been a dead end. He hasn't found any connections between him and anyone politically connected, but he's still looking."

"Good," I said, crossing the room to my desk and sitting back down. I nodded to the papers he was holding. "Was there something else? Did you come in here to give me those?"

Ian's gaze dropped to the stack of papers, and he fell silent. I watched him, impatiently waiting for him to say whatever he was trying to build up to saying. I wasn't sure what more could go wrong. My life was already in difficult mode, with the settings switched to worst-case scenario.

"I did some digging into Adam's proposed development." His words were measured, intended to carefully tap dance around the point. "I wanted to see what might have given him the upper hand."

"Did you find anything?" I asked.

"I managed to get a list of tenants."

"Okay…" I waved him on impatiently. I didn't need to know the entire research process, I just needed to know the result. "What's your point? Did Adam snag some golden anchor tenant that won over the mayor?"

Our tenant roster was solid, a nice mix of local businesses and corporate chains. The commercial spaces were small, fairly standard 1100-2000 square foot units, only suitable for a few types of commercial activities. I didn't see what Adam could possibly have that we didn't.

"Not exactly." Ian slid the stack of papers across my desk to me. "Did you know about this?"

CHAPTER THIRTY-NINE

Thayer

WITHIN SECONDS OF WALKING INTO BENNETT'S OFFICE, I knew something was wrong.

Maybe it was the fact that when I opened the door, he didn't even look up from the sheaf of papers in his hands. Or the way he was hunched over his desk with a deep frown across his face. But I think it was the tension radiating off him in waves so palpable they practically knocked me over the second I entered into the room.

I closed the door behind me, and its click echoed ominously through the quiet office. "Hi."

"Hi," Bennett muttered, attention still focused on the document in front of him. After a second, he set it down, glancing up. When his gaze locked with mine, I nearly flinched. There was a look in his dark blue eyes that I hadn't been on the receiving end of in a long time. One I'd hoped to never see again. It wasn't just cold; it was glacial.

I took a few tentative steps toward his desk, and he straightened in his chair but didn't stand to greet me like he normally would have. His dress shirt wasn't as neatly pressed as usual, either. His dark hair was mussed like he'd been running his hands through it, and his undereye circles told me he'd slept very little, if at all. Which was no surprise, considering how much he had at stake. I guess that explained his frosty reception.

"If you got caught up with work," I said gently, "we could have rescheduled for dinner tonight instead."

He shook his head, not meeting my eyes. "It's not about work. We need to talk."

My stomach did a skydive. Everything had been perfect since we'd gotten back from Mexico—too perfect. I'd been waiting for the other shoe to drop. For everything to come crashing down. For Bennett to change his mind and bail on me again.

And now he was.

I swallowed the gravel in my throat and eased into the cream leather guest chair facing his desk, bracing myself. "About what?"

Bennett turned the stack of papers in front of him and leaned forward, wordlessly sliding them across the polished desk to me. I glanced down, confused. It was a commercial lease agreement between AM Developments as the landlord—with Lace & Grace as a tenant.

My jaw dropped. "What the hell is this?"

"What does it look like?" he asked evenly.

I grabbed the contract and began rifling through the pages, certain there had to be some kind of mistake. Much to my dismay, Quinn's signature and initials were all over every single page. *Quinn Montgomery. QM.* Over and over again.

Disbelief barreled into me. We were still in the process of getting the third location off the ground and she'd made an executive decision about a fourth without even consulting me. She'd committed to fourteen thousand dollars in rent per month for five years, with an option to renew for an additional five years. What on earth we she thinking?

Oh, that's right. Quinn wasn't thinking. She was caught under Adam's spell, letting him manipulate her for his own self-serving purposes. But that was no excuse for doing this, especially not when it directly affected me.

"I've never seen this before in my life." I gestured with the papers. "I didn't even know Quinn signed this."

Bennett's eyebrows lifted, but his expression was one of disbelief and not surprise. "You're telling me you didn't know about the lease."

"I had no idea," I insisted, reading through the termination and default clauses again. Maybe there was a loophole, or some kind of no-fault provision that applied prior to the commencement of construction. But as far as I could tell, the agreement didn't contain an exit mechanism beyond a hefty financial penalty. "If I had been aware of this, I would have told you."

"Right."

The papers crumpled in my hands. "You think I knew?"

"You're saying Quinn signed a lease for a fourth location and you had no idea." He nodded to the wrinkled contract.

I bristled. The way he kept repeating back what I'd just said both stung and irritated the hell out of me.

"Do you see my signature on this contract?" My voice climbed and I caught myself, lowering it a notch. "Have you met my sister? This is exactly something Quinn would do—act without asking me, like always."

Bennett drew in a slow inhale, holding it for a beat before he let it go. "It just seems like a stretch, that's all." He studied my face, his own expression devoid of the warmth he usually regarded me with.

An ice pick stabbed at my heart. "You don't believe me?" Without even thinking, I pushed out of my chair, coming to stand awkwardly in front of his desk. Bennett stayed seated and his demeanor remained infinitely calmer than mine, which made me feel even worse.

"I want to believe you."

"But you don't."

He gave a one-shoulder shrug, saying nothing. The room

started to swim around me, and I lowered myself back into my seat. This version of Bennett who sat before me was a completely different person than the one I'd spent the weekend with. I tried to tell myself he was on edge about the bid, but that didn't make his callous demeanor hurt any less.

My gaze dropped to the papers in my hand. On some level, I knew the lease was a big deal—potentially catastrophic, even—but while things with Bennett were unraveling before my eyes, it was impossible to care.

Before I could stop myself, feelings I had been repressing for weeks tumbled out. "You pushed me away for years. Stupidly, I let you waltz back into my life without so much as an explanation. And you have the nerve not to trust *me*?" I huffed, fighting to restrain the hot tears welling up in my eyes. I couldn't believe this was happening. "Do you honestly think I'd sit here and lie straight to your face? Do you think that little of me?"

Bennett's face fell, his tone softening a fraction. "Thay. I didn't mean it like that."

I tossed the papers back onto his desk and they slid into the middle, coming to a stop halfway between us. "Either you believe me, or you don't."

"I just think you might be afraid to tell me the truth," he said carefully.

Pretty ironic, when he was one of the only people that I did tell the truth to.

"Why don't you trust me?" I pressed. "When have I ever given you a reason not to?"

He didn't respond.

Realization hit me like a wrecking ball to the gut. Bennett had completely side-stepped my remark about him bailing from my life. He was intentionally avoiding the subject. There had to be a reason why.

"Is this why you stopped talking to me in high school?" My

hands balled into fists, and the hurt came rushing back to me all over again. "Do you think I did something to break your trust back then?"

Bennett's entire demeanor instantly shifted, and he looked away. He stared at the desk in front of him, working his jaw, as if weighing what to say. Time slowed to a crawl while I waited, brimming with trepidation.

Finally, his gaze snapped back up to mine, brow furrowed. "Do you really want to get into this? We were just kids."

"Get into what?" I asked. "I didn't do anything."

"I'm willing to move past it, but the least you could do is own up to it."

Panic skittered through me. I didn't even know why. I never did anything to Bennett; that was the whole problem. One day we were friends—verging on something more—and the next, it was like we were strangers. He cut me out without any explanation.

"Own up to what?" I felt like a broken record, but I had no idea what he was talking about.

His expression clouded over like a category five storm rolling in. "You sold me out."

"How?" I demanded, leaning forward. My panic multiplied exponentially, tangling with threads of anger and disbelief to form a knot in my belly. After all this time, Bennett actually thought I wronged *him*.

"My dad?" Bennett's throat bobbed. "The whole school knew he'd been carted away in handcuffs from our house like some kind of common criminal. It was the only thing people talked about for months. There were even rumors he'd killed a guy. That ring a bell?"

A pang of sympathy surged through me. I remembered—it was impossible to forget witnessing Bennett's life implode from the sidelines—but I still didn't know what it had to do with me. I could tell he wasn't done speaking, so I nodded silently.

He continued, "Holden was out of town for a soccer tournament when my dad was arrested. My mother didn't even get a chance to tell him what happened in person, because he found out about it on the trip—in a text message from one of his fucking friends."

My stomach lunched. "Oh my God."

Growing up, Holden had been the quiet, sensitive type; the opposite of Bennett in nearly every way. He donated all his birthday money every year to the local animal shelter and wrote depressing poetry about subjects like global warming as a tween. I could only imagine how he'd taken that news.

"By the time Holden got back, he refused to go back to school. Failed freshman year. Had to attend summer classes and nearly got kicked out of the academy altogether." Bennett paused, cords in his neck tensing. "All his little dipshit friends turned on him, too. He was on suicide watch for months. Let's just say that issue hasn't exactly been put to bed, either."

"Bennett," I whispered, my hand flying to cover my mouth. A fresh wave of tears pricked at my eyes. It wasn't a huge secret that Holden struggled with his mental health, but I hadn't known the full extent of it, and it was clear that it weighed heavily on Bennett. "I'm so sorry."

He rolled his shoulders and loosened his tie, tugging it off and setting it aside on the corner of his desk. Unbuttoning the top of his dress shirt, he continued. "People began to make up wild stories about what my dad had done. The gossip turned vicious and started to include stuff about my mom being involved, too. She was so humiliated that she quit her position on the hospital fundraising board, which, as you may remember, was one of her favorite pastimes. And it all started because word got out about my father's arrest."

His last sentence hung in the air between us like an allegation I didn't quite understand. Bennett looked at me pointedly, waiting for a response. I shifted in my seat as I tried to make sense of what he'd said, but there were still missing pieces of the puzzle.

"I'm not trying to be difficult," I said, "but I'm afraid I don't follow. What does this all have to do with me?"

Incredulity crossed his face. "You were the only one who knew."

The words landed at my feet like a grenade.

"You think—you seriously think I told everyone?" My grip on the upholstered armrest tightened. I wasn't sure whether I was more hurt or offended. There was definitely a hefty dose of shock mixed in there, too.

Nearly ten years of estrangement, all because of...this? Something I hadn't even done?

"The only people who knew were me, my mother, our family lawyer, and you." Bennett held up a hand, ticking off his fingers. "Once I told you, our entire school knew by the next day. The whole town, by the day after that."

"You know I would never spread something like that around."

"Sometimes, even telling one person is enough. You used to tell Quinn everything." He sighed and raked his fingers through his hair, leaving it even more disheveled. "That was my fault. I should have known you would."

"But I didn't tell Quinn," I said, suddenly realizing this must have explained his apparent distaste for her. "I didn't tell a single soul. I would never do that to you, Bennett."

"Then how did everyone find out?" He gestured, growing visibly frustrated.

"I have no idea." While I could see how it looked from his perspective, it gutted me to know he thought I'd do that. I frowned, mulling over the possibilities. Bennett was popular in high school, and he had no shortage of other friends to confide in. "I figured you must have told Pierce or one of the other guys on the team."

"No. I didn't trust any of them with that information. I knew none of them would be able to keep their mouths shut."

Everything about that day came rushing back, and a sickening recognition dawned on me.

I stood up again, fraught with adrenaline. "I think I might know how it got out. Do you remember the day you told me?"

"Sure," Bennett said. "I was cutting bio, smoking a joint by the side entrance. Hard to forget a day that shitty."

"Did you happen to see who I was with?"

He took a sip of coffee from his black mug, placing it back down. "No, I didn't even see you coming until you swooped down and snatched that joint out of my fingers."

"Millie and I had just left AP Biology when I spotted you, and then I blew her off to go intervene. What do you think is more likely? That I'm lying to you nine years later, or that the biggest gossip in the entire town circled back, eavesdropped on our conversation, and blabbed to everyone?" Despite the molten anger churning within me, my voice cracked. I'd never been so furious, devastated, and resentful all at once in my entire life.

I leaned against Bennett's desk, mind reeling. I was going to find Millie after this and ream her out until I lost my voice. Even that wouldn't make up for what she'd done. She cost me something that could never be replaced. But Bennett played a role in that, too.

"Fucking Millie," Bennett murmured, more to himself than to me. "Makes perfect sense, though. She even tried to 'console' me."

A sliver of doubt crept into the back of my mind. "We both know Millie's always had a crush on you, so why would she blow up your life?"

Her involvement was the only logical explanation, yet it was still illogical in its own way. While I hated to punch holes in my only plausible alibi, I needed to understand her motives.

"Wanted to drive a wedge between us, obviously. She was jealous of you."

"Of me being your study partner for AP Chemistry?"

Bennett stood up and pushed his chair back. His eyes darkened, expression smoldering. He stepped around his desk and came to stand in front of me. His fingertips landed on my hips, thumbs pressing in possessively. My breath stuttered and my body instinctively started to lean into him, eager for more.

"I can't tell if you're messing with me right now or if you're actually this oblivious." His nose brushed mine, breath warm against my face. I almost tilted my head to close the distance and crash my lips into his, but my brain slammed on the brakes and stopped me.

I took a step back, withdrawing from his grasp. "Let's go with the second answer."

"I liked you," he said. "Sitting next to you in AP Chem was the highlight of my week. Why do you think I asked you to homecoming?"

My heart crumpled like a fender bender. Back then, I'd harbored an enormous schoolgirl crush on Bennett. I had no idea he'd felt the same way. We wasted years—almost a decade—apart all because of one stupid misunderstanding. Because of his pride.

"If you liked me so much, why didn't you talk to me? We used to tell each other everything." I tried to catch my breath, but it snagged in my throat. It was taking every ounce of strength I had to keep my tears at bay. "I was your friend, and you were supposed to be mine."

"I'm sorry." There was anguish written across his face. "I was a fucking wreck. As far as I knew, my mom was dying, my dad was about to serve life behind bars, my little brother was liable to kill himself the next time I left him unattended—then I went and ruined all of our lives by letting news about my dad's arrest get out. Plus…" Bennett scrubbed a hand across his jawline, shaded with a day's worth of rich brown stubble. "I was embarrassed."

"Embarrassed? Why?"

"When I thought you betrayed my trust, I assumed you didn't like me anymore because of what happened with my dad." He peered down at me, deep blue eyes gleaming with sadness. "That sounds really fucking stupid, doesn't it?"

I didn't know what to say. It was a lot to process, especially when I'd had less than twenty minutes to do it.

"I was pretty torn up when you went to homecoming with Archer after that," he added.

Oh, that was rich. *He* was torn up. The guy who persecuted me for a crime I didn't commit. Meanwhile, I cried so hard I burst a blood vessel in my eye, lost ten pounds from not eating, and couldn't even look in his direction at school without nearly breaking down into tears all over again.

"You may recall that I was supposed to go with someone else, but he decided to stop speaking to me. I went with Archer to save face, and I had a terrible time." I gritted my teeth, fighting back another wave of tears that threatened to overflow.

Bennett grunted, and something that looked like jealousy flitted across his face. He took a step closer. "You seemed okay to me."

"How would you know?" I crossed my arms, hugging my body to maintain the distance between us. "You weren't even there."

"I went to try to talk to you," he said. "I missed you, and I was starting to think I'd made a mistake. When I saw you two kissing, I figured I'd fucked things up for good."

All of his goddamn assumptions had been wrong. Every single one. I opened my mouth to argue, but he held up his hand, cutting me off.

"That was sixteen-year-old logic, Thay." He leaned one hip against his polished desk, facing me. "I know I have no one to blame for that other than myself. You had every right to go with him and do whatever you wanted, no matter how much I hated it."

"Archer kissed me. I didn't kiss him back," I said, recalling that horrendous homecoming dance. His breath had smelled like the cheap beer he and his friends somehow managed to smuggle in. He also tried to get handsy with me over in the corner of the dance floor. "You must have had the world's worst timing if that's when you came across us. Want to know what the rest of the evening looked like? I cried in the bathroom twice. Hated every minute of the dance. And made Archer take me home early because I was too upset about you. Does that make you happy?"

"No," he said. "It makes me feel like shit."

"That makes two of us, then." A lone tear slipped out, trailing down my cheek, and I brushed it away with my finger. "You're the only person who ever broke my heart."

He looked stricken. "Don't you think I know I made a huge mistake?"

"How do I know you won't make the same one again?" Another tear escaped and he lifted his hand like he was going to reach for me, but when I leaned away from him, he let it fall to his side instead.

"Thay, I would never. I'm not going to screw up a shot with you twice. That's why I talked to you about the lease."

"Talked to me, or accused me of knowing about it? Which one do you think you did?"

Bennett's lips pressed into a line. "You're right, my delivery sucked. I assumed the worst, and I'm sorry for doing that."

My issue wasn't the delivery itself so much as what it meant.

I'd already lived through him doing that once. My heart wouldn't survive a second round.

A weighty hush fell between us while the chrome analog clock on his desk ticked away. Twelve ticks passed, and neither of us spoke.

"Please don't shut me out," he said quietly. "I can't imagine my life without you now."

His plea eroded my resolve until it nearly broke, but I knew it was the only logical course of action. The only sane course of action, too. Right now, I could stomach the idea of walking away because what we had was never technically real. It was infinitely better than having him walk away once it was.

"Look…" I faltered, unable to bring myself to verbalize what I was really thinking. "This is a lot to process. I need some time, okay?"

"No." His voice was firm, like he knew what was actually running through my mind. "I'm not going to let you walk away like this." He reached for me again, but I took another step back, gathering my purse from off the chair. I clutched my purse against my coat, trying to conceal my trembling hands.

"Remember the favor you owed me?" I asked. "I'm cashing it in. I need you to leave me alone until the engagement party."

It was a week and a half away, longer than we'd gone without talking since this all began. The idea of not talking to him for that long killed me—which was exactly why I needed the space. Cut my losses now or have my heart cut to pieces later. It would be better this way, even if it hurt.

He blinked. "You're still willing to go through with that?"

I didn't want to; the idea of pretending everything was okay with Bennett in front of an audience seemed akin to psychological torture. I already told him I would, though, and I always kept my word.

"I will. But it's the last time I'm going to pretend."

CHAPTER FORTY

Thayer

THE ELEVATOR RIDE DOWN FROM BENNETT'S OFFICE TOOK LESS than five minutes, but it felt like five hours. I was working overtime not to break down while I was surrounded by office workers coming and going from their lunch breaks, blissfully oblivious to the fact that my heart lay in a thousand tiny pieces on the elevator floor.

By the time I reached the safety of my SUV in the underground parking garage, I was distraught. I barely managed to lock the door behind me before I buried my face in my hands and burst into huge, ugly sobs. Tears streamed down my cheeks, dripping onto my shirt and my lap, as I drew in shaky gulps of air, trying to catch my breath. I tried to remember the last time I cried like this and realized it had also been over him.

What just happened? How did everything go from the way it had been with us all weekend—since Mexico, really—to this? It made my chest ache in an all-too-familiar way. Not only did Bennett actually believe I'd hide something as major as a lease from him, but he also assumed I destroyed his family's reputation back in high school.

Here I was, thinking he was one of the only people who understood me, when it was clear he didn't even know me at all.

I didn't understand. I needed to understand. Between spending the weekend together and those moments in the car, I had let myself start to believe he actually felt something for me. Did none of that mean anything to him? Was I reading everything wrong?

Then another horrifying possibility crept into my mind.

Was *any* of it even real?

Nausea bowled into me, and my tears restarted again in earnest. Convincing everyone we were an item, salvaging his reputation, winning Callaghan over...All of Bennett's reasons for being with me were rapidly coming to an end. Was that why he'd been so cold to me upstairs about the lease?

A text from Bennett popped up and I swiped away the notification without reading it, tossing my phone in the center console. What was going to happen after our engagement party? Once Callaghan signed, and Bennett got what he wanted? Had he ever even planned to stick around until Adam and Quinn's wedding? Maybe our expiration date had been closer than I realized.

Maybe I'd let myself get played by the chess master himself.

I hiccupped, fumbling in my purse for a pack of tissues, and blotted my eyes in the mirror. They were glassy and bloodshot, impossible to conceal. Going back to work wasn't even remotely an option. I grabbed my phone and quickly texted Quinn to inform her I wouldn't be returning to the store because I was under the weather. It was true, anyway; I had a severe case of heartbreak flu.

Once I was marginally calmer, or at least calm enough to drive, I quickly checked my surroundings to ensure Bennett hadn't followed me downstairs and witnessed my complete breakdown. Then I started the ignition, determined to get out of Flux's parkade as quickly as possible.

Anger, sadness, resentment, and grief mixed together, the

chemical reaction forming a cloud of despair. If I'd possessed the ability to string together a coherent sentence, I'd have called Quinn on the spot to chew her out about the lease. Not only did she deserve it, but I also almost wanted to pick a fight with my sister so I could take the way I was feeling out on someone else.

The following day, I holed up at our north location when I knew Quinn would be busy changing up the retail displays at the south store. Bennett stopped by, but I stayed in the back and had our sales assistant, Kyla, send him away. I wasn't ready to talk to him. He might have had time to get over what happened, but I hadn't. He'd texted and called multiple times, too, completely disregarding my favor request. Not that I'd expected him to honor it.

By Wednesday, I'd been crying and moping for the better part of two days. Lola had tried to lure me out of my apartment for a drink, but I'd insisted on hibernating instead. Bennett was still a gigantic question mark, and I was going to delay facing that for as long as possible. But I knew I had to handle Quinn.

When I arrived at Lace & Grace shortly after nine, Quinn was perched on a stool by the cash register, sorting a pile of lacy white bras by size. She was the picture of perfection, with a fresh set of beige-blonde highlights, perfectly applied makeup, and a well-rested air about her. I was the polar opposite, with my hair desperately in need of a trim, puffy eyes, and hastily applied makeup after waking up late this morning. After very little sleep and entirely too much caffeine, I was simultaneously both wired and tired. Not to mention, lacking a single shred of patience.

Jaw clenched, I strode up to her and tossed a copy of the lease agreement on the counter. It landed with a loud, confrontational slap. I'd intended to approach the subject in a calm, diplomatic way, but the minute I laid eyes on her, that was no longer an option.

I guess I was taking a cue from Bennett on how to start difficult conversations.

Quinn paused, glancing up at me. "What's gotten into you?" She scanned my face and her eyes turned to saucers. "You look like you've been crying. Are you okay?"

I shrugged off my camel Moncler Fleole coat, placing it on the far end of the counter beside my canvas tote. It was bitterly cold outside, but I was already growing hot under the collar at the thought of having this conversation.

"You signed a lease in Adam's development on our behalf without discussing it with me first? What the hell were you thinking?" I gestured to the papers, but Quinn didn't bother to look. Why would she? She already knew.

"Oh, that?" She waved me off, her freshly manicured, mauve-colored nails gleaming under the store's LED lighting. "I was helping Adam with the bid. The Mayor is all about supporting local businesses. In order to win him over, Adam needed some independent stores on the tenant roster to counterbalance the big corporate chains."

"Well, Adam won." While I knew going in that this had to be the result of Adam's machinations, Quinn's flimsy justification was infuriating. She was oblivious to the destruction she'd inadvertently triggered in my personal life and was apparently unconcerned about the potential fallout for our stores, too.

I added, "Now we're stuck with a fourth retail space we don't want or need. You do realize a lease is a legally binding contract, right? There are financial penalties for breaking them, and they're generally steep." Maybe she didn't realize that. I was the one who handled all the legal and regulatory matters—not to mention, all the money. Based on her blasé attitude, I was sure she hadn't read the lease before signing it, either.

"It's fine. Adam said he'd let us out of the lease after the project was approved."

Of course, he did.

OTHERWISE ENGAGED | 333

"And you believe that?"

Quinn's tone chilled. "Of course. He's my fiancé." She pushed the neatly stacked pile of thongs aside and tore open a plastic bag containing black lace bikini underwear, dumping them out on the counter.

It was a mighty big leap of faith on her part. With no paper trail and zero proof, Adam could easily strong-arm us into fulfilling our obligations contained within the lease agreement. If they were to break up tomorrow, we would be screwed. Quinn's willful ignorance was exasperating. How was I supposed to stay in business with her when she did things like this without any remorse?

Even more disturbingly, there was a clear relationship between her problematic behavior and when Adam entered her life.

My nails dug into my palms. "We need to talk about Adam."

"What do you mean?" She stiffened but continued to sort through the pile of black bikinis.

Here goes nothing.

"Let's take a look at how all this went down, okay?" I said. "Adam randomly bumps into you at a Starbucks, you two hit it off, and he proposes almost immediately—right when he's trying to get his business off the ground."

I'd bet good money the Starbucks encounter wasn't random, either. I wasn't sure how, but I was certain he'd orchestrated this whole scheme with my sister from the ground up.

A surge of revulsion coursed through me. That probably meant Adam tried to hustle me, too. But he must have seen the writing on the wall when we were having drinks and I confirmed my anti-marriage stance hadn't changed. Didn't stop him from sleeping with me, though. Creep.

Then again, I still couldn't explain why I'd slept with *him*, except for having been drinks deep—and maybe a little lonely. I'd have taken it back a thousand times if I could.

"What exactly are you trying to say?" Quinn asked. Through the window, a woman pushing a stroller walked by and I held my breath for a beat, praying she wouldn't turn and come into the store, but she continued past.

I tried to keep my tone non-confrontational, knowing my words were anything but. "Don't you think the timing of your relationship is a little suspect? And the fact that he needed a large amount of money that you ended up securing for him?"

"I already told you," she snapped. "That was my idea."

"Are you sure?"

"Positive." She huffed a sardonic laugh, shaking her head. "I know you're new to the whole 'relationship thing,' but this is how serious relationships work, Thayer. You're a team. You help each other. Once you're talking marriage, you have to think about what's best for you as a family."

Her last words confirmed what I already knew. Adam had used Quinn's dreams of starting a family to entice her into helping him—while manipulating her into thinking it was her idea. After all, it's hard to stay at home with your carload of kids in your big suburban mansion, like she'd always wanted, if your husband's company has gone belly-up.

"Don't you see? Adam is taking advantage of you, Quinn. He's using you."

"Oh my God." She shot to her feet, planting her hands on her slender hips. "What is your problem? Are you mad because I'm getting married first?"

More proof that my sister was completely out of touch with reality. I'd never cared about getting married, and even if I did, I wouldn't see it as some kind of race down the aisle. She knew that, too. Or at least, she would have if she was in her right mind.

"My problem is that you're in a vulnerable place right now, and I don't want to see you get hurt." Vulnerable was putting it mildly. Lately, the slightest hint of stress caused her to crumble like a macaron from her favorite French bakery.

"Are you having problems with Bennett? Is that what all of this is about?" Quinn demanded. She flopped back onto the stool and crossed her bare legs, anchoring the heel of her pump on the foot rail, and threw me a haughty look. "Kyla said he stopped by the store yesterday and you had her ask him to leave. Is that where this is coming from?"

My throat closed up at the mention of Bennett's name. For a few painful seconds, I wasn't able to respond for fear of bursting into tears.

Finally, I choked out, "This has nothing to do with him."

Quinn tsked in disbelief while I scrambled inwardly to formulate an effective case. If I wanted her to see how selfish Adam's motives were, I knew I had to resort to the big guns—even though she was guaranteed to pull out her own verbal assault rifle in return.

Even then, I still wasn't entirely convinced Quinn would listen to me; I could tell her the facts, but I couldn't make her believe them.

"When did you and Adam start dating?" I asked. "Specifically."

She glared at me. "Why?"

"Humor me."

"Late June. Happy?" Quinn returned her attention to sorting through the underwear at the counter, making a point to ignore me.

Though it was closer than I would have liked, there was no overlap. A small silver lining. I closed my eyes and inhaled through my nose, channeling the emotional strength required for what was about to come next. Nausea, which had been my default setting for the past two days, threatened to overtake me again.

"Quinn…" I reopened my eyes, fixing my gaze on her. The words were difficult to force out, syllables jagged in my mouth. "Adam and I slept together a month before you started dating. While you were in Napa with Millie.

"You what?!" Quinn's attention snapped back over to me, and she dropped the underwear in her hands onto the table. Her voice was shrill. "Are you serious? Why didn't you tell me?"

"It was a one-night mistake. He blew me off after and I was embarrassed. When he showed up with you on his arm a few weeks later, I felt like the way he'd treated me was my fault somehow—like

maybe he was going to be better to you. But then Bennett said…"
My courage faded, along with my voice. If my first bombshell hadn't
set her off, this surely would.

"Oh, this should be good. What did Bennett say?" Quinn
placed an elbow on the counter and leaned forward in mock interest.
"I mean, he's known for being so reliable and upstanding himself."

I chose to ignore her jab. Bennett had at least been faithful,
which was more than I could say for Adam.

"He said that Adam was being inappropriate with other women
at the club in Mexico. He told me he's heard rumors about Adam
cheating on you, too. From credible sources."

Quinn laughed, caustic and sharp. "I'm supposed to believe
that a womanizer like Bennett has magically morphed into the perfect fiancé, and that my *actually* perfect fiancé is a player? A player
who's using me for daddy's money?"

I clamped down on the frustration building within me. Quinn
was determined to bury her head in the sand about everything: the
lease agreement, Adam, and reality in general. She'd always been
this way to an extent, but before, it had been more annoying and
harmless than anything. Now, it verged on intolerable and hazard-
ous. What would be next? Was she going to sell the business without telling me?

"It's pretty clear Adam's not perfect, according to some of the
things you've told me. You can't honestly tell me you think he's faithful to you. Bennett's intel just confirmed what you already know,
deep down inside." It came out harsher than I intended, but it was
the truth.

"This is hilarious." She slapped the glass counter with her hand.
"The two most dysfunctional people I know, giving me advice about
my own relationship. Glass houses much, Thay?"

"This isn't relationship advice, Quinn, I'm worried about you. I
genuinely believe Adam's intentions are bad, and it breaks my heart.
Especially with everything you're already dealing with."

Quinn shook her head, raking a hand through her loose curls.

"You think you're so perfect, but you're a control freak. All you care about is everyone following the rules and doing what you think is right, even if it's not right for them."

"That's not even a little—"

She continued before I could finish. "Your issue with daddy investing in Adam's company sounds a lot like a 'you' problem, Thay. It's not my fault your relationship with Bennett isn't as strong as mine and Adam's."

My stomach sank to the floor. Little did she know, there was no relationship with Bennett. Just a broken pile of what-ifs, almosts, and could-have-beens.

As for my sister, if this is how it was going to be from now on, continuing to work together was an impossibility. It was like we inhabited two different planets. Two different realities, even. Something had to give; either our relationship or the store, hopefully not both.

A heavy silence fell over the room while I tried to work out what to say. For years, I'd allowed myself to be derailed from pursuing what I wanted in order to make Quinn—and my mother—happy. Postponing business school for one year had turned into two years, then three, and now I was staring down the end of year four. I'd sacrificed too much to stand here and be walked all over like this.

"What?" Quinn snorted. "You've got nothing to say all of a sudden? You were full of such helpful insights a minute ago. I can't believe—"

Something in me snapped.

"I can't do this," I blurted out, cutting her off before the tirade could continue. "I'll help you replace me, but I quit. I can't keep bending to what you want, what you think, what you say. If you want to run the show, have at it. I'm out. Done."

It was like a huge weight had been lifted off my chest; one that I hadn't even known was there.

Her eyebrows shot up, quickly lowering into a scowl. "Fine."

She leapt out of her seat and spun away, high heels clicking angrily against the hardwood while she stomped into the office.

I watched the door close behind her, my eyes blurring with tears. They started to overflow, warmth streaming down my cheeks. Drawing in a jagged breath, I gathered up my purse and coat, crying in big, ugly sobs. I knew Quinn could see me on the security camera, but I didn't care. She must not have cared, either, because she stayed in the office until I left.

On some level, I knew I should have been devastated, but all I felt was numb. My life was vacant. No job, no Bennett, no Quinn.

A few days ago, everything had been almost impossibly perfect, and now, everything was broken.

CHAPTER FORTY-ONE

Bennett

WAS SERIOUSLY CONSIDERING SELLING ALL MY BELONGINGS and becoming one of those guys who lived in a van down by the river. At this point, it seemed easier than facing the fallout that was imminent in my life.

No Thayer, because I fucked that up. No Flux, because I fucked that up too. And probably no Ian when all was said and done, because he wouldn't appreciate being taken down with me. Bankruptcy would strain even the strongest of friendships.

The only literal silver lining was that my mom had gotten encouraging news from her doctors. It was early, but so far, her cancer was responding to treatment. I was thankful for that. I just wished everything else wasn't shit.

"We have to keep going," Ian said, bringing me back to reality, where I was seated across the table from him at Saltlick, an upscale steakhouse down the street from our office. He'd dragged me out in some attempt to cheer me up, or maybe just to get me to eat something.

I stared at him blankly. "Why?"

"Because we can't lay down and die?" He waved his fork at me, loaded with a bite of medium-rare steak. "That's your favorite motto."

"I'm tired." I scrubbed a hand along my chin, clad with enough stubble that it was now more like a beard. A full plate of food sat in front of me, untouched. I poked at my filet with disinterest. "Really fucking tired."

"That's what Adam wants," he pointed out, trying to goad me into being angry. Normally, it would have worked, and I would have perked right up on a mission to destroy. But I hadn't slept in several days, and I didn't have the energy to care.

"It's not done until it's done," Ian added. "The planning department hasn't issued a decision on the bid yet."

"We both know what it's going to be," I muttered.

He studied me over the rim of his glass of ice water, eyes assessing. "How much of this has to do with Thayer?"

All of it.

Even if we did manage to bail out the sinking ship that was Flux, it would be a hollow victory without her. In fact, if I had to pick one or the other, I would have chosen her. But that didn't matter, because she didn't want me back. Which was fully my fault.

I shrugged helplessly. "It isn't helping, that's for sure."

"All couples fight," Ian said. "A fight isn't necessarily the end of the world."

"It is when she won't talk to me."

CHAPTER FORTY-TWO

Thayer

I HADN'T SPOKEN TO BENNETT OR QUINN IN DAYS. AS THE WEEK dragged on, I woke up every morning even lonelier than I had been the day before, and it only intensified over the course of the day; an aching emptiness that no amount of distraction could fix. Every night, I turned off my ringer and went to bed early, desperately trying to avoid the bitter reality of my life.

Of course, Bennett had texted me several times. Called a handful of times, too. Even stopped by the store once more. But I didn't know how to face him. I didn't even know what to say.

Quinn had been radio silent, however. Sharing our calendars turned out to be a great way to avoid each other by working at opposite stores.

Half an hour into an episode of Emily in Paris, my phone buzzed with another text from Bennett.

Talk to me, Thay. I miss you.

The show continued in the background while I stared at the screen, debating whether to reply. Or how to reply, if I did. Before I could decide, there was a soft tap on my front door. My heart leapt into my throat, but I stayed glued to my spot on the couch. If it was Bennett, I didn't want to answer it. Fine, that was a lie. If it was Bennett, I did want to answer it—but I knew I shouldn't.

I also knew if I checked and it was him, I'd give in and open the door immediately. There was no way I could look him in the eyes and keep my resolve about, well, anything. That posed a fairly big problem with respect to our impending 'engagement' party.

When the keypad started beeping, my hopes deflated like a leaky tire. Bennett didn't know the code to my door. Quinn was the only person who did.

At first, I thought she was coming over to grovel via a bottle of rosé and pretend nothing had happened, which was her usual method of apology. But when I laid eyes on her, alarm bells sounded in my head. Her hair was limp and unwashed, and she was wearing a baggy grey hooded sweatshirt with black leggings. For many people, this might have been a fairly normal state of affairs, but for Quinn, this was rock bottom.

"Hey." I paused the show, standing to greet her. When she drew closer, I realized her eyes were puffy, skin blotchy and red. She'd been crying—a lot. Just like me. That explained the outfit, too.

Quinn set down her keys on the coffee table and buried her face in her hands, bursting into heaving sobs. Guilt seized me, along with a sisterly sense of duty, and I stepped forward, wrapping her in a hug. No matter how badly we'd left things between us, seeing her in so much pain hurt me almost as badly. Her shoulders racked with each frantic gasp for several minutes before they finally slowed, and she calmed down.

"I'm sorry, Thay." She pulled back, wiping away her tears with her sleeve. I reached behind me and grabbed a box of tissues, handing them to her. Sniffling, she dabbed at her eyes. "I wanted to believe Adam so badly that I turned into a total jerk. But when I started digging, I saw that you were right."

In this case, vindication didn't bring any sense of satisfaction. It simply stoked sheer, unadulterated rage toward Adam for hurting my sister. She'd been too good for him all along, and he had the nerve to be unfaithful to her? The only upside to this twisted situation is that now, she would be free of him. We all would be.

Except for our father, I guess, who was still tied to him through his investment. I wished Quinn hadn't facilitated that. Maybe there was some way he could get out of it or unload the shares on someone else.

"I didn't want to be right." I steered her over to the sectional, gesturing for her to sit. "Do you want something to drink?"

"Yes," she said immediately. "All the drinks. Hell, bring me the whole bottle."

I'd meant something more like water or tea, but I supposed getting drunk on a weeknight was a valid strategy right now, too. I disappeared into the kitchen, grabbing two highball glasses and some ice from the freezer to mix the drink with. Two vodka sodas in hand later—which were more vodka than soda—I joined Quinn on the couch.

"Do you want to talk about it?" I asked gently.

She took a gulp of her drink and set it down on the glass coffee table sans coaster. I cringed inwardly, but let it slide.

Quinn drew in a breath, brows drawn together. "Adam is away on business until next week and he forgot his iPad. It's signed into his account, so it receives all his text messages. After what you said yesterday, I decided to go digging to prove that you were wrong. All I had to do was guess his pin, which is his birthday because he's an idiot, and..." Her voice cracked. "It was all right there in front of me."

Dread bubbled in my gut. "What did you find?"

"You'll never believe it... Adam is having an affair with Millie." A mouthful of my vodka soda went down the wrong pipe and I started to cough. Her lips twisted into a grim smile. "Actually, I think I'm the affair, because it sounds like this started before I entered the picture."

"What?" I croaked, clearing my throat. I definitely hadn't been expecting that. Another girlfriend, maybe, but Millie? Quinn was her best friend; one of her only friends.

"Uh-huh." She nodded, pursing her lips. "Gross, right? Millie told me she was going on a spa retreat with her mom this week, but she failed to mention the part where she was meeting Adam for a weekend in a hotel after."

Oh, ew. Quinn was right; that was gross. The mental image alone was beyond disturbing.

"But what… why…?" I gestured vaguely, unable to make sense of what she was saying. I knew Adam was a garbage human being, and Millie was no saint herself, but this was beyond the pale.

"You were right about the money, too. It almost sounded like they were conspiring together the whole time." Quinn downed another half of her drink, shuddering at the alcohol burn.

I knew it. That that was how Adam ran into Quinn: Millie was playing puppeteer. She probably knew where Quinn was going to be and helped orchestrate their 'chance' meeting. I bet she'd even told him things to help win Quinn over, too. And Millie definitely, definitely knew about Quinn's fertility struggles, which made the entire conspiracy even more disgusting.

"Why would he do that?" I asked. "Millie has plenty of money of her own. Why not use hers?"

Quinn snorted. "No, she doesn't. When the stock market crashed back in college, her parents blew through her trust fund trying to make it up. They have nothing. Financed to the hilt, leased luxury cars, you name it. It's supposed to be some big secret, but fuck that. Now I'm going to tell everyone I know."

It would be sweet justice after what Millie did to Bennett, too.

"Do you have some cookies or something? I need sugar." She craned her head, looking into my kitchen.

"Let me go check." She'd made a remarkably quick recovery from hysterical tears to searching for processed carbohydrates in the span of minutes, but I wasn't going to question it. Pushing to stand, I went into the kitchen and returned with two bowls of cookie dough ice cream.

"Best I could do," I said, offering her a pink-patterned bowl.

She grabbed it out of my hands, diving into it with her spoon and eating the cookie dough first, like she always did.

"You know what the worst part is?" Quinn asked, as if reading my mind. She stirred her ice cream around with her spoon. "I don't even think I loved Adam. Because when I saw those messages, I was more angry than sad. And right now, I'm…embarrassed. Embarrassed I bought his phony act, or thought I was falling for such a jerk."

"Maybe you liked the idea of him," I said gently. "You know, the whole family thing."

"Yeah, I think I did." Quinn hiccupped, and sadness stretched across her face again. Something about her expression seemed almost childlike, and her voice turned small. "Are you still going to quit the store?"

Guilt plunged over me like a bucket of ice water. I felt bad saying yes, but I couldn't lie and say no, either. Quitting had been such a relief, that the instant I had, I knew it was the right choice all along. I'd already submitted a few MBA applications and was finalizing a couple more. With the way things were going, I didn't even know if I'd stay in our city for school. While my first-choice program was in the area, maybe I'd be better starting over somewhere else. It still came down to where I was accepted—though with a high GMAT score, I was hopeful I'd have several options to choose from.

I gave her an apologetic look. "I think we both know it's for the best, Quinn. For me, as well as our relationship."

"I don't know if I can handle the stores all alone," she admitted. "I know you shoulder a lot of the work."

I did, and I didn't. It's not that the things I handled were difficult, necessarily, it's that they were boring.

"I'll stick around until you get everything sorted out. I can teach you how to manage some items, and you can hire a bookkeeper for the rest. It's not too complicated, I promise."

That was the whole issue. At times, I could finish all the work I needed to do in an hour or less, which left me drifting aimlessly without anything else to occupy myself. Being left feeling like I hadn't accomplished anything of value at the end of the day made me a little empty on the inside.

Her jaw dropped with a sudden realization. "Oh my God. Did you and Bennett get into a fight because of the lease? Am I the reason you two are having problems right now?"

Problems was a diplomatic way of putting it. We'd imploded.

"Partly," I said. "That's what started our argument, but that wasn't all of it."

"What do you mean? You two are perfect together. I can't even imagine you arguing. Well, unless it's that cute little bickering thing you two always have going on, but that doesn't count. Everyone knows that's just foreplay."

Courage surged through me. "We were faking it, Quinn. When I told you I had a date to the wedding, I didn't." As humiliating as it was to own up to it, I felt like she deserved to hear the truth after what she'd just been through herself.

She laughed. "Nice try."

"No," I said. "I'm serious." I gathered up what was left of my dignity and tossed it straight out the window, telling her the truth in detail. After I finished explaining everything, from beginning to end and everything in between, Quinn looked more confused than when I started.

"First of all," she started, "I am so sorry I ever made you feel like you needed to lie about something like that. But I still…" She shook her head, blinking rapid-fire. "Bennett is in love with you, Thay. I guarantee it."

My heart contracted in my chest. I wanted to believe her, but it didn't make sense.

"Then why was he so mean to me about the lease?" It sounded

juvenile to phrase it that way out loud, but that's the only way I could explain it. He'd been mean; cold.

"Male pride?" Quinn offered. "Men are stupid creatures sometimes. Adam went by earlier that day to gloat about the fact that he was going to win the bid, so Bennett was probably riled up going into that conversation with you."

Bennett hadn't told me that, but an unpleasant encounter with Adam would have definitely put him on edge more than usual. I still didn't think that excused accusing me of hiding the lease from him, though. Or any of the other things that happened in the past.

The net result was me questioning every single thing about us. He'd had information I hadn't. It had been an uneven playing field from the start, and I'd lost a game I hadn't known I was playing.

"Think about it," she said, scooping up her last piece of cookie dough with her spoon, pointing it at me. "Bennett thinks he's about to lose everything—again—with you watching."

Sympathy and skepticism warred in my brain, and my gut twisted like a towel being run out. I clutched the cold ice cream bowl between my hands, letting it chill my skin in some warped form of catharsis.

"What if it's not that?" I asked. "What if none of it was real?"

Quinn put down her bowl and took mine out of my hands, setting it aside. Then she took my hands in hers, ducking to catch my eye. "From what I've seen, and from all the attempts he's made to get you to talk to him since you left his office, there's no way that this is just pretend. For either of you. I think you know that, deep down inside."

"But I *don't* know."

She raised her eyebrows pointedly. "Your heart knows."

My heart was telling me to get in the car, drive straight over to Bennett's, and pretend none of this ever happened. Clearly, my heart needed a breathalyzer, because it was drunk behind the wheel.

At any rate, my brain knew that was a terrible idea. With the mess I'd made of my life, I was kicking my heart out of the driver's seat for a while. Otherwise, it was going to drive me straight off a cliff.

When I didn't respond, Quinn waved her hand, prompting me. "And your heart is saying…"

"Run," I lied.

"You're not a good liar, Thay." She inclined her head, putting a finger to her bare lips thoughtfully. "Which is pretty telling, if you think about it. How were you able to convince so many people you were in love with Bennett if it was all fake?"

"But that doesn't mean his feelings for me are real, or that I should be with him." I grabbed my favorite fuzzy throw blanket from the basket beside the couch, draping it over my legs. Quinn scooted closer, joining me underneath it.

"You're scared," she mused, rubbing my arm soothingly. "It's normal to be scared when you fall for someone, especially if it's the first time you've ever done it."

I wasn't scared; I was terrified.

"I've had other boyfriends." But I was being contrary more than I was actually protesting. I could count the number of men I'd been emotionally invested in on one finger.

"How many of them have you cried over?"

We both knew the answer to that. A big, fat zero.

I shrugged and looked away. "Some people cry over commercials. Crying doesn't necessarily mean anything."

"With them, it doesn't. But it means plenty with you."

I tried to catch my breath but couldn't. "He already broke my heart once."

"So you're going to break it yourself for a second time?" she asked.

Ugh. I hated it when she was right.

"Think of it as a mitigation strategy," I said, digging in my heels. "Little break now, or big break later?"

"First of all"—Quinn gestured to me, rose-gold nails glinting in the light—"I wouldn't call this heartbreak you've got going on right now 'little.' Second of all, you have no way of knowing that Bennett will break your heart down the line. For all you know, you two could get married for real and live happily ever after."

Much as I liked to think that could happen, I was skeptical. Especially when it involved a man who was vocally opposed to marriage. Wait. I was opposed to marriage, too. Wasn't I? But then why did it sound so appealing when Quinn said it?

"Adam is such a shit," she muttered suddenly. "He's gunning for Bennett when he's the one who deserves to fall on his smug, stupid face." She paused, a look of pure contempt taking over her face as she turned to look at me. "But... I think I know how we can get Adam back."

"How?" I asked. I'd love nothing more than to see Adam go down, especially if Bennett triumphed as a result. No matter how hurt I was right now, I still didn't want to see him fail.

"I know how Adam was going to win the bid."

CHAPTER FORTY-THREE

Bennett

I CHECKED MY PHONE FOR THE TWENTIETH TIME IN AS MANY minutes, even though the ringer was on full volume. My text had gone unanswered, just like all the rest. Thayer still wouldn't talk to me.

For the first couple of days, I wrote it off as her needing time to cool down. Now, I was starting to panic.

Regret wasn't a strong enough word for what I'd done. It was more like self-loathing. I worked so hard to get behind those fucking walls of hers, and then I pushed her into building them right back up.

Ian was practically dragging me around by my tie at the office, trying to force me to deal with my responsibilities, from the menial to the critical. There was no shortage of work to be done; I just didn't care. Having witnessed it firsthand with Holden, I was beginning to wonder whether I was depressed.

As I walked out of the kitchen with a beer in hand, a soft knock sounded at my door. Only a handful of people knew the code to my building, and I was praying to God it was the one I wanted.

In some bizarre act of superstition, I didn't check the peephole before opening the door. And when I cracked it open, my prayers had been answered. Thayer was standing at my front door in black yoga pants, an oversized grey sweater, and not a trace of makeup. While she looked beautiful, like always, she also looked like she'd been crying. Knowing I was the cause of that made me feel even worse, and the dull ache I'd been carrying around for several days turned into a stabbing pain in my chest.

Our eyes locked and her mouth twitched, but I couldn't tell if she was fighting a smile or trying not to cry. Which was sort of where I was at, too.

My hands itched to reach out and grab her, but I knew I shouldn't. At least, not yet.

"Thay?" I opened the door all the way to find Quinn standing beside her. "Er, hi, Quinn." Relief and hope gave way to an epic amount of confusion, along with a hefty dose of disappointment. I couldn't imagine any scenario that would explain why the two of them were standing at my doorstep, but I was sure it didn't involve Thayer coming over to reconcile with me.

"Can we come in?" Thayer asked. "It's about Adam."

That lying, cheating, sneaky, bribing bastard.

I made another lap around my living room, raking a hand through my hair, which I was certain was standing straight on end at this point. Quinn and Thayer sat on the couch in front of me, looking mildly alarmed at the level of my anger. They didn't know how well I was actually hiding it. If I'd run into Adam right now, I would have maimed him with my bare hands.

"Did you get screenshots?" I asked Quinn. Receipts proving

he'd bribed the mayor were exactly what I needed to put a bullet through Adam's career.

"No," she admitted.

What little remained of my patience vanished and I slapped my thigh in frustration. "Fuck!" Quinn was a zero out of ten on the common sense scale.

"Bennett," Thayer reprimanded me, nudging me with her foot as I passed by. It was warped, but the bodily contact gave me hope. Despite the fact that I was half out of my mind, she'd softened toward me since she first arrived.

"Adam's still out of town," Quinn added, evidently unfazed by my outburst. "I can get them. I'll do it when I get home tonight."

I made a sharp right, beginning another lap from one end of the room to the other. I'd long since lost count of how many laps I was at in total, but I'd been pacing for over twenty minutes, and at the rate I was going, I'd be pacing all night. The amount of adrenaline surging through my veins was unparalleled. I knew Adam was a slimeball, but bribing an elected official for the sole purpose of one-upping me? That was ballsy.

What I hadn't figured out was how to leverage it, however.

"I know you guys want to help," I said, "and I appreciate that. But outing his bribery and causing a big scandal will mean this development gets put on hold indefinitely, and that still leaves me in a bad position." I hated to admit that, especially to Thayer, but it was an open secret at this point. We all knew Flux was in trouble.

"Well..." Thayer hesitated. "If AM Developments is going to win the bid, what if we take AM Developments?"

I came to a stop. "What do you mean?"

"According to the prospectus, Adam only owns thirty percent right now. My father has thirty-five, and his other investor holds the remaining thirty-five."

"Who's his other investor?" Quinn asked.

I couldn't believe she didn't know. Had she and Adam talked about anything of substance at all?

"Richard," Thayer and I both said.

We pored over the prospectus Adam had provided Thayer's father, stress-testing AM Developments. It took a few hours to determine whether our plan was financially feasible, and then we double-checked the figures to make sure Adam hadn't padded them to paint himself in a more favorable light. Quinn tried to help as much as she could, but she didn't understand most of it.

When Quinn excused herself to use the bathroom, Thayer and I found ourselves alone for the first time since our fight. While being around her could have been awkward, it wasn't. Partially because we were so occupied crunching numbers, but also, I thought, because of what was still between us. The ever-present magnetism was just as strong as it had always been. After spending a couple of hours with Thayer, I was confident I hadn't ruined things forever; I just didn't know how to make her see that.

"AM Developments is in a pretty good position right now," Thayer pointed out, running her finger along the totals at the bottom of the spreadsheet.

"Of course, it is," I said, failing to keep bitterness out of my voice. "Look how liquid he was when he started. Flux has never had the luxury of that much operating capital. I floated the entire company myself when we started out." And then Adam stole from me, which meant I'd floated his company, too.

Her tone softened. "I wasn't blaming you, Bennett. I know he screwed you over, but we're going to get him back."

We. The simple two-letter word did something to me. Was there still a "we"? I wanted there to be, but I didn't want her to be on my team right now out of pity.

I turned to face her. "You don't have to do this for me, you know."

"Don't think of it as me doing it for you, think of me doing it for Quinn," Thayer said, offering me a weak smile. "Plus, you told me that parcel of land AM owns downtown is worth over five million dollars on its own, right? I'm not worried about it. Adam aside, the figures justify the investment my father made."

I was deeply torn. On the one hand, this was my only way out of this mess alive. On the other, I didn't want Thayer to save me. Plus, if we pulled this off, Adam was going to be out for blood. I didn't particularly care when it came to myself, but I didn't want to put her in his crosshairs.

"I don't want you to make an enemy out of Adam," I told her.

"We aren't exactly BFFs as it is," she said. Her fingertips landed on my arm and we both startled, like she'd breached some unspoken barrier. But she let her hand stay there, and warmth spread through my body in response to the contact. "I know what I'm doing, Bennett. Adam deserves to go down in flames."

"We can both agree on that."

Quinn tiptoed back into the room, like she was afraid she was interrupting something. I only wished that were the case. If they'd driven separately, maybe I would have had a shot at Quinn leaving first, but as it was, I was stuck with both or neither of them.

"Sorry," Quinn said softly. "Can you run me through what I'm supposed to do one more time?"

Thayer removed her hand, and we exchanged a brief look. Something clenched in my chest, like all the unsaid words I couldn't tell her in front of Quinn had formed a gigantic knot.

When I walked them to the door a few minutes later, Thayer let Quinn go ahead, lingering behind. She fidgeted with a button on her grey wool peacoat, looking back up at me.

"You're going to run this by Ian tonight?" she asked.

"I will." I wasn't sure whether Ian would be amenable to a forced takeover of Adam's company. It did mean taking on a significant amount of additional work and responsibility, especially until we absorbed the expansion internally and eliminated staff redundancies, but I hoped he'd be on my side once he saw the assets we would acquire. Plus, being able to pay off the IRS was a fairly significant benefit. We'd both sleep better at night once that happened.

"Thanks for the help," I said.

And I miss you, I wanted to add, but I wasn't sure she wanted to hear that since she hadn't replied to my earlier text. Still, something flitted across her face that made me think she might miss me, too.

"Thank me when we get your money back," Thayer said, stealing a glance over her shoulder at Quinn. "I'll see you Friday."

"See you then." Our plan was risky. It probably wouldn't even work. But I had to try.

The following day, it was do or die.

Last time I met with my Uncle Richard at his office, it had been a last resort. This time, it was still a last resort, but I had a few more cards to play. Ones he wouldn't see coming, for a change.

I tilted the iPad screen so Richard could see, swiping through the image files Quinn had sent to me.

"Here, you can see a large campaign donation to our recently-elected mayor," I said. "Timing's a bit odd, don't you think? Especially because he publicly stated this would be his final term in office. Could be construed as a bribe, especially if Adam received something in return, like preferential treatment for a development bid. Which, incidentally, is exactly what the mayor promised him in this lovely little email here."

You'd think between Adam and the mayor, someone would have been smart enough not to leave a paper trail; but their stupidity was to my advantage in the end.

Richard's jaw tensed as he scanned the email on the screen, and he nodded tersely, indicating for me to continue.

I swiped to the next image, a cash flow statement from two years ago. "But this one is my favorite. Turns out, these figures highlighted in red were part of an elaborate framework to embezzle funds from Flux. Quite creative on Adam's part, really. I've got to give him credit where it's due." Adam probably got his knack for concocting schemes like that from Richard, but I knew better than to say that out loud.

Richard harrumphed, studying the screen with a frown. His eyes ping-ponged back and forth along the columns of numbers, connecting the dots. It was obvious once it was laid out in plain sight.

Finally, his hawkish gaze landed back on me. "Are you trying to blackmail me, son?"

"Would I ever skirt the rules of the law like that?" I asked.

He cocked a salt-and-pepper brow. "I don't know, Bennett. Would you?"

"I'm merely bringing the situation to your attention since you're an affected party. Of course, I don't particularly want to involve the IRS and the Securities and Exchange Commission—but I can't let misappropriation of my company's funds go unaddressed, either."

This was a bluff; I couldn't afford to involve the IRS or the SEC, or I risked running into trouble due to some of the gray-area things I'd done myself. Luckily, Richard didn't appear to know about any of that. He knew I was destitute, but not that I'd basically kited checks to stay afloat.

"All I'm saying is, I don't think any of us want to see a second family scandal, especially not with your history of previous SEC investigations. Might be perceived as one of those smoke and fire situations. I'd hate to jeopardize your securities license. We both know how limiting that's been for my father."

As in, it ruined his entire life.

"That's what this is really about, isn't it?" He picked up his glass of scotch, swirling it.

"The fact that you walked away scot-free while he lost everything? It could be a factor."

"Your father was going down either way," Richard said. "The informant had him on tape. Do you honestly think that taking him down with me would have somehow improved the outcome for you?"

Part of me knew he was right, even if I hated hearing it. It still didn't excuse him working my father to the bone in a lower-level position, underpaying him for his level of expertise and experience. Even a lateral move to a different firm would be difficult, if not impossible, with my father's history.

He added, "I took care of your family, Bennett, and I made sure Lydia had everything she needed when she was sick. I still do."

"Now," he said. "I do concur with your assessment of the situation and that the optics of this blowing up publicly would be undesirable for everyone. What do you propose?"

"Again, I'm not looking to coerce you in any manner. But if you happen to be looking to divest yourself of the equity in Adam's company, I'd be happy to take it off your hands."

Richard regarded me skeptically. "You're not liquid enough to do that."

Little did he know, I was about to be. But I was in no hurry to tie up that much capital in one place.

"I'm sure we can work out a payment schedule that we both deem agreeable," I told him. "If I default on the payments before the balance is paid, I'll even ensure your equity will be returned to you in full."

I was practically holding my breath, but I tried not to look like it. This was the last step in our plan, and without it, everything Thayer had done would be for nothing.

"How much?"

I slid a piece of paper across the table to him. Frowning, he picked it up, and his frown deepened. His eyes flicked back up to me.

"Your call," I said.

He studied me for a beat before finally giving me a nod. Something a bit like begrudging respect emerged across his face. "I'll have my lawyers draw something up," he said gruffly.

"I'll have *my* lawyers draw something up," I said, "and yours can review it."

CHAPTER FORTY-FOUR

Thayer

"I CAN'T BELIEVE YOUR FATHER AGREED TO SIGN THOSE SHARES over to you," Bennett said, leaning back in his office chair.

I shrugged. "It's for the greater good. He doesn't want to be in bed with Adam after what he did to Quinn."

Quinn made sure of that after she spoke to our father and gave him all the gory details, along with the sad little girl act she had always excelled at. Since the share transaction had already gone through, there was no way of forcing Adam to reverse the sale. That's why we were at Flux in the middle of the afternoon with Bennett and Ian, finalizing the paperwork required to complete the last step of our plan. This was the only feasible course of action.

While we were waiting for Bennett's assistant to return with signed copies of all the documents, Quinn's phone started to go off the hook with texts. One, two, three pings chimed in quick succession.

She looked up at us, pale blue eyes wide. "It's Adam. He's pissed, and he wants to know where Thayer is." It was the first day since Adam had returned from his business trip, which meant she'd left early in the morning to avoid him. At least she'd only had to fake it via calls and texts for the past week. Pretty soon, she wouldn't have to pretend to tolerate him at all.

Bennett caught my eye, his expression questioning. A slight ripple of fear shot through my body. Not because I was afraid of Adam, but because I hated confrontation in general.

"Go ahead," I said. "Tell him I'm here."

Ian looked at us dubiously. "Are you sure you want to let him come up?"

"Might as well get it over with." I crossed my legs, pretending I actually believed that myself.

The mood in the room shifted, turning tense. Bennett's assistant returned and we signed our respective documents, trying to make small talk as we waited for what was coming next.

Not even ten minutes later, Adam stormed into Bennett's office. His face was scarlet, eyes bulging with anger.

"Why does this share certificate my lawyer sent over say Thayer Montgomery?" Adam roared. He weaved around the chairs, ignoring the fact that Quinn was sitting with us, and thrust a sheaf of papers in my face. "Know anything about this?"

"What's that now?" I peered over at the papers in his hand, playing dumb.

"My company," he snapped. "It says you own thirty-five percent."

I pretended to frown as I scanned the document. "I guess it does say Thayer Montgomery, not Thomas Montgomery." I smacked my forehead. "Oh, that's right. Daddy signed his shares over to me as an engagement gift. Us women folk have a hard time keeping track of that stuff sometimes."

The color drained from Adam's face. "Thomas did what?"

"Wasn't that sweet of him?" Quinn chirped. "Then again, he wasn't too happy with you when he found out about you and Millie."

"*Millie?*" Adam whirled around to face her, doing his best

impression of an innocent man. It wasn't a very convincing act. "What are you talking about?"

"Save it, Adam. I saw everything in your text messages." Quinn gave him a disdainful 'you're beneath me' look, and I couldn't have been prouder. "The movers are packing up your stuff as we speak. They'll leave it for you in the building lobby."

Adam's jaw tensed, but he clearly thought better than to argue with her in front of us. Likely, because he had other dirty laundry that would come out if he did. He returned his attention to me, eyes gleaming with malice. "Why do you want shares in my company, anyway?"

"That's where you're confused," Bennett told him. "It's not your company anymore."

"That's right," I said, leaning against the desk beside him. "Bennett picked up a few shares privately from your other investor. That makes for seventy percent ownership between the two of us."

Adam's mouth hung open. He blinked, rapid-fire, and for the first time since I'd known him, he was lost for words. Quinn watched the spectacle unfold from her chair beside us, her expression impassive.

"According to the bylaws, two-thirds of the shareholders have to agree to pass a motion. Which means we amalgamated AM and Flux under one umbrella this afternoon. Still kept the name Flux, obviously. I guess you work for me now." Bennett smirked. "Or did, anyway. You're fired—for cause. Which means you won't be receiving two weeks' pay in lieu of notice."

"You can't do that." Adam waved the papers like a weapon. "I have rights, even as an employee."

"At-will employment laws say otherwise. Though if you'd like to fight about it, using your position within Flux to further your interests is also a valid reason, according to my lawyer. And we haven't even touched on your little donation to the mayor. Or misappropriating company funds."

"Speaking of your share." Bennett paused. "I'm going to buy you out for sixty cents on the dollar. And you're going to take it."

"Or else?"

"I don't think I need to spell that out for you." Bennett thrust a paper in his face. "Here are the details of the offer."

On paper, it would raise too many flags to take Adam's company without compensating him in some form. But the amount he was about to walk away with meant he was taking a massive hit.

Adam's hands were dirtier than Bennett's, which meant there wasn't a whole lot he could do, either. If push came to shove, Bennett might have gotten a regulatory slap on the wrist, maybe some penalties from the IRS, but bribing an elected official could earn Adam time in prison.

Adam's face reddened, vein in his forehead bulging. He looked back up. "This is less than sixty cents on the dollar."

"I subtracted what you stole from Flux."

"I have personal debt," he snapped. "This would leave me underwater."

"Am I supposed to give a shit?" Bennett asked.

Adam spun around and sneered at Quinn. "I suppose you're in on this too?"

"You bet I am," she said. "Couldn't happen to a nicer guy."

"Look on the bright side," I said. "The store's always hiring. How do you feel about underwire versus soft cup bras? Don't worry, I'm sure you're a fast learner."

"Fuck you," he spat. "Frigid bitch."

Bennett must have teleported, because one minute he was seated at his desk, leaning back in his chair with a smug look on his face, and the next, he was across the room standing toe to toe with Adam with a homicidal gleam in his eye.

"Bennett. Don't let him get to you." I stepped between them and touched his forearm, trying to move him back, but he was a wall of solid muscle, and he was pissed.

Bennett's hand landed on my hip, gripping firmly, and he wordlessly moved me aside, which I took to be a bad sign.

"What the fuck did you just say to her?" He took another step toward Adam, who looked back at him with a defiant smirk.

"I said, she's a frigid bitch," Adam repeated. "Good luck marrying that."

Before I realized what he was doing, he lunged forward and punched Adam square in the jaw. Adam staggered back, holding his face with a look of disbelief. Bennett backed away, shaking out his fist, but the smile on his face was clear. And while I normally didn't condone physical violence, it was hard to hold back a smile of my own. I think I managed, but barely.

Quinn, on the other hand, was beaming like a Cheshire Cat.

"What the fuck?" Adam glanced back up at him, leveling him with a searing glare. "You just assaulted me. I hope you look good in orange, Bradford."

"I think all the witnesses here would agree that you hit me first." Bennett scanned the room, and the three of us nodded. "That was merely self-defense. It's not my fault you can't land a decent hit."

Adam gaped at Bennett, apparently lost for words, while Bennett walked around to his desk and paged his assistant. I couldn't remember the last time he'd looked so relaxed. "Please have security come escort Mr. Matthews out of the building. And bring me a bag of ice."

After security dragged a ranting, raving Adam out of Bennett's office, Ian and Quinn claimed they had other obligations, leaving the two of us alone. Bennett and I stood on opposite sides of his desk and looked at each other, neither of us sure what to say. The tension in the room was tense, ridden with angst and full of unsaid words.

"You shouldn't have hit Adam," I finally said. "Especially not because of me." The last thing Bennett needed was some kind of legal trouble from punching Adam, no matter how much he may have deserved it.

"Are you kidding?" Bennett grinned, and I tried to ignore the flutters it stirred in my belly. "I've been dying to do that for nearly a year. He just finally gave me a good enough reason."

"Well." I cleared my throat, reaching for my wool peacoat and leather handbag. "I guess everything is settled. Adam is out of Quinn's life, and you got what you wanted."

His smile faded as quickly as it had emerged. "Not everything."

"Don't start, Bennett. I don't want to fight." My throat tightened.

"Neither do I," he said, stepping around the desk to close the distance between us. His cologne permeated the air, evoking a kaleidoscope of emotions that I couldn't even begin to process. "That's why I apologized. And I'll keep apologizing until you forgive me."

Tears swelled behind my eyes, and I nestled my head against his shoulder so he couldn't see. Being close to him felt so familiar; so easy. But I still wasn't completely convinced that meant it was right.

"I told you," he said, gently rubbing my back. "I'm not making the same mistake twice. You can be pissed at me for not listening, but at least then I can say I tried."

Words failed me, and I didn't respond. It was like standing on the precipice of a cliff. I didn't know what was at the bottom. It could have been the best decision of my life, or the worst. The biggest gamble I'd ever make… but I wasn't sure my heart could take the loss.

After another bout of silence, I spoke up again. "Bennett?"

"Yeah?"

"Why didn't you kiss me in the bathroom at the party, back in high school?" The very act of asking was like ripping off a scab, transporting me back to when I was an insecure sixteen-year-old again.

He huffed a low laugh, shaking his head. "I should have, but I choked. I didn't want our first kiss to happen with Millie on the other side of the door."

"But our first kiss was a fake kiss."

"Was it? Because the only person I've been lying to is myself."

Another wave of tears sprang to my eyes, overflowing before I could stop them. I wiped them away with the back of my hand and tried to blink them away, but it was futile.

"Thay." Bennett turned to face me, ducking his head. There was a sadness in his eyes that cut me to the core. "I'm sorry. I didn't mean to—"

"It's fine," I cut him off, pushing away from him. There were too many things swirling around my brain, too many conflicting emotions warring within my heart. "Let's just get through the engagement party tomorrow, okay?"

His expression fell and he looked like he wanted to argue with me, but then his jaw set, and he nodded. "Okay. I'll see you tomorrow."

CHAPTER FORTY-FIVE

Thayer

NEVER EXPECTED TO BE ATTENDING MY OWN ENGAGEMENT party on the tail of Quinn's engagement falling through. Even though she and I both knew it wasn't real, somehow it made me feel even more sorry for her. Attending our party tonight would be like rubbing salt in a fresh wound.

After a grueling spin class, followed by brunch with Lola, I went home and obsessively scrubbed every inch of my apartment to avoid thinking about what awaited me later. Even the fridge, which was my least favorite and often-neglected cleaning task, got the full-service treatment. Despite all of the physical activity, I was still wired with nervous energy when I finished. My place had never been cleaner, but my head was more of a mess than ever.

I was a basket of contradictions, wrapped in a blanket of confusion. I couldn't wait to see Bennett, but I was dreading it, too. Every day apart was torture, but the idea of getting hurt again was torture of its own. All I wanted to do was go back to when things between us were perfect, but whenever I tried to move past what had happened, my brain hit the brakes and kept me firmly stuck in limbo.

In the late afternoon, Quinn texted offering to come over to get ready together, but I declined because I wasn't in a good mood, and I didn't want to take it out on her. Styling my hair and doing my makeup went smoothly enough solo, but once I started to get dressed, I regretted turning down Quinn's invitation. Nothing I tried on seemed right. Ten dresses later, they were all too bright or too dark; too sexy or too frumpy; too formal or informal. I needed a second opinion, because I knew the real problem was with me and not the clothes—I was dramatically unprepared to face the evening. It had nothing to do with which dress I was going to be wearing, and everything to do with my heart.

Finally, I texted Quinn full-length photos of four dresses, plus three shoe options. With her help, I settled on a deep blue cocktail dress and champagne-colored pumps. The fitted crepe bodice and gathered chiffon skirt of the dress were feminine, and the details made me feel pretty, even in light of the otherwise dismal situation. Bennett's tendency to compliment me whenever I wore blue may also have been a factor in my selection, though that was difficult to admit.

Applying bronzer and highlighter, I dabbed and blended until my lack of sleep was nearly concealed. Unless you looked closely, at least. Then, I gave myself a final once-over in the mirror, checking to make sure I didn't have any traces of scarlet lipstick on my teeth or stray flyaway hairs. On the surface, I appeared perfectly pulled together. Hopefully, I could convince everyone else that was actually the case.

I doubted I'd be able to convince the one who mattered most, though.

One nerve-wracking twenty-minute drive later, I pulled into the driveway of Bennett's parents' home on the outskirts of town. It had been ten years since I'd been here, though it was largely unchanged aside from an updated paint job on the exterior and larger trees lining the property. Memories of hanging out with Bennett after school and in the summer came flooding back, weakening my already fragile sense of composure.

I put the ignition into park, and my heart slammed into my chest as Bennett exited his car, where he'd been waiting, and walked over to greet me. We'd driven separately, due to obvious reasons, but had agreed to enter together to avoid raising any questions. And of course, his dark blue silk tie matched my dress almost perfectly. We couldn't have planned it better if we'd tried. Now it looked like we had.

Bennett reached over and pulled open my car door for me, stepping aside. I was nervous, and it showed—my hands were shaking as I grabbed my purse from the passenger side seat before sliding out and coming to stand beside him. A frigid breeze kicked up, chilling my bare legs. At least I could blame my jitteriness on being cold.

He dipped his head, eyes meeting mine. "Ready?"

"Ready." It was a lie, but I didn't have a choice.

He shut the driver's side door behind me, and I locked it remotely as we made our way up the paved sidewalk leading to the entry. With each stride I took in my heels, my heart rate climbed a little more, until it was practically vibrating in my chest. When we reached the steps, he shot me a sidelong, apologetic glance and slid his arm around me before opening the front door. The heavy weight of his body pressed against mine in a way that was all too familiar, and a pang of sadness hit me like a punch to the diaphragm.

We stepped into the marble foyer, and Bennett's mother, Lydia, rushed over to greet us and wrapped us both in a warm hug. Her emerald green sheath dress hugged her slender frame and she felt thin in my arms, though Bennett had said treatments were going well.

"Look at the beautiful couple." Lydia released us, taking a step back and clasping her hands. "Thayer, you look stunning."

Bennett gave me an affectionate squeeze, sending a thrill down my spine. "She does."

I didn't know whether I was flattered or annoyed. Maybe both. He'd seemed nervous a few moments ago, but he was slipping back into his usual role a little too easily. It was going to make it even more difficult to keep him at arms' length. I'd spent the last couple of days trying to convince myself I wanted to, but now that he was standing next to me, that was a much harder lie to sell myself on.

Deep down, I still wanted him—even if I didn't want to want him.

"Thank you," I said, sliding off my coat and handing it to Bennett, who hung it in the closet next to us. "Everything looks lovely, Lydia. You've done a wonderful job. We really appreciate it."

"Of course." She beamed at the two of us. "It makes me so happy to see the two of you together again after all this time."

Bennett wrapped his arm around my waist. "Must have been meant to be."

"Must be," I agreed, ignoring the lump in my throat.

Being back at Bennett's house, talking with his mother, was more than a little surreal. It was the first time I'd seen Lydia in nearly ten years, and it felt like no time had passed at all. She was as warm and effusive as ever, which compounded the guilt I felt over our fib. Or was it even a fib, anymore? I still didn't know how much of it was real. Bennett and I would have to clear the air eventually, but I was more concerned with making sure tonight went smoothly so he could close the deal with Callaghan.

We lingered, chatting, while Bennett shared some funny stories with his mother from our trip from Mexico—including ziplining, which he refused to let me forget—and we humored her questions about our plans for our upcoming "wedding". After a few minutes, Bennett's mother excused herself to go check on the caterers, leaving the two of us alone. From the other corner of the room, Jared Callaghan spotted Bennett and waved him over. Bennett's gaze fell back to me, his expression torn.

"You should go talk to him," I said, jutting my chin. "That's why we're here, right? Get him to sign those papers and lock him down."

Bennett nodded, but he didn't move. His eyes stayed fixed on me, and he took my hand in his, tracing his fingers along my inner wrist. Another pang hit me, this one squarely in the heart. "Come get me if you need anything, okay?"

"I will."

He looked at me for another beat before reluctantly releasing his hold on me and turning, weaving through the groups of people and greeting them as he passed. Ian was in the crowd as well and Bennett signaled to him on his way over.

Like she'd been waiting to pounce, Quinn bustled over to me with two glasses of champagne, placing one in my hand. I accepted, taking a small sip. I hadn't eaten much all day due to my nerves, and I didn't want to get sloppy in front of all of the guests—or in front of Bennett.

She nodded at me, pale blue eyes gleaming affectionately. "Glad you went with that one. You look amazing."

"Thanks," I said, but I didn't feel amazing; I felt like a fraud. A fraud who hadn't slept a wink last night, because all I could think about was the look in Bennett's eyes when I walked away from him in his office yesterday. Seeing how broken he'd looked had been like having my heart ripped out all over again.

And seeing him now, well, that only left me confused.

Quinn and I made small talk while countless people milled about Bennett's parents' home, and our mother made rounds socializing like it was her job. As I'd expected, the party was like a Who's Who of the city, dotted with politicians, businesspeople, and the odd local celebrity. When Bennett had said our mothers had gotten carried away planning, he wasn't kidding. And by 'our mothers,' he meant mine; at a glance, it was clear more than half the guest list consisted of her invitees. Fortunately, his mother hadn't seemed to mind too much. She seemed to be enjoying herself, and I was glad.

Across the room, Bennett and Callaghan reappeared and Bennett caught my eye, giving me a nod that I took to mean everything had been finalized. They were immediately accosted by a group of people I didn't recognize, but they both seemed to know. Bennett already looked noticeably more relaxed than when we'd first arrived, probably because the ink was drying on the papers with Callaghan.

Everything had been wrapped up into a nice, tidy bow…except for us.

"Where's Lola?" Quinn asked, scanning the crowd. I felt a pang of sympathy for her, given that she'd recently lost her own best friend. Much as I'd never liked Millie, and much as Quinn was better off without a backstabbing bitch in her life, Quinn seemed a little adrift without her usual right-hand woman.

"Work emergency," I said. "The alarm at the art gallery went off while she was on her way over, and she had to go see what was going on. She'll be here pretty soon."

"Ah."

"Are you okay?" I touched her arm, leaning closer so no one would overhear. "You don't have to stay, if you don't want. I wouldn't blame you if you wanted to duck out early."

Hell, I was impressed she'd come at all. If I were her, I wouldn't have wanted to.

"I'm fine." Her tone was cheerful, but the fact that she was already on her third glass of champagne strongly suggested otherwise.

The one silver lining to Quinn's situation was that our mother had been shockingly supportive; she said that she knew what it was like to marry the wrong person, and she'd rather see Quinn realize it now before walking down the aisle. Which really begged the question of why I'd gone to such extreme lengths of my own to create the illusion of a boyfriend—now alleged fiancé—but it was a little late for that now.

"What about you? How are things with Bennett?" Quinn kept her face nearly immobile, almost like a puppeteer trying not to show their mouth moving.

I glanced over to him, where he was now talking to his brother, Holden, and their mother. Bennett laughed, shaking his head, and said something to Holden. Holden gave him a playful punch on the shoulder in return.

"I don't know," I said.

Bennett must have sensed me looking at him, because he turned, and his gaze fell to me. His mouth tugged into a half-smile, but it was laced with sadness beneath. If I thought pretending at my mother's dinner party had been difficult, this was ten times more complicated.

"Go talk to him," Quinn urged. "Play the part, at least until you decide what you're going to do."

Bennett leaned closer to his mother and said something to her, then nodded to his brother and added something. Before I could decide whether I should join them, he turned and crossed the room to join the two of us. As our eyes locked, his smile broadened, growing more genuine. His charcoal suit was freshly pressed, stretching across his broad shoulders, and there was a determination about him as he approached.

"Can I borrow Thay for a moment?" he asked Quinn, like I wasn't standing right there. I'd have been irritated, if not for the part of me that was desperate to be alone with him. And by part, I mean all of me. I missed him so much there was a physical ache inside of me.

"Of course." She scanned the crowd and spotted our mother from across the room, giving her a little wave. "I have to go discuss what to do with some wedding-related deposits anyway."

I was fairly certain that was the last thing Quinn felt like doing right now, but I appreciated her making an excuse to leave us alone. Maybe all the champagne would take the edge off for her, at least.

Bennett's arm wrapped around my waist, grip more firm than I'd expected, and he began to forcefully steer me out of the room. I breathed in his cologne and felt my body relax against him in response, my feet automatically following the direction he was setting. Stupid, traitorous body.

We stepped around people huddled around the room, offering them smiles as we did, until we passed through the doorway into the hallway.

"What are you doing?" I asked him quietly, once everyone else was out of earshot.

He leaned in, nuzzling the side of my face, and every nerve in my body came alive. "What does it look like?"

With a few more steps, he took me by the arm and practically pushed me up the winding hardwood staircase, into his old bedroom. Nostalgia hit me like a tsunami, breath freezing in my lungs. It was like stepping back in time. Rugby trophies lined the desk and shelves, and the dark blue walls were covered with sports posters and old photos, including several with me in them. Why didn't he get rid of those if he'd been so upset with me?

The noise from the party downstairs faded away as Bennett shut the door, spinning me to face him. His dark blue eyes pinned me to the spot. "You really do look beautiful."

"Thank you. You look pretty handsome, yourself." Then again, he always did.

His chest rose with a deep inhale, and he let out a cross between a growl and a sigh. "I fucking miss you."

"I saw you yesterday." My gaze lingered on his lips, which were pulled into sulky frown, and my emotional barricades threatened to collapse.

"That's not what I mean, and you know it." He reached down, taking my hands in his. His warm palms were rough against my skin. "Are we done with this pushing me away thing yet? Because you and I both know it's total bullshit."

My mouth went dry, and I swallowed, inwardly scrambling for the right response. Finally, I landed on the truth.

"I need to know you won't shut me out again."

"Never," he said, rubbing the backs of my hands with his calloused thumbs. "I know I fucked up. I wanted to talk to you about everything, Thay. I just didn't know how to. I was afraid it would blow up in my face and set us back to square one—or worse. I couldn't stomach the idea of jeopardizing a good thing. All I wanted was to move past it, so I forgave you."

"For something I didn't do."

"I know that now. But even when I thought you had, I realized I love you too much to let that—" He stopped short, and his brow furrowed. This was a new expression; one I'd never seen on his face before. It was an 'oh shit, did I say that out loud?' face, and it was adorable.

"You love me?"

His mouth tugged into a boyish grin. "I've loved you for as long as I can remember."

My breath snagged and tears sprang to my eyes; the first happy tears I'd had in my life. It was the best thing I'd ever had someone say to me, especially coming from him.

"Don't get me wrong," Bennett said. "You're beyond stubborn, incredibly opinionated, and sometimes I'm pretty sure you disagree with me for the sake of it." He gently tucked a lock of hair behind my ear, eyes gleaming with affection. "And every second I'm apart from you, those are just a few of the things that I miss."

A wave of warm tears began to spill down my cheeks, evading my fingertips and dripping down onto my dress. Looking up, I tried to blink them away, but they continued to spill over. For so long, I'd felt like I didn't belong, wasn't enough, wasn't outgoing or warm or all of the things I felt like everyone else expected me to be. I never fit into any of those boxes. But Bennett saw me for who I was and loved me for it, not in spite of it.

"I love you, too." I sniffled, half-laughing through my tears. "Even when you're being impossible, which is pretty much always."

"That second part is fair." Bennett slid his arms around my waist and pulled me closer. "Do you have any idea how long I've waited to hear you say the first part?"

Happy tears continued to leak from my eyes as I nestled against him, and the fabric of his shirt grew damp from my tears. I was certain there would be streaks of mascara and foundation left behind.

"I'm getting makeup all over your shirt," I said, muffled by crisp white cotton and the taut muscle that lay beneath. "Probably going to ruin it."

"Fuck the shirt." His voice rumbled in his chest, firm finger-tips kneading along my lower back through my dress. I drew in a breath, inhaling the comforting scent of his cologne, and soaking up the warmth from his body against mine. It felt so natural to be in his arms. My tears receded, breathing slowing into a regular, easy pattern. Bennett let out a low, satisfied hum and kissed the top of my head, stroking my hair.

"I'm sorry I ever made you doubt the way I feel, Thay. I'm bad with feelings and even worse when it comes to talking about them, but that isn't an excuse."

Sadly, I was even more deficient in both of those areas than he was. Which was why I didn't know what to say, so I just let out a quiet sound of agreement.

"But I'll do better," he added, pulling back slightly to peer down at me. "I promise. I would do anything for you."

I nodded, feeling my cheeks pull into a smile so broad I thought my cheeks might crack. We looked at each other for a few seconds, the energy in the air shifting. His gaze darkened and he leaned in, mouth covering mine. My lips parted instantly as his tongue swept inside, and the chemistry between us ignited, setting off a cascade of fireworks throughout my body. I'd missed him in every way.

Our kiss deepened and everything started to fast forward as he steered me backward until I bumped into the wooden desk behind me. Bennett scooped me up, setting me onto the surface, and his hands slid up my thighs, beginning to inch up the hem of my dress.

"There are people downstairs," I reminded him.

"So?" he murmured, tilting my jaw up. His lips brushed against the sensitive spot beneath my ear, sending tingles down my spine. "We both know most of those guests aren't here for you and me."

"True," I admitted. "But we should probably make it quick."

Bennett chuckled, sinking his teeth into my neck. "I can't prom-ise that."

In a flash, my underwear came off, followed by his suit jacket, and he was standing between my legs. His fingertips glided along my inner thighs, leisurely teasing without touching me where I wanted him most. I looped my arms around his neck, tugging him closer for another kiss, but each time one ended, I was left wanting another. Maybe the high from kissing him would wear off someday, but I doubted it would be any time soon.

His fingers slid against me, sending off a frenzy of pleasure, and I let out a soft gasp. His teeth sank into his bottom lip, and he watched my expression as he pushed a finger inside me, followed by another.

"Small problem," Bennett said, curling his fingers and hitting my G-spot. I whimpered. "For once, I wasn't prepared for this."

My hips arched in response to his touch, greedily seeking more. "Birth control."

His gaze lifted to mine, questioning. "Are you sure?"

"Yes." Our mouths came together again while I unfastened his belt and pants, wrapping my other hand around his hard length. Bennett slid me to the very edge of the desk but stopped short before pushing inside. My fingertips dug into his back, urging him on, and he let out a low laugh. I was impatient, and he knew it.

His mouth tugged in a crooked, wolfish smile. "For the record, this is fulfilling a major fantasy of mine."

"Sex in your childhood bedroom?"

"Fucking *you* in this bedroom." He thrust into me, and the sudden fullness took my breath away. "That's the fantasy. Ticking all the boxes."

Bennett wrapped his hands around my lower back, pinning me in place, and circled his hips. Immediately, pleasure started to overtake every other sense of mine, and our surroundings faded into the background, including any thoughts about the party downstairs. The only thing that existed in the moment was our bodies joined together, him moving against me in perfect rhythm. His mouth

crashed down on mine, muffling my needy cries, and he continued to take me closer and closer to the edge with each movement.

He broke away from our kiss, letting out a low groan. "Move
in with me."

"I'm sorry, what did you just say?" Was I hallucinating from
pleasure overdose? He was good, but that would be a first.

"I said, move in with me." Before I could respond, he slammed
into me, sending the trophies on the desk rattling. I saw stars, eu-
phoria building within me.

"Fuck." Bennett let out a hiss, and slowly pulled out almost all
the way before thrusting back inside me again. "Or I can move into
your place. I don't care which."

"Hold on." I grabbed his face, my fingers and thumb landing
on his rough, stubbled jawline, and turned him to look at me. "Is
this sex talk, or are you serious?"

He stopped thrusting and rested his forehead against mine,
trailing his fingertips down the side of my face. His thumb brushed
my bottom lip. "I'm serious, Thay. We've wasted too much time
being apart as it is."

It was incredibly sweet, even if the timing was a little unortho-
dox. Then again, doing something like this in the middle of sex was
on-brand for Bennett, and I loved him even more because of that.

Before my brain could catch up enough to voice my agreement,
he started to move against me again, and I let out a quiet, involuntary whimper. It was like his body was made for mine with the way
we fit together. I never in a million years could have imagined finding what we had, inside the bedroom or otherwise.

His voice turned strained. "I want to wake up next to you every
morning. I knew that after Mexico."

My heart swelled to the point where I thought it might burst.
I never imagined wanting to live with someone before him, but
now I couldn't imagine not saying yes. Or trying to, because I was
halfway to an orgasm and making a considerable effort to be quiet.

"I'd love that," I managed. "As long as you're sure."

"I've never been more sure of anything in my life." His grip on me tightened and he pushed into me deeper, hitting a spot inside I didn't know existed. My breath caught, toes curling with pleasure. He did it again and we both moaned, likely louder than we could afford to but unable to hold back. With a few more thrusts, we both came undone, clinging to each other as each wave washed over us until we were both tired and sated.

Bennett tilted his head, planting a soft kiss on my mouth. "Fuck, do I ever love you."

"I love you, too." I placed my hand on his chest, feeling his heart pound against my palm.

We stayed together for a few more moments, snuggling as much as we could given the situation and position. He looked over his shoulder and grabbed a few tissues before he pulled out of me, quickly helping clean me up. Then he stepped back to let me hop off the desk and began to get dressed again.

"I'm holding you to living together," he said, fastening his leather belt. "I hope you realize that."

"We can call moving companies first thing Monday morning. But for now, we should get back to the party." A quick glance at the clock revealed we'd already been gone far longer than could easily be explained away.

I straightened my dress, knowing my hair and makeup had probably been ruined. I'd have to send Bennett out first while I did a massive touch-up in the bathroom. And while I thought of a way to pretend like our extended disappearance together wasn't incredibly suspicious.

"Unfortunately, you're right." He fixed his shirt sleeves and pulled his suit jacket back on, smoothing his rumpled clothing. Glancing down, he straightened his cuffs, and with that final fix, he was back to his pre-romp normal. He looked the way he had when he'd walked through the door earlier. It was patently unfair.

Despite all of our talks, one final unspoken question still lingered between us. One that I was finally feeling brave enough to ask.

"Um, Bennett? What do we do about the ring?"

Bennett looked up, lips quirking. "Leave it on."

"Why? So people don't ask questions?"

He walked up to me and wrapped his arms around me from behind. A warm wall of muscle enveloped me, securing me to the spot. His nose traced my cheek, breath warm against my skin. "No," he said. "Because I want you to have it."

Contentedness settled in my body, because it was the answer I hadn't known I needed until I got it.

When I appeared downstairs a few minutes later, Quinn and Lola immediately accosted me, thrusting a fresh glass of champagne in my hand and dragging me off to the side.

"Where were you?" A smile played on Lola's glossy nude lips.

"Where do you think?" I asked, fighting the rush of heat to my cheeks.

Quinn smirked. "Called it. You two are a little freaky, and I love that for you."

"Does this mean…?" Lola's amber eyes studied my face, widening. She dropped her voice to a hush. "Are you two together-together? Or back together? Whatever you want to call it?"

"Yeah," I said. "We agreed to keep the ring on, too."

Both of their faces lit up with excitement, but we shared a glance of silent understanding that this wasn't the time or place to discuss it. Good thing, too, because a few seconds later, my mother appeared from out of thin air like always. Her chilly hand landed on my bare shoulder, and I wondered if she could tell how fevered my skin was from what had just happened upstairs.

"There you are," my mother said. "I've been looking everywhere for you. Your fiancé is waiting in the dining room. I was going to make a toast to you both."

She led me through the double doors to where Bennett was standing at the front of the oversized dining room, a mixture of amusement and irritation on his handsome face. Every eye in the entire party was trained on us, and I immediately hated it. My mother turned her back on us, trying to get everyone to quiet down.

"I hate being the center of attention," I whispered to Bennett.

"I know," he muttered. "I tried to stop her. She also wants us to have a 500-person wedding. And that was with me talking her down from 750."

"In that case, eloping someday is the only option."

He reached over and interlaced his fingers with mine. "Agreed."

EPILOGUE

Bennett

DIMMING THE LIGHTS TO OUR APARTMENT'S LIVING ROOM, I gave the room a once-over. Music was playing, the mood lighting was set, and everything looked perfect. Despite that, I'd never been so nervous in my entire fucking life. I felt like I'd mainlined ten espressos and followed it with some lines of cocaine.

Objectively, it made no sense. Thayer and I had been living together for the better part of the past year, acting like a married couple for all intents and purposes besides the paperwork behind it. Hell, Thayer was already wearing an engagement ring. Everything was unbelievably perfect between us, from the daily routines we'd fallen into, to the odd silly squabble that resulted in hot makeup sex. I was pretty sure she didn't care about coasters nearly as much as she pretended to, but when it meant we ended up naked, I was going to keep forgetting to use them.

But despite all of that, we hadn't set a date to take that next step. Hadn't talked much about marriage at all in the past few weeks, actually, because she'd recently started her MBA program and had been adjusting to classes and studying again. While I knew she was a brilliant student, her perfectionist ways meant she had been more than a little stressed, even though she was crushing everything so far—just like I'd said she would.

Needless to say, she'd been preoccupied lately and wouldn't be expecting this, which meant it was either brilliant or terrible timing. And I was about to find out which.

After readjusting the candles on the counter for the tenth time in as many minutes, I realized I was on the verge of having a nervous breakdown and decided to crack a beer. Three-quarters of the way into it, I was a little less riled up, then the lock rattled, followed by the door swinging open and slamming shut in the hall. Go time. My nerves surged again, and I quickly finished off the rest of the bottle, setting it aside.

I could do this. I pitched venture capitalists. Spoke at conferences. Had the IRS breathing down my back until not too long ago. Hell, I'd been deposed in lawsuits before. Proposing was no big deal, right?

Wrong. It was a huge deal, especially when I thought I never would. Finding someone who made me change my mind about so many things was like winning the lottery; a one in a million win, and I didn't want to screw it up.

Keys clinked in the dish, footsteps echoing, and Thayer appeared in the doorway. She was wearing a dark green velvet dress that tied in the back with her hair loose around her shoulders, and she looked like a present I wanted to unwrap. Hopefully, I would be doing that in a little while, but I had something else to do first.

Because she also looked like the person I wanted to spend the rest of my life with, and I wanted to make that official.

Her eyes widened in surprise as they landed on me, then scanned the darkened living room, complete with a handful of decorations on the wall and a portable color-changing light. It was a rough approximation of what our junior year homecoming looked like; or at least, as close as I could stomach without getting too cheesy. I may have been walking that line already, but I was going to roll with it.

"Hey." Thayer's mouth pulled into a small smile. She took a few steps closer, gesturing to the room. "What's all this?"

"I owe you some slow dances," I said, taking her in my arms. "About nine years' worth."

Her smile broadened, and I knew I'd made the right choice with the set-up. "This certainly is a nice surprise after a long day of financial analysis and trying not to strangle my group project partners."

"Stick to strangling me. That way you can avoid jail."

"Good call," she murmured, resting her head on my shoulder, and nestling closer to me. I never could get over how perfectly she fit in my arms, or how right it made everything else feel when she was. I could be having the biggest garbage fire day ever, and I'd instantly be able to forget about it when I came home and saw her face.

We pivoted a turn along the makeshift dance floor and her perfume drifted over; it was spicy and sweet, something like cinnamon and vanilla, and entirely edible. Like her. Which was also something I was planning to do later when I...

Fuck. Focus, Bradford.

In the background, the song changed. It was one we'd listened to obsessively on the flight to Italy for our school trip. Or Thayer had, rather, while I'd pretended to hate it because my insecure fifteen-year-old self thought it would seem uncool for a guy to like a slow song. And because it made me feel a little outed when it came to my feelings for her.

Her eyes brightened. "Oh my God, I remember this song. You said you hated it because it was too...what was it?" She pursed her berry-painted lips. "Sappy."

"Maybe I said that because it made me feel called out for having a massive crush on you."

"Yeah, right." But a tiny flush appeared on her cheeks in the dim light.

I winked at her. "True story. By the way, we have reservations at Alloy in two hours."

Also known as her favorite restaurant in the entire world. We hadn't been there in a few months, mostly because I'd been intentionally avoiding it. I even pretended it was booked up one night not too long ago, which had made me feel guilty, but it was for a good cause. I wanted it to be special when we did go there again.

"Alloy?" Her brows knit together. "What's the occasion?"

"Acing your first set of exams," I said. "Plus, maybe one more thing." I took her left hand in both of mine, turning the band of her engagement ring from side to side between my fingers. "Lately, I've been thinking this looks a little bare, like something is missing."

"Is that so?"

"Definitely." Reaching into my pocket, my fingers glanced upon the delicate band with pave diamonds set on all three sides. I pulled it out and slid it onto her left finger, placing it on top of the engagement ring. Technically, I knew it put the rings in the wrong order since the wedding band should have been first, but it was the best I could do while trying to be smooth—and I was trying pretty fucking hard. "See? I was right."

Her gaze dropped to her hand for a beat, then she looked up at me and her lips curled into a smile. "Is this a…"

"Wedding band? Sure is." I leaned closer, capturing her mouth in a kiss. Her lips parted and she melted against me, kissing me back, and digging her fingertips into my shoulders. Before I knew it, I started to get a little lost in her and realized I hadn't actually popped the question. Catching myself, I pulled back, mouth hovering over her lips.

"Marry me," I said. "I'll spend the rest of our lives making you glad you did."

"Yes." She bit back a grin, nodding. "Of course."

Whoosh. All the tension I'd been holding left my body with those three simple letters. Between Thayer back in school and my stressful, sometimes volatile self-employment situation, I had no idea what the future held for us, but it was a future we would have together, and that was all that mattered.

"But I still don't want a big wedding," Thayer added, a hint of apprehension appearing on her face.

"Me neither. Let's elope on a beach somewhere, just you and me. I want to set a date, though. Tonight, over dinner."

"Are you sure you're okay with eloping? What about your family?"

I laughed, pivoting her a quarter turn. "What about yours?"

"Elopement it is," Thayer said. "How's next month? Turks and Caicos? Maybe we can have a small party when we get back."

Ducking my head, I kissed her again. "Done. Let's book a flight."

THE END

Enjoyed the story? Sign up for my newsletter and follow me on social media by visiting beacons.ai/averykeelan to receive bonus materials, updates, and more!

ACKNOWLEDGEMENTS

Thank you to my family for putting up with me when I am on deadline and lock myself in a room, making up stories about people who don't exist. To my parents, for telling me I can achieve anything and truly believing it. To my husband, for being my sounding board and helping me work out plot problems, particularly with my hockey stories. And to both of my boys, without whom I never would have had the courage to begin writing and pursue my own dreams.

To my editor Mackenzie, for providing great insight and suggestions, putting up with my chaos, and working with the fact that I can't keep track of timelines in stories for the life of me and probably never will. Thank you for being so encouraging and for helping me bring Bennett and Thayer to the life on the page.

To my writer friends, thank you for your support, critique and feedback, and for being an ear when I need one. Writing can be a lonely pursuit at times, and I am lucky to have a great network filled with other authors who understand the sometimes wild, and never boring, world of publishing in a way that only other authors can.

And finally, to my readers. Writing is very personal to me, and I truly appreciate all of your reads, comments, reviews, and aesthetics bringing my characters to life. Thank you so much for all of your support along the way, both with Otherwise Engaged as well as with my other stories.

ABOUT THE AUTHOR

Avery Keelan is a writer of hockey romance & adult contemporary romance, a gym addict, and a diehard coffee lover. Her stories contain swoon-worthy happily ever afters with lovable characters, snarky banter, and enough steam to fog up a mirror. Plus, of course, a hefty dose of drama and angst along the way. When not writing, Avery can be found spending time with her husband and two sons, reading, or enjoying the great Canadian outdoors.

OTHER BOOKS BY AVERY KEELAN

Rules of the Game Series
Offside
Shutout

Lakeside University Hockey Series
The Enforcer

Top Shelf Series
Playmaker

STANDALONE NOVELS
Otherwise Engaged
Breakaway

SOCIAL MEDIA

Website: averykeelan.com
Instagram: www.instagram.com/averykeelan
Twitter: twitter.com/averykeelan
Goodreads: www.goodreads.com/author/show/18114417.
Avery_Keelan

Made in United States
Troutdale, OR
11/11/2023

14477583R00239